I'm Maid For You

Luxx Monroe

Copyright © 2015 by Luxx Monroe

All rights reserved.

Cover design by Blazing Covers

Edited by Aquila Editing

No part of this book may be reproduced in any form or by any electronic or mechanical means including information storage and retrieval systems, without permission in writing from the author. The only exception is by a reviewer, who may quote short excerpts in a review.

This book is a work of fiction. Names, characters, places, and incidents either are products of the author's imagination or are used fictitiously. Any resemblance to actual persons, living or dead, events, or locales is entirely coincidental.

Luxx Monroe

Printed in the United States of America

First Printing: September 2015

ISBN-13 978-1517015343

Dedication

This is dedicated to everyone out there that believes in love and happily ever afters. You never know when you'll meet 'the one', so always be ready.

If you've already found them, well, enjoy the ride.
It's a sweet one.

Table of Contents

	Acknowledgments	i
1	Chapter One	1
2	Chapter Two	13
3	Chapter Three	18
4	Chapter Four	28
5	Chapter Five	34
6	Chapter Six	45
7	Chapter Seven	66
8	Chapter Eight	72
9	Chapter Nine	77
10	Chapter Ten	82
	Epilogue	86

Acknowledgments

I need to give a huge thank you to everyone who made this happen. Aquila, for being a kick-ass editor. Blazing Covers for making Natalie come alive, and making a freaking awesome cover. And of course, my wonderful beta and proof-readers out there. This book would be a mess without you.

I also want to thank all of the book bloggers, reviewers, and fellow authors who gave me such strong support for releasing my debut novella. It would have been impossible to do this without you, so thank you.

Chapter 1 - Natalie

The minute you hear the words out loud that your mother is dying, it sends something through your body that is indescribable. I'd never lost a loved one, by death anyway, and I didn't want to start with my mother as the main target for the Grim Reaper. Instead of worrying if the cancer will spread, we should be planning our future trips together, talking about how crazy my wedding day will be, and about our next spa visit.

The other craptastic part about this new life endeavor? Her place of employment got wind that she was sick, and fired her right in the nick of time so they wouldn't have to pay for her treatment. It goes to show you that there really are horrible people out in our world. So now, my mother had cancer, and couldn't afford to save her own life.

That's where I stepped into the picture. When I found out that she'd been canned, I decided that it was my job as a daughter, the only one on her side, that I needed to be the one to make sure she got the care she needed. Even if it meant finding another job, working sixty-hour weeks, and basically draining myself daily. After all, the woman did give birth to me.

My father split when I was a little girl, and it's just been her and me for the past twenty-four years.

I called in my best friend, Maggie to brainstorm ideas, when she proposed something that would change the whole course of my life plan. I had my degree in culinary arts, and dreamed of someday owning my own swanky downtown restaurant that was all the rave, but until then, I worked at an upscale place that was making it's own waves in the market.

"Why don't you just come and work for me?" Maggie asked as she threw the classifieds section of the newspaper across my living room. "I mean, I don't think there's anything out there, except maybe an escort service or something."

I rolled my eyes and went to retrieve my now crumpled paper. "Don't be dramatic, and I'm almost considering selling my body."

That earned me a slap against my arm, and a dirty look. "Quit it. I'm being serious. Think about it. Please?"

I sat there and looked at my best friend. She was probably right, even though I would never admit that defeat out loud. Maggie had taken a small home-cleaning service and made it into a six-figure business in a very short amount of time. I let out a deep breath and knew if I wanted to make any extra cash, her cleaning business was the best way to go. My cooking career hadn't taken off yet, and I couldn't hold my breath waiting. "I just don't want anything to affect our friendship. I love you too much to ruin it with business."

Maggie grabbed my hands and held them to her chest. "Nothing will ruin us, you silly woman. You should know that by now." She winked at me and let my hands drop back down to my side.

I let out a little laugh and thought about all of the moments where we really could have called it quits: boys, sports, high school drama, and don't get me started on college. But now that we were adults with our own adult lives, we should be just fine working together.

"Besides, we really won't even be working together. I'll get you some high-end clients, and you'll be doing your own thing. You'll be doing me a huge favor. I'm having a hard time taking new clients, Nat."

"Are you sure? You have to be truthful with me, and you better not be doing this out of pity."

"Natalie Mae Rifton. I will slap your cute little cheek if you ever speak like that again." Maggie said in a more serious tone than I would have liked. I wouldn't put it past her to give me a little smack, so I shook my head and turned around to walk in to my kitchen.

"You really have no idea how amazing you are. Even if you resort to violence, you're the best." I said the last part quietly, because I felt the dam in my eyes about to break.

"You're really doing me a favor as well. Do you know how hard it is to find reliable help in this crazy ass city? I mean, one time I had a girl sleep with the owner of the house she was cleaning during her shift! That was messy, and so now, of course, I have to have strict rules in place. I feel like a mother hen sometimes."

I walked over and embraced Maggie in a genuine hug and whispered, "Thank you," into her ear.

"You'd do the same for me. Oh, and I have the perfect first client for you. Kent Bryant. He's some big wig with investments and has a corporation downtown. Apparently he's had a hard time finding good help as well and a friend of his who had used our cleaning service gave us a glowing review. His secretary and I just made a cleaning schedule, and the girl I was going to use is moving next week. Something about her boyfriend getting a modeling job in New York City or some bullshit that won't work out."

I chuckled about Maggie's thoughts and her notion that nothing ever ends with a happily ever after. "Well, good luck to them. When should I start, boss?"

"Don't call me that," Maggie said and scrunched up her nose a little. "It sounds weird, but oddly I kind of like it." She wiggled her eyebrows and walked over to her bag that was by my door. As she pulled out a notebook, I started to have a feeling that this actually might work out. My mom would get her treatments, and we would save her life. "Okay, here we go. Looks like Mr. Bigwig himself wants you to start on Monday. He seems picky, but I know you can handle him. I have a list of everything he's expecting you to do, and he needs you out at his house every other day."

"Let me see." I took the list from Maggie and scanned quickly down the line. "This looks like basic cleaning demands. I can so handle this." I smiled and placed the list down on my counter, so I could study it later that night.

"I know you can. One more thing, when dealing with some of the wealthiest people in this city, you might find they can be total assholes. Just do your job, and ignore the rest. Okay?"

I patted Maggie's shoulder as she was heading to my door. "I will, and I have the address. I'll stop by and get the cleaning supplies before I head over to Mr. Bryant's house on Monday. This really is working out great, Maggie. I owe you one."

Maggie smiled and gave me a reassuring hug. "Everything's going to be okay. You know that, right?"

I told myself I wasn't going to cry, but when I felt a tear slip down my cheek, I tilted my head back and saw that Maggie's own flood gates were down. We both silently cried for a few seconds before she wiped her eyes and headed out my door.

I leaned back on my front door once Maggie was gone, and looked over the details of my new client, my new job. "Okay, Mr. Bryant. Please don't be too crazy. I really need this."

**

"It looks like you're all set, Nat. How are you feeling? Are you sure you're ready for this?" Maggie was monitoring my every move, and quite honestly she was driving me a little insane.

"I'm fine, and ready. I'll give you a full update when I'm all finished, and I'll even take pictures. Okay?"

Maggie nodded once and saluted me as I headed for my first cleaning client through her service, Maid For You.

As I was driving through the hills just outside the city, all I noticed were some of the largest houses, or mansions really, I had ever seen, and I started to doubt my decision. Who the hell was I kidding? I barely liked to clean my own house. What made me think I knew a thing about cleaning a freaking mansion. I needed this, however. My mom needed this. I had to remember that the end prize would be my mother's life.

When I looked down at the address and saw a matching number outside a wrought-iron gate, I knew I had arrived at my destination. "17239 Vine Hill," I whispered out loud and pulled right up to an intercom to my left. I pushed the large green button and waited for a response.

"What's your business?" a scratchy old voice said through a little bit of static.

I tilted my head in confusion and was shocked by how old Mr. Bryant sounded. I guessed for some reason I had pictured a younger man in my mind, but it made sense when Maggie told me he was single, and living in a huge palace. Apparently, he's an older guy living in a castle by himself. "Yes, Mr. Bryant. My name is Natalie and I'm here from Maid For You."

"Right. Mr. Bryant is expecting you."

When the intercom clicked off, I placed my hand over my mouth and let out a little laugh. So that wasn't Mr. Bryant. God, I was more nervous than I thought. Of course Mr. Bryant wouldn't answer his own intercom. He had a maid service for crying out loud.

I wasn't used to meeting my clientele face to face. Cooking in the background is what I was used to. I knew making this extra money would help, but now I wasn't so sure.

I let out a deep breath and gripped my steering

wheel as I headed to the front of Mr. Bryant's house. It's just cleaning, what the hell was I so freaked out for? Well, one thing, this was my best friend's business and I didn't want to screw things up for her. So, with that being said, I knew I needed to put on my big-girl panties and do my job.

I stepped out of Maggie's cleaning van, and looked down at my attire. She told me that all of her maids wore the same outfit, and I had never felt more ridiculous in my life. I honestly was wearing a typical black-and-white French maid's outfit. I laughed and touched Maggie's company logo on my right shoulder. *Oh, Maggie.*

I turned around and looked up at the house that was mine to clean for the next four hours. *Holy shit.*

I walked up to the front door and lightly pushed the doorbell.

A few seconds later, I was greeted by an older man who was wearing a typical bellhop outfit. It took everything in me to hold in my laughter, but I managed to do it. "Hi, I'm Natalie with Maid For You. Is Mr. Bryant here?"

The elderly man did a little bow, and asked me to follow him. I may have made a small strange sound, because for some reason this whole thing was absurd. There were really people like this still in our world?

I followed Joe, I knew the name because as least Mr. Bryant was kind enough to have it embroidered on his shirt, and looked around the most beautiful home I had ever been in. The entire place seemed to be made out of wood, and it made me feel like I was in a mountain cabin. I used to stay with my dad when I was younger, before he took off and decided he didn't need us in his life. A sudden feeling of sadness crept through my body, but I instantly pushed it aside, and admired the structure of this beautiful home. "This is gorgeous," I said, more to myself but I got Joe's attention. He gave me a slight nod and motioned for me to follow him down a hallway.

"Mr. Bryant is in his office and asked if you could wait outside for a moment."

"Of course. Thanks, Joe." I smiled at Joe and he returned it instantly. Joe had one of those smiles that made his eyes light up, and I knew instantly I would like this guy.

"Any time, Ms. Rifton. If you need anything, please let me know."

I gave him a little wave goodbye, and sat on a plush lounge chair right outside Mr. Bryant's office. I looked down at my watch and noticed I was a few minutes early. I hoped Mr. Bryant appreciated punctuality and wasn't annoyed by my early arrival.

A few minutes later I heard the sound of a phone being clicked off, and I sat up straight, ready to meet my new client.

When the door finally opened, I stood to meet Mr. Bryant, and when I saw the gorgeous face that was staring back at me, I totally clammed up. Holy. Fucking. Shit. This was Mr. Bryant? I started to remember Maggie saying something about one of her girls sleeping with a client on the job. I wondered if it happened to be the man I was looking at? No, it couldn't be. This was the first time he was using her service. Me. Using me. He could use me all he wanted. I started thinking how long it had been since I'd had sex, not counting any time I used my vibrator. Months. Shit. I was in trouble. Just when I thought my ears had failed me and I had gone completely deaf, I noticed Mr. Bryant's lips moving.

"Natalie, right? Are you okay?"

I blinked a few times and sank my teeth into my bottom lip. I was speechless, but quickly gave myself a pep-talk to get me back to normal. "Hi, Mr. Bryant. Yes, I'm Natalie from Maid For You."

"Yes, that's what I asked you. I'm glad you made it. And early, too. I like that." He smiled at me and I swear I could feel a drop of warm liquid saturate my panties. No guy had never had an effect on me like this before.

I just smiled back and followed him into his office. When he clicked the door shut behind me, every fantasy I had of me dressed in my naughty maid outfit and him inside me flashed through my mind. I had to stop this, though, and get it together.

Mr. Bryant motioned for me to have a seat across from a beautiful mahogany desk, and he walked over to lean against the front of it.

"So, Natalie. I'm sure your boss told you what I'm looking for, and I understand you've agreed to all of my terms."

I cleared my throat and pulled out my notes from Maggie. "I believe so. I need to be here every other morning to make sure the house is in order, in case you have any business contacts coming by or for any dinner parties. I'll also have all of your laundry pressed and ready for you on Wednesdays, and on Fridays -"

Before I could finish, Mr. Bryant held up his hand, indicating he wanted me to stop.

"Yes, that's what I asked for. But I also had a note asking if the service ever offered a live-in maid. I assumed your employer talked to you about that and you've agreed."

I must have had a frantic look on my face, because Mr. Bryant placed his hand to his chin like he was equally confused.

"Well, no, sir. Let me look again and see if Maggie, my boss, put that note somewhere. Live-in maid? As in I would live here with you?"

Mr. Bryant chuckled and stood to walk around his desk. "Yes, Natalie. As in live here with me. Would you mind if I made a quick phone call while you think about this out in the hall?"

He picked up his phone, and I slowly rose out of my chair to make my way back to the hall. I smiled at him, and it was then that I noticed a small dimple in the middle of his chin. I wondered what it would be like to lick that little jewel, and found myself walking almost straight into the door. "Shit," I said as quietly as possible, but I knew he'd heard me by the lift of his brow. "I mean, yes, of course. I'll be out here when you're all finished."

I shut the door and quickly grabbed my cell out of my bag. I pulled up Maggie's number and pushed the green call button. Maggie answered after a few rings.

"Hey, girl. Everything okay? Did you find the place?"

I covered the phone with my hand and bent over a little to hide my face, just in case Mr. Freaking Gorgeous Pants decided to come back out into the hall. "Are you fucking kidding me? A live-in maid service? I didn't even know you did this. What the hell am I supposed to say to this man? Sure, I'll move in with you, but you really should buy me dinner first?"

Maggie made a weird sound and whispered back to me. "What did you just say? A live-in maid service? You've never heard of it because we don't do that."

"Well, that's not what Mr. Bryant said. He said it was in the paper work."

"No way it said that, I would have definitely remembered that. Wait, hold on. Something's coming through on the fax."

I could hear a few sounds that indicated Maggie had picked up some papers and was wrestling around with them. "Wait, his secretary just sent me something. It looks like they amended it and didn't send the final list. Oh shit, Nat. He does want a live-in maid. I didn't know, and we don't do this at all. If you want me to, I can talk to him and tell him there's been a misunderstanding. I can fix this."

Just as I was about to respond, the door opened again and there he was. Dark, beautiful hair, and eyes that were partly green and blue, almost like they couldn't make a decision and decided that both colors could stay. I pulled the phone away from my face and clicked if off. I could handle this and figure it out.

"I'm sorry about the confusion, Natalie. Please come back in and let's sort this out." He pushed the door open some more, and when I walked through I could feel his hand on the small of my back. A slow burning sensation formed around his touch, and if I thought my panties were wet earlier, well now they were just plain drenched. I couldn't believe the effect this guy was having on me, and he was only touching my back.

"That's okay, Mr. Bryant. My boss, Maggie, didn't quite understand what you were looking for."

"Please, call me Kent."

I gulped and watched his eyes roam down my totally inappropriate maid outfit. I could kill Maggie for letting her staff go out in public in these things. No wonder she had to have a set of guidelines. I felt like I was in a bad porno. "Okay, Kent."

I noticed his eyes flared for a split second, but then in an instant he was back behind his desk. "Please, have a seat. It looks like I have a proposition for you."

Well, now he had piqued my interest.

Chapter 2 - Kent

What the fuck was I doing? A proposition? A live-in maid service? I wasn't looking for either, and yet there went my mouth. I couldn't believe how I was acting, and never in my life had I felt more out of control. Natalie was right when she read off the list I'd created. I did just need a maid in the mornings. Hell, I already had a whole slew of workers that could take care of everything else. What would I do with a live-in maid? My mouth had made that decision for me before my mind could comprehend what I was saying.

However, for some reason, when I laid eyes on the woman before me, I decided right then that a live-in maid was what I wanted. I wanted her. I had never wanted something so much in my entire life, and here she was, sitting in front of me, in every man's fantasy outfit. Now I just had to persuade her to agree to my new plan. I also had to send flowers to Nancy, my secretary, for getting that new contract sent out so quickly.

"Yes, a proposition. You see, Natalie, my full-time housekeeper just had a baby, and has asked for a little maternity leave. I agreed that it was important for her to be home with her husband and child, so I decided to give her some time off. Jenny lived at home and had a half-hour commute both ways every day. It was hard, and I decided the next housekeeper I was going to hire needed to be able to live here. If this is something you'd consider, I'll make it well worth your time."

Natalie stared at me like I was standing in front of her wearing a black cloak and asking her for her soul. She must have thought I was crazy, but my excuse sounded plausible to me, even though I made half of it up. Yes, Jenny had a baby, but she didn't ask for time away. Her husband ended up getting a huge promotion and she decided to quit and be a stay-at-home mom. I couldn't argue with her decision, and her commuting wasn't a big deal, but for some reason my new mission was to get Natalie in my house.

Finally, she cleared her throat and started to fidget a little in her seat. "Well, you see, Mr. Bryant, I mean, Kent." She cleared her throat again and lifted her beautiful porcelain-like hand to her neck and stroked it softly. I felt the bulge in my pants grow by the second and tried to readjust myself without her noticing.

"Would you like a drink?" I asked and she quickly shook her head.

"No, no. I'm fine. It just seems a little warm in here." She uncrossed her legs and crossed them again, exposing a small glimpse of white cotton between her thighs.

I leaned forward and grabbed a pen and paper before I totally lost it. "Tell me, Natalie. Are you working anywhere else? Do you have a boyfriend who would have a problem with this? Anything that is an obstacle, I'm sure we can get it figured out."

Natalie sat up a little straighter and clenched her legs together. I wondered if I was having the same effect on her as she was having on me, but I chalked it up to nerves. "No. No boyfriend at this moment, and as far as work goes, I'm a chef at a small restaurant. I only work evenings and I'm really not making that much. I would have to quit, though, and I'm not sure I'm ready to do that."

I analyzed Natalie for a minute and started to really think about my rash decision. I was praying she wasn't crazy, but I also knew I wanted this. *Her.* I wanted her. I also replayed in my mind the fact that she didn't have a boyfriend. Perfect. "I promise that what I'll be paying you will make you never think about your past job."

Natalie looked down at her purse, and I could hear a quick vibration coming from inside it. She reached down and clicked her phone, to ignore a call, I assumed.

She looked back at me and sucked in her bottom lip. I wondered what she tasted like, and clearly had to readjust myself again.

"Well, I'm making close to twenty-five-dollars an hour with my current job, and I know that's low for a chef's salary, but I'm really close to getting my dream job. I can't just pass that up for a cleaning job, no offense."

I noticed a soft blush rise in her cheeks, and it made me want to make her blush every chance I could get. "What if I paid you double that and gave you full benefits? Would that change your mind?"

Natalie gulped and looked down at her hands. "Double that? You would pay me fifty dollars an hour? How would that work?"

I leaned back and thought about that. I obviously hadn't thought about my plan in great detail, but she didn't need to know that. "We'll clock you in at forty hours a week, and you'll get paid double for any extra time you put in. I'll have a system that you'll use to monitor your hours. You'll have your own suite, which will be on the west side of the property. You'll have access to the pool, gym, and any other amenities whenever you're not on clocked hours. I'm also intrigued by your cooking history and I would like to hire you as my personal chef. I would pay you for that service too, making your annual income almost triple what you make now. Does that sound like something you could do?"

Natalie's eyes were as big as saucers. I thought maybe I'd lost her, but just as I was feeling there was nothing else I could do, she finally responded.

"Okay, I'll take it. I'll be your live-in housekeeper and chef."

It took everything in me to hold back the grin that was threatening to take over, and I stood to shake her hand. "Great. I look forward to working with you, Natalie. Please make whatever arrangements necessary for the rest of the day, and I can have you moved in here tomorrow."

"Tomorrow?" Natalie gulped and placed her hands behind her back.

"Is that a problem?"

She shook her head and reached down to grab her purse. I got a perfect view of her large breasts and knew I'd made the right decision.

"No, not a problem at all. Thank you, so much Mr. Bryant, I mean Kent. I'll be here tomorrow, ready for our new arrangement."

Natalie and I walked back out into the hallway, and I could feel the electric energy between us. I hadn't felt this way about a woman in a very long time. I was used to the usual quick hook-ups, but by the second time, I was bored and ready to move on. For some reason, I wasn't too concerned that was going to happen with Natalie.

Chapter 3 - Natalie

"You're freaking kidding me. He said that?" Maggie was pacing around her office, stunned at the news I'd just shared with her. "He wants to pay over one-hundred-fifty grand for you to live in his mansion, swim in his pool, and all you have to do is cook and clean? Who is this guy? I don't know, Nat, it seems sketchy. I'd like to run a background check on him."

I watched Maggie as she lost her cool, and I tried to contain the snicker that was stuck in my throat. I did, however, appreciate that she was looking out for me. "Of course we'll run a background check. Maggie, the guy seems harmless. He has way too much money, but if I'm going to get my mom the treatment she needs, I have to do this. It's the best option so far."

Maggie walked over to a chair next to mine and sat down, facing me. "What else did he say? I just don't want this to affect my business, you know? I've never allowed a live-in maid service, and I don't want to start."

"Right, but what if all of his colleagues notice how great I am and want to hire more? You could really make some money off of this idea."

Maggie looked up at the ceiling, and I could tell she was contemplating my idea. "You're right. Except for one thing, one huge thing that you have to promise me."

I sat up a little straighter and gave her a quick nod. "Anything."

"Is he handsome?"

I let out a small laugh and placed my hand to my chest. "Why does that matter?"

"Nat, is he good looking?"

"He's fucking hot, but that doesn't matter. I'll do my job, I promise."

"Natalie Mae, you cannot sleep with Kent Bryant. I almost lost half of my clients when my last girl slept with the man of the house she was cleaning for. I'm not hosting an escort service, and I can't have my name ran through the mud."

I patted Maggie's cheek and let out a little sigh. "Mags, I would never do anything to jeopardize your business. I won't sleep with him. Besides, if I did, he'd probably be done with me and throw me out. Then what would I do? I'm about to quit my job and lease my apartment. I'd have nothing. I'm not stupid. I know how much I need this money."

"You know I'll lend you as much as I can. You don't have to do anything."

I stood up and walked over to a picture that captured Maggie receiving an award for her new business. "I know, hun, and I appreciate everything you're doing for me. You need to keep your money in your business. This is my problem, and I want to take care of it."

Maggie stood so she was standing right beside me and wrapped her arm around my waist. "Well, just think. You'll be living the dream for the next little bit, and if it doesn't work out, we'll just get you set up somewhere else. This is going to work out, I can feel it."

"Thanks. I don't know what I'd do without you, but now it's time to totally alter my life. I'm a little nervous, but I can't believe this opportunity. I'm going to call my mom's doctor and tell them we have a new payment plan."

We hugged each other and I headed out of her office, so I could be on my way to my new life.

The first thing I did was call my boss to tell him I had received a new job offer. He wasn't very happy and ended up offering me more money, but it wasn't close to what I'd be making with Mr. Bryant. I also let my landlord know about my new living situation and she was so sweet and generous. It ended up working out well because her niece was moving to the city and needed a place to stay. I agreed to leave my furniture, because frankly I wasn't quite sure how long my new arrangement would last. I was hoping for the next year, at least, because that way I would be able to save and have a great cushion for my mom and me to live off. Maybe by then I'd land a new chef career with Mr. Bryant's recommendation.

Later that night, when I was packing my belongings, I looked around my room and decided I was excited about doing something different with my life. I was stuck in a rut and everyone around me knew it. My love life was hopeless because of my odd working hours, and I barely had enough time to think about myself. Living with Kent would hopefully give me that sense of adventure I was looking for, and it would be especially fun looking at his gorgeous face everyday.

Speaking of his gorgeous face, I couldn't

seem to get his beautiful eyes out of my head. When I noticed I hadn't thought about him in a span of minutes, there his face was again, flooding my mind and holding it hostage.

I glanced at the clock next to my bed and couldn't believe it was already midnight. I decided to call it a day and pulled back my covers. The minute I closed my eyes, Kent's face appeared and sent a pulse of pleasure straight to my core. I let out a small hum and reached down to try to relieve some of the pressure that had been building up all day. Not sleeping with Kent, that was probably going to be one of my greatest achievements to this day, but I could at least pleasure myself while picturing his own hand in my panties.

I rubbed the top of my clit and let out a loud moan. I imagined Kent's rough hand pleasuring me, and his five o'clock shadow brushing across my face. Within minutes I was pulsing so hard I thought I was literally going to see stars. I'd hoped that having an orgasm would relieve some of my want, but it only intensified it. It made me want Kent more, and I hadn't thought that was possible.

**

I awoke the next morning with a huge bubble of nerves in the pit of my stomach. I hoped I was making the right decision as I looked at my packed bags by my door. I'd called my mother last night, and she was in tears when I told her I'd found a way for her to receive all of her treatments. I also called her doctor and told him to go ahead with our previous plans. She was going to get her mastectomy at the end of this week, and would start her chemo next Monday. I was ecstatic with how quickly her team was moving forward, and I had a really good feeling that we would beat the beast living inside of her.

I needed to talk to Mr. Bryant, however, and make sure I'd still be able to sneak away for my mother's appointments. I also didn't want to get too personal and tell him quite yet about her sickness.

I decided it was now or never, and I loaded up my new life and headed to my new mansion. I hoped I wasn't going to blow this and end up losing everything. I couldn't think like that now, because I had more important things to take care of. Like Kent Bryant. Fuck me, living with him was going to be hard. Literally.

When I pulled up to Mr. Bryant's estate, Joe greeted me and had another man with him to help me with my bags.

"Ms. Rifton, it's a pleasure to see you again," Joe said with a wink and continued to show me into my new home.

"It's nice to be here, Joe. Is Mr. Bryant home? I have a few questions I need to ask him."

Joe continued walking and motioned to the man who was carrying my belongings to continue up a large wooden staircase and he nodded as a reply.

"I'm sorry, Ms. Rifton, but he had some early business to take care of this morning. He sends his apologies and asked me to give you this." Joe handed me a letter, and I made sure to hold it tightly in my hand. "He should return later this evening, and has already set up a menu to his liking in the kitchen. If you need anything, please push the little red button that is located in every room."

I looked over at an intercom by the front door and realized it was setup throughout the entire house.

"Thank you, Joe, and please call me Natalie. It seems way too formal for you to be calling me Ms. Rifton." I smiled at my new friend and squeezed his arm.

He smiled back and gave me a quick bow before heading back outside.

I looked down at the letter I was holding from Mr. Bryant and did a quick survey of my living quarters. This place was massive. Who was I kidding? It was fucking huge! Why did one man need so much living space? I didn't understand it, but it also wasn't my job or my business to be wondering about my boss and his money situation.

I couldn't help but wonder how in the world I was going to clean all the windows in this place. The floor-to-ceiling glass was way beyond my reach, and I couldn't mention my fear of heights now. I also noticed all the wood and etched detail that was built into the design. I loved it. If I was ever able to design my own home, it would be a mirror image of this place.

I felt giddy all of a sudden and did a little happy dance that this place was actually my new home. I ripped the side of the envelope I was holding, and pulled out a lined piece of paper.

Kent had hand-written me a letter, welcoming me to his home. He also told me which room would be mine, and that all of my new job requirements were listed in an envelope on the desk in my new room.

I walked up the grand staircase and easily found my new living area. Kent wasn't kidding when he told me I would be staying in the west wing. I basically had my own living room, small kitchenette and en-suite. I gasped when I looked out my window and saw my view for the very first time. I loved living in a big city, but I also loved the rugged mountains that edged the suburbs. I'd never been in a more spectacular home, and it felt like my heart was about to jump right out of my chest.

After I finally composed myself and settled down, I walked over and retrieved my list for the day. It was a list of your basic cleaning requirements and I decided to get started right away, that way I would have dinner ready by the time Kent made it home.

I slipped on my work outfit and rolled my eyes when I looked at myself in the mirror. I did my hair in a quick side braid, put on my stupid little white hat, and found my cleaning supplies. I'd promised Maggie that I would wear her uniform, just in case one of Kent's business associates stopped by and noticed her logo. The things you do for friends. Truthfully, I owed Maggie a lot, so this was the least I could do.

When I was just about finished with my cleaning duties, I ventured to the kitchen and almost lost my bottom jaw. "Holy freaking shit. This is my new kitchen?" I said to myself and looked around one of the most topnotch kitchens I'd ever seen up close. I'd watched a few cooking shows on TV that featured kitchens that would compare, but I'd never seen anything like this in real life. I did another little happy dance and noticed the stove, or should I say, stoves. Yes, I had multiple stoves. I was in cooking heaven.

I looked over my menu for the week and decided Kent had impeccable taste in food. I loved everything that was written down, and decided I would add a few of my own touches to spruce things up a bit.

After I had finally finished cleaning most of the kitchen, I decided it was time to run to the store and grab the groceries I needed for the week. I noticed a credit card Kent had left with the list on the counter, so after I'd put on some more appropriate day clothes, I slipped it in my purse and made my way to the store. I'd never had an unlimited amount of money to spend while grocery shopping so this was a new experience that I had a feeling I'd love.

**

When I returned home, I slipped on my maid's outfit and headed to the kitchen to get dinner started. On the menu for the evening was southwestern maple glazed salmon with pineapple salsa. I was thrilled when I found a shop that sold flash frozen Alaskan salmon just a few minutes from the grocery store.

I always lose track of time and my surroundings when I get into my cooking mode, so the minute I heard a deep voice say, "Something smells amazing." I couldn't help the shriek that flew out of my mouth and almost caused the finished salmon to go crashing down onto the marble floor.

"Oh!" I yelped after I safely placed the dinner back onto the counter. I turned around and faced my new boss, my new lust obsession whom I couldn't touch. "Mr. Bryant, I didn't know you were home."

Kent ran one of his large hands through his hair and looked around the kitchen. He closed his eyes and smelled the air, as if taking in a scent that had never invaded his senses before. "I'm home a little early. I see you found your way around. The house looks great, and this salmon is making my stomach ache. When will dinner be served?"

I smiled at his kind words and glanced at the clock that was hanging on the wall. "It's cooling now, so it'll be ready to serve in fifteen minutes. Does that work for you, Mr. Bryant?"

"That's perfect, and please, call me Kent."

I just nodded and turned around to finish dinner. I didn't want to tell him that I felt very uncomfortable calling him by his first name. I could also feel his eyes on me, and I didn't know why, I guess I felt like playing with fire because I slowly bent over, opening the oven to retrieve the prosciutto-wrapped asparagus. When I heard Kent's breath hitch behind me, I smiled to myself and guessed the thigh highs I was wearing were to his liking.

I knew I was being a tease, but honestly, it felt good. It felt really good. I hadn't had a man look at me like Kent did in a while. I'd been too busy with my cooking career and didn't make time for a dating life. It was time I had a little fun. Besides, Maggie never told me not to flirt. No harm, no foul. Right?

Just to add a little salt to Mr. Bryant's wound, I spread my legs farther apart and reached in just a bit more, placing my ass higher in the air.

I slowly turned my head, and saw the want in his eyes. I knew I could have probably continued on, but there was no need to torture myself, especially because the only thing I'd have to satisfy myself at the end of the night would be my own fingers.

"I'll bring dinner into the dining room, Kent, in a few minutes. The table is all set."

I heard Kent leave the kitchen, and I assumed we both needed a minute away from each other. I replayed Maggie's plea not to sleep with my new employer, but I had a feeling it was going to be harder than I expected.

Chapter 4 - Kent

When I turned around to leave the kitchen, I about blew my load before I stepped through the doorway. Holy fucking shit did Natalie look hot in her little outfit. And paired with those thigh highs? Shit. I knew I couldn't just fuck her and send her packing, so I needed to play this out as long as possible. I didn't want to ruin our arrangement, but dammit, I needed her underneath me. Preferably tonight.

I closed my eyes for a moment to regain my composure, and when I felt my cock was ready to handle seeing Natalie again, I headed to the dining room.

Dinner smelled amazing, and I had a tinge of guilt when I thought about my regular cook, but she never looked like Natalie did in her uniform.

"This smells amazing, Natalie."

It almost looked like Natalie blushed a little, but she hid it well as she set down the main course in front of me. I almost asked her if she'd like to join me, but I felt like that was crossing a professional line. Hell, I was about to cross that line in more ways than one.

"Would you like a glass of wine to go with your salmon, Mr. Bryant?"

I didn't know why Natalie calling me by my last name bothered me, but I knew I loved hearing her same my first name more. I let it go, however, and decided to enjoy my meal. "That would be great. Thank you."

I watched her gently slide her hand around the glass bottle, and I could only imagine what that hand would feel like around my dick.

When Natalie reached me, she bent over me slightly, exposing her large and heavy breasts. I hadn't seen such a perfect chest in a long time. I noticed the black lace peeking through her uniform and pictured what she was thinking when she put that beauty on. Was she lusting after me just as much as I was lusting after her?

The wine started to flow into my glass, but I could only think about pushing her down onto the table and taking her from behind. I would keep that little maid's uniform on and give her the ride of her life. I knew, though, that it couldn't happen now. Not on her first night. I didn't know if her company had a policy about sleeping with their employer, but fuck it. I didn't really give a shit.

I tore my eyes away from her double Ds and told her that was enough wine. I took a sip and enjoyed the warm liquid flowing down my throat. "Thank you, Natalie. I think everything looks set."

Natalie gave me a nervous smile and stepped out of the dining room. I devoured her meal in just a few minutes and found myself wanting another helping. That rarely happened. I had just eaten the most delicious salmon I had ever tasted in my life. So not only could this woman clean, she cooked amazingly as well.

When my supper was finished, Natalie swooped in immediately and cleared my place. I would have to write to the owner of this company and say how wonderful Natalie was already. After dinner, I excused myself and finished up on a few business proposals. I was typing up my last document when I heard a light tapping on my door.

"Yes?" I asked, curious if everything was okay.

Natalie slowly opened the door and peeked through the crack. I couldn't make out what she was wearing, but it looked like some sort of see-through-top with boy shorts. I could tell she was trying to hide herself, but she wasn't doing a very good job.

"Mr. Bryant, I'm so sorry to bother you, but my shower isn't working in my suite. Is there another one I could possibly use?"

I looked her over, and noticed her hands covering her chest. It took all my energy not to walk over and move them so I could get a better look. But, I didn't and I said the first thing that came into my head. "Yes, use mine."

Natalie's shocked expression matched mine, but she didn't reply. She just simply nodded her head and closed the door.

Use mine? What was I thinking? I didn't know Natalie from the lady working at the grocery store down the street. Yes, I'd done an extensive background check on her last night, but that didn't mean I needed her going through my things. The damage was already done, so I needed to forget it.

When I was finished emailing my last document to a recent client, I shut down my Mac and called it a night. Natalie had taken up most of the space in my brain, so I wasn't able to focus on my normal nightly work tasks. Her long dark hair was flawless, just like her porcelain skin. I found myself noticing her small imperfections, like her nose lifted a tad at the end. I found it adorable, and it made me want to run my tongue across it. She also had a small scar above her lip. It piqued my curiosity and I wanted to find out how she got it. Her ice blue eyes were a complete contradiction to her hair, and it made me wonder why she was still on the market.

I finally made it to my room, and pushed my door open. The sound of the shower stopped me in my tracks, and I almost forgot that there was a beautiful naked woman cleaning herself just a few feet away. I decided to let it go, and I undressed for the night. I slipped into bed, and rolled over to my right side, hoping that sleep would take me, and I wouldn't have to think about my new maid.

Just as I was finally feeling the pull of slumber, the shower turned off and I noticed a beam of light coming from my master bathroom. The door was partly cracked open, and I could just make out the silhouette of a woman's leg. That got my attention, and it took everything in me to roll over and look the other way.

The sound of running water broke my strength, and it had me turning toward the light in a matter of seconds. I looked in wonder as Natalie propped one leg perfectly on the sink and ran her hands up and down her smooth, silky skin. I assumed she was applying lotion, but never could I have imagined her towel was going to have an opening that featured a perfect shot of her glistening lips. I licked my own lips, and continued to stare like a young teenage boy, getting his first look at a woman's treasure.

Damn, and she had a perfect one. Shaved, no less. I watched in amazement as she continued to lotion her body, unaware that she was putting on a show for her new employer just a few steps away.

I reached under the covers and found my rock-hard cock. It was almost painful when I began to stroke my soldier from tip to base. I thought about the women I had taken home lately, and I couldn't remember one that had me as hard as Natalie did at that moment. I could only imagine what she would do if I pushed the door open and pulled her towel down, exposing those amazing tits, and wet pussy. I had a feeling she would deny me, but I also wasn't brave enough to test out my theory.

I continued to stroke my member and briefly closed my eyes, imagining Natalie's hands on my dick. I was so close to coming, I needed one more look at her perfect, wet lips. I opened my eyes, and what I saw about nearly made me come right there. Natalie had dropped her towel, just enough to expose her full breasts. The towel was hanging on her womanly hips, and she had switched legs. She now had her left leg propped up on the bathroom counter. Her head was thrown back, and her wet hair cascaded nearly to the tip of her ass. I loved long hair, and I knew I would be wrapping her mane around my hand very soon. What totally made me lose it was what her hand was doing. I could only see her wrist, but her fingers looked like they were moving in a circular motion between her legs. I scooted up a little farther in my bed, and finally captured what I was after. Natalie was rubbing her clit, right in front of me. How she didn't know I could see her, was beyond me. Maybe she didn't even know I was in my bed yet.

I started to stroke myself faster and a groan slipped past my lips before I even knew it was coming.

Natalie's head snapped up and our eyes met for a split second. I couldn't break our contact, and just when I thought she was going to scream and slam the door, she did something so far out of the blue, that it made me instantly hard again.

She finished pleasuring herself and threw her head back again with pure bliss. I couldn't stop watching. Finally, after what felt like hours but was actually only a few seconds, Natalie reached behind her and clicked the door shut.

I lay in bed and replayed what had just happened a million times in my mind. I wasn't quite ready to barge through the bathroom door and have my way with her. I didn't want this amazing woman to get scared away on the first night.

Chapter 5 - Natalie

I couldn't control my breathing when I finally reached back and closed the door to Kent's master bathroom. I don't know what had come over me, but I felt more alive than I had in the last twenty years. Pulses of pleasure were still coursing through my body, and I finally looked at myself in the mirror. I wasn't sure how long Kent was watching me, but I couldn't will myself to stop when I found him eyeing me through the crack of the door. It was so hot, and I had come so hard that I had a hard time staying standing up.

I was sure the few extra glasses of wine I'd consumed earlier that evening had a little to do with my new-found courage, and I wasn't complaining. Getting off in front of Kent wasn't the same as sleeping with him, so in my eyes I hadn't broken my promise to Maggie.

I quickly finished my nightly routine in Kent's bathroom, and was ready to head back to my side of the house within fifteen minutes. I suddenly felt awkward walking through Kent's master bedroom while he was sleeping in his bed. If he was sleeping.

I flipped off the light in the bathroom, and made my way to the door that led out to the hall. I willed myself not to look in Kent's direction, and I started to feel somewhat shy when I made my way through his bedroom. I couldn't believe I masturbated in front of my new boss. What the hell was I thinking?

I picked up my pace and let out a breath when

I finally made it back out into the hallway. I closed Kent's door behind me and made a beeline for my end of the house.

When I made it back, I decided flirting with disaster wasn't worth it. I had my mother to remember, and if I messed up my new arrangement, I'd regret it for the rest of my life. I knew what I had to do. I had to apologize, and tell Kent that it was totally inappropriate of me to do that in his bathroom.

**

"Natalie, we need you to sit down. We have some news that is going to be very hard to understand and take in. First, please listen, and then if you have any questions, you may ask me after I explain everything."

I nodded and took a seat in the doctor's waiting room, where I heard soft sobs. I looked around and noticed I wasn't the only one receiving horrible news.

"Okay, just tell me what you found out."

The doctor sat down beside me, and flipped a few pages on her notebook before speaking. "Your mother's cancer had spread further than we had initially thought. We're afraid it has metastasized and we would like to do a full body scan."

I could feel the blood drain from my face, and I had to grip my chair's arm so I didn't tumble out of it. The doctor grabbed my arm and asked if I was okay. Okay? I knew what she was saying. My mother was dying. The only person I had in my life, and she was going to die, right in front of me.

"I'm fine." I sat up a little straighter and started to take in a few deep breaths. "We'll do whatever you need us to. So, it's stage four?"

The doctor squeezed my hand, and gave me a reassuring smile. "We don't know that yet honey, but we will after her scans."

I placed my hands over my face and thought about how much our lives were going to change.

When the doctor stood to leave, she cleared her voice and patted my shoulder. "One more thing, your payment has been declined. We're sorry, but we won't be able to take your mother as a patient anymore."

I lifted my head and the world started to spin. I couldn't make out the doctor's face and suddenly the room turned into Kent's large bathroom. I was naked and sitting on his counter with my legs spread. Kent stood before me, wearing an evil smile and wiping his large hand across his mouth. "You tasted exactly like I expected you to. Sweet and juicy."

I shook my head and tried to get back to the hospital, so I could explain to my mother's doctor that I had a new payment plan that was going work. I was just about ready to push Kent away from me, when he leaned forward and inched his huge cock toward my entrance.

This was the most real thing I'd ever felt, and just as the tip of his dick brushed across my clit, I let out a moan that rattled me awake from one of the strangest dreams I'd experienced in a very long time.

I quickly looked around the room and sighed.

I was in my bedroom in Kent's house and it took a few minutes for me to fully comprehend that it was all a dream. My mother didn't have stage four cancer, and Kent wasn't about to push himself inside of me. I reached down and felt my panties. They were about as wet as they could be, and I started to curse myself for waking up when I did. I probably could have used him inside of me for a minute to relieve the ache between my legs.

I lay in bed for a few more minutes before I finally admitted to myself that I was wide awake. I glanced at my nightstand and when I saw an angry 3:46 glaring at me, I decided a glass of cold water was what I was really craving.

I swung my legs out of bed and looked down at what I was wearing. I had on a tight, see-through white cami and some pink boy shorts. I looked over at my robe and decided that I was only going to my own little kitchen, and nobody better be in there.

When I made it over to my sink, I turned the handle and waited for the water to appear. Nothing. *What the hell is up with the plumbing in this house?* I thought to myself and looked at the empty cup in my hand.

My body was now screaming for water, and because the water must have been turned off on my side of the house, that meant I had to make a dash for the kitchen. My stomach must have heard my thoughts, because I felt it make a small rumble.

I tried to remember what I'd had for dinner, but all I could remember was the amount of wine I'd consumed. I had forgotten to eat.

I decided to give in to my cravings, and I

headed out toward the large kitchen that contained some very delicious salmon that was calling my name.

The minute I opened the large refrigerator and spotted my meal, I knew I had made the right choice. I rubbed my hands together and had made a grab for the salmon when someone behind me cleared their throat.

"Excuse me. What are you doing, Miss?"

I turned around so quickly I ended up banging my elbow on the refrigerator door. "Oh, Joe. Holy crap you scared me," I said, and rubbed the spot that was throbbing on my arm.

Joe let out a little laugh. "I'm so sorry, Natalie. I noticed some commotion in the house, and I was coming to see if everything was okay."

Commotion? Didn't this guy ever sleep? "I'm fine. I was just getting a little something to eat. I must have forgotten to eat dinner, and my stomach woke me."

I smiled back at Joe, and I felt almost like a teenager getting caught sneaking in late by her parents. "Is this okay?" I asked and pointed to the salmon sitting on the ledge in the fridge.

"Of course, Miss Natalie. I was just checking in. Carry on." Joe waved his hand in the air and disappeared before I could get another word in.

I turned and grabbed the salmon before anything else could get in my way. I decided to just eat it cold, right there on the kitchen counter. I hopped up and tore in to some seriously amazing salmon. I high-fived myself and decided I would have to make this dish again in the near future.

I was about halfway through when I heard a noise behind me. I figured it was Joe, again, and yelled before looking. "Back for a taste for yourself?" I asked in a teasing voice.

What I didn't expect was a deep cough and a noise that sounded like someone choking. I whipped my head around and saw Kent, my new boss, standing in the door way, holding his chest.

"Well, I wasn't expecting you to say that," was all he said while catching his breath.

I jumped off the counter as quickly as I could and started to put the lid back on the salmon.

"No, please, stop. You don't have to put that away. I didn't mean to startle you either. I've just had that damn salmon on my mind and decided I could use a midnight - "

Kent stopped mid-sentence and stared at me the second I turned around to face him. I had forgotten what I was wearing and was standing practically naked right in front of him. The way he was staring at me had my core tingling, and I could feel a small drip of moisture saturate my panties.

Kent raked his eyes over my body and stopped at my legs, which were crossed tightly to hide my obvious lust for him. I folded my arms across my chest, which only pushed my girls higher up. "I'm sorry. I woke up and realized I hadn't eaten anything tonight. There's still plenty left, and it's all yours."

I reached out and motioned for Kent to take the container of salmon. He, however, only had one thing in his sights, and it was me.

He walked over and pushed the salmon away

from me. "Why didn't you look away from me earlier?" he asked in a rough and gravelly voice.

I could feel the blush rise in my cheeks and I tried to look away from him. It didn't work, because I felt his hand grab my chin and he pulled my face back to his.

"I asked why you didn't look away."

I let out a breath and looked at him, right into his beautiful ocean-deep eyes. "Because I like the way you look at me."

Kent lost it and grabbed the other side of my face. He pulled me up to his mouth, and just as our lips were about to touch, he whispered, "And I like the way you look at me."

When our lips crashed together, a powerful jolt went straight to the spot between my legs that could barely take anymore. Kent reached around my head and wove his hand through my long hair. When he yanked me back, I opened for him and his warm tongue caressed my mouth.

"You taste so fucking good. Like pineapples." He came back to me, parting my mouth with his.

I moaned in approval, which only fueled his fire. He let go of my hair and placed his hands around my waist. Before I knew it, I was lying back on the counter, while Kent's mouth trailed a path of kisses up my stomach.

"This shirt, if you can call it that, needs to go. Now." I felt him pull and I heard a loud ripping noise. "Fuck me." I looked down as I felt the cool air hit my chest. Kent was looking at me like I was some kind of top filet mignon at an exclusive restaurant. "I've wanted to taste these too, from the minute I saw them in that maid's outfit."

I leaned my head back and moaned again as Kent bent and sucked one of my nipples into his mouth. This guy was freaking good with his mouth. Holy shit, he was good. I could feel the pleasure build in my core, and I had no other choice but to reach down into my panties to relieve some of the pressure.

Kent went over to my other breast, licking and sucking as I continued to make noises I had never heard myself make before. I would have been more embarrassed, but I didn't care what was happening, as long as he kept doing what he was doing to my chest.

When Kent finally pulled away from my breasts, he looked down and noticed my hand in between my legs. When he placed his hand around my wrist, I wasn't sure if he was going to join me or pull me away from pleasuring myself. What I wasn't expecting was for him to pull my hand to his mouth and suck my juices from my fingers.

"You taste like fucking candy."

I didn't know it was possible, but I became more turned on and put one of his large fingers in my mouth.

"You taste like sin."

Kent let out a low growl and pulled my panties right off me. I looked down at my naked body and watched Kent place his hands on my thighs. When he pushed them far enough apart to his liking, he bent down and went straight for my clit. I let out a scream when he sucked on my sensitive spot and reached up to cup one of my greedy nipples.

The feeling of pleasure that rocked through my body had me sailing to another place and screaming out words I didn't know were in me. "God, yes! Kent, that feels so fucking good! Don't stop!"

Kent pulled his tongue off me for a second and reached up to suck my nipple quickly into his mouth again. He must be a boob guy. "I knew you'd be this good. From the minute I saw you walk in, wearing that sexy little outfit, I knew it. You have no idea how much I wanted to throw you over my desk and fuck you from behind. You and that sweet cunt I knew would taste this divine."

I pulled Kent towards me for another quick kiss, and his words began to sink in. My maid outfit, when he first saw me, and wanting to fuck me. "Maggie," was all I said and I knew I had to stop this.

"Maggie?"

I pushed Kent off me and nodded. "I'm sorry, Kent. You're unbelievably hot, but I can't screw this up. I need this job more than you could possibly understand. I just can't."

Kent looked at me with bewildered eyes. "You can't?"

I crossed my legs and covered my bare breasts with my arms. "I can't. I promised my boss, my best friend, that I wouldn't sleep with you. She doesn't want her business ran through the mud. She's doing me a huge favor by letting me live with you, and I can't mess it up. Like I said, I need this job."

Kent backed up against the refrigerator and a look of understanding replaced the look of desire in his eyes. "Are you in some kind of trouble?"

My eyes unwillingly pooled with tears, and I quickly blinked them away. It had been a very long time since a man in my life asked a caring question. "No, nothing like that."

Kent leaned forward and ran one of his hands down the side of my bare leg. "Sleeping with me won't ruin your job here. We'll keep it casual. We'll fuck, but all in fun."

I loved what he was proposing, and it was right up my alley. I wasn't in the right place for a relationship, but a fuck buddy sounded damn good. I had still, however, promised Maggie. "As much as I want to say yes, can we just keep it a strictly professional relationship?"

Kent ran a hand through his hair and closed his eyes. "I guess if it's that important to you. Maybe it would be easier to say yes when you're clothed." Kent reached down and grabbed my ripped tank top. "I don't know if this is going to do any good."

We both started laughing and I held up a finger, indicating I'd be right back.

I hopped off the counter and headed to my room. I slid on my robe, and was back in the kitchen before Kent had even finished heating the salmon.

"There, is this better?" I asked and did a little twirl for him.

He looked me up and down and shook his head. "No, because I know you don't have any underwear on underneath."

I rolled my eyes and walked over to meet him by a small table at the edge of the kitchen. "Thank you, Kent, for hiring me, for understanding my predicament, and for keeping this professional. You have no idea how much this means to me."

Kent just smiled while he finished up placing the salmon on two plates. "Well, after this meal you made today, I would be a fool to let you go."

I chuckled as I sat down in the chair opposite him. We spent the rest of the night talking and laughing about our childhoods. He listened as I told him the story of how my dad liked gambling and drugs more than my mother and me, and I heard story after story about his uncle, and how he was more like a father figure to Kent than his own dad was. It was nice to have someone to talk to who'd also had a rough childhood with their father.

I almost told him about my mother a few times, but I wasn't ready to say it out loud. It would mean that her cancer was real, and I was still in a state of denial, I guess.

I did remind him that I would need this Friday off, but that I would work Saturday instead. He was so easy going, and didn't even flinch when I mentioned that I might need random days off during the week, but that I would always make them up.

I don't know how, some may call it luck, but I had just landed the best damn job in the entire universe. Even if I wouldn't be getting any sex on the side.

Chapter 6 - Kent

Doing the 'just business' relationship with Natalie was fucking ridiculous, but I could see it in her eyes the night we found each other in the kitchen that it meant a great deal to her. I would never force a woman to be with me sexually, so business it was. For now.

I didn't know why, but talking to her about our lives was actually quite pleasant. I couldn't remember the last time I sat and talked to a woman when I knew it wasn't going to lead to sex. Some of my friends would say I had an issue, that it wasn't normal to not want a relationship, but they didn't know what it was like growing up with my parents. They fought more than they breathed. I vowed at a very young age that I was never going to get married, and I still felt as strongly about it today, as I did when I was seven.

About a week later after staying a little later than normal at work, I found Natalie in her room. She was sitting on a chair rubbing her shoulder.

"Hey, is everything okay?"

Natalie turned around and smiled at me. "Yeah, I'm just a little sore. I haven't worked this hard, well, ever."

I chuckled a little and noticed a swimsuit on her bed. "Are you thinking about going for a swim?"

Natalie blushed and looked over at her suit. "I was thinking about maybe using the hot tub. It might relax my muscles. If that's okay?"

I thought about her in that small white bikini and it started to make me hard. Hell, everything she did made me hard.

"You can use the pool any time; I've already told you that."

She smiled at me and looked relieved. I was ready for her to loosen up more around me, especially if it involved a bed. For now, however, I was doing what she needed me to do. Keeping our relationship strictly business.

"Thank you. I'm going to get dressed then and head outside. I've got dinner for you in the oven. It should still be warm."

"Great. I'm starving. Help yourself to anything; you should know that by now." I walked over and squeezed her shoulder gently. As I was walking out of her room, I had to tell myself to calm down. Seeing her in that bikini was going to make it difficult for me to behave, but I could handle it.

After I inhaled some chicken parmesan that would even put the best chef's to shame, I decided to check on Natalie and see how her swim was going.

I walked out the back French doors and stopped dead in my tracks. Natalie was stepping out of the pool and hadn't noticed me yet. "Fuck," I said under my breath, and readjusted myself.

She looked around, maybe checking to see if anyone was looking, and then slipped into the hot tub. Her back was to me, and I noticed that she was fidgeting with her top. Holy hell, she better not be thinking about taking it off. I could understand how wonderful it would feel, but to have her topless just feet away from me would be my undoing. Promise or not.

I sat down in a chair by the back door and watched with amazement as she pulled off her top and sank deeper into the water. I could hear her groan from where I was sitting, and I knew I wasn't going to be able to take it much longer.

Natalie dunked her head under the hot water and came up on the opposite side, finally noticing that I was sitting outside watching her every move.

"Oh, Kent. I'm so sorry. I didn't know you were out here." She leaned forward to grab her top, but I put my hand in the air and started walking towards her.

"No, it's okay. I should have said something. I didn't know you were going to go topless, so I decided to let you have your fun."

I could tell that my words made her blush, but I couldn't stop myself.

I knew she wouldn't be able to reach her top without me seeing her full, gorgeous breasts, so I stopped a few feet away from the hot tub. "I'll go back inside to give you some privacy."

I could tell that Natalie wanted to say something, but she didn't, and started to look around the back yard.

Finally, she looked back at me and smiled. "If it isn't totally inappropriate, it would be nice if you joined me."

I coughed a little and thought about sitting with her in the water, with her naked breasts only mere inches away from me. "That actually sounds nice, but you'll have to put your top back on. I won't be able to keep our agreement if not."

I earned a quick head nod and walked over to a lounge chair where I started to remove my shirt and pants.

"You aren't going to get your suit?"

I laughed and pulled my socks off, leaving me in my boxer-briefs. "No, these will work just the same."

I noticed her eyes roaming my body and I had to admit that I really did love how she looked at me. "I'll turn around so you can get your top on."

When my back was to her, I heard a little splashing noise. When I finally heard a soft, "Okay," I turned around and Natalie was securing the back strap to her top.

When I slipped into the water, I could feel my body thanking me. This was a fabulous idea and it made me make a mental note to get in this bad boy more often.

"Did you have a nice day at work?" she asked.

I leaned back and tried my best to keep my eyes off her cleavage. "I did. It was a long day, but I got a lot accomplished. You?"

Natalie also seemed to relax a little and told me about her day cleaning and cooking. "I've got to admit, I like this job way more than I expected to. It's not so bad. It's a lot of work and I have sore muscles that I didn't even know I had. But, I like it."

I smiled at her and reached over to hit the jets. I loved the way the hot pulses eased my muscles.

Natalie leaned back and looked up at the dark sky. "God, this feels amazing." She became quiet, but then turned to look at me. "Would you like something to drink? I could go and grab you a glass of wine."

I loved the sound of that. "That sounds perfect, but make it two."

Natalie looked at me skeptically, but then seemed to relax and started to climb out of the tub. "It does sound perfect. I'll be right back."

I didn't hide the fact that I watched her as she lifted her leg over the side and gave me a perfect shot of the hidden spot between her legs. That white swimsuit hid nothing. It was as if she was naked.

I reached down to my cock and gave it a quick pat. Poor guy, I could literally feel his pain.

A few minutes later, Natalie was back with two glasses and a bottle of pinot. "I hope you like this wine. I found it at a market last Sunday in town, and it looks really good."

I watched as she set the glasses and bottle down, and I held out my hand to help her back into the hot tub. She must have missed her footing because instead of gracefully entering one foot at a time, she ended up slipping and landed practically on my lap.

"Shit, I mean, dammit. I'm sorry."

I pulled back and was face-to-face with her huge breasts, but I wasn't complaining one bit. She quickly stood-up and returned to her side of the tub. I grabbed the bottle and poured us both a glass of wine. She was right, the wine was delicious.

After thirty minutes of talking and sharing

more stories about our pasts, I decided my body was done, but I wasn't ready to leave yet.

"I'm starting to overheat. Want to go for a little swim?"

Natalie smiled and jumped up, splashing water in my glass. "Oh! I didn't mean to splash you."

I waved my hand and followed her out of the hot tub. Fuck me and that little white suit. I stood back and watched as Natalie finally jumped into the water. I started to walk down the pool stairs, when she came up and faced me. Her top had slipped and one of her nipples was visible, and I swear that I was being punished for all the naughty things I'd done in my past.

I couldn't look away and when Natalie finally realized she was hanging out, she blushed and fixed it immediately.

"Geez, this swim suit is being a pain."

"I think you're trying to kill me."

Natalie looked back and me. "I'm not, and why would you say that?"

"Are you fucking kidding me? Look at you in that suit. I've been practically sporting a boner all night."

If I thought I'd seen Natalie blush before, apparently it wasn't full force. Her cheeks turned a rosy red as she looked away from me.

"Look at me."

She did, but she didn't hold eye contact very long. "I'm sorry, Kent. I'm not trying to be a tease, but it's hard for me too. I just can't screw this up."

I started to inch down the steps. "You said no

sex, right? With each other? What if we do something that will at least relieve some of this tension we're feeling, but we don't break any rules?"

I could tell that I had gotten her attention. "Okay, what do you have in mind?"

"I want you, and you obviously want me. We can keep this relationship strictly work related, but who says we can't pleasure ourselves while watching each other?"

Natalie looked a little nervous, but then glanced at my naked chest. "I guess that would be okay. As long as it only happens this one time."

I crossed my fingers over my heart and reached down to remove my underwear. It didn't matter that I was now standing in cool water, my cock was so hard and I knew that it wouldn't take long to get the relief I needed.

"I'm not taking my suit off. I'll just pull it to the side."

The hell she wasn't. That wasn't going to work for me. "The fuck you aren't. I want to see you and that perfect little pussy of yours."

I could tell my words shocked her, but she did what I asked. She pulled her top off, and reached down to remove her bottoms.

"I promise after this, we'll go back to being strictly business."

I knew I was lying and I had a feeling she knew it too.

I placed my hand on my dick and slowly started to stroke it. I walked over to a shallow area and went to stand on a step. Natalie had a perfect

I'm Maid For You

view of my cock, and I could see her eyes widen.

She followed, but sat on the opposite side of the stairs.

"Spread your legs. I want to see that cunt of yours before you touch it."

Natalie let out a small breath, but did what I asked. When I saw her pinks lips, I started to stroke myself faster. "Fuck, yeah. That's it."

Natalie reached down and started to slowly touch herself. Her moans had me pick-up my pace, and before I could stop myself, I stood and walked closer to her.

Her eyes were closed, and when she finally opened them and saw me standing right above her, she gasped and picked up her own pace. "No touching. You promised."

"I won't touch you, but I need to be closer."

Natalie stood and went to sit on the highest step, exposing all of her naked body to me.

"God, you're beautiful."

I knew I was close, and I could tell she was too. "Come with me, and then we can put this behind us. I needed this. Fuck, I needed this."

"Me too. I doesn't matter what I do, I can't get this pressure to leave my core."

I leaned closer to her and pushed her back against the edge of the pool. "I promise I won't touch you anywhere else."

I kneeled down and had my dick so close to her entrance that it took everything inside of me not to just thrust it inside of her.

"God, this is so hot. I've never done anything like this before," she said in a breathless voice.

"I'm close. I'm going to come on your stomach."

Natalie's eyes shot open, and before I could stop, I came so hard, my white liquid covering her huge tits and tight stomach. "Fuuuck!"

Natalie leaned her head back and yelled, indicating that her own orgasm took over.

I pumped my cock a few more times and sat back down in the water.

I looked over at Natalie. I couldn't help but love seeing her covered in my liquid. I thought, however, that she was going to be upset that I did that, but she didn't say another word. She dipped into the water and cleaned herself off. Then she stepped out of the pool, retrieved her towel and suit, and headed inside. I knew she was regretting what we'd just done, but I sure as hell wasn't.

**

Natalie and I had gone an entire week keeping our relationship purely about work after the pool incident. Every night when I went to bed, I tried to relieve the hard-on she gave me, but for some reason I had an insta-boner the minute I thought of her ripe pussy. I didn't know how I was going to keep going this way, but she was staying true to her word. This Maggie friend must really be important to her.

I even tried to call one of the many women who were in my little black book, but when it came time to schedule a place and time, I hung up the phone. They weren't Natalie, and they wouldn't do.

I needed her. I knew if I could just have her one time, get my cock in her tight little pussy one time, I'd get over this obsession with her. The only thing was I had to persuade her to believe the same thing.

Later that evening when I finally made it home from work, Natalie had dinner on the table and it smelled amazing. "What did you make tonight?" I had given up on my own menu, because she already knew how to make some of the best dishes I'd ever had.

Natalie smiled and lifted up the cover of my plate. "I made beef Wellington with green peppercorn sauce. This was one of my most popular dishes at my last restaurant, and I hope you enjoy the cabernet I paired it with."

I licked my lips when I noticed how perfect everything on the plate looked. I also noticed how hot Natalie looked in her skimpy little uniform. I didn't understand how Maggie made her girls wear that outfit, but didn't want any of the clients to have sex with them. It was every man's wet dream come true.

"It looks amazing." Before I could help it, I blurted out something I had never asked my help in the ten years I'd owned this home. "Would you like to join me tonight?"

Natalie's eyebrows shot up and she looked down at her outfit, running her hands down her sides. "Oh, no Kent. You don't have to do that. I enjoy eating with Joe and Benny in the butler's kitchen." She smiled, but I could tell she was slightly embarrassed.

"I wouldn't ask if I didn't mean it. Please,

join me. This looks too good to enjoy by myself. Besides, I need to talk to you about my dinner party this weekend. We could go over the menu together."

Natalie looked down at herself again and finally shrugged her shoulders. "Okay, let me go and get an extra plate. I'll be right back."

A few minutes later, Natalie sat across from me and we both began eating one of the best beef Wellingtons I'd had in my life. "This crust around the meat is amazing. Natalie, you're one of the best cooks I've ever had. I'm very surprised you don't have your own restaurant already."

Natalie took a sip of her wine and blushed a little at my words. "Thank you, that's really kind of you to say."

We spent the next hour talking about the menu for my party, and more about our lives. Natalie mentioned that her mother was the only person in her family she was close to. I also only had my uncle, but he passed away a few months ago. I connected with her, and something inside me started to feel diffcrent. I started to think what it would be like if Natalie wasn't sitting here, if she wasn't in my life.

I shook those thoughts away, and asked Natalie if she wanted to open another bottle of wine.

"I can't believe we already finished the cabernet. It was so good, but I think I have a better one. I'll be right back."

Watching her walk out of the dining room had me thinking about that fine little ass under her outfit. How it would feel when I finally cupped it in my hands. She would fit perfectly, I just knew it.

My cock was now at full attention, and I cursed myself for thinking about Natalie naked.

She was back quickly and poured us both a full glass of wine. When she sat down, one of her buttons popped free, exposing the tops of her full breasts. How she fit those girls inside that uniform all day was beyond me. She didn't seem to notice, and as I was a bit sexually frustrated, I didn't let her know anything had happened either.

We finally had a good plan for Friday night. Any time Natalie spoke, it took everything in me not to stare at her cleavage spilling out over her top. Just when I was about to lose it, a second button came free and I got a glimpse of the hot pink lace bra that was holding those babies in.

I let out a huge breath and downed the last of my wine. "If your breasts keep falling out of that damn outfit in front of me, I'm going to forget our deal."

Natalie gasped a little and looked down at her chest. She covered it quickly and tried to button the two that had come undone. "Oh geez, I'm so sorry. All of my friends used to be jealous of my boobs, but they have no idea what a pain in the ass they can be sometimes. Oh shit! I just broke one of the buttons. Dammit, I'll be right back."

I held up my hand and told her to have a seat. I went into the kitchen and found a safety pin in the drawer by the door. "Here, this should work."

Natalie thanked me and started to fix her top button. She flinched and cursed a little under her breath, and I tried really hard not to laugh. "Having trouble?"

She admitted defeat and waved the pin toward me. "Obviously. A little help?"

I knew I should have said no. I knew what was going to happen the minute I walked over and took the safety pin in my hands, but I didn't give a flying shit. "Here, lean back so I don't poke you."

We both fell quiet, and then the sound of laughter filled the entire dining room. "Shut up, you know what I mean."

Natalie pushed her chest out so I could get to the button hole, but just as I was about to run the sharp end through her fabric, I dropped the pin into the darkness between her breasts. "Dammit," I cursed and without thinking reached down to retrieve the pin.

Natalie tried to push my hand away, but in doing so, two more buttons came loose and her outfit practically fell to the sides and exposed her entire chest.

"Fuck," I breathed and looked into Natalie's crystal blue eyes.

I didn't care about anything at that moment, except having my mouth on her exquisite tits.

I reached down and pulled her up onto the table, sending her plate crashing to the ground. Her yelp didn't deter me, and before either one of us could speak, I had her maid outfit around her waist and her bra unsnapped.

"Tell me to stop and I will. Tell me you don't want this as much as I do."

When she didn't say a word, I removed her pink bra, hurling it across the room. Her small, peachy nipple was calling my name and when I sucked that beauty into my mouth, Natalie's moan only intensified my desire.

I kneaded the other nipple with my finger, and I felt Natalie spread her legs. She wanted me, and there was nothing that was going to stop me this time.

"You taste so good. I can't stand not having you. Please, think about my proposal. No one would have to know. You have my word."

Natalie slipped one of her hands down my pants and wrapped her soft fingers around my cock. "I've dreamt about this, and you feel exactly the same as in my dreams."

I snapped my head up and I looked at her. "You dream about me?"

"Every. Single. Night."

I grabbed the back of her head and brought her mouth to mine. I didn't know how, but it was even hotter than the other night in my kitchen, or our little moment in the pool. We kissed like we couldn't get enough as Natalie continued to stroke and cup my dick.

"You're so hard. You're going to feel so good."

"So you'll do it? I promise nothing will get in the way of work. You'll continue to work here, I give you my word."

I must have hit a chord, because Natalie pushed me off her again and grabbed her uniform. She dressed in a hurry and stormed out of the room.

I wasn't giving up this time. I knew we could make this arrangement work. We had to. "Natalie, wait!" I hollered and grabbed her arm before she made it into the kitchen.

"Stop, Kent. I didn't mean to lead you on, again, but I just can't. You have no idea how much I need the money from this job."

Natalie looked away from me, and I could tell she was about to cry. "Just tell me. I would like to say we're friends, and maybe I can help."

When she placed her hands over her face, I knew I was getting closer to breaking through the wall she had built up.

"My mom has breast cancer. Stage three. That's why I was gone last Friday and why I need Wednesday off. They're starting chemo. I'm all she has, and we need the money. She doesn't have insurance, and she'll die if I can't make this work."

"Shit." That was not at all what I thought was going on. I figured she had some kind of gambling debt, or shopping addiction. "I can't believe you didn't tell me this earlier."

Natalie wiped away a tear that was running down her face and tried to look away from me. I pulled her chin to make her face me and made sure she could see my eyes. "You have my word that your mother will be taken care of."

Natalie lost it and sobbed into my chest. I held her, for what seemed like hours, and let her get it all out. I let her long hair down, and stroked her locks while telling her over and over again that it was going to be okay.

"I can't lose her. She's all I have."

"You have me now too. I know I'm just your client, but I'm here for you. I'll help you get through this."

"Why? Why me? You don't have to do this; you don't have to feel sorry for me."

I didn't know what to say, so I let my mouth do the talking. I cupped her chin with my hand, and gently brought her lips to mine. She tasted like salt water, and I never wanted to stop.

She finally gave in to me and I could feel her relax underneath me. I grabbed her hand and led her out of the kitchen, up the stairs to my bedroom. When I clicked my door shut, I started to unbutton my shirt. "You don't have to do anything, but I'd like you to lie with me tonight. In my bed."

Natalie nodded once, and started to shimmy out of her maid's outfit. I told myself to be a gentleman, and for once in the past week, I felt I had control of my cock.

"Come here." I pulled her over to my bed and laid her down under the blankets.

I walked to the light switch and clicked it off, which only left a small beam of moonlight trickling in through the curtains.

"You're being wonderful, Kent. Thank you."

I slipped into bed beside her and pulled her to me. "I can't imagine what you're going through, but know that you won't lose this job. I promise."

Natalie looked up at me with wanting eyes. "Okay. I want this, you, so bad. I'm trusting you."

I didn't waste a second before I had her mouth on mine. We kissed and our tongue's tangled like they were long-lost lovers.

I sat up and cupped Natalie's bare breasts in each hand. "Have I told you how fucking hot your tits are?"

Natalie giggled and shook her head.

"Well, they are. Fucking spectacular."

I leaned down and kissed all around her areola. I could feel her wiggle beneath me, and it made me want to take my time even more. I licked, and nipped, and took my time with each nipple. By the time I was kissing a path down her stomach, Natalie was about to lose it.

"Please, you're taking too long."

I chuckled and pulled down her pink thong. "If I would have known what you've been wearing under your uniform, I wouldn't have made it this entire week without touching you."

I took in her scent when I finally made it to the place I had been thinking about nonstop. It was recently shaved, and I could practically hear it calling my name. I pushed her legs apart and noticed a small amount of moisture drop onto the sheet below her. I started at the base of her opening and licked to the very top. I took her clit in my mouth and gave it a hard suck. Natalie bucked beneath me, and placed her hand's above her head.

I continued to lick and suck, and soon she was calling my name, and pulsing sweet juices in to my mouth.

I crawled back up her body and took her mouth with mine. I wanted her to taste herself on my lips, to show her what made me so crazy.

"Now, I'm going to fuck you. Hold on."

I grabbed my dick and stroked it slowly up and down Natalie's slit. She moaned with approval and reached down to open herself to me.

"Patience, dear."

"Please, I need you inside of me."

Without thinking, I pushed my cock deep into the folds of her heavenly bliss. We both cried out and I knew I wasn't going to last long. Just as I went to pull out, I remembered that I didn't have a condom on. No wonder it felt so amazing. I had never done it bareback before. I decided a few more thrusts wouldn't hurt anyone, and so I took my time, enjoying this new sensation. "Fuck me, you feel wonderful. I knew you would. So fucking tight. Dammit, I'm not going to last long. I promise I'll make it up to you."

Natalie grabbed one of my nipples and gave it a hard pinch, which made my dick throb deep inside her pussy. "Fuck, don't do that."

She laughed but then quickly moaned when I reached down and found her clit with my finger. I began to rub and push into her at the same time, making her call out unrecognizable words.

I finally pulled out completely, and almost told her to grab a condom from my nightstand. For some reason, something completely unnatural crept into my mind. Natalie, with a round belly. Carrying my child. It was the first time an image like that didn't send me running for the hills.

Natalie looked at me in bewilderment, and I could tell she thought I was having second thoughts. She couldn't have been further from the truth. I wanted this woman. I wanted her every night in my bed, and I wanted her to have my children. I couldn't believe what I was thinking, and I'd only known her for a week.

I leaned down and kissed her gently on the

lips, before thrusting into her core a few more times.

"Fuck!" I screamed as I came so hard, my cum had to have filled her entire body.

Natalie was breathing hard, coming down from her own orgasm. I slowly got off her and walked into my bathroom to get a washcloth. I looked at myself in the mirror and thought about what it would be like to be a dad. Who knew if she was even able to get pregnant? Or hell, maybe she was on the pill. That's probably why she didn't say anything. A sudden feeling of sadness crept through my body, and I decided I was going insane.

When I walked out to clean her up, she was already standing by the door, slipping on her work outfit.

"What in the hell do you think you're doing?" I asked, and stalked over to her.

Natalie's surprised expression told me she thought she was doing what I wanted her to. "I'm getting dressed and going to my room."

"The hell you are. Get back in bed. Now."

Natalie pulled her outfit tighter and looked back at me with angry eyes. "You can't talk to me like that. Just because we had sex -"

I couldn't take it anymore, and picked her up and threw her over my shoulder. "You are sleeping here tonight, because we aren't done having sex. Did you really think I'd want to have you one time and call it a night?"

"Well, no I -"

"Then get your naked ass back in bed. We aren't even close to being done."

Natalie finally let out a little laugh when I set her down and discarded her uniform on the floor. "You're bossy."

"Yes, I am. I tend to get what I want."

"I didn't notice," she said in a sarcastic tone.

Natalie crawled back in bed, and I retrieved the wash-cloth I had originally gotten to clean her. "Spread your legs."

She did, and I wiped the remnants of our sex off her. "Are you on the pill?"

Natalie's face went from a blushing pink color, to stark white. "Shit! No, I'm not. Oh, shit, Kent! I didn't even think about it. It's been so long, and I figured you had a condom on. I don't know why, but shit, shit, shit."

I chuckled and lay down beside her. "I figured you weren't."

Her shocked expression turned to fear when she looked up at me. "I'm clean. Are you?"

"Of course I am. That was the first time I'd ever had sex without a condom. It was so fucking amazing, I didn't want to stop."

"What if I get pregnant?"

"Would it be the worst thing?"

Natalie stared at me like I had two heads. "You barely know me."

"I know you're the most beautiful woman who's ever been in my bed. I know that you drive me absolutely insane, and all I want to do is know more about you. I know that picturing you with my child inside of you is one of the most wonderful things I've ever imagined. So, yes. I do know you."

Natalie huffed out a breath and closed her eyes for a second. "Well, I'm only a few days away from starting my period so we should be okay. I don't know, Kent. I'm not ready to have a baby. I'd like some other things to happen first."

I smiled down at her, but made the mistake of looking at her tits again. I felt my cock spring to attention, and I know she did too. If she thought she was getting any sleep tonight, well she thought wrong.

Chapter 7 - Natalie

I couldn't believe it when I felt Kent's dick get hard beside me. We literally just had the most mind-blowing sex minutes before, and he was already set for round two? I smiled. I wasn't complaining one bit.

It probably should have scared the crap out of me to hear him talk that way about having kids already, but I knew the chances of me getting pregnant were pretty minimal. My mother had an extremely hard time getting pregnant with me, and my high school boyfriend and I occasionally used protection. I know it's a stupid thing for kids to do, but we timed it right and we both loved the feeling of not wearing condoms. I hadn't gotten pregnant then, and I knew my chances now were so slim that I didn't even give it another thought.

I pushed Kent on to his back and licked my lips when I saw his erection standing to attention. He had a very beautiful penis. It was long enough, but not so huge that it made me run away screaming. "It's my turn to taste you."

Kent leaned back and groaned when I took his swollen head into my mouth. I sucked him and drew my tongue up the sensitive vein that ran from tip to base. He weaved his fingers through my hair and gave me an encouraging push to continue on. I sucked, and licked as my boobs glided along the rough skin of his legs.

Kent reached down and pinched one of my nipples, causing me to sink my teeth into the tip of his dick. He jumped and looked down at me. "Easy, you about got bit."

Kent laughed and continued to rub and play with my boobs while I gave him one hell of a blow job, if I do say so myself.

Right before it felt like he was close to his release he said, "Okay, I need to be in you."

He stood, grabbed my waist, and flipped me around so my ass was right in front of him. "I've wanted you like this since the minute I saw you. I knew fucking you from behind would be one of the greatest things in the world."

I held my breath and placed my arms in front of me on his bedspread, while he made a licking sound, and placed a wet finger at the entrance to my core. "So wet and ready."

I pushed my ass in the air as Kent grabbed my hips and scooted me to the edge of his bed. He lined up his dick with my entrance, pushed once, and filled my pussy completely. "Oh my God! Kent, fuck me."

"With pleasure." And he set a harsh but blissful pace, pumping in and out of me, while squeezing my ass.

I was about to lose it, when his finger started to trail a little too close to a hole that wasn't meant for anything to enter it. "Um, no." I said quickly and started to pull away from him.

He laughed and grabbed me again by my waist and sank back into me. "Let me just try something. If you don't like it, we'll stop."

I closed my eyes and hoped none of my dead relatives could see what I was doing, and gave him a quick nod.

He placed his finger again right at the entrance to a place I never thought I'd let anyone close to. The pressure of his finger entering me and his cock pounding the hell out of my cunt had me screaming at the top of my lungs.

"You like it? I knew you would, because you're a dirty girl. I could tell. I'm going to fuck you so hard, that I'll make everyone around us hear you scream."

I didn't know why, but having someone talk so dirty to me turned me on more than anything else ever had. I lifted my ass higher in the air and matched his thrusts. I could feel him swell, and I knew he was close to coming again. "I love it. I didn't know I'd like it so rough and dirty."

Kent pulled out and grabbed my butt, pulling my cheeks apart. Before I could object, he slowly entered my ass, and had me squealing. "Ow!"

He quickly pulled out and started to massage my hole. "You're not ready. We'll save that for later."

I didn't say anything because frankly I wasn't sure that I would ever let him have anal. "Just fuck me."

Kent pushed into me so hard, I almost face-planted onto the bed. He grabbed my ass and started to squeeze and massage it every time he pumped into me. "God, you're so fucking hot." He picked up his pace, and when I felt his finger by my forbidden hole again, I lost it and had one of the strongest orgasms I'd ever had.

"Yes! Fuck! Yes!" Kent's liquid spilled into

me, and I felt the warm surge flood my insides.

He reached down and ran his finger along my entrance. I turned around and grabbed his hand, placing his finger in my mouth.

"You are a dirty girl."

I smiled and bit the tip of his finger, causing him to pull it out.

We had sex one more time before sleep overtook us. I wasn't sure what to think of my new situation, but I also knew that having sex with Kent was one of the best things I'd ever done. I wasn't even close to being ready to let that go.

**

Early the next morning, I woke from a magnificent dream. Kent's lips were on my wet, eager pussy and he was showing me how good he was with his mouth. When I batted my eyes open, I found that my dream was actually reality. Kent's head was under the sheets, and he was having his way with me. No wonder I thought it was such a realistic dream.

"I could wake up like this every morning."

I pushed the covers back, and Kent raised his head and licked his lips. "Me too."

He went back and not only used his tongue, but had his fingers doing ungodly things to me. I came so hard, I wasn't sure if my body was going to survive him.

"I can't believe I really thought I wasn't going to sleep with you."

Kent laughed and pulled himself up my body.

He played with my breasts until he had me begging for more. I never understood when my friends would say that a guy drove them crazy in bed, until now.

"Please don't make me beg. I need you inside of me."

"But, I love your boobs. They're so big and fun to play with."

Kent pushed them together, and started to rub his dick in between them. I sucked his tip right when it came close enough, and he leaned back and let out a loud moan. "That's so hot. I love titty sex."

That wasn't the first time I'd heard that. Guys loved my boobs.

He continued to fuck my tits, until I finally couldn't take it anymore. I flipped him over, so he was underneath me. "It's my turn to have a little fun."

Kent agreed and sucked one of my nipples into his mouth while I positioned his cock underneath me. We both gasped and cursed when I slowly sank down and took him inside of me. I rode him and rubbed on him, all while he played with and sucked on my breasts.

"You're so tight, I can't last long with you."

I laughed and picked up my pace. I could feel the pressure inside me build, and just as I was about to cum, Kent pulled me off and flipped me around so he was on top of me again.

"My turn." He smiled deviously at me and pushed into me, making me orgasm and pulse as he pumped a few more times, spilling his own orgasm inside of me.

"You're amazing," Kent said and licked the tip of my nose. "I've been wanting to do that for a while, too."

I looked at him like he was losing it, but he just laughed and jumped off the bed. "I have a busy day at work. We just picked up a new client, and I have a lot of work to do before we get his business out there. I'll be back late, but let me know if you need anything."

"Yeah, my boss is a real hard ass. I better get to work as well." I squealed as he walked back over to me and swatted my ass. "See? He's abusive too."

"I'll show you abusive..."

But before Kent could smack my ass again, I rolled over to the other side and grabbed my uniform.

"Get ready for work. I'll be downstairs." I ran out of his room and shut the door behind me. I didn't know what was going on between us, but I did know that I kind of liked it.

Chapter 8 - Kent

Natalie had cast some kind of spell on me. She was all I could think about, dream about, and I was constantly surrounded by her scent wherever I went. I'm pretty sure she bewitched me. I'd never felt that way about a woman, ever.

I had a few guy friends who told me that when they met their wife, they knew instantly that they were done. Well, I was done searching and wanting other women, because I couldn't imagine anyone being better than the woman I had found. I now knew what they meant. Thinking about being with another woman was like buying a suit from a different tailor. I knew what I liked, and I didn't want anything else.

The next few weeks flew by, and Natalie and I meshed together like we'd been doing this for years. She would mostly stay in my room, and we would spend the night tangled up together, or pass the hours talking about the future.

Except I noticed she seemed a little distant. She'd come up with some kind of excuse to sleep in her suite, and had been at the hospital more with her mother. I'd tried to get her to talk to me about her mom's cancer, but every time I got close, she shut down.

I decided I needed to do something nice for her, something different. I had a great surprise for her, and I was hoping it would take us a step further in our soon-to-be relationship.

I came home a little early with white roses,

which she told me were her favorite flowers after our first time in the shower.

I walked in and heard music flowing from the living room into the front entrance. Natalie was dancing around, dusting while shaking her perfect ass. I couldn't help myself and snuck up behind her.

"Has anyone ever told you that you look absolutely fuckable when you dance?"

I must have really startled her because she flew around and screeched when I held my hands up, showing her it was just me.

"Holy freaking shit, Kent. You scared me."

I laughed and took the cleaning spray out of her hands and set it on the table. "Have I also told you how hot you look in that outfit?"

Natalie blushed, making me feel crazy. It had been a few nights since we had sex, and I could almost hear my cock begging for her.

I leaned down and captured her mouth, having my way with her tongue. My instant hard-on pushed up at her, calling out to be touched.

She must have heard him, because soon she was reaching down into my pants to stroke him.

"He's missed you."

Natalie laughed and pulled back. "It's only been a few days."

"A few days too many."

I pulled open her outfit, exposing my favorite two girls. "Why hello, pretty ladies. Have you missed me?"

I pulled her cup to the side, and licked her taunt, pink nipple. I knew I had her, the minute I heard her moan.

"Come here, I've been wanting to do this for a while now."

I pulled her over to one of the floor-to-ceiling windows, and pushed her against it.

"Kent, what if someone walks in?"

"Well, then they'll probably turn around or wait for us to finish."

Natalie rolled her eyes, but couldn't get a word out, because soon I had her almost naked.

"It'll be quick. I won't last long when you're looking like that."

She turned around and placed her hands on the glass.

"That's a good girl. Now, lift your ass up, yeah, just like that."

I pulled my dripping cock out, and lined it up with her wet pussy. I used some of her juices to make sure I was nice and lubed before pushing in.

"Oh, fuck yeah." I pushed her against the cool glass, and cupped one of her breasts.

She threw her head back and matched me thrust for thrust. "This feels so good, the cool glass and your warm, your warm -"

"Hey, don't get shy on me now. I've heard your dirty mouth."

Natalie didn't say anything else because I was pumping so hard, and her huge tits were pounding against the window. I'm sure someone noticed what we were doing, but I didn't give a shit. I was in heaven. In *my* heaven.

I reached around and found Natalie's clit. I started to rub and tease it, while she started to scream out my name.

"Kent, fuck, that feels good. I'm going to come."

"Wait for me, hold it. I'm close."

I picked up the pace, and when she bent over slightly, the movement made me lose it. "Oh shit! That feels fucking good."

Natalie and I came hard, and fast.

"Baby, I could come home like that every day and be a happy man for the rest of my life."

I don't know what I had said, but something about it struck a nerve. Natalie's eyes started to water, and she ran out of the room.

"Hey, wait! Natalie!"

Pulling on my underwear, I chased after her, but she was quick and made it up the stairs before I could grab her. I was just about to get a door slammed in my face when I placed my foot in the crack to stop it.

"Hey, what the hell is going on?"

Natalie ignored me and went to lie on her bed, covering her face with her hands.

"Nat, come on. You can tell me anything. I'd hoped you knew that by now."

Natalie looked up at me with those blue eyes that I knew were my undoing. Not her breasts, not her tight little pussy, but those damn eyes.

"You keep saying stuff like that to me. Forever, home, you and me. I'm just so confused, and I don't want to get my heart broken, or lose my mom."

I walked over and sat next to her, placing my hand on her cheek. "I'm serious with you, Natalie.

I'm falling for you. Hard. I'll never let anything happen to you or your mom."

"Do you love me?"

I sat back a little, and stared at her. I tried to say the words, I really did. I knew I did, that I loved her with all of my being, but for some stupid reason my mouth wouldn't work.

"Get out. Now!"

I leaned forward again and tried to touch her. "It's not like that. I ...you -"

"Leave now. I'm serious."

Instead of telling her I was an idiot and that of course I loved her, I stood up, and walked out of her room. I didn't know what the hell I was doing, but I knew I wasn't doing the right thing.

Hearing her soft cries made my own eyes pool with tears, and I knew I needed to show her how she'd changed me. How I was ready to move on in my life, and I wanted her by me. There was only one thing I could do, and I needed to do it right away.

Chapter 9 - Natalie

I was a fool. A damn fool to think that a guy like Kent would just fall head over heels in love with me in just under a month. I knew the minute I had sex with him that first night, that I had basically bought my mother's coffin. Who could live with themselves after doing such a thing?

Kent had tried to talk to me about my mom, but how was I supposed to tell him that my mother's chemo wasn't working, and that her cancer was more aggressive than they had originally thought.

I also knew something else was different. I hadn't started my period. I was hoping that the stress of my mother's illness was to blame, but after staring at a positive pregnancy test, I realized I had now not only put my mother's future in jeopardy, but I was bringing an innocent child into this uncertain life as well. I wasn't sure how Kent was really going to react. Sure, he had said sweet nothings in bed, but I also knew how much guys liked it bare. Nothing but skin on skin.

I was shocked. I really truly believed that I wouldn't ever have a child, but now, after watching a man I was falling in love with refuse to tell me the one thing I needed to hear, well I was done.

I packed a small bag, and called Maggie.

You know you have a good friend when you royally screw them over but all they care about is you. Maggie didn't take it very well when I told her Kent and I had slept together, but she also said she knew my fate was sealed when she heard me talk about him the way I did.

When I told her I was pregnant, she was excited, but also nervous for my future.

I looked down the staircase and didn't see Kent anywhere. I walked down to his room, and placed my work uniform on his bed. I had really hoped that we would have had a future, but I guess you can't always get what you want.

**

Walking into my mother's room, was something that never got easier. Watching her sleep made me feel like we'd switched roles. That I was the worried parent, looking at my frail, weak child. My mom had already lost her hair, and had also lost so much weight that I could see a perfect outline of her collarbone.

I sat down beside her, and when her eyes fluttered open, I completely lost it. "Mom," I said in a breathless voice and started crying about everything that had been happening.

"Honey, what's wrong?" She placed her hand on my head, and started to rub her fingers through my hair. It's what she would do when I was younger and was sad about life.

"Oh, Mom. I've made a real mess of things."

"Nat, come on. Life isn't that bad." She smiled at me and lifted my chin. "I can tell this is about that man, the one you're working for? It will all work out in the end. I promise."

I snapped my eyes up and looked at my

mother. "What do you mean, the guy I work for?"

My mom's laugh threw me off guard, and I looked over at her IV to see if the doctors were giving her something new that was making her a little crazy.

"I'm not on anything so quit giving me that look."

I still didn't say a word and watched as my mom took my hand in hers. "He's a really great guy, and I know you two will be happy together."

"Mom, how do you know about, how did you-"

"Oh, come on. I might be sick but I'm not an idiot. Maggie told me a little, and when I found out what you were doing, I decided I needed to meet this man."

My eyes were practically bugging out of my head, and I felt like the room started spinning. "You met him!"

"Shush, honey. You know old Miss Riley next door gets all fussy if we wake her up."

I looked out the door and then back to my mom. "You need to tell me what's going on."

"Okay, dear. Just listen to me before you say anything, okay?"

I nodded and leaned a little closer to her, making sure I could hear everything she was about to say.

"Well, it all started when you quit your job at the restaurant. I'm not a fool, and I could tell something was going on. I cornered Maggie, and got her to spill about the new job. I didn't say anything to you, well because I knew you were just trying to do what was best for us. I noticed, however, that you were changing, that you seemed really happy. Probably the happiest I'd seen you in a very long time. Then, when I found out that all of my medical bills were going to be taken care of, I knew I needed to see what was really going on."

I held up my hand and tried to speak.

"No, now be quiet. I've got more to say."

I closed my mouth and blinked a few times before I waved my hand for her to continue.

"When I finally received the name on my billing account, I put two and two together and decided I needed to meet the man who saved my life and my daughter's heart."

"Wait, Kent paid for all of your medical expenses?"

My mom nodded, and I could see a few tears break through her lashes. "He's a good man, honey. I approve of him."

"You met him?"

"Of course. I called him right away and invited him to come and meet me. He was a perfect gentleman, and I could tell how much he cared for you. I'm surprised he didn't tell you."

I instantly felt guilty about keeping my mother's illness to myself. Everything he had said was true. He was going to take care of my mom, and me. I placed my hand over my stomach, and started to cry.

"What's wrong? Did something happen that I don't know about?"

I reached over and grabbed a Kleenex, and I spilled about the baby. "I'm pregnant, Mom. Kent doesn't know. I've been too nervous to tell him."

My mom's face brightened the moment I said the word baby. "You're having a baby? I'm going to be a grandma?"

I laughed and went in for a hug. "You are. I'm glad you're happy, and not disappointed in me."

"I would never be disappointed in you, and a baby is a celebration. Never a disappointment. You need to make this right. Go find him and tell him right away. He has a right to know."

I wiped a fresh tear off my cheek, and looked up at the ceiling. "Well, that's the thing. I asked Kent if he loved me, and he couldn't say it. How can he not love me, and have a child with me?"

My mother's laughter was the last thing I expected to hear, and when I had decided she was definitely on some sort of high pain medication, she reached over and slapped my arm. "For such a smart girl, you sure can be an idiot."

"Mom!"

She laughed again and shooed her arms towards the door. "He loves you. Now go find him."

I stood-up and headed out of her room. I looked back at my mother and hoped she was right. A few emotions ran through my body, and I'd never been so nervous to tell someone such wonderful news before.

Chapter 10 - Kent

When I finally made it home after my overdue errand, I called for Natalie, but she was nowhere to be found. I rushed up to her suite, and stopped when it looked like she'd been robbed. There were clothes thrown everywhere, and some of her things were missing.

Panic coursed through my body, and I started yelling her name. I made my way back to my room hoping she was taking a bath, or a shower, and that's why she wasn't able to hear me.

I knew it was bad when I saw her maid outfit on my bed. She'd quit. She'd given up on me.

I sank down and laid my head against my bed. I had never felt this kind of emotion before. My uncle's death was tragic, but my heart never felt like it was going to explode right out of my chest.

I grabbed Natalie's outfit, and held it against my nose. Her scent was intoxicating, and I felt a sudden pain run through my body. Just when I was about to stand up, I could hear someone behind me.

"Are you smelling my dress?"

I jumped up so fast, that I must have startled her as well because she backed up like I was some kind of wild animal.

"You came back," I breathed as I moved toward her.

Natalie lowered her head, and gave me one quick nod. "I did. I need to tell you something."

I started to speak but she put up her hand to

stop me. "You don't have to say anything, In fact, it would be better if you didn't."

I knew I needed to let her get out whatever was on her chest. Then, I would do the one thing I knew was right. The one thing I should have said and done the minute I laid eyes on her.

I gave her a weak smile and walked her over to my bed. "Okay, I won't say a word until you're done."

Natalie was so serious that I became nervous I was too late.

"Okay, sit down. I need to tell you something."

We both sat, facing each other. I tried to hold her hand, but she pulled away before I could even touch her.

"Don't. Just listen. First, thank you for your generosity towards my mother. I know you met her, and she fell for you, just like I did."

I tried to interrupt, but I could tell it wouldn't have done any good.

"Wait, please. I also need to tell you something else. Something about our future together."

I began to feel hope again, and I must have shown it because I could tell Natalie was close to losing it. I couldn't see her cry again, so I let my emotions calm down, and told her to continue.

"I know we both knew there was a possibility, that without us using protection that I could possibly be pregnant. So, I took a test and - "

There was no way I could let her finish that sentence. The amount of joy filling my heart was more than I could handle. Natalie was pregnant with my child.

I jumped off the bed and held her in my arms. "You're pregnant. You're having my baby."

I pulled back and saw the dam break. Natalie was crying, and it looked like I had caused her pain.

"Shh, don't cry. You have no idea how happy I am."

I knew the time was now, that I had to ask her this one question before I lost her.

"Natalie, my Natalie. I love you, more than anything on this Earth. I wished and prayed that you were growing our child, and that we will have more in the future. I want you by my side, forever. Now and until we are so old we only have sex missionary style."

That earned me a small laugh, but she still looked a little skeptical.

I pulled out a baby blue box, and got down on one knee.

"Natalie Rifton, will you marry me? Will you make me the happiest man on the planet? Will you make a home for our child and be my wife?"

I looked at Natalie's loving face and watched it transform from doubt to complete and utter happiness.

"Yes! Are you kidding me? Yes!"

I was tackled to the ground and our lips instantly found each other.

"I'm not going to hurt you, am I?"

Natalie giggled and shook her head. "No, not at all."

I picked her up, and laid her on our bed.

"Make love to me. Show me that we are in this forever."

When she pulled her shirt off, I knew I was going to be a happy man for the rest of my life.

We made love that night, not once or twice, but three times. I couldn't seem to get enough.

I wasn't sure what our future would hold, but what I did know was that I found a woman who was maid for me.

Epilogue
Two Years later - Natalie

"Kent, come on, you know Mason is going to be awake any minute."

I knew no matter what I said, there was no getting that man off my boobs.

"But they're so big and juicy. I love it when you're pregnant. They double in size."

"Yeah, we'll they're sensitive as hell."

"Your mom will get Mason, don't worry."

I smiled when I thought of my mother, living in our home, and in full remission from that evil stuff that was living inside of her. The doctors found an approach that kicked the living hell out of her cancer, and to this day she was still receiving clear scans.

"I guess you're right. Play away."

Kent chuckled and moved over to my other breast. His warm tongue licked and nipped at my sensitive peak, and the pleasure and pain made me drip with anticipation. I felt my boobs start to harden, and I knew I was close to leaking.

Kent pulled away, and just when a small stream of milk ran down the side of my breasts, he licked it up, and wiggled his eyebrows at me.

"That's so weird."

He let out a loud belly laugh, and trailed a path of kisses to my round stomach. "How's my little Sophie girl doing?"

"She's still quite the acrobat. I'm pretty sure she's going to come out doing cartwheels."

Kent laughed again, and placed his lips on my stomach. "I love you, sweet baby girl."

I looked down at my husband, the father of my children and smiled with pride. Kent was one of the best daddies, and I knew I was so lucky to have him.

I pushed him off me, and rolled over to my side. When you're eight months pregnant, there's really only one way to have sex.

"You dirty girl, always liking it from behind."

I rolled my eyes, but forgot about everything when his hands spread my legs apart, and his warm tongue lapped up my cream.

"Oh my God, I'm so sensitive. That feels amazing."

I heard Kent grunt, and his tongue picked up the pace. He reached around and gave my boob one more squeeze before I shooed him off, hoping I wouldn't leak anymore milk.

"You taste so damn good, I could eat this pussy every day of the week, and still not get enough."

Maggie never believed me when I told her how much Kent liked to go down on me. She said I found a unicorn, and men like him weren't real. She had that right, I did find someone special.

"Fuck it, I'm not going to last with you so fucking wet and my cock not inside of you."

Kent flipped me onto my hands and knees, and lifted up my ass. "This will always be my favorite. Your perfect ass begging me to take that greedy cunt of yours."

I smiled, loving his dirty talk, and reached

around, well as best as I could, to open my slit for him.

"Baby, that's hot." He slid the tip of his dick in and took a moment to let me adjust. I knew he loved that I had a C-section with Mason, and told me that my walls were still as tight as when he first had me, but I secretly wished I would have been able to have a baby naturally. However, when he was pounding in and out of me, I didn't care either way, only that we still had amazing sex.

"I can't take it anymore. Please, fuck me."

"I'm going to fuck you, honey, but not too hard. That's my baby girl in there."

I smiled at his words, and rubbed our little Sophie.

When I felt him slide all the way in, I moaned out in ecstasy. "Yes. Oh, yes!"

Kent grabbed my ass cheeks, and started to move in and out. He pumped at a steady pace, and moved his hand down to a different entrance.

I finally let him try anal after Mason was born. I drank enough wine that I braved the new experience, and I actually enjoyed it.

"I'll get in this tight little ass of yours again. After Sophie is born, it's game on."

I laughed, but was quickly panting when his finger found my clit. "Come for me, baby. Come hard."

I moaned and felt his cock grow bigger. "I'm going to come, but not inside of you. We don't need our princess here early."

His last two pumps sent me over the edge, and when I felt his warm liquid spread across my back, I knew he had come with me.

"Shit, hun. That was fucking amazing." When he pulled back, he grabbed his shirt off the floor and wiped his seed off my back. "Lie down, and I'll get a wet cloth to clean you."

I could still feel my walls pulse with pleasure when I lay down on my side. Sophie was kicking up a storm, and I pictured what our little girl would look like. Would she have Mason's turquoise eyes, or would she take after her daddy?

Kent walked over and pressed a warm cloth to my back. "I love you, Natalie Bryant."

I sat up and kissed my husband on his cheek. "I love you, Kent Bryant."

"And I love you, baby girl." Kent gently rubbed the underneath of my belly. "I can't wait until your pregnant with number three. Maybe Sophie will have a little sister."

I rolled my eyes, and laughed about Kent's obsession with me being pregnant. We did, however, agree on four so I knew he was right. Maybe Sophie would have a little sister.

I looked over his shoulder and caught a glimpse of my maid's outfit. Before I was pregnant with Sophie, I would wear it sometimes to get a rise out of him.

"Who knew that taking a maid's job would land me you."

Kent reached over and kissed the end of my nose. "Well, baby, as I always tell you. You were maid for me."

I always laugh at his joke, but this time I couldn't have agreed more.

A Note from the Author

I want to thank you so much for purchasing my debut novella, I'm Maid For You. I had a wonderful time writing this story, and even made myself get a little steamy when writing Kent's dirty words.

If you loved Natalie and Kent's story, there is nothing greater you can give an author in return than a review on Amazon and Goodreads. They mean a lot, and I thank you from the bottom of my dirty heart.

I'm Maid For You may be my debut novella, but it certainly won't be my last. Here are a few titles to look for in the near future.

*Snowed In With You
*Yes, Mr. Mitchell
*Take Me Home

I also love connecting with you! Come find me at:

Facebook
https://www.facebook.com/pages/Luxx-Monroe/1012618672111014

Goodreads
https://www.goodreads.com/user/show/45782706-luxx-monroe-author

Twitter
@LuxxMonroe

Printed in Great Britain
by Amazon

TiMEI
FLiGHT

The Definitive Biography of

THE BYRDS

Johnny Rogan

SQUARE 1

SQUARE ONE BOOKS LTD

By the same author
Timeless Flight: The Definitive Biography Of The Byrds (Vol.1)
Neil Young: Here We Are In The Years
Roxy Music: Style With Substance
Van Morrison: A Portrait Of The Artist
The Kinks: The Sound And The Fury
Wham!(Confidential) The Death Of A Supergroup
Starmakers And Svengalis: The History Of British Pop Management
The Football Managers

©Johnny Rogan 1990

All rights reserved.
No part of this publication may be reproduced,
stored in a retrieval system, or transmitted
in any form or by any means, electronic, mechanical,
photocopying, recording or otherwise, without the prior
permission of the Publisher or copyright owner.

First published in 1981 by Scorpion/Dark Star
This edition first published in 1990 by
SQUARE ONE BOOKS LTD

ISBN 1 872747 00 0

Publisher: Colin Larkin
Editor: John Orley
Production Assistant: Susan Pipe
Special thanks to Jim Dickson for his co-operation
and to Bob Hyde at Murray Hill Records

Typeset in Linotype Plantin 10 point on 11.5
Printed and Bound in England by Biddles Ltd

Contents

Acknowledgements	vii
Introduction	ix
1. Journey To The Troubadour	11
2. And Then There Were Five	19
3. The World Pacific Recordings	24
4. Fame and Fluctuating Fortunes	30
5. The British Tour	39
6. From Fistfights To Former Glories	47
7. Eight Miles High	59
8. The Leaving Of Gene Clark	65
9. Beyond The Fifth Dimension	70
10. Younger Than Yesterday	78
11. Mutiny From Stern To Bow	85
12. Wanted: The Notorious Byrd Brothers	94
13. Gram Parsons: The Struggle For Supremacy	102
14. The Great South African Disaster . . . And Its Aftermath	109
15. A Period Of Transition	118
16. The Easy Riding Byrds	126
17. The Byrds Enter The 70's	134
18. Dares And Dreams And . . . Gene Tryp	142
19. Melcher And Maniax	145
20. Farther Along The Road To Disunity	152
21. The Creative Nadir	160
22. The Final Dissolution	167
23. The Phoenix Rises . . . And Falls	171
24. We'll Meet Again	180
25. McGuinn, Clark And Hillman	189
26. Circle Of Minds	195
27. The Dark Decade	203
28. Tomorrow Is Never Before	217
29. The Third Coming	223
Discography	235
Videos	249
Bootleg Albums	250
Bootleg Tapes	255
Sessionography	262
Unreleased Recordings	272

FOR CATHY SHEA

Life-lines of THE BYRDS

Left to right: **CHRIS HILLMAN**   **GENE CLARK**   **JIM McGUINN**   **MIKE CLARKE**   **DAVID CROSBY**

	CHRIS HILLMAN	GENE CLARK	JIM McGUINN	MIKE CLARKE	DAVID CROSBY
Real name:	Chris Hillman.	Harold Eugene Clark.	James J. McGuinn.	Michael Clarke.	David Van Cortlandt Crosby.
Birthday:	December 4, 1942.	November 17, 1942.	July 13, 1942.	June 3, 1944.	August 14, 1941.
Birthplace:	Los Angeles.	Tipton, Missouri.	Chicago.	New York City.	Los Angeles.
Personal points:	5ft. 9in.; 155 lb.; blue eyes; brown hair.	5ft. 11in.; 155 lb.; blue-green eyes; brown hair.	5ft. 11in.; 145 lb.; blue eyes; brown hair.	6ft. 2in.; 160 lb.; blue eyes; blond hair.	5ft. 9in.; 140 lb.; brown hair; brown eyes.
Parents' names:	Betty.	Kelly George and Mary Jean.	James and Dorothy.	James and Suzy.	Floyd and Aliph.
Brothers & sisters:	1 brother, 2 sisters.	None.	Brian, 14.	Debbi, 7, Judi, 14.	Chip.
Present home:	Hollywood.	Bonner Springs, Kansas.	Los Angeles.	Los Angeles.	Hollywood.
Instruments played:	Bass guitar, mandolin.	Guitar, harmonica, tambourine, vocals.	Lead .12 string guitar, banjo, bass vocal.	Drums, harmonica, congas.	6 and 12 string guitar.
Educated:	San Diego County.	Raytown, Missouri, Bonner Springs, Kansas.	Chicago Latin prep, high; Grammar schools in N.Y., Chicago, Florida.	Stockbridge, N.Y.	Grammar schools: Cate school, Laguna Blanca; Santa Barbara City College.
Musical education:	None.	None.	Old Towne School of Folk Music.	School band in high school.	Five years of singing folk music and blues.
First entered show business:	At 16.	After high school.	At 17.	When joined Byrds.	Little Theatre during high school.
First public appearance:	Coffee house.	Folk music gatherings.	Coffee house long ago.	Coffee houses in New York.	Don't remember.
Biggest break:	The Byrds.	To left leg !	Limeliters tour 1960.	Joining Byrds.	The Byrds.
TV debut:	Country Music Time.	Yes.	Bell Telephone Hour.	" Bash " show with the Byrds.	KOOP " Bash."
Biggest influence on career:	Music.	Music.	Bob Gibson, Elvis Presley, Pete Seeger.	Day I saw r-and-b bands growing their hair long.	Probably Jim Dickson.
Former occupations :	Cowboy.	Everything.	None.	None.	Folk singer.
Hobbies:	Rhythm-and-blues.	Raising pets.	Jet pilot.	Talking.	Sailboats.
Favourite colour:	Green.	Marigold, orange.	Blue, brown.	Orange.	Green.
Favourite singers:	Muddy Waters, Mose Allison, Sleepy John.	Bob Dylan.	Everly Bros., Carl Perkins, Bob Dylan.	Bob Dylan, Mick Jagger, John Lennon.	Bob Dylan, John Lennon, Goldie.
Favourite actors/actresses	Melina Mercouri.	None.	Jimmy Dean, Peter O'Toole, Peter Sellers.	Steve McQueen, Paul Newman, Burt Lancaster.	Paul Newman, Steve McQueen, Peter Sellers.
Favourite food:	European cheese.	Good.	Gourmet.	Cheeseburgers.	Steak, Guacamole.
Favourite drink:	Coke.	Wet water.	Grape juice.	Pepsi Cola.	Chocolate.
Favourite clothes:	Jeans, boots.	Suedes and denims.	Vests-designs and non-good taste colours.	Jeans, T-shirts, Turtleneck sweaters.	Leather, suede, jeans, boots.
Favourite composers:	Bob Dylan.	Bob Dylan.	Bernstein, Bob Gibson.	McCartney-Lennon.	Miles, Evans, Coltrane.
Favourite groups:	Rolling Stones, Them, Kinks.	Beatles, Rolling Stones.	Zombies, Phil Spector, Supremes.	Beatles, Rolling Stones, Them.	Manfred Mann, Them, Searchers.
Favourite car:	Rolls-Royce.	Ferrari.	Ferrari, navy blue.	Aston Martin.	Modified Porche, Ferrari.
Likes:	Listening to music.	Don't know.	Love, creating, trusting.	Tall girls with long hair.	Life, love, freedom.
Dislikes:	TV, newspapers.	Nothing except bugs.	Fear, worry, hate, anxiety, distrust.	Barber shops.	Innocence, stupidity, prejudice, war.
Most thrilling experience:	Folk festival in Hawaii.	First time I rode a cow.	Hearing applause at first Carnegie show.	Going 180 miles an hour in a Ferrari.	Standing watch at night by myself.
Tastes in music:	Everything.	Strawberry.	Universal, international.	R-and-b, Jazz.	Jazz, Indian, classical, rock 'n' roll, blues.
Best friend:	No " best " friend.	George Greif.	God.	Lots.	The other Byrds.
Personal ambition:	To be happy.	To be a goody-goody.	To be a good soul; to have own jet.	To lay around Big Sur and paint rocks.	To own and sail a large schooner.
Professional ambition:	Successful with Byrds.	Human being.	Jazz guitar, TV direction, movie direction.	Want to learn all I can about music.	To help the Byrds be the best group.

COMMON TO ALL
Current hit and latest release: " Mr. Tambourine Man " (No. 2 this week).
Present disc label: CBS (in Britain); Columbia (in U.S.A.).
Personal managers: Jim Dickson and Ed Tickner.

Acknowledgements

The interviews that I have conducted for this book span approximately 13 years from the genesis of *Timeless Flight* in 1977 through to this new edition in the spring/summer of 1989 when I returned to America to undertake new research. I am indebted to the following individuals who agreed to lend their time and support in order to provide me with interview material: Roger McGuinn, David Crosby, Gene Clark, Chris Hillman, Michael Clarke, John York, Gene Parsons, Skip Battin, Michelle Phillips, Jim Dickson, Eddie Tickner, Terry Melcher, Jim Seiter, Derek Taylor, Camilla McGuinn, Dorothy McGuinn, Al Hersh, Bob Hyde, Steve Green, Bill Siddons, Linda Loo Bopp, Lizzie Donohue, Michelle Kerr and Patti McCormick. Acknowledgement is also due to the following publications for permission to reprint material in their own copyright: *Crawdaddy!*, *Dark Star*, *Hit Parader*, *Melody Maker*, *New Musical Express*, *Omaha Rainbow*, *Sing Out! The Folk Song Magazine*, *Sounds* and *Zig Zag*. A big thanks to Bob Hyde at Murray Hill for providing session details on request and also for allowing me to reprint the stupendous sessionography from *Never Before*. I would also like to thank Pete Frame for allowing me to use selected quotes from previously unpublished interviews with Clarence White, Roger McGuinn and Byron Berline. Indeed, the Clarence White quotes serve as a last testament on his time in the Byrds and were recorded shortly before his death. The photos presented in the book are courtesy of CBS Records, Capitol Records, WEA Records, and Sierra (formerly Sierra/Briar) Records. Additional thanks to the following contributors: Pete Frame, John Delgatto, Jim Seiter, Dorothy McGuinn, Raffaele Galli,

Chrissie Oakes, Pete Long, Michael Ochs, Nick Ralph and Lou Cohan. Over the years a number of people have corresponded with me about the Byrds. Some have disappeared, others return infrequently. Chief amongst them remains Chrissie Oakes, now the editor of the excellent fanzine *Full Circle*, available from 61 Silverbirch Close, Little Stoke, Bristol, BS12 6RN, England. It is a pleasure to write thousands of words therein at the birth of each new issue and I trust that myself and others may maintain the same enthusiasm for re-investigating the Byrds in years hence. Barry Ballard, as busy as the rest of us, certainly retains his enthusiasm for the group two decades on and can safely be described as one of the best sources of Byrds news around. His support throughout the period of rewriting this text has been greatly appreciated. May the flame burn eternal. George Guttler, and his historically-minded wife Nancy and sister-in-law Alice, still catch up with various Byrds whenever they appear within a certain radius of Massachusetts. My favourite American hosts, they make every US Byrds expedition eminently enjoyable and worthwhile. Those continental correspondents, Jean Pierre Morisset and Rafaelle Galli continue to write about the Byrds when they can and I'm sure we will continue to read each other's views, even if the letters have ceased. Pete Long still carries the flame for CSN&Y and retains a spare torch for the Byrds too. His consistency is to be admired. Nick Ralph, I haven't seen in years but I still remember his contribution to the original edition of this book, and I thank him. Other first edition absentees include Roger Leighton, Jo Saker, Stephen Peeples and Douglas Coates, all of whom deserve the same old thanks. Debbie Bennett still shares record labels with David Crosby ten years on, this time at A&M rather than Capitol, and her friendly cooperation is appreciated more than she may ever realize. Peter Doggett has emerged as a new enthusiast in recent years, intent on rivalling his elders. Tony Poole still sings 'She Don't Care About Time' on request as perhaps only he would. Then there are those correspondents from afar, most of whom I have lost contact with: John O'Brien, Tom Pickles, Geraint Davies, David Prockter, David Blackmore and Keith Bickerton, to name but a few. Finally, I wave a swift hello/goodbye to the people from the Byrds concert days: Anne Cesek, Deborah Novotny, Wally Hammond, Alan Roberts, Alan Russell and the rest of the ghostly cast. In conclusion, it is the Byrds themselves that keep the passion burning and that is why the story is important. It is also why I have tried to be as unsycophantic as possible and always avoided getting close to any of the factions that surround the various Byrds. What that also means is that you end up offending everyone somewhere along the line. But whether they love, hate or ignore you is scarcely relevant to their story. Every interview, however tough, is still an experience even after all these years. Here's to the next edition in the 21st century – may we all be alive for that.

Introduction

The common wisdom with new editions of ageing books is that the author tags on a couple of short, badly researched chapters at the end. Usually, the author has moved on to other projects and can hardly be expected to muster enthusiasm for a dead project. However, this is no ordinary book, this is *Timeless Flight Revisited*. That means drop everything, fly to America, spend lots of money, and live it all again. This was my first book and I find myself as deeply involved with it today as I was a decade ago. I still remember my regret about not reaching manager Jim Dickson, a failure for which I was taken to task by David Crosby. One of the highlights of revising this book was the chance to hear his comments on a remarkable series of events and add them to the narrative. Looking back to the first edition, I remember McGuinn, Clark and Hillman reuniting when I first put pen to paper and on the brink of dissolution by the time I reached the last chapter. A decade on, the events are no less dramatic. This time the scenario reads McGuinn, Crosby and Hillman versus Clarke, with Gene Clark watching anxiously from the sidelines. Will it all end in tears and litigation or a grand onstage reunion of the original five for the first time since 1966? Even as I write, nobody knows for sure.

People occasionally ask me when I first decided to write about the Byrds. It has never been an easy question to answer. I was writing about the Byrds before I was a teenager! If I had to construct a capsule filled with Byrds' 'moments in time', it would probably read as follows: observing a strangely named group and their equally odd titled record entering the *Billboard* charts; hearing 'Mr Tambourine Man' on the radio and watching it zoom to number 1 in the US and the UK; *Top Of The Pops* 1965, entranced by Crosby's incredible cape and McGuinn's weird glasses; skipping part of my paper round to watch them take over *Ready Steady Go!*; faking a letter and imaginary record token award from Radio Luxembourg in order to justify the extravagant purchase of their first two albums; wandering round a Pimlico bombsite with a transistor playing 'Set You Free This Time'; staying up till 2 am to catch 'Eight Miles High' on the pirates; the intense disappointment over Clark's departure; Alan Culligan raving over my copy of 'Captain Soul' on his 3 foot bass heavy speaker; hearing 'Time Between' on the Light Programme's *Newly Pressed*; frustration that the *NME* and the other music papers did not even bother to review *Younger Than Yesterday*; blasting out 'Renaissance Fair' from the barracks in Tramore; never hearing 'Lady Friend' played once on commercial radio; the body blow of Crosby's firing; the fiasco over Clark's return; wearing a suit at their Royal Albert Hall gig in 1968 to see them with new boy Gram Parsons (also in a suit!); depressed that it was apparently all over at the end of 1968; relief that they were back again in 1969 with 'Bad Night At The Whiskey'; singing 'Mr Tambourine Man' onstage at the Golden Lion, Fulham, on St Patrick's Night; sleeping in a graveyard after watching them at the Lincoln Folk Festival; bunking in to see them on *Top Of The Pops*; disbelief upon hearing about the reunion in 1973; a celebration cake for the 10th anniversary of 'Mr Tambourine Man'; being asked to interview and write about them in *Zig Zag* and *Dark Star*; all the interviews over the years too amazing in their detail to document; securing an extra scholarship in Anglo Saxon to finance a trip from Canada to Beverly Hills to complete *Timeless Flight* in 1979; walking the freeway from Universal City to Hollywood after a confrontation with McGuinn and Hillman; stranded on the Sunset Strip, accosted by prostitutes at 4 am and being picked up by the police; Crosby copiously freebasing in Denbigh Street; asking Crosby how long he thought he had left; Oxford and presenting Gill Chester and Cathy Shea with copies of *The Original Singles*; the amazing realization that the Byrds' work still sounded as good, if not better, 25 years on. It is still a timeless flight.

Johnny Rogan

1
Journey To The Troubadour

With musicians as respected as the Byrds one of the toughest problems for an author is searching for a starting point. Rock mythology insists that the legend had its beginnings in early 1964 when Gene Clark, Jim McGuinn and David Crosby combined their talents and formed a Beatle-influenced trio, the Jet Set. Without question, the Beatles' invasion of America in early 1964 set in motion a series of events that culminated in the creation of the Byrds, but that was far from the entire story. In order to appreciate what the Byrds represented when they first rose to prominence it is important to appreciate that they were not garage group aspirants in search of quick glory but accomplished musicians whose individual histories and musical experiences stretched back over a decade.

James Joseph McGuinn, born in Chicago on 13 July 1942, had a colourful pre-Byrd history worth a book in itself. His parents, James and Dorothy, were involved in journalism and public relations and during his childhood penned a best seller humorously titled *Parents Can't Win*. They toured extensively across the States and James Jnr attended a variety of schools. His interest in popular music intensified after hearing Elvis Presley's 'Heartbreak Hotel' which hogged the top of the US charts for eight weeks in the spring of 1956. The Presley phenomenon so captured McGuinn's imagination that he asked his parents to buy him a guitar for his 14th birthday. In his spare time he began playing the rock 'n' roll hits of the period and soon had a repertoire which included the work of Buddy Holly, Gene Vincent, Carl Perkins, the Everly Brothers and, of course, Elvis Presley. The fascination for rock 'n' roll would soon be displaced by another musical passion which unexpectedly emerged in the school classroom. McGuinn's teacher was acquainted with the folk musician Bob Gibson and invited him to play some songs for the kids one afternoon. This made a great impression on McGuinn who soon turned to folk music as his new love. His teacher suggested that he enrol at Chicago's Old Town School of Music where for $10.00 a lesson he rapidly mastered the five-string banjo as well as honing his guitar skills. One of his tutors was Frank Hamilton (formerly of the Weavers) whom McGuinn credits for teaching him a formidable folk repertoire. During his final days in high school McGuinn, although only a minor, began visiting Albert Grossman's Gate of Horn folk club where he remembers hearing the entire Ewan McColl songbook of sea shanties. Years later, he would remember those impressionable moments in the tribute song 'Gate Of Horn', which appeared on his second album, *Peace On You*.

McGuinn's growing confidence encouraged him to get up and play some songs in the non-intimidating atmosphere of the local coffee houses and small clubs. There he was spotted by a member of the Limeliters and immediately offered a job. Ever practical, he declined the offer explaining that he wanted to finish his final year at high school. The Limeliters still needed an accompanist some months later and within days of graduating from school McGuinn received a telegram requesting his presence in Los Angeles. He played at the celebrated Ash Grove and appeared on their album *Tonight In Person* but hopes of further glory were postponed when the cost-cutting Limeliters dispensed with his services after only six weeks. McGuinn continued to work as a solo act and moved to San Francisco. Soon, he found himself in demand again when the Chad Mitchell Trio telephoned through an irresistible offer. Mitchell and his cohorts were part of the more commercial area of folk music and could afford to pay good wages. McGuinn stayed with them for two-and-a-half years, toured across America and played on their albums *Mighty Day On Campus* and *Live At The Bitter End*. Although the experience was valuable, McGuinn gradually became disenchanted and found that he was missing the spotlight. The Trio were all singers and merely required a sharp guitarist to accompany them from the back of the stage. McGuinn needed a new challenge and was about to accept a job in the New Christy Minstrels when, one evening in 1962, a surprise guest turned up backstage.

Bobby Darin, one of the most astute pop singers of his era, had seen McGuinn at the Crescendo club in Los Angeles and wasted no time in securing his services. Darin had moved from pop to the supper club circuit and needed McGuinn to add a musical punch to his folk routine. Playing upmarket cabaret was quite a revelation to the ex-folkie, but the early 60's were not all good times. During a Darin tour, McGuinn's first marriage ended and when his pop star mentor lost his voice and temporarily retired from playing, the future looked bleak.

Settling in New York, McGuinn accepted a job in Bobby Darin's publishing company for the princely sum of $35.00 a week. Soon, he was hard at work in the cubicles of the Brill Building which also housed such prodigies as Neil Sedaka, Gerry Goffin and Carole King. While there, McGuinn co-wrote a Beach Boys pastiche entitled 'Beach Ball', which was released on Capitol under the banner of the City Surfers. It was a typical studio creation and in spite of the presence of Terry Melcher (piano) and Bobby Darin (drums) failed to sell. Although McGuinn was a skilled arranger, he was not yet a natural songwriter, yet one of his compositions became a minor hit in Australia for an Elvis Presley look-alike. Outside of the Brill Building, McGuinn continued to seek less demanding work and sought Darin's opinion on how to become famous. Bobby's reply was perceptive: 'The way to start off is to be a rock 'n' roll singer'. It would be some time yet before McGuinn actually followed this good advice.

From his conversations with Darin, McGuinn realized that his best move was to gain live experience as a soloist. He was already a good musician and had gained valuable experience in session work, arranging for and accompanying Hoyt Axton, the Irish Ramblers, Judy Collins and Tom and Jerry (who later emerged as Simon and Garfunkel). While playing at Greenwich Village hootenannys he had also seen the competition whichincluded the soon-to-be-famous Bob Dylan.

By the end of 1963, McGuinn had become aware of the Beatles and when the group exploded onto the American charts soon after, he was ready to embrace Darin's rock 'n' roll dream. Before leaving New York for Los Angeles, McGuinn appeared at a club which had a sign begging for 'Beatles imitators' and although he still had short hair and wore glasses he could sing their tunes. Taking his quasi-Beatle repertoire to the West Coast, McGuinn hit lucky when his friend (and later co-writer) Bob Hippard secured him a gig at the Troubadour. After a couple of solo residencies, he began to think about the possibility of finding a partner.

Harold Eugene Clark had yet to assimilate McGuinn's vast experience of the different spectrums of the music business, but his road to the Troubadour was far from uneventful. Born in Tipton, Missouri on 17 November 1941, Clark was reared on country, bluegrass and rockabilly and, like McGuinn, became a folk music aficionado in his teens. At high school in Kansas City, he formed his first notable group, the Sharks, and began that prolific songwriting spree which was to characterize his later stint in the Byrds. In 1955, the Sharks recorded one of his compositions 'Blue Ribbon' for a local label and the song was actually played on national television. For 14-year-old Gene, it was quite an ego boost. School groups seldom last, however, and Clark went through several including the Rum Runners and the Surf Riders. The latter looked particularly promising and during late 1962 could be seen playing Kingston Trio-influenced material at the Castaways club in Kansas City. One night, the New Christy Minstrels came to town and a couple of their members caught the Surf Riders' set and were pleasantly surprised. Christys' supremo Randy Sparks next appeared in order to gauge their potential and wasted no time in commandeering the entire group. Clark's erstwhile partners, Jimmy Glover and Michael Crumb, were despatched to the Back Porch Majority while he was offered a support in the Minstrels.

The timing could not have been better. The Christies had just recorded their *Ramblin'* album and their latest single 'Green Green', featuring the gravel-voiced Barry McGuire, was about to become a smash hit. The Minstrels toured extensively and slotted in recording schedules whenever time permitted. On one hot summer's day, Gene found himself in the studio putting down tracks for a festive album, *Merry Christmas*. When a second Top 30 hit occurred with 'Saturday Night' in November 1963, Clark began to grow weary of the seemingly endless touring rota, which included long, tension-filled aeroplane flights.

During the first ravages of American Beatlemania, Clark was entertaining President Lydon B. Johnson at the White House. However, the prestige of Minstreldom could not entirely compensate for his subordinate role in the ensemble. He contributed towards one more album, *Land Of Giants*, before half-reluctantly returning to California to stake out the local clubs. One evening, he visited the Troubadour and saw McGuinn playing Beatle-songs on a 12-string guitar and introducing rock arrangements of famous folk songs. Suitably impressed, Gene suggested that they form a duo in imitation of the British group, Peter and Gordon. McGuinn remembers the short-lived career of the duo:

'Gene and I actually started it. We met at the Troubadour and we were both guitar-playing, singing, writing people and we wanted to get a thing going. We were playing around in coffee houses and running around trying to find places to play all night long, and there weren't many out here. So we'd wind up at somebody's house and that was the pattern – no pressure at all, no responsibility, just get up and feed yourself, find a place to play all night.'

At the same point in time, another young, impressionable folk singer was regularly frequenting the Troubadour. Born in Los Angeles on 14 August 1941, David Van Cortlandt Crosby hailed from a high society family. His mother Alphi was a former debutante and his father Floyd was a respected director of photography. As well as winning Academy Awards for his work on *High Noon* and *Tabu*, Floyd was also responsible for the photography on a whole series of Roger Corman films, including such classics as *The Raven*, *The Pit And The Pendulum* and *The Fall Of The House Of Usher*. Music was very much a part of David's early life and even before he learned guitar he enjoyed scat-singing along with his elder brother, Chip.

By the time he reached late adolescence Crosby had a long history as a troublemaker. An incorrigible pupil, he was expelled from some of the best private schools in Hollywood and was generally regarded as a precocious, car-crazed, girl-chasing, rich brat. In spite of his affluent background, Crosby briefly took up housebreaking with a couple of local kids, but it all ended in tears:

'I used to make a joke that that was the way I worked my way through school but the truth was that we did it more for the rush than anything else. We did it a number of times. I worked out a system which worked pretty well. I did it until once I had to confront a woman whose house we had ransacked. She wanted her wallet back. It had the only existing picture of her old man who had died in the war. She was in tears, you know. And it changed it completely. It was not just taking stuff. All of a sudden it was somebody's precious things. It made quite an impression on me and I would never take anything now. It's just not right.'

Crosby's punishment was a term of probation and a visit to a therapist. His mother was mortified.

After finally graduating from Santa Barbara College, Crosby made a failed stab at acting school, then took up singing in coffee houses with a repertoire that included 'Motherless Children', 'God Bless The Child' and, surprisingly, Gershwin's standard, 'Summertime'. After getting his girlfriend pregnant, Crosby ignobly fled from responsibility and took off across America, living out a Woody Guthrie fantasy. He met a number of influential musicians including Travis Edmunson and Fred Neil, who greatly influenced his guitar playing. After a year on the road, he journeyed to San Francisco where he shared a houseboat with Dino Valenti. Eventually, he moved into a semi-communal household in Venice that boasted some interesting names, including Paul Kantner and David Freiberg.

The proto-hippie lifestyle was eventually replaced by an urgent need for cash so Crosby joined the Les Baxter Balladeers, another of those commercialized folk aggregations. Dressed in cute, red jackets, Crosby and his friends (including brother Chip, Bobby Ingram and Michael Clough) toured the States and were even captured on vinyl on the rare *Jack Linkletter Presents A Folk Festival*. Life as a Les Baxter 'Little Dear' eventually took its embarrassing toll and Crosby returned to play solo and hung out at the Unicorn club in Hollywood. The patrons were largely unimpressed with his jazz-tinged repertoire, but there was one man who listened closely and spotted something special.

Jim Dickson, ten years older than Crosby, had already lived a full life by 1963. From the army to motor cycle gangs and sales work, he suddenly found himself in the music business after discovering and recording the legendary satirist Lord Buckley. For a time Dickson worked in films, both as a sound engineer and assistant camera man. Inspired by his good friend, Barry Feinstein, he took up photography as a possible career, but this always overlapped with music. Dickson was wonderfully eclectic in his tastes, equally at home with jazz, folk and bluegrass. He had recorded various jazz musicians at the Club Renaissance and albums by a number of artistes including the Dillards, Odetta and Hamilton Camp. Jac Holzman of Elektra Records respected his taste so much that he hired his services as a freelance A&R man. Dickson, meanwhile, sought to increase his own standing in the industry by branching out into the potentially lucrative field of music publishing. By late 1963, he had formed a partnership with a business manager named Eddie Tickner:

'I knew Jim Dickson from the Club Renaissance days. I was doing business management, working with Odetta, a black folk-songwriter. Jim was producing records and since I was experienced in accounts he asked me if I'd like to go into publishing. He was working mainly in jazz and he was in a position to get the publishing and needed somebody to take care of the publishing work. So, during the latter part of 1963, we each put up $100.00 and formed Tickson Music.'

The first song that Tickson Music published was Dino Valenti's 'Get Together', although they later were pressurized into selling the copyright. The fact that Dickson had recorded Valenti impressed David Crosby as he came offstage at the Unicorn. More importantly, Dickson had access to World Pacific Studios after midnight and was in a position to offer his chosen artistes a shot at recording some demos. Towards the end of 1963, Crosby recorded several songs under Dickson's supervision, two of which popped up in the late 60's on a rare album titled *Early LA*. The tracks provide a revealing insight into Crosby's pre-Byrd repertoire. Ray Charles' 'Come Back Baby' displays his youthful voice, strikingly higher in range than some of his later work. 'Willie Gene', written by Hoyt Axton, is even better, an absolute showcase for that crystal-clear diction with some sparse backing, unobtrusive percussion and surprisingly effective blues guitar. Two other demos, the aforementioned 'Get Together' and Crosby's 'Brotherhood Of The Blues' completed the session and Dickson was hoping that a major label might be interested. He approached Joe Smith of Warner Brothers, but met with a cool response. According to Dickson, Crosby as a solo act was not quite strong enough to secure a deal:

'When he wrote songs with verses and choruses in them they were OK. They weren't great though. Certainly, they weren't enough to found a career on. They tended to be songs that showed him off as a singer. Nobody ever denied that David had a distinctive recording voice. How he used it is a matter of opinion!'

Never a prolific songwriter, most of Crosby's unreleased recordings from 1963-64 were adaptations of public domain songs such as 'Jack Of Diamonds' and 'Motherless Children'. One notable exception, however, was the extraordinary 'Everybody's Been Burned, which remained dormant for several years before finally appearing on *Younger Than Yesterday*. Although the song is regarded, particularly by this author, as one of Crosby's greatest, Dickson was less than overwhelmed:

'I used to have tapes of David doing it on his own and they're not that good. I suspect that when he was complaining about being burned somebody said to him: "Everybody's been burned, David", and he wrote the song . . . It reflected the period of his life before he had approval of any kind from anybody, when he tried to deal with his unhappiness by himself. We published it before the Byrds. In fact, it was one of the first songs we published. If I had been able to get that deal from Warner Brothers for David Crosby as a solo singer with a back-up band then it would have been one of the best songs on the album. No question. That's assuming we were going to use stuff from him. I was also impressed by David singing "Motherless Children", which is in a similar vein. Hundreds of people have sung "Motherless Children" but I think it's a better song. "Everybody's Been Burned" is a nightclub ballad that would fit into the late 50's or early 60's. It would have been sung well by a Ruth Price, Chris Connor or Kinky Winters. The people that sprang from singers like Peggy Lee and Ella Fitzgerald, the later imitators of that kind of person. A girl torch singer would be the one to sing the hell out of "Everybody's Been Burned" – somebody with a lot of feeling . . . David, in fact, sang that kind of ballad similar to a girl singer . . . It's gentle, it's reaching for a shared experience, it doesn't have the aggression of Sinatra.'

One of the saddest realizations is that the tapes of these and many later songs have been either lost, taped over or destroyed. Although Crosby had yet to reach his full potential, the early recordings demonstrate a unique talent, all the more fascinating in light of his subsequent success.

Without a record contract, Crosby had little choice but to continue furthering his career as a folk singer. It was during a performance at the Troubadour that he discovered McGuinn and Clark. Gene recalls the eventful evening:

'McGuinn and I started picking together in the Troubadour bar which was called "The Folk Den" at the time . . . We started to write a few songs and then one night we went along to a hootenanny at the Troubadour and there was this guy called David Crosby who came on stage and played a few songs. I told McGuinn that I thought he was good and he said that he had worked with him before and that they were friends and had hung out in the Village together. We went into the lobby and started picking on the stairway where the echo was good and David came walking up and just started singing away with us doing the harmony part . . . We hadn't even approached him.'

Crosby immediately introduced the duo to Jim Dickson, who was quick to see their potential. Dickson was sufficiently impressed to take on the responsibilities of management and even gave the group rent-free accommodation at his house. It was a loose arrangement and much depended upon what the trio could produce in the studio over the next few months.

2
And Then There Were Five

Jim Dickson's friendship with World Pacific's Dick Bock meant that he had a luxury that many fledgling producers and inchoate groups would have envied: unlimited studio time. McGuinn, Crosby and Clark soon became nocturnal creatures, playing on into the early hours of the morning. During the first months of painful rehearsal, the boys sought a catchy stage name and McGuinn whose hobby was aeronautics came up with the Jet Set. Although Dickson felt it was highly inappropriate, the monicker was accepted, at least for the present. The first recording made by the Jet Set was 'The Only Girl', which came out as a cross between the Beatles and the Everly Brothers. The soaring harmonies and acoustic guitar work sounded somewhat derivative yet extremely interesting. Certainly, the trio was unique: three solo folk singers, each with a 12-string acoustic guitar, attempting to play rock 'n' roll. The transition from folk to rock, however, was not as sudden or remarkable as it appeared, as Crosby remembers:

'I really wasn't suited to folk music. They used to say, "Hey, you sing like a rock 'n' roll singer", and I used to play with a flat pick on a very loud acoustic 12-string. I used to play rhythm guitar on it because I couldn't pick; I don't know how to pick. I played rhythm guitar all along. I made a terrible folk singer, I was very upsetting. McGuinn too. We were ill-suited to the folk field because we were already half grown into rock 'n' roll. We were aware of it.'

Inspired by the Beatles' recordings and entranced by the film *A Hard*

Day's Night, the Jet Set began to incorporate Merseybeat elements into their songs. The leading light in the group at this stage was probably Gene Clark, who excelled in the studio and contributed the bulk of the songs. In fact, during the early World Pacific period Clark was the only member who sang lead vocal.

Dickson, with his interest in photography, was keen for the Jet Set to develop a strong visual image. They were already starting to grow their hair in imitation of the Beatles, but still had a long way to go before they looked the part. Meanwhile, they needed a drummer whose presence would make them appear more like a pop group than a long-haired folk trio. The perfect candidate soon appeared like a ghostly vision on Santa Monica Boulevard, almost as though he had been scripted for the part.

Michael Dick was born on 3 June 1944 in New York City, the eldest of three children. With his blue eyes, Brian Jones' styled sheepdog hair and Jaggeresque lips, the 6 foot 2 inch Stockbridge boy was classic pop star pin up material. Like Crosby, he was something of a traveller having left home at 16 and journeyed to Mexico, London, Sweden and San Francisco. His musical education was rudimentary, although he had played in several high school groups and was doing fine until they discovered that he could not read music. He had hung out in similar beatnik clubs to Crosby during the early 60's and even played alongside Dino Valenti for a time. Anybody associated with Valenti generally received Crosby's approbation and Michael was no exception. In common with Bob Dylan, Michael had long since jettisoned his surname and chosen a new nomenclature borrowed from one of pop's most famous broadcasters: Dick Clark. An 'e' was fortuitously added which later helped to distinguish him from his namesake and best friend in the group, Gene Clark. McGuinn recalled the sudden recruitment of Clarke and their first impressions of the man:

'I remember Michael was walking down Santa Monica Boulevard on his way to the Troubadour. He had this Brian Jones haircut which looked really neat. We said, "Hey, how would you like to be our drummer?" and he said, "Sure". David already knew him from Big Sur and I'd seen him play congas when I was in this folk club in San Francisco. I reckoned he could learn to play drums pretty quickly, though he really couldn't play when we hired him. At that point we couldn't afford a set of drums, so Michael had to practise on cardboard boxes using a tambourine.'

While Michael Clarke was banging away on his cardboard boxes, Dickson decided that the time was right for a new experiment. Having saved some money, he decided to organize a professional recording session with studio musicians. Ray Pohlman, musical director of *Shindig* and an important ally during the group's early days, appeared on bass while the drums were handled by the renowned session player Earl Palmer. With Gene Clark on acoustic guitar, McGuinn on electric 12-

string and Crosby adding harmony vocals, the results were primitive yet endearing. Two tracks were cut for a projected single, 'Please Let Me Love You'/'Don't Be Long' (the b-side being an earlier version of 'It Won't Be Wrong') with Dickson in the producer's chair, assisted by Paul Rothchild. A one-off deal was struck with Elektra which, Dickson confesses, erred on the side of caution:

'I didn't know where we were going to take it. I didn't know what we had in mind when we were recording it other than to see what we could do. We were trying to see what a finished record would sound like, trying to get it going. I made a deal with Jac Holzman to release the record but he couldn't associate it with them. He couldn't use their names or the group name. It would have prejudiced our chances of signing to another label. We didn't want to use it up.'

Faced with the problem of finding a pseudonym for the Jet Set, Holzman decided to exploit their long-haired Beatle image. He needed a quintessentially English-sounding name and suddenly realized that the answer was staring him in the face. On a gin bottle nearby was a brand name that conjured up visions of the Tower of London: 'Beefeater'. Although nobody liked the name or took it seriously, the opportunity to record professionally was a real buzz, especially for David Crosby:

'It was a funny thing. We just thought it was great to be able to make a record. I guess we didn't know what to think really. We were kids. We didn't have any idea.'

Jim Dickson was neither surprised nor upset by the failure of 'Please Let Me Love You'. He knew that a small independent label like Elektra had only a slim chance of breaking a single nationally, but the experiment had given the Jet Set some valuable studio experience, not to mention a $750.00 fee.

In many ways the Beefeaters' saga precipitated the move away from Beatle-imitation. Although they all adored the Fab Four, Crosby, Clark and McGuinn were never mere copyists. In fact, it was impossible for the Jet Set/Beefeaters to imitate the Beatles effectively because their backgrounds were so far removed from the British beat tradition. Without even realizing it, the trio were on the brink of discovering a new sound which would transform their lives and alter the direction of pop music during the next few years.

Immediately after the Beefeaters recording, there was a significant addition to the Jet Set line-up. Crosby's attempts to play bass were not proving fruitful and both Dickson and the group realized that something had to be done:

'David had got a six-string bass and tried but couldn't do it. Playing the bass was very hard for David. He found it hard to play the brute of anything. He plays accent rhythm; he wants to be the one to make it swing, not to be the one to put the mark down where you swing from. But he struggled along with it for some time. Finally, we knew we couldn't make it work with David.'

Intriguingly, Crosby's replacement as bassist would be a musician who was even less experienced on the instrument.

Christopher Hillman was born on 4 December 1944 and brought up in San Diego County. The youngest of four children he suffered a traumatic moment at the age of 11 when his father committed suicide. The powerful remembrance of that incident and its effects on Chris' life were poignantly revealed in the song 'Running' years later. Within 12 months of his father's death, Hillman had taken up guitar, inspired by the rock 'n' roll explosion of the mid-50's. Like Crosby and McGuinn, he became disillusioned with the state of pop music towards the end of the decade and turned towards more traditional forms. His elder brother and sisters encouraged his interest in country and bluegrass and before long Hillman emerged as an adept mandolin player. During his final year at high school he was already playing professionally with the Scottsville Squirrel Barkers and recorded an album titled *Bluegrass Favorites* for supermarket distribution.

One of Hillman's favourite bluegrass ensembles was the Golden State Boys who performed for Cal's Corral, a local country show hosted by Cal Worthington. During late 1962, Chris was overjoyed to receive an invitation to join his idols and soon he was playing in country bars and appearing occasionally on television. When guitarist Hal Poindexter left the Golden State Boys the remaining trio became the Blue Diamond Boys before receiving a significant name change. Eddie Tickner remembers how his partner unexpectedly promoted the youngest member of the group: 'Dickson recorded the Golden State Boys and we managed them. We then changed their name to the Hillmen after the 17-year-old genius mandolin player'.

The newly-christened Hillmen were regular visitors to World Pacific Studios throughout 1963 and Dickson persevered with them in the same way that he nurtured the Jet Set. Unfortunately, the big break remained frustratingly elusive as Dickson remembers:

'I'd been taping Chris for over a year at World Pacific long before there was any Byrds. He was there overlapping the stuff I did with Crosby independently. I'd recorded 16-18 sides with him and the Gosdin Brothers and we'd done the same thing, taping over and over until we'd built an entire album with choices. It was aimed at Elektra Records, but they turned it down.'

It would be a further six years before Chris' work was revealed to the world on the archivist album *The Hillmen*. What was most interesting about the sessions was the inclusion of two Bob Dylan songs, particularly 'When The Ship Comes In', which featured Hillman on vocals. Already, the crucial links between Dylan and the Beatles and folk and rock were within Dickson's grasp.

Hillman's recruitment to the Jet Set was by no means certain. He had recently left the Tickner/Dickson management in order to play in a group formed by the ubiquitous Randy Sparks, but, like McGuinn and Clark in their earlier ventures, he became disillusioned. Although attracted by Dickson's offer, Hillman did not want to lose the $100.00 a week that he could earn playing bluegrass. Dickson recalled his protege's dilemma:

'He was very flighty. He'd already gone through a long period with me of recording as the Hillmen and nothing had come of it. On the other hand, this new group looked like the future. He didn't play with the Randy Sparks group because he had respect for them. It was just like working at Woolworth's to him.'

At first Hillman intended to join the Jet Set on a temporary basis before finally committing himself, but after visiting World Pacific to watch their set he was converted:

'I was a mandolin player and didn't know how to play bass, but they didn't know how to play their instruments either, so I didn't feel too bad about it. None of us were rock 'n' rollers; we were all folk musicians and, although it was tremendously exciting, it was such an alien thing to be getting into . . . The original idea was for Crosby to be the bass player but it wasn't coming naturally to him, so they asked me to have a go. So, when I first joined, the line-up became me on bass, McGuinn on 12-string, Gene Clark on rhythm guitar and Crosby was just singing.'

The recruitment of Chris Hillman as a bass player was an illogical but satisfactory solution to the group's problems. At this early stage, the lack of sufficient funds meant that Hillman was forced to practise on a cheap little red Japanese bass, which was probably as effectual as Clarke's cardboard boxes.

3
The World Pacific Recordings

Depriving David Crosby of a musical instrument did not detract from the Jet Set's appeal until they played an informal live date at the Troubadour. Thereafter, the most flamboyant of the group began to concern himself with the competence of his fellow players. Eddie Tickner remembers a flurry of activity which culminated in another crucial change:

'David was more negative about Gene's guitar playing than he was positive about his own bass playing. There was a hustle, and in came Chris, and Crosby took the guitar out of Gene's hands.'

Crosby, while stressing that he did not physically remove the guitar from Clark's hands, does remember feeling frustrated by Gene's timing:

'Gene played very poorly and his time sense was atrocious. He would play really monotonously and very behind the beat. He would start behind the beat and slow down from there. He dragged heavily, and with a drummer like Michael Clarke (who at that time wasn't a drummer) it was a disaster. And I was a good rhythm guitar player already.'

Dickson was not convinced by Crosby's criticisms of Clark for he knew that every member of the Jet Set was still learning. While agreeing that the rhythm was far from perfect, he argues that Crosby exaggerated its relevance:

'David started telling Gene his timing wasn't good and started shaking his confidence. There wasn't anything wrong with Gene's timing. It wasn't imaginative, but it was straight. He played straight time. He was pretty much on the money, as good as the rest of them. We tried them all with a metronome and he certainly wasn't the worst. But I'd seen it happen in jazz where you could shake someone's confidence. I saw one bass player shake the confidence of another by just circulating the rumour that his timing was bad. By the time it got around, it had become bad. David did that to Gene. It was a self-fulfilling prophecy, to use your phrase.'

Crosby maintains that his finely-attuned sense of rhythm made him sensitive to such flaws and his views were certainly not challenged by the other Byrds. The role switch was effected quickly and surprisingly painstakingly. The fundamental differences in the quality of the Jet Set's playing, however, did not emerge until some weeks later when the resourceful Eddie Tickner managed to secure a loan of $5,000 to purchase new instruments:

'I was doing business management, and one of my clients at the time was Naomi Hirschorn. I solicited her to invest $5,000 for an interest in the Byrds. She was an artist and an art collector and an off-Broadway producer of shows and small theatre.'

Michael received his long-overdue drum-kit; Chris was given a Fender; a Gretsch Country Gentleman rhythm guitar was purchased for Crosby, and McGuinn bought himself a George Harrison-style 12-string Rickenbacker. With gleaming new instruments to practise on, the Jet Set's morale improved and so did their work at World Pacific. They were already regarded as something of a curio by local musicians and many of Dickson's friends passed by to check them out. Among the earliest visitors was Bob Dylan who betrayed none of his legendary moodiness and seemed the perfect gentleman. Characteristically, he saw facets of the Jet Set that had bypassed other critics and seemed positively enchanted by Michael's cardboard boxes. This was minimalism taken to the limit.

Another celebrity guest who visited World Pacific was the controversial comedian Lenny Bruce who had previously been recorded by Dickson. Bruce liked what he heard and soon afterwards his mother Sally Marr offered the Jet Set their first paying gig: an afternoon performance at East Los Angeles City College. The $50.00 fee was greatly welcomed.

The live performance was another test for the Jet Set whose progress over the months was impressive. Even Crosby began to appreciate the speed with which the group was improving and commends Jim Dickson for having the foresight to play back rehearsal tapes endlessly until the quintet righted their flaws:

'It might have taken us a couple of years to learn how to play and sing together but because of that we were ready in eight months. But it was brutal. You can hear it on *Preflyte*. It wasn't good enough at that point. I would never have put those songs on a record and released it.'

Preflyte (later issued with additional tracks and alternate takes as *In*

The Beginning) was a retrospective collection of recordings from the World Pacific period that provides a revealing insight into the Jet Set's experimentation. Although Crosby appears to have objected to its release, it should be stressed that he signed a release form agreeing to the project. According to Dickson, the quality-conscious Crosby was won over by his perennial partner, Graham Nash:

'Graham Nash said that the songs were charming baby pictures. You have to get a little older before you can tolerate seeing your baby pictures out there. We were all babies once! Graham just charmed David's socks off.'

Eight months of sterling work was undertaken at World Pacific but, two-and-a-half decades on, only a small cache of tracks remain. Forty-five takes spanning approximately 100 minutes provide an intriguing insight into the Jet Set's primal sound. Sadly, only 15 different actual songs (excluding the Beefeaters' tracks) are now in existence and one of these, 'Maybe You Think', is still unreleased. The remainder show the Jet Set at various stages of their evolution from their most primitive to the moments when they were close to major label stature. Dickson recalls their development and provides a cautionary word about the tapes:

'It was an exciting process, a struggling process. But it had its rewarding moments in the studio. I wouldn't say the best things they ever did in the studio were saved or ended up on *Preflyte* and *In The Beginning*. They were just the best of what was left in the boxes when we moved on. When we went back through everything there were just reels of takes that hadn't been pulled. We just went and looked.'

What Dickson discovered was a veritable treasure trove of Byrds juvenilia. Only five of the thirteen songs appeared on their first official album and the prototype demos are, not surprisingly, weaker, both vocally and instrumentally. On 'You Won't Have To Cry' the vocal range is positively restrained and McGuinn's Rickenbacker work has yet to reach the high standards evident in later recordings. Clarke's drumming is unvarying in its beat and he seems content with just keeping time. 'Here Without You' is minimalist by comparison but Clarke manages to keep time and sounds as though he is enjoying himself, having just discovered how to over-use the cymbals. 'I Knew I'd Want You', with its equally sparse backing and incessant, pounding tambourine, probably emanates from the early 'cardboard box' sessions. 'It's No Use' with its denser sound seems strangely out of place and was probably recorded later in the year.

Understandably, the strangest cut to emerge from World Pacific was the original version of 'Mr Tambourine Man' which sounds quite remarkable. McGuinn's lead guitar work is already good and will soon be better; Crosby shows signs of uncertainty and nervousness in his harmony work, but, as always, the diction is crystal clear. The most perplexing feature of this early version however is Clarke's drumming. For some reason he has adapted the song to a military school style of drumming which sounds completely inappropriate, yet extremely interesting. The attention of the listener is distracted from the lyrics as a result of the unusual arrangement, which partly transforms the number into an old-fashioned marching song. The story of how the song reached the Jet Set has always provided conflicting replies. McGuinn maintained that it was a gift from the composer:

'Dickson knew Dylan, and Dylan laid this dub on him with Dylan and Jack Elliot singing. It hadn't been released on the previous album because of a contract release problem with Jack. It was sloppy, kind of "Hey, Hey Mr Tambourine Man" – the words weren't all clear – it was groovy though . . . had its charm.'

Eddie Tickner provided a more plausible explanation of how the song reached the group:

'Dickson had heard Dylan do "Mr Tambourine Man" in concert but it hadn't been recorded. He requested a demo of the song from the publisher and when it arrived it had Jack Elliot on it too.'

Dickson himself credits a genial promotions person named Jack Mass for securing him the acetate that would shortly transform his group into international stars. Even when presented with such opportunities, the Jet Set could be frustratingly obdurate and all of them rejected 'Mr Tambourine Man' outright. It was only a personal appearance at World Pacific from Bob Dylan himself that finally changed their minds.

It is evident that a tremendous amount of work went into perfecting the Jet Set's vocals during 1964 and Dickson recalled some of the intricacies:

'Gene and McGuinn would both be singing melody, like a double lead, and Crosby would sing the only harmony. I tried to get Gene and McGuinn to drop down and sing a third part in the chorus sometimes. They had difficulty trying to do three-part harmony. But the three-part harmony gave David more freedom. The only problem with those early attempts at freedom is that the chord structures didn't support some of the lyrics. Crosby would rehearse the songs vocally with them and they'd sound great. But when you put them on top of the music they were playing they sounded a little sour. Crosby later found the chords that would fit the harmonies.'

One of the more extraordinary tracks to emerge from World Pacific in vocal terms was Gene Clark's 'Tomorrow Is A Long Ways Away'. His deep voice almost conjures up a vision of P.J. Proby, and it was precisely for this reason that the song failed to reach the vinyl stage, as Dickson revealed:

'Gene's vocal prevented the song from being a contender. It bothered everybody. We tried to get the vibrato out and find some way to deal with it, but we couldn't.'

Several other Clark songs were rejected outright even though they appeared on various rehearsal tapes. 'She Has A Way' with its distinctive harmonic blend almost won a place on their first Columbia album, but was deleted in favour of extraneous material. 'You Showed Me' was regarded as overtly sentimental but eventually gained Clark considerable songwriting royalties when the Turtles transformed the song into a Top 10 hit five years later. The pleasant but derivative 'You Movin'' and the extremely dated 'Boston' (complete with plodding bass) are perplexingly simplistic but, according to Dickson, these were merely warm-up tunes, specially designed for live performances and never intended for vinyl release.

The final oddity from *Preflyte* was the very last song recorded during that period: 'The Airport Song'. Crosby's fragile vocal is perfectly augmented by the sparse backing, which includes Gene on harmonica, and there are even a few moments of early jingle-jangle Rickenbacker at the end of the song. McGuinn recalls the origin of the composition:

'I collaborated with Crosby on "The Airport Song" but it was basically my idea to do it. It was written about LA Airport where we used to spend a lot of time just hanging about getting drunk and watching the planes coming in . . . Looking back I guess the song was OK. It's a pity it didn't make the first album but these things happen.'

A lovely missing link, 'The Airport Song' was always considered a potential film theme rather than a contender for their first album. When the movie idea foundered so did any interest that they may have had in re-recording the song.

Overall, the World Pacific demos and rehearsal tapes capture a group revelling in the excitement of discovery. There is an almost tangible feeling of lost innocence and yearning eroticism that permeates every cut, but such qualities were no guarantee of securing a record contract in 1964. Dickson felt that a major deal could be achieved and also realized that much depended on the reception afforded 'Mr Tambourine Man'. What the Jet Set urgently required was a lucky break and this came about in a typically unexpected way.

One afternoon, the group visited the home of a local impresario, Benny Shapiro, to play him some demos on their portable tape recorder. Nothing amazing was expected of the meeting, but as Shapiro could get them gigs his support would be an asset. The Jet Set unpacked their equipment in the promoter's cathedral-like living room and McGuinn, Crosby and Clark sang along to the tape, creating an impressive double-tracked three-part harmony. Suddenly, Shapiro's daughter Michelle ran into the room, overwhelmed by a sound which conjured up visions of the Beatles. Her father related this funny episode to Miles Davis shortly afterwards and the great horn player duly informed his record company, Columbia. Communication links were now open and Dickson found himself discussing the future of the Jet Set with CBS's West Coast A&R representative, Allen Stanton.

Miles Davis's recommendation, coupled with Dickson's rhetoric, proved sufficient to secure a recording contract with Columbia. The actual contract was dated 10 November 1964 and contained only three signatures: Jim McGuinn, David Crosby and Harold Eugene Clark. Although Hillman and Clarke were regarded as fully fledged Jet Setters by this time and not merely a live adjunct to the group, CBS insisted on signing vocalists only. What seemed a major breakthrough was cautiously viewed by Dickson. He knew that the signing far from guaranteed long term commitment, let alone imminent success. In fact the agreement covered only six months and Columbia's obligations did not extend far beyond recording, as opposed to releasing, four titles.

What everyone now agreed on was the need for the Jet Set to find a new name. There had already been much discussion about possible titles and the whole issue was finally concluded 16 days later when the Byrds convened for a Thanksgiving Day celebration. Gene Clark recalls the discussion that culminated in the grand christening:

'We were having Thanksgiving over at Ed Tickner's house and we were still trying to think of another name and I remembered a song that Dino Valenti had written called "Birdses", so I suggested that we call ourselves the Birdses because I really liked the song. They were serving turkey dinner – that's how I flashed on it.'

The group were less than impressed with the title 'Birdses', in spite of Jim Dickson's involvement in the recording of that single. McGuinn, however, was keen on finding a name that represented soaring flight similar to the Jet Set. At this point, Tickner suggested 'The Birds' as a possible alternative but the others reminded him that it was English slang for girls and might therefore cause confusion about their sex. At the same time, the name did fit McGuinn's requirement of 'soaring flight'. It was at this moment that one member suggested that they should alter the spelling of Birds, in imitation of the Beatles' vowel shift. Tickner told them to go through the vowels, but neither the Berds nor the Burds sounded plausible. With McGuinn still discussing the importance of flight, the name of the famous aviator Admiral Byrd entered the conversation, and the group unanimously insisted upon Byrds as their chosen title. Both McGuinn and Dickson were especially impressed with the name, as Tickner remembers: 'They thought it was a great idea because it had the magic "B" as in Beatles and Beach Boys'. So after weeks of considering possible names the Byrds were at last formally christened and could boast of their new status as Columbia recording artistes.

4
Fame And Fluctuating Fortunes

The Byrds' first producer at Columbia was Terry Melcher (Doris Day's son) who, in spite of his youth, appears to have been the one person in the company suitable and experienced enough to deal with the group:

'I was a staff producer at Columbia and at the time they didn't have any rock 'n' roll groups. The next youngest producer was about 20 years older than me, so the Byrds were allocated to me. CBS had originally signed me as an artiste, then I met Bruce Johnston and formed a duo. I'd produced about four or five hit records and was well known as part of the Jan and Dean, Beach Boys, LA rock 'n' roll set.'

Initially, Melcher and Dickson proved a superb combination and were in total agreement that the Byrds' first single should be 'Mr Tambourine Man' backed with 'I Knew I'd Want You'. Although McGuinn and company had previously voiced their dislike for the Dylan composition, Dickson's proselytizing had finally convinced them of its merits. Only David Crosby retained strong doubts, but, faced with the opportunity of recording at Columbia he, not unnaturally, bit his lip. It was evident from the World Pacific demos that, instrumentally, the Byrds were not yet competent enough to record a sufficiently impressive single within the limits of the allocated studio time. Dickson made the inevitable decision that session musicians would have to be employed, a view with which Melcher concurred:

'McGuinn was the only Byrd who played on the first session, then Crosby and Clark came in to sing the harmony. Hillman and Clarke didn't appear on either of the two sides. We used Leon Russell, Hal Blaine and Larry Knechtel.'

Much has been made of the fact that only one Byrd played on 'Mr Tambourine Man', but Dickson was mystified by the storm-in-a-teacup controversy and has always argued that the session musicians were not only desirable but necessary:

'CBS weren't obligated to do anything beyond the audition. That was it. Terry Melcher was more interested in the fact that the people I'd chosen to back them were heroes of his and had played on Beach Boys records. Hal Blaine, not Dennis Wilson, played on those Beach Boys hits. Nobody in California would have questioned our use of those session musicians. They were the guys that everybody used in some sort of combination. Their techniques were designed for the studio. They wouldn't go on the road.'

The evolution of the song was a story in itself with Melcher employing a rhythm feel inspired by the Beach Boys' 'Don't Worry Baby' and suggesting that most famous of opening bass lines. McGuinn, meanwhile, was approaching the song like an actor. Dickson had already convinced him to study Stanislavsky and remembering his acting classes, McGuinn programmed his voice to sound like a cross between John Lennon and Bob Dylan:

'In the spectrum of music at the time, that was the niche I saw vacant. I saw this gap, with them leaning towards each other in concept. That's what we aimed at and hit it. We caught it from there and worked it up in a more contemporary style at the time, the beat and the wispy kind of freaked out vocal treatment. The unison sounds came from the 12-string guitar doing plagal cadences – like the Joan Baez thing. It sounded different with electric.'

The gap between the World Pacific 'Mr Tambourine Man' and the Columbia version is staggering in itself but nobody has ever pointed out the song's biggest irony. At an even earlier date than the *Preflyte* demos, the Dylan number had been assigned to Gene Clark yet, within a year, circumstances had thrust him into a subsidiary position. Dickson explains how the tambourine-playing Byrd's voice was buried in the Columbia recording:

'Terry mixed out Gene Clark's vocal. You've got to be magic to hear that. It's only bleed from the other mikes four feet away. He also mixed out Leon Russell. It wasn't out of disrespect though. The electric piano just wasn't working. By the time they added the drums, they had enough. It had come together.'

At the last minute Dickson suggested that they should hire his old friend Douglas Dillard to add a banjo to the recording. Terry looked around quizzically and simply said: 'Man, you'd be gilding the lily. You've already got a *great* record'. Melcher was correct and the whole ensemble agreed that the end product had a marvellous sound.

Having successfully completed 'Mr Tambourine Man' in January

1965, the Byrds were left in limbo because Columbia delayed the release of the song for several months, arguing that it might get buried in the forthcoming release of several big name singles. In the meantime, the Byrds began their career as a live performing group, but their opening gig, at a bowling alley, was nothing less than a disaster, as McGuinn remembers:

'It was awful. I think there were about 20 people scattered around the room that held 100, with cocktails in their hands, totally apathetic, all looking at the floor. We'd had two sets of suits to wear which were both stolen, so we started wearing blue jeans which stayed. Anyway, we played to these mannequins with their martinis, and the bowling pins were going smash as we sang.'

According to Tickner, the Byrds almost broke up immediately after that gig, but eventually decided to struggle on. However, the indecision resulting from the delay in the release of 'Mr Tambourine Man' caused McGuinn to re-examine the Byrds' progress and, for a brief period, he seriously considered leaving the group to join Dino Valenti. The whim passed, however, and the Byrds continued gigging, having received a booking at the night club Ciro's in March. The following month 'Mr Tambourine Man' was at last released and became, quite literally, an overnight smash. Crosby recalls the day that the Byrds fully realized the enormous potential of the single:

'We were driving along in a black station wagon that we'd bought from Odetta. All of us were in the car. We were driving along and on radio station KRLA comes 'Mr Tambourine Man' three times in a row. The biggest radio station in LA and they played it three times in a row. We just sat there and drooled. We went crazy. It was so good. We knew we'd won. It was a good feeling.'

Gene Clark recalls the progress of the disc during its first few weeks of release:

'It was picked up by Tom Donahue at KYA in San Francisco because David Crosby was a friend of Tom's and David flew up there with an acetate which Tom listened to and right away he decided to put it on the radio. He put it on air, Top 40 air, and from San Francisco it was picked up in Sacramento, Fresno and into LA and the thing broke within three weeks. It was getting pretty crazy.'

In order to control and exploit the 'craziness', Dickson decided to appoint a press officer. A photographer friend recommended Derek Taylor, the urbane Beatles' publicist who had recently moved from London to Los Angeles. Taylor was doing some work for KRLA at the time, so Dickson accosted him with an acetate of 'Mr Tambourine Man' and terms were discussed. Dickson knew that he lacked the financial resources to afford a figure as prestigious as Taylor but came up with the intriguing idea of offering the Liverpudlian a 2 per cent commission on the group's earnings. It was a loose arrangement which proved highly successful and the terms were never revoked or challenged even after the Byrds' rise to fame:

'Two per cent! It wasn't even on paper. We never talked about it. It never came up. I guess when Derek left we never paid him anymore. It wasn't ownership the way Naomi Hirschorn, who actually put up cash, continues to get paid.'

The induction of Taylor coincided with the rise of Eddie Tickner, who elected to take on the responsibilities of organizing the Byrds' road work and performing commitments. Dickson recalls Tickner's evolving role in the Byrds' story:

'When I first started with Eddie I saw him as somebody to keep the books, to be a partner and keep track of it. To me, a partner was an equal partner. I didn't think of him as an equal contributor, but if you make somebody a partner you play straight with them. I can't imagine a 60:40 partnership. It's beyond my imagination to do that. Eddie never came to World Pacific that I can remember and he didn't interfere in the music. He didn't have anything to say about the music then. He took over the responsibility of dealing with all the live performances first and then he began to enjoy the Byrds.'

It was Tickner who secured the group their now legendary first season at Ciro's, a once glitzy supper club from the golden era of Hollywood. The debut performance in March occurred before the release of 'Mr Tambourine Man', but they returned the following month for a second series of dates amid scenes of mayhem. Derek Taylor recalls the highlights:

'When we first turned up there was hardly anyone there, literally about 16 of us. From then on, though, it was always packed. The sound was new and exciting. McGuinn was terrific. He had a certain abstraction about him which was fascinating; and then there were those incredible dancers. I can vividly recall this young girl dancing on her own, wearing McGuinn's glasses. I was captivated.'

Michelle Kerr, the mysterious girl whom Taylor so vividly recalls, takes the not uncontested credit for providing McGuinn with one of his earliest trademarks: 'I was wearing these glasses and Jim McGuinn asked me where I'd got them and he went out and got a pair'. The whole scene at Ciro's had actually begun in the unlikely setting of an artist's studio, as Michelle remembers:

'Vito was a sculptor who had a studio, a store and his living quarters in the same building. People used to go over there for sculpting lessons and exercise classes. He was a weird artist, the original beatnik – he looked about 61 then! Carl Franzoni lived upstairs. Kim Fowley had seen me and Karen Yum Yum at Ciro's and asked us to come over to Vito's. The Byrds began rehearsing in Vito's basement and got to know

Carl, and gradually it all came together.'

The Byrds' dancing followers were an incredible sight with their outlandish clothes and exotic names such as Beatle Bob, Karen Yum Yum, Linda Bopp, Emerald and Butchie. After seeing the Byrds' opening nights at Ciro's some spectators felt that both the group and their followers were permanently stoned. Michelle, however, feels that this was an exaggeration:

'I was never on drugs. Ciro's was such a high. I'd be just in another world. None of the Byrds were really gone on drugs either. They weren't into it to any great degree, and Gene's drinking wasn't a problem as far as the early Byrds were concerned.'

The excitement generated at Ciro's was enough to encourage Bob Dylan to check out these new, young hopefuls. He had already seen them rehearse, and apparently was so puzzled that he did not even recognize their renditions of his own songs. Dylan was sufficiently intrigued by their electric versions of his old material to make an impromptu guest appearance with them onstage at Ciro's. Derek Taylor rationalizes his motives:

'Dylan was then super-hero but his impact had yet to be measured in record sales. It looked as if he was bestowing his presence upon them, but the Byrds were doing him a favour as much as he was doing them. I always thought they had a good deal going together.'

When McGuinn casually explained their arrangement of 'Mr Tambourine Man' Dylan, observing the audience, retorted: 'Wow, man, you can dance to that'. According to McGuinn: 'We played him some of his other stuff at Ciro's and he didn't even recognize them'.

The appearance of Dylan merely increased the fervour that the Byrds were causing at Ciro's. Suddenly, the night club became one of the most hip and fashionable places at which to be seen, and scattered amongst the fans were a combination of established stars and the soon-to-be-famous: Jack Nicholson, Barry McGuire, Major Lance, Little Richard, Judy Henske, Mary Travers, Buffy Saint-Marie and Sonny and Cher. Dickson remembers when Ciro's was filled to the rafters with his friends, associates and rivals:

'We had all the up-and-coming elite who wanted to know what was going on. All the young Hollywood people came there. If you were in Hollywood and on the way up, or even trying to be, it was too big an event to miss. Even people who had nothing to do with it came. Sal Mineo arrived in a tuxedo because the last time he'd been at Ciro's that's what you wore. He had that tuxedo and a black tie and ordered champagne in a bucket. He was the only one in the room with that kind of set-up. None of us were impressed with Sal Mineo as an actor, performer or hero. But to have him show up and to be able to say: "Hey, that's Sal Mineo over there!" was neat. Jack Nicholson was a more familiar part of our community. All these actors came in, lots of people I'd known. We'd call them up on the phone every day, everybody. They'd have a good time then come back with somebody else. Everybody had a great time at Ciro's. That's why they're still talking and writing about it 25 years later. It was just mind-boggling – and for Eddie Tickner too! For me, to see Eddie at a Byrds show *every* night was surprising then.'

Other people who attended the shows were no less extravagant in their praise and speak in epochal terms about the performances. Michelle Kerr maintains that the happening at Ciro's was the start of a cultural revolution:

'We started the hippie movement. We were the first groupies who were known. Jim Dickson started calling us groupies, but at that time it wasn't a put down. After that when everybody else started following the groups around it became a lower-class thing.'

The Byrds' stage performance was unpredictable and daringly erratic. During the first couple of sets they seemed nervous, off-key and out of place. McGuinn appeared tentative, Crosby 'looked at the guitar as if it was a foreign object' while Clarke appeared to be asking 'What do I do with these drum sticks?' Once Crosby's mood lightened, however, the entire group would surge. Dickson pinpoints David's backing vocal on the Beatles' 'Things We Said Today' as the pivotal moment in the third set. As soon as he uttered the words, 'Me, I'm such a lucky guy', he seemed to realize the full implications of the words and, smiling that crooked smile, would take the Byrds towards musical nirvana. For Dickson, the other hero of Ciro's was Michael Clarke whose drumming on his home territory, orchestrated by a legion of dancers, was so magnificent that it defied belief and logic. The Byrds' erraticism was to remain a constant for virtually the remainder of their career. During those early days of 1965 they moved from poor to brilliant in the space of an evening and the following night the process would be repeated. It was this aberrant quality which won them a fanatical following in Hollywood and would shortly create enemies abroad.

Although the Byrds live shows seemed almost wilfully casual, no pressure was placed upon them to fashion an image. Rather, they created their own image of 'unpredictability' and 'eccentric genius' both in their unconventional dress and their moody, erratic performances. Derek Taylor explained the Byrds' 'image':

'The Byrds' management let them control their own image. The group did it all themselves. The Tickner/Dickson thing was just right for the Byrds, just relaxed enough for them. Had they had an Elliot Roberts or Irv Azoff, it might have frightened them. They were so scruffy, and their attitude towards the audience was so blase. They were often quite bad on stage, but they had this relaxed management who said: "That's cool!" Dickson really knew what being laid back meant. He was so laid back himself; no middle-aged, middle-class hang ups. Everything went with Dickson. His attitude was, "If David Crosby wants to do this, let him do it". Eddie curbed Jim's wilder instincts. It was a good partnership.'

Dickson feels that Taylor's analytical comments needed to be qualified:

'Eddie Tickner is more laid back than me. He's more organized. I don't know if I'm as laid back as Derek says. To him, I was. To East Coasters I guess I was. But I didn't think I was any more laid back than the average Californian goof-off. I came from a community that felt that if you had to get a job to make a living then you were a failure. If you couldn't make it by your wits, you weren't worth it.'

If Dickson had some elements of Californian cool in his personality, then the Byrds were masters of the form. The image that they created made them sex symbols and their pop star trappings, such as McGuinn's rectangular granny glasses and Crosby's extraordinary green suede cape, sanctified their appeal. According to Crosby, however, their otherworldly ambience and groomed prettiness was not premeditated:

'We didn't look at it that way. I naturally smile all the time. I didn't do it as an act. I have no act. The green cape and the glasses we did use to look far-out to jazz people. I admit that. But we dispensed with them pretty quickly and rested it almost solely on the music . . . None of us bought the star bullshit. Star is the *übermensch* mistake – it means somebody bigger than life. And nobody is. There's no such damn thing. They try and tell you that you're solid chrome, 11 foot tall, you've got wings, and sweety baby everything you say is deathless prose. But it's pure, unadulterated, misleading bullshit. It's one of the peripheral things that pulls you away from the music. That fame and glory shot, and the chicks and money and "Oh my God, I must be smart, look at how many people are listening to me". All those things are mistakes. They all pull you away from the music. And we tried very hard, consciously, to avoid them and to stay concerned with the music and with what we were saying. We thought we were wordsmiths too by the time we got into it, and we at least liked the things that we were saying. But I don't think that any of us bought that star bullshit. Not any of us. I'd give every guy in the band credit for not going for it. I can remember McGuinn, before we even really started saying, "Man, we'll be like princes". But even he didn't buy it in terms of thinking of himself as any different. Maybe he did, but I don't think he did. I'd give him credit for being smarter than that.'

While the momentum gathered, Billy James (the Columbia publicist) worked overtime by promoting the group at every opportunity, recruiting new fans and encouraging them to spread the word. The overnight success of 'Mr Tambourine Man' earned the group a support spot on the Rolling Stones tour, and during the same period they made their television debut on *Hullabaloo*. McGuinn remembers the big moment:

'We'd never experienced the pressure of a live television show before, and this was a national broadcast. They had these big colour television cameras coming in on us and it was pretty unnerving. The guy at the mixing board couldn't get our voices right and I didn't like my vocal on "Tambourine Man", which came out very shaky, probably because we were so nervous.'

Much of McGuinn's account is true; the Byrds performed three numbers, a slightly slower than expected 'Feel A Whole Lot Better', a marginally different arrangement of 'Chimes Of Freedom' and a nervous, but ultimately rewarding, 'Mr Tambourine Man'. Certainly, the live performance of 'Mr Tambourine Man' proved that the Byrds were already capable of performing their hit single without the assistance of session musicians. The playing was competent, and Clarke, abandoning his unusual military style of drumming, as demonstrated on *Preflyte*, effectively duplicated Hal Blaine's work on the single. The Byrds were a little ragged but nobody could have guessed that McGuinn was the only member to have played on the single.

While the single began to break internationally, the Byrds continued gigging from coast to coast without a break. It was a gruelling but extraordinary tour, as the Byrds were accompanied by several members of the Ciro's dance troupe. The extensive touring schedule was masterminded by Eddie Tickner:

'We went out on a dance tour and played five sets a night in ballrooms. We brought our own go-go dancers, but we put them on the floor and not in costume and created a scene. I felt that was the next step in the evolution of rock. I thought my vision was correct but they weren't ready for it. It wasted them.

Lizzie Donahue, a leading member of the dance troupe, recalls the events of the tour:

'I was 17 when we went on tour. We took a Trailways bus – the Byrds, Bryan MacLean, Carl, Karen Yum Yum, Jeanine and me. Linda Bopp and Butchie followed in a car. I remember we all got high in a bathroom on the bus, especially David Crosby. In Duluth, Minnesota, the police searched the bus and I remember David having to throw his stash out of the window.'

When the Byrds arrived in town the result would often be close to pandemonium, as Lizzie confessed:

'It was amazing. I don't think the Mid-West was ready for Carl Franzoni and the whole troupe of us. We'd go into restaurants in the Mid-West and they wouldn't wait on us. They thought we were something from Outer Space. In Paris, Illinois, they actually threw us off the dance floor. I think they cancelled the gig that night.'

Within weeks 'Mr Tambourine Man' had topped the US charts, and its success was repeated in Britain under similarly surprising circumstances. The pirate station Radio Caroline was playing the song before CBS had even decided to issue it, and public demand precipitated its release. Within four weeks it was number 1 and impresario Mervyn Conn hastily negotiated a British tour for the month of August. Meanwhile, the Byrds had recently completed their first album which was immediately released in the States.

5
The British Tour

Having rehearsed the material for the first album over many months, it was not surprising that the sessions were completed quickly. According to Terry Melcher the recording sessions went very smoothly, but Lizzie Donahue remembers one clash of personalities:

'I went to a recording session for the first album and it was clear that David Crosby wasn't getting along with Jim Dickson. Jim had David on the floor and he was choking him. David seemed to have a problem with everybody; he was always at odds with someone, but we all got on really well.'

The incident that Lizzie Donahue remembers actually occurred on the final day of recording their all important debut album and Dickson had already reached the end of his tether:

'Lizzie said I was choking him! It probably looked that way from the booth. I wasn't choking him though, I had him by the shoulders. David Crosby had cut the last track for the album, "Chimes Of Freedom". He then announced that he wasn't going to sing on it, he was leaving. Trying to get him through the first album, I sat on his chest and said: "The only way you're going to get through that door is over my dead body. I will physically stop you with every bit of energy I have. You're going to stay in this room until you do the vocal". And David broke into tears. There were a lot of people there apart from Lizzie. People were there from CBS who'd come to see them for the first time. It was not the moment that one would choose to have that kind of conflict, but it was either finished or to hell with it all.'

Dickson's heavy persuasion was vindicated by the completed version of 'Chimes Of Freedom' which highlighted Crosby's subtle harmonic blend.

The released recordings that emerged from the conflict were so polished and professional that some uninformed commentators suggested that session musicians were once again employed. This, however, was not the case as all the Byrds and everybody associated with them will testify. Hillman was outraged by the suggestion and retorted: 'All you have to do is listen to hear it's us'. Melcher concurred with an impatient riposte: 'I produced that album and Hillman and Clarke definitely played on *every* cut apart from the two sides of the single, "Mr Tambourine Man" and "I Knew I'd Want You". 'At one point, it seemed likely that the Byrds would have to submit to the use of session musicians but they remained firm and as Crosby explains: 'Columbia wanted us to do the first album with session men and we threatened to quit. We didn't like that at all'.

What the first album showed most clearly was that the Byrds had already moved away from Beatle imitations. Although the arrangements of 'It's No Use', 'Here Without You' and 'You Won't Have To Cry' were unaltered from their World Pacific demos, the vocal and instrumentation were improved to such a degree that the songs appeared totally underivative. The Byrds were now the innovators of a new musical style: 'folk rock'. The early repertoire of Gene Clark songs was by and large replaced by new interpretations of Dylan's material. In addition to the title track, the Byrds included new arrangements of 'All I Really Want To Do', 'Spanish Harlem Incident' and 'Chimes Of Freedom'. The decision to continue covering Dylan songs, however, was no longer solely due to the insistence of Jim Dickson, as McGuinn remembers:

'After Dickson picked "Mr Tambourine Man" we got into Dylan – it was a mutual decision. The whole group were responsible for the arrangements – I'd come up with the guitar part and Chris would come up with the bass part. Dylan was aware of what we were doing and liked the idea.'

One of the most satisfying tracks on the album was a new Gene Clark song, 'Feel A Whole Lot Better'. It seemed to contain the essence of the Byrds sound, the pounding tambourine and some exceptional jingle-jangle Rickenbacker work from McGuinn. Terry Melcher was overwhelmed by the quality of the song, which was way beyond his expectations. Dickson seemed equally impressed and years later would record Gene Clark singing the same song as a solo artiste. The Byrds' management even laid on a special budget for the song, such was their commitment to its commercial potential. For Dickson, it represented the perfect bridge between Clark's more simplistic love songs and the surrealistic Dylanesque material that he would compose later in the year:

'There was always something to unravel in those songs – the nonexplanation of the complex feeling. For instance, if you remember "Feel A Whole Lot Better", it doesn't say: "I'll feel a whole lot better when you're gone", but, I'll *probably* feel a whole lot better". For me, that makes the song. There's a statement followed by hesitation: "Hey, I'm a little unsure!" I've heard Gene sing the song without the "probably". He got tired of singing it for awhile. He'll sing it now in 1989 because Tom Petty has done it. But I remember him laying behind the beat and not having that right-on feeling that he had in the beginning. He started economizing on words because of gum disease. I said to him: "But, Gene, you can't leave out the *probably* – I can't live with that Gene!" He said: "What do you mean?" The part that was most remarkable to me was probably just some way that he filled up the chorus at the time. I think we all tend to find things in songs that songwriters don't necessarily intend. But that's OK. A good song always allows the listener to make up his own mind.'

The durability of 'Feel A Whole Lot Better' was further demonstrated by its continual re-appearance in the Byrds live sets, long after its composer had moved on. Even the overly-critical Crosby maintains that the song was one of Clark's finest of the period:

'Gene did try to emulate the Beatles, and he would try to play folk changes rather than standard rock 'n' roll changes. His songs had good chord structures. You'll notice that they never had just three chords; there were several chords involved, and they were good chord structures with good melody. Gene had a pretty good way of stringing the melody across chords. "Feel A Whole Lot Better" was probably the best of them.'

A late addition to the Byrds repertoire was an old favourite of McGuinn's from the Judy Collins days. 'The Bells Of Rhymney', a song adapted by Pete Seeger from a lyric by Welsh poet Idris Davies, told the tragic tale of a coal-mining disaster, but the listener would never have guessed the theme from the tone of the Byrds' electrified rendition. Here the group had made a crucial development demonstrating that the move away from Merseysound was now complete, the familiar Byrds' 'aaahhs' replacing the Beatles' 'oh yeah' phrasing. Although Dickson was mesmerized by the Byrds' adaptation of Seeger's lament, he felt that the finished recording lacked one crucial ingredient:

'The only mix of Terry's that I was disappointed with was "The Bells Of Rhymney" because he automatically shut Michael's cymbals down. It was the only time Michael ever had something important on the cymbals that was part of the music. It was just overlooked in the process. Ordinarily, it would have been a good idea to turn them down and just concentrate on the snare and bass drum and forget about Michael's tom-tom and cymbals. He wasn't that good at them, but on *that* song, he had it. The fact that we never got "The Bells Of Rhymney" on tape anything like the way it was at Ciro's was just a terrible thing. Later on, I wanted CBS to release "Chimes Of Freedom" with "The Bells Of Rhymney" on the back as a single so that we'd have a chance to remix it as a single. Terry would always remix for singles and do a much better job.'

Another song that had arrived in the Byrds' set between the World Pacific and Columbia recordings was Jackie De Shannon's 'Don't Doubt Yourself Babe'. The group had already betrayed a strong inclination for her material and Dickson was determined that they should record at least one of her songs. With its marraccas and tambourine, the number came out sounding not unlike the Rolling Stones' 'Not Fade Away'. In retrospect, the song was a fairly minor league Byrds cover, but Dickson regarded its inclusion on the album as a matter of personal honour:

'Jackie De Shannon was the first professional person in rock 'n' roll to risk her credibility by saying that the Byrds were great and helping them to get work. She had put herself on the line. Jackie had a reputation good enough to have sung with the Beatles when they first came over. She was a little piece of the American new dream and already had a career and success. She'd written hit songs and made hit records. With no hesitation at all, Jackie looked everybody in the eye and said: "The Byrds are the greatest!" She said wonderful things about them. I wanted to do one of her songs to repay her and "Don't Doubt Yourself Babe" became that one. McGuinn decided that this was the time to do the Rolling Stones' rhythm part with the Bo Diddley feel. They'd lapse into it, come out of it, go into straight time and then play it again. Michael always wanted to play something like that anyway. He'd try to figure out how to do it. They played it and they didn't think much of it. In truth, it never amounted to that much. But I had a feeling, and it came from an older part of Hollywood, that you paid back debts and didn't overlook favours.'

While 'Don't Doubt Yourself Babe' emerged as unusual, the final track on the album was positively bizarre. With unintended whimsy, the Byrds provided a unique reworking of the war-time classic 'We'll Meet Again'. The group had adapted the song to their repertoire by re-arranging the tempo and adding a three-part harmony. The idea to record the song was inspired by the ending of the film *Dr Strangelove*, and at Ciro's the Byrds dedicated the number to Stanley Kubrick, Peter Sellers and Slim Pickens (the directors and stars of the film, respectively).

While the album climbed the US charts, the Byrds continued their rigorous touring schedule and found themselves in great demand among the 'teenzines'. It was suddenly impossible to pick up any teenage magazine that did not include a long list of the Byrds' vital statistics and various likes and dislikes. The Byrdmania that was sweeping the States was already gaining a foothold in England and the group was being hyped to gargantuan proportions. Unknown to the Byrds, Mervyn Conn was promoting them as 'America's Answer To The Beatles'. All over London, posters began to appear with the message: 'The Byrds Is Coming'. Articles were already published in the music weeklies (courtesy of transatlantic phone interviews) and although most English journalists had only heard the 'Mr Tambourine Man' single, they were more than willing to echo the words of Mervyn Conn's posters, with such headlines as 'Byrds Biggest Craze Since Beatles' and 'Byrds – America's Biggest Ever Group'. Chris Hutchins was convinced that the Byrds' visit would be the greatest single event this side of the Apocalypse, and we were warned to take heed:

'Unless I am very much mistaken August is going to see Britain gripped by a new phenomenon – BYRDMANIA. Stand by for the biggest explosion of hysteria since the Beatles first sent love From Me To You, when the Byrds fly from Hollywood to cash in on the success of this week's haunting chart topper. Mothers should take heed of the warning and lock up their daughters, for I have it on good authority that the group has Pied Piper habits, and at this very moment birds are following Byrds by the coach-load across the breadth of America.'

With all the pre-flyte publicity, it was no surprise when, upon arrival in London, the Byrds were greeted by coach loads of fans who had waited patiently just to get a glimpse of the group. A less amiable greeting came from a representative of the British group, the Birds, who presented the group with a writ claiming infringement of his clients' registered name and gaining them some useful publicity in the process. Undeterred by such an affront, the Byrds retired to the Europa Hotel in Grosvenor Square until dark fell. Then they crept out for a night on the town during which they fulfilled Michael Clarke's ambition of meeting the Beatles.

The following night the Byrds appeared at a warm-up gig before the tour in a small London club called Blaises owned by John Carter Fea. It was a select gathering, including John Lennon and George Harrison. Derek Taylor remembers the evening with mixed feelings:

'Blaises was a place where people wouldn't mind being seen, but it wasn't an ideal gig. The stage was the size of a sofa and the Byrds played extraordinarily loud and appeared both awkward and temperamental. Still, I loved them, and George Harrison and John Lennon were also impressed.'

After the gig, the Byrds were wined, but not dined, by the Beatles duo. The entire troupe returned to Brian Jones's flat, where they stayed up until the early hours of the morning smoking dope. On their way to the Europa they at least managed to purchase some well-deserved hamburgers. These nights of riotous entertainment, however, would shortly take their toll.

Prior to leaving the States, the Byrds issued their second single, 'All I

Really Want To Do', and it was released in Britain during the first week of their visit. The single was a different cut from the album version, with a more abrasive sound and forceful vocal. Terry Melcher was surprised to be reminded that the Byrds had taken the time to re-cut the song:

'I remember remixing it for the single. I used to always speed tracks up for singles but I can't remember the details of any re-recording. But it you say the words are different then we must have re-recorded it. It was put on the album first but I thought it was a bad move for a single because Cher's version had just entered the US charts.'

The Byrds felt that they could climb above their imitators without difficulty, but on this occasion they were proved incorrect. Cher's version became a US Top 20 hit while the Byrds failed to manage a Top 30 entry. As a follow-up to a number 1, it was nothing less than disastrous. The Byrds had now experienced their first major setback.

In Britain, the situation initially looked more promising. The music papers were predicting 'Another Byrds No.1', and indeed, within its first few days of release, the single smashed into the Top 20. With the Byrds on tour to promote the single it appeared a certain chart topper. The timing seemed perfect; after all, it was August, and as everyone in the music world knows, the summer months are invariably the dreariest for quality singles. Unfortunately for the Byrds, a series of catastrophes transformed their summer of glory into a month of nightmare. Firstly, Cher's version also became a Top 10 hit and although the Byrds outsold her in Britain, they were seriously affected by the split sales. The sleepy summer months might normally have left the Byrds relatively unaffected by a cover version, but this was no ordinary August. Incredibly, three of the year's finest singles were released almost simultaneously, and the Byrds found themselves sandwiched between the Stones' 'Satisfaction' and Dylan's 'Like A Rolling Stone', while competing against the Beatles' 'Help!'.

Meanwhile, the ill-fated British tour had opened at Nelson in Lancashire on 4 August and the Byrds suffered their first casualty. A doctor was rushed to the Imperial Ballroom to give emergency penicillin injections to Chris Hillman who had collapsed in his dressing room suffering from 'acute asthma and bronchitis'. Thirty minutes later, he had recovered sufficiently to appear on stage. The tour continued, and television appearances were arranged for *Ready Steady Go* and *Top Of The Pops*. At this point, the Byrds suffered their second casualty. McGuinn:

'I got sick. I had something like 103 temperature fever. We were at the BBC studio doing some show and the doctor came in and said: "This guy shouldn't work, send him home to bed". And they said: "He's got to work". So I'm laying on a couch or something there and everybody's going crazy, nobody has any organization any more.'

While the doctors were attempting to revive McGuinn, Beatlemaniac Michael Clarke became the third victim of the Byrds' plague. Taylor remembers the chaotic scenes:

'Mike Clarke was also ill during a BBC session and I seem to remember that the others weren't particularly sympathetic, so he imitated Ringo's stunt in *A Hard Day's Night* and vanished. He returned literally one second before the live show was due to begin.'

The Byrds then began arguing among themselves whether Mike ought to be fired or not, and by the end of the evening they had all decided to call it a day and return to the States. The crisis passed, however, and the tour resumed once more, although the Byrds were in a severely weakened state. Still recovering from their arduous bus tour of America, they were in no condition for a stamina-sapping major British tour. Dickson had been sceptical from the outset, but was overruled by his partner and the group. Now the Byrds were paying for their heavy socializing and hard work with undisguised exhaustion. 'Dr' Derek Taylor diagnosed their problems most perceptively:

'Mike was ill, Hillman was ill, McGuinn was ill. As soon as you took them out of Hollywood and put them into a proper climate it seemed to affect them. They were not leading healthy lives or eating good food, and they were overworked by Mervyn Conn.'

While the Byrds' super-cool stage persona had worked wonders at Ciro's, the response at the Finsbury Park Astoria was slightly different. The press objected to the Byrds' Dylanesque moodiness and complained about the over-amplification and atrocious sound quality. It seemed that 'America's Answer To The Beatles' were nothing more than pretenders to the throne, and the press spared no adjectives in exposing them. Luckily, the recently released *Mr Tambourine Man* had received reasonable reviews so all the hostility was directed against the Byrds' stage act. Many of the adverse comments may have been justified, but there also seemed to be strong overtones of partisanship. Derek Taylor summed up the attitude of the British press:

'The press was, as usual, the press. Unfortunately, the British press tends to get together on such occasions and there was a lot of aggression over the Byrds. One of the Byrds' characteristics was that they could be objectionable by not performing very well and not being consistently good. I loved them as if they were my own children, but unfortunately they weren't as well behaved as my own children! I found the concerts very unnerving. I had tears in my eyes every night, I thought it was so wonderful. But the audiences had gone expecting heaven. They'd been told that this was a very important group.'

The reactions of the audiences were expressed in letter form to the music press which resulted in such captions as 'The Byrds Get The Bird'. One letter summed up the expectations of the British audiences:

'My friend and I went to Slough to see the Byrds and thought they were terrible. The sound was awful, they didn't bother to introduce any of the songs, they tuned up on stage, and altogether they had no talent or personality.'

As the disastrous tour reached its completion, the Byrds found themselves facing another threat. Their rivals, Sonny and Cher, having already caused them problems with 'All I Really Want To Do', now chose to descend on England at the very time when the Byrds were experiencing their greatest problems. Within days of their arrival, the fickle teenzines, which had devoted so much space to Crosby's green suede cape and McGuinn's fab, groovy, rectangular mini-shades, were now obsessed with Cher's hair and Sonny's furs and striped trousers. The Byrds, it seemed, were no longer trendsetters in fashion. But weren't the Byrds still the 'kings of the protest movement', the non-conforming voice of youth, the darlings of the anti-establishment? No! While the Byrds were safely ensconced at the Europa and had given receptions at the Savoy, Sonny and Cher gained themselves a great deal of publicity and public sympathy by being refused admittance to London's more elite hotels because of their eccentric clothing. The Byrds left England just in time to see their single trapped at number 4 while Sonny and Cher's 'I Got You Babe' by-passed Dylan and the Beatles and moved effortlessly to the coveted number 1 spot.

The Byrds flew back to the States in a fairly depressed state, with a severely damaged reputation and personal losses including both a stolen Rickenbacker and the gold disc awarded to them for sales of 'Mr Tambourine Man'. At least David Crosby managed to perceive some humour in the face of disaster. On the plane back to America he turned Derek Taylor on to drugs and announced: 'If we did nothing else, even if our music is shit, we got you high'.

6
From Fistfights To Former Glories

Upon returning to the States, Derek Taylor immediately placed an advert in the music press thanking Britain for its hospitality:
'There was enough good press to extract some warm quotes but, by and large, what we left behind was a feeling of disappointment. I think the Byrds felt they'd blown it. The next thing to decide was how we were going to cheer them up. One of their many acolytes, John Barry, organized a concert at the Palladium in Hollywood. Traditionally, it was an MOR joint but they put on a "welcome home Byrds" concert which was not entirely successful either, in terms of turn out. The "right" people were there, such as Peter Fonda and company, but the punters were not there in large numbers. September 1965 was not a good period in any of our lives.'

The Byrds were depressed and confused; less than eight weeks before they had been hailed as a cult, but now they seemed half in danger of extinction. Sonny and Cher had totally outmanoeuvred them and were now reaping the rewards. The intensity of this rivalry affected those surrounding the Byrds in different ways. Characteristically, Dylan taunted the group, as McGuinn remembers:

'What really got to me most was Dylan coming up to me and saying, "They beat you man", and he lost faith in me. He was shattered. His material had been bastardized. There we were, the defenders and protectors of his music, and we'd let Sonny and Cher get away with it.'

Eddie Tickner placed the blame on the Byrds' record company:

'We resented Columbia issuing "All I Really Want To Do". Columbia decided that they were going to bury Atlantic. Dickson got upset about that and wanted them to give it up. We were willing to let Sonny and Cher get away with it. We were against releasing it. We weren't interested in a fight. It became a political thing between the two companies.'

Reacting more strongly, Derek Taylor was extremely disappointed:

'I was not only disappointed, I was disgusted. Sonny and Cher went to Ciro's and ripped off the Byrds and, being obsessive, I could not get this out of my mind that Sonny and Cher had done this terrible thing. I didn't know that much about the record business, and in my experience with the Beatles, cover versions didn't make any difference. But by covering the Byrds, it seemed that you could knock them off the perch. And Sonny and Cher, in my opinion, stole that song at Ciro's and interfered with the Byrds' career and very nearly blew them out of the game.'

You overexaggerated

'Dickson always said that: "You're overexaggerating Sonny and Cher's impact, the Byrds will outlast them".'

In the late autumn of 1965, however, it seemed as though Taylor's worst fears were about to be realized. While the Byrds sat around reviewing the situation, Sonny and Cher, as a duo and as soloists, notched up no less than six Top 30 entries in two months: 'I Got You Babe', 'All I Really Want To Do', 'Laugh At Me', 'Baby Don't Go', 'Just You' and 'But You're Mine'. The Byrds were also facing competition on the folk rock front. While 'All I Really Want To Do' had failed the Byrds, the Turtles' interpretation of Dylan's 'It Ain't Me Babe' was a sizeable hit. Another figure from Ciro's, Barry McGuire, had pulled off a number 1 with the controversial 'Eve Of Destruction', while the writer of the song, P.F. Sloan, was being acclaimed as the voice of youth.

The Byrds were in a very difficult position, and they knew it. However, they still had the patronage of the Beatles and, in spite of the competition their original entourage had not deserted them completely. The group desperately needed another hit single to restore them to popular favour, with a successful album as a follow up. The tensions resulting from the British tour, however, had made them unhappy and irritable, as Taylor explained:

'Suddenly there were insecurities and cracks in the relationship. David was getting awkward and they were getting on each other's nerves. They were too busy arguing and as a result they were not singing well'.

The sessions for the projected second album were long and arduous and continued for several months while their tempers frayed. Loyalties were divided, and the continual arguments created warring factions in the group, as Melcher remembers:

'There was friction between McGuinn and Dickson and it became a sort of McGuinn and Melcher versus Dickson and Crosby situation. I think that McGuinn figured that with me on his side he'd have a greater say in the albums. Gene, Chris and Michael were pretty much neutral at this point. Crosby had probably the biggest ego and he was causing a lot of problems in the studio. In the middle of one session, Crosby became extremely objectionable because Gene had been playing a rhythm guitar. Anyway, Mike was always a fairly passive guy but, shortly after this incident, I remember he left his drums, walked over to Crosby, and smashed him in the mouth. He literally knocked him off his stool and just said: "I've wanted to do that for a long time". Not long after this, they all ganged up on Dickson – they felt he'd been bullying them. They were doing some filming on the beach, and suddenly they jumped him.'

McGuinn remembers the incident on the beach with a mixture of incredulity and amusement:

'Someone wasn't looking right or something, some dumb thing like that. Then, Michael started to get really uptight, you know, he said: "This is stupid". And Dickson said: "You'd better stay in" and got everyone back in line. So then Crosby just hauled off, let off and punched Dickson in the mouth. And Dickson said: "Wow, you loosened my tooth" or some number like that, and he had him down in a stranglehold. Dickson was twice as big as Crosby. This is on the beach, and Gene Clark went and grabbed him off of Crosby . . . and we straightened everthing out.'

Eddie Tickner recalls his partner's comments on the fracas shortly afterwards: 'Dickson told me that Gene Clark had his arms round him and he'd never felt such strong arms in his life. Clark's an animal!'

David Crosby remembers how he was also 'restrained' after punching his mentor in the face:

'I slugged Jim once. Hard! I was mad at him. Fortunately, for me, Barry Feinstein (Byrds photographer) threw me up on the ice plant and helped to restrain him. Dickson could have beaten me to a pulp. Jim's a big man: 250lb, 6 foot 2 inches'.

Dickson was amused by Crosby's precised portrayal of the incident and adds a few memories of his own:

'Barry Feinstein arrived, went up to Gene Clark and wouldn't let him grab me again. Barry was unfamiliar and had enough authority that Gene obeyed him. To Barry, from a distance, it must have looked like one guy was going to hold me while the other beat me up. He wasn't going to allow that to happen. Barry had been a football player and was the guy that stood at the goal posts with his arms out when his team played Notre Dame. He got creamed by 11 Notre Dame players who broke his face for making fun of Jesus. Barry Feinstein was fearless and a lot more gifted at handling himself than any of us. I find it really funny reading your book that on that day I was 6 foot 2 inches and 250lb. I've never been more than 5 foot 10 inches, an inch taller than David. I may weigh 250lb now but then I wasn't more than 180lb. David likes to blow things out of proportion. But that wasn't who I was! In order for him to hit me while I was being held by Gene Clark I better be a pretty *big* guy. David was 24 years old, he wasn't a child but a full grown man. I was 34. I was almost too old for that kind of shit. I didn't feel that I had any intrinsic advantage over David Crosby other than that he would be frightened.'

What is interesting. however, is that the normally reliable McGuinn also pictured Dickson as 'twice as big as Crosby'. It wasn't so much Crosby's post-rationalization as the event itself which took on a mythical status in the Byrds story. The incidents as described are reminiscent of the way adults remember key childhood experiences. Physical objects and charismatic characters somehow become bigger and brighter than they actually were. In later years, it sometimes comes as a shock to revisit a favourite spot or meet an elder relative only to see that they have inexplicably shrunk and the recollected sense of dimension had been seriously awry. What is notable about McGuinn and Crosby's recollections is not the all action sequences, which are accurate enough, but the almost child-like way they perceive Dickson's size, power and importance. The paternal overtones were echoed in Crosby's description of Dickson's role in the group:

'He was the father figure to us. He did everything he could to keep that band together and to keep us working with each other. He was a practical man and he was a lot older than any of us and he knew how to make it work. He did exactly that and it worked very well for all of us.'

The ever-increasing pressure to release a new single was causing further problems. The common wisdom was that the Byrds should record another Dylan song so Melcher went outside the group camp and commissioned arranger Jack Nitzsche to produce a demo. Nitzsche found a local group and came back with two songs 'I Don't Believe You' and 'It's All Over Now, Baby Blue'. The demos were deliberately produced to sound like the Byrds so that the group could quickly duplicate the sound and arrangement. The unnamed rented session group boasted a female vocalist with a fairly strong, bluesy delivery. Melcher wanted to experiment with the demos, using McGuinn's vocal and Rickenbacker, but the results were inconclusive and only 'It's All Over Now, Baby Blue' appears to have been attempted. Terry claims that there was a star-studded gathering in attendance during the recording:

'Lennon and McCartney sat in the booth on "It's All Over Now, Baby Blue" which was really sloppy, largely due to the fact that Dylan was there too. It was enough to make anyone nervous.'

Dickson has no memory of the attendant superstars, but recalls that the initial recordings were curtailed. At that point, Melcher departed for a weekend in Palm Springs and Dickson took all five Byrds to another studio in a determined attempt to complete the recording. A rough, preliminary take of 'It's All Over Now, Baby Blue' was cut and Dickson was optimistic that it would be released as the new single. The circumstances of the recording suggested that there was a rift between Dickson and Melcher, but Jim denies that this was the case:

'I didn't do it behind his back. I did it to cut the track, not to trick Melcher. He wasn't standing waiting for the Byrds. He had a life outside of the group. If Melcher or the Byrds didn't want to do it, he'd walk away. He'd go to Palm Springs. "You don't want to do it? See you next time". I thought we should do the song. I liked "It's All Over Now, Baby Blue". What I expected to do was to go in and cut it with Tom May on Saturday, bring it back, have Terry polish it, transfer it to 8-track and finish it up. I didn't expect him to be upset by it. I wasn't trying to defy him. He just wasn't there and we had a chance to go in and do it. I felt they did a pretty fair performance although we didn't have Ray Gerhardt (the engineer) to help. You're not allowed to touch the knobs at CBS. Whether I could have done it better at the time, I'm not sure, but I think I could have with the right help. We didn't have our A-team. I thought when Terry finally came back and listened to it he'd say: "Let's take it back down into the studio, clean it up and make it better". We thought he'd make a good mix and be delighted.'

What no doubt soured Melcher was the impromptu decision to allow his friend, the programme director of KRLA, to broadcast the song. Terry was appalled by this turn of events, perhaps feeling that his authority had been usurped. His comments on Dickson's version of the song were pithy and scathing: 'It was sloppier than anything on the first album in terms of playing'. Although the song might have been salvaged and could have been used to plug that long gap between 'All I Really Want To Do' and 'Turn! Turn! Turn!', it was instead unceremoniously abandoned. Years later, Dickson attempted to resurrect 'It's All Over Now, Baby Blue', but this proved only partially successful:

'It was canned. The multi-track is lost. It was probably thrown out. All we had to put on *Never Before* was a quick rough mix. We had a better mix but it had a flaw in it. McGuinn sounded much better on the guitar. Unfortunately, the drums were lost, so we couldn't use it.'

As the months passed, the pressure upon the Byrds to release a new single became intense. Dickson was still adamant about recording a Dylan song until McGuinn suggested 'Turn! Turn! Turn!', which he had previously arranged for the third Judy Collins album. He realized that the song would fit well into the folk rock idiom when played on a 12-string Rickenbacker with a rock beat. Interestingly, the idea to revive 'Turn! Turn! Turn!' had come up during the Byrds' first bus tour when

McGuinn's wife, Dolores, requested the song from the back of the bus. Even then, McGuinn's version sounded fresh and distinctive, as he recalls:

'It was a standard folk song by that time, but I played it and it came out rock 'n' roll because that's what I was programmed to do like a computer. I couldn't do it as it came out with the samba beat. We thought it would make a good single. It had everything: a good message, a good melody and the beat was there.'

Unfortunately, not everybody was convinced of the merits of the song, as Melcher points out:

'McGuinn and I were the only people who thought it was a good idea. Dickson and I disagreed over it. He felt it didn't have hit potential because it was a lyric from the Bible'.

Dickson's reservations were perplexing. At this point in their career it would have been inappropriate for the young rebels to sing, for example, 'The Christian Life', but 'Turn! Turn! Turn!' was hardly a religious song in the psalmodic sense. The sentiments of the song were essentially philosophic and included mild political overtones: 'A time for peace, I swear it's not too late'. At the height of the folk rock protest boom, nothing could have been more appropriate. Strangely, Dickson chose to ignore the overwhelmingly positive aspects of 'Turn! Turn! Turn!' and focus entirely upon its supposedly dogmatic content:

'I thought "Turn! Turn! Turn!" was an either/or song that didn't fit with the kind of poetry we could get from Dylan. The philosophy that you've got only two alternatives went against everything that I thought we were about. It conflicted with that. It wasn't that it was biblical or that I was uninterested in purveying religion. That hadn't stopped me from doing all kinds of bluegrass songs if they were appropriate for the time. McGuinn and Melcher chose to think that I didn't like it because it was from the Bible, but the real reason was that it was philosophically simplistic. The whole problem was Aristotelian. There's an insanity in it in my mind. Read *Science And Sanity: A Guide To Non-Aristotelian Thinking*. One chapter deals with the confusion of orders of abstraction.'

One cannot help feeling that Dickson was so distracted by what he considered the distasteful dualism in the song that he chose to overlook its appeal, not merely to the young pop audience but to the more discerning listeners who applauded the Byrds for their sophistication. Within the context of pop music, 'Turn! Turn! Turn!' was far from an intellectual sell-out, but rather another step forward.

Although the arrangement for 'Turn! Turn! Turn!' had been worked out on paper, it took between 50 and 78 attempts (depending upon who you ask) to achieve the final take, with Melcher spending five days in the studio in order to get five instruments playing together in time. A Gene Clark composition, 'She Don't Care About Time', was chosen for the flip-side, complete with McGuinn's guitar arrangement of Bach's *Jesu Joy Of Man's Desiring*. Beatle George Harrison was impressed with the memorable Rickenbacker break, as was Melcher:

'McGuinn liked Bach. The centre section of "Chestnut Mare" had a similar arrangement. It's a pity "She Don't Care About Time" wasn't included on the album. Perhaps they felt Clark already had too many songs to his credit.'

Once again, a white label copy of the single received radio play, and this time the reaction was favourable, in spite of some departmental rivalry, unwittingly caused by Taylor:

'I slipped the single to KRLA and got into trouble with CBS. Their promotions man said, "I'll bury that bloody record", but he couldn't and it made number 1.'

The success of the single was enough to restore the Byrds to public favour and re-establish them as America's top group. Although the single held the American number 1 spot for three consecutive weeks in December, and sold over a million copies worldwide, it was a comparative flop in Britain, barely scraping into the Top 30, a fact that caused George Harrison to comment: 'I feel sorry for the people who didn't buy it'.

Turn! Turn! Turn! quickly followed and, capturing the Christmas shoppers, became their second hit album. In retrospect, the album lacks the consistent excellence of their debut effort, yet, at the end of 1965, it appeared to be a major step forward and showed that the group were capable of moving beyond the limited boundaries of folk rock. The weaker tracks on side two seemed less noticeable in 1965-66, partly because the general musical standard of pop albums was low and mainly because the remaining tracks were unquestionably excellent. A closer analysis of the album reveals its strengths and weaknesses.

As with the first album, the Byrds chose to begin this latest work with their current chart topper. Crosby explained the extent to which 'Turn! Turn! Turn!' was a progression from their earlier work:

'We thought that it was better, it sounded more real. It had gone from being the commercial meat-grinder process to a wholly organic thing that we were doing ourselves. McGuinn did the arrangement and I thought up that opening lick.'

Following the brilliance of the opening title track was a revival of the Beefeaters' 'Don't Be Long', retitled 'It Won't Be Wrong'. The difference between the two tracks in terms of quality was remarkable. The lacklustre Beefeaters' version was replaced by the driving beat of a Byrds rock classic, complete with strident guitars and improved harmonies, that transformed the sentiments of the song from an ineffectual statement to a passionate plea. Terry Melcher summed up the Byrds' attitude to the revamped version: 'We were all satisfied with "It

Won't Be Wrong". The production was really tight'.

The most astonishing song on the album, however, was Gene's 'Set You Free This Time', which I have always regarded as one of the Byrds' finest lyrics. The song was written during the British tour, following a late night drinking session with Paul McCartney and various members of the Animals at London's Scotch of St James. Gene Clark remembers what happened next:

'When I reached my room, I got out my acoustic guitar and started picking out a tune. In a couple of hours I was finished, literally! I slept for a full 12 hours after that'.

Observing from a booth at the recording session, George Harrison was impressed enough to comment on the composition and its unusual metre. While the song should have established Gene Clark as a singer-songwriter of distinction, it was largely ignored, particularly by the other Byrds. Melcher recalls the session:

'The Byrds left the studio before Gene had even completed the vocals. Gene was always very tolerant, but I remember him being a little upset about their attitude. There seemed to be an element of resentment on the part of the other Byrds because he was making the most money as the main songwriter in the group.'

An additional factor was more pressing, for, unknown to Melcher, an FBI agent had been stalking the recording studio in search of illegal drugs. Fortunately, Derek Taylor persuaded him that the Byrds were innocent and he departed happily.

'Lay Down Your Weary Tune' has always caused controversy among Byrds fans. Many regard it as a classic Byrds Dylan interpretation, while others, myself included, feel that the arrangement is uninspired and unnecessarily lengthy. Surprisingly, Melcher agrees with the latter point of view: '"Lay Down Your Weary Tune" was really sloppy from start to finish. I have to admit that the production was really lousy'.

McGuinn provides an alternative perspective:

'Well, it was "Lay Down Your Weary Tune" that finally convinced Dylan that we were really something. I was at this apartment in New York and Dylan came up to me and said: "Up until I heard this I thought you were just another imitator and didn't like what you were doing. But this has got real feeling to it". That was the first time he'd realized that I could do something different with his material.'

'He Was A Friend Of Mine', like all the best tribute songs, succeeds precisely because it is an understatement. The sparse backing complements perfectly McGuinn's personal statement:

'I wrote that song the night John F. Kennedy was assassinated (22 November 1963). I suppose you could say it's one of the earliest Byrds songs. The arrangement used for *Turn! Turn! Turn!* was as I'd always sung it. I just thought it was a good idea to include it on the album.'

David Crosby was less than pleased with one aspect of the production: 'Remember that organ note that goes all the way through it that seems very out of place? Terry put it on after we finished the song without even asking us, and mixed it that way. And the tambourine . . . I could have popped him in the lip for that'.

'The World Turns All Around Her', which opens side two, is an interesting example of the way in which a plaintive love song may be applied to a rock beat in such a fashion that the lyrical impact is not negated but reinforced. The two-part vocal harmony is another impressive feature of the song, possibly the best of its kind on the album. Although the instrumental work is far from stupendous, Gene was clearly satisfied with the song: 'I liked the song very much. I thought the fast, electric treatment worked out OK'.

'Satisfied Mind', which Dickson had previously produced on an album by Hamilton Camp, seemed a little too self-conscious an attempt at folk rock to be convincing. The playing is, to say the least, unspectacular, and the vocal lacks that necessary spark of commitment. Perhaps, as Taylor hints, the Byrds were unconvinced by the philanthropic sentiments of the song: 'I remember at the end of 1965, Crosby told me that he wanted a yacht and a lot of money'.

'If You're Gone' was one of Gene's less impressive songs of the period, but the harmony work is unusual enough to be interesting. Terry Melcher gives McGuinn credit for suggesting the unusual harmonic blend:

'He had this good idea for using a fifth harmony to create a droning effect, like that of a bagpipe or drum. On the album it really does sound like another instrument'.

'The Times They Are A-Changin'' sounds so contrived that it appears almost sardonic. McGuinn tries desperately to sound full of venom and conviction, while Clarke's deliberately ostentatious drum rolls and clashing cymbals create a curious dichotomy. Most people connected with the Byrds were disappointed with this version, as Taylor explains:

'"The Times They Are A-Changin'" was a shame! They could have done it so much better had they recorded it once more, but they gave up on it. They just said: "We can't!" Dickson was crazy with anger about it because he was a perfectionist in his own way. I'd seen them perform a beautiful version of the song on stage, but in the studio they couldn't get it right.'

'Wait And See' is another less than spectacular song, partially redeemed by one of McGuinn's impressive lead guitar breaks. It is difficult to decide to what extent this Crosby/McGuinn collaboration was included for aesthetic reasons, rather than simply to break the Gene Clark songwriting monopoly. Eddie Tickner hints that the latter may have been the case: 'There was a movement away from Gene Clark songs.

Crosby and McGuinn wanted to move away from the simple boy/girl songs'. Ironically, however, 'Wait And See' was far more a 'simple boy/girl song' than most of Gene Clark's compositions.

The rocked-up 'Oh Susannah' which closes the album is further evidence of Byrds humour, the 'banjo on my knee' being replaced by McGuinn's Rickenbacker. As with 'We'll Meet Again', McGuinn sings the song straight without betraying any sense of the subtle underlying humour. Clarke is given leave to resurrect his bizarre military style of drumming which, surprisingly, proves both an appropriate and effective accompaniment to Stephen Foster's traditional standard.

With a critically acclaimed number 1 hit single and a commercially successful second album, the Byrds looked poised to reach even greater heights. The dissension in the camp, however, was not totally resolved and, upon returning from a trip to England, Melcher was informed that he had been fired. McGuinn believes that the decision was a political manoeuvre:

'Jim Dickson believed that if he got rid of Melcher then he would be the one to produce us. He didn't realize that CBS would stick another of their producers on us. It was Jim Dickson's political ambitions. Melcher was doing a fine job though.'

McGuinn adds that Dickson '. . . convinced everybody that Melcher was getting drunk on the set and all that stuff. He made us all believe that he could do a better job'.

Melcher's response to McGuinn's account was dismissive: 'Getting drunk on the set? That's funny, especially when you consider that they were all high'. Searching for additional motives, Melcher came up with an intriguing proposition:

'My theory has always been that Dickson was embarrassed because he made such a great point about "Turn! Turn! Turn!" being such a blatant error on my part'.

Eddie Tickner remains convinced that Melcher misconstrued Dickson's attitude to 'Turn! Turn! Turn!':

'It wasn't so much that Dickson didn't want to put it out. He wasn't opposed to the "Turn! Turn! Turn!" release as much as the timing. He felt that something was needed before it. Dickson felt that "Turn! Turn! Turn!" was too good to put out then. He said that if it was released at that point then they would never get another number 1 – and they never did.'

Unlike McGuinn and Melcher, Tickner maintains that there were definite reasons for the sacking beyond 'Jim Dickson's political ambitions':

'The opinion was that Melcher was playing favourites in the group. He became fast friends with McGuinn and was isolating the other members of the group'.

Dickson had been difficult to work with during the latter part of 1965, but so too had the Byrds. And as Tickner quite rightly reminds us, Dickson's original ambitions for his proteges extended far beyond a chart-topping single:

'Dickson's vision of the Byrds was beyond Terry Melcher's imagination. There are people who have such a strong vision, such an intense vision and sense of direction that nobody else's voice can be heard. Dickson found it difficult to compromise when something interfered with that vision.'

With hindsight, Dickson concurs with his partner's personality reading:

'When I read Eddie's reference to my vision I found it very perceptive. Good or bad I was probably guilty of that. I knew what I wanted the Byrds to be and I was as inflexible as I could get away with being. I compromised when I felt I had to and I did it reluctantly. I felt sincerely that I was a better judge of material than anybody else available for those purposes. I wasn't prepared to say: "David Crosby is a better judge of material for what he wants to do". If those directions weren't left to me they'd break down the team and send a message of who the Byrds were that wasn't what I thought would be pertinent to the future.'

Of all Dickson's champions and Melcher's critics, it was David Crosby who, not surprisingly, proved the most inflammatory. His harsh comments on Melcher seem partly to be prompted by an enormous respect for Dickson's work:

'Melcher had almost nothing to do with it. Terry's a nice guy but he's a dummy. He didn't understand what we were trying to do and I don't think he does yet. He was just in the way. He was a hindrance, as was Columbia. What Terry said about us taking sides was somewhat true, but McGuinn wasn't really on Terry Melcher's side. McGuinn thought Terry Melcher was a dummy too.'

Although Jim Dickson was not always in agreement with Terry Melcher he did not share Crosby's aggressive dismissal of the man's contribution. On the contrary, he credits Melcher for fighting tooth and nail for 'Mr Tambourine Man' and suspects that without his influence the song might never have been released. Dickson even suggests that Melcher deserves recognition for inspiring the song's magical opening bass line: 'There's no disputing that. He contributed it'. Another plus for Melcher was his credibility among studio engineers which Dickson claims helped the Byrds enormously:

'He was Doris Day's son, so he had the respect of the engineers. I don't know whether it was a respect for what he could accomplish or a respect for who he was. You don't mess with Doris Day's son! Doris Day was one of the biggest things that ever happened in music, especially during World War II. And she was on Columbia.'

Far from being consistently at loggerheads with Melcher, Dickson stresses that they found common ground instantly in their mutual respect for Leon Russell, Hal Blaine and Larry Knechtel. For Melcher, these guys were musical giants and the fact that Dickson had campaigned for their inclusion made him an ally. It was only after the first sessions that friction emerged.

The theory that Dickson attempted to oust Melcher is also qualified by his revelation that it was a signed letter from all five Byrds which precipitated the producer's removal. Although there was certainly a disagreement over the release of 'Turn! Turn! Turn!' and some concern over politicking within the group, Dickson claims that he never seriously believed that he would ever produce the Byrds at Columbia:

'I couldn't produce at CBS. The fact was you had to be a musician or a Columbia employee. They only used in-house producers, so when I signed them to Columbia I never felt that I would be able to produce. Allen Stanton, when he got Terry, suggested that he take his lead from me. I could work on all the sessions but I couldn't produce. Once Terry cut "Tambourine Man" and did such a great job I didn't feel any real need to be the producer. Although certain things about Terry were disappointing, there were others which were very pleasant. I never felt that he had to be exactly like us.'

The loss of Melcher may have been no big deal to Crosby and the rest but it weakened their political power at CBS. As ever, of course, they were more than content to fight their own battles and there were many more on the horizon.

7
Eight Miles High

Following Melcher's departure, the Byrds decided to move forward in search of a new musical direction. Meanwhile, Columbia released 'It Won't Be Wrong' as the follow up to 'Turn! Turn! Turn!', but it merely became a Top 40 hit. The Byrds were hardly disturbed by the news, however, because the song was already regarded as a remnant from an old set. Their ideas were far more attuned to the future, and revolutionary changes had already occurred in their live performances. During their residency at the Trip, in January 1966, they began to replace their folk rock songs with hard rock and jazz rock numbers, while speculation grew about the formulation of a *new* Byrds sound. More than ever before, the Byrds began to present themselves less as pop stars and more as intellectual musicians. Although they still required hit singles, they were equally determined to investigate different forms of music in order to develop their own ideas. Along with the Yardbirds, the Byrds became one of the first groups to incorporate elements of Indian music into their repertoire. It was a brave move in the pop world of early 1966 but, fortunately, public interest was awakened by the fact that the Beatles (*Rubber Soul*) and the Rolling Stones ('Paint It Black') were travelling the same road. The Byrds suddenly found themselves spearheading a new musical phenomenon which the press named 'raga rock'. Interest in the Byrds grew as rumours began to circulate that they had introduced the Beatles to the sitar. McGuinn recalls the incident that prompted the rumour:

'Well, I remember in 1965, Crosby and I were both at the house where the Beatles were staying. We were sitting around on acid, playing 12-

strings in the shower. We were in this large bathtub which used to belong to the Gabors. John, George, David and I were just sitting there playing guitars. We were showing them what we knew about Ravi Shankar and they'd never heard of him.'

The interest in ragas had been spearheaded by David Crosby after Dickson had invited him to attend a Ravi Shankar recording session. The Byrds effectively repaid that debt in December 1965 when they introduced a new composition, 'Eight Miles High'. Chris Hillman explained how the original version of the song was effectively suppressed:

'We cut it at RCA Victor and Columbia wouldn't let us release it because it had been cut at another studio. In those days that was the law. We cut this really hot version and were trying to sneak it on to an album but they caught us and we had to recut it'.

McGuinn confirmed Hillman's account:

'That's true. We did it at RCA with Dave Hassinger. We took the master tape over to CBS and they said we couldn't use it because it hadn't been recorded with their union. They forced us to recut it, which we did, begrudgingly, and it came out OK.'

While McGuinn felt that the RCA cut had a more spontaneous guitar break, he was not willing to concede that the later version recorded at Columbia was inferior. David Crosby obviously had no such reservations in championing the Dickson original:

'It was better. It was stronger. It had a lot more flow to it. It was the way we wanted it to be. When we did the other one, we had to force it. I promise you, it's better. It had a better solo on it. A lot better. Dickson used to get so mad at them. It must have been the biggest frustration of his whole life. He could mix that stuff ten times as well as they could. He could hear the music really well. He knew what we were trying to do. He knew how to structure it, and he knew how to get it out of us.'

Although the legendary RCA 'Eight Miles High' was finally transferred onto vinyl 22 years later, Dickson stresses that the original was not intended for release without adding considerable work:

'It was just demonstration vocals on the RCA version. The problem with it when we finally put it out on *Never Before* was that it came from a quick mixdown on the four track. The whole band is on one track, McGuinn's on another and two tracks are vocals. That's only four track and you can't open up the mix and get it all back. The way we had intended to do it was to take the four band tracks that had the drums and guitar separated, transfer them to eight track at CBS, then do the vocals on a new guitar. We had the choice of saving the guitar because it was on a separate track. We could have used part of it, all of it or we could have given McGuinn several passes at bettering himself.'

The Byrds were clearly reaching new peaks of musical development and their eclecticism was intriguing. Apart from the Indian music of Ravi Shankar, the Byrds also became strongly influenced by jazz saxophonist, John Coltrane. Before embarking on a coast-to-coast tour at the end of 1965, they had discovered that they had no background music to entertain them on the long trip and so they hurriedly taped a couple of their favourite Shankar and Coltrane albums. For the next few weeks, they were forced to subject themselves to repeated plays of their solitary Shankar/Coltrane tape, and upon returning to their first studio session they discovered that the jazz and raga influences had permeated their own work. David Crosby explained the phenomenon to the raga-hungry journalists:

'Every kid practically in the United States now knows what a sitar is because George Harrison played it on *Rubber Soul*. Most of them are becoming aware of where the sitar comes from – India. Some are even aware of Ravi Shankar, John Coltrane and a lot of other people too. I'm not trying to justify what we're doing with Indian music. We didn't plan it that way. We went into a room, sat down and played. And what came out was what we put down later on the record. It'll be our next single. We didn't write it or arrange it. The five of us just played music to each other until it gelled. And that's what it comes out as. I don't want to justify it either. We don't plan anything we do, we don't try to scheme trends. We just play music.'

Do you think the public is ready to accept raga?

'We'll find out. Somebody's got to turn them on to it. It might bomb completely, you might never hear of the Byrds again. When we did "Tambourine Man" everybody said it was too far out. I think it's been to number 1 in all the English-speaking countries. We're not wanting to brag, it's just that the blue-chip thinkers were wrong.'

The new recut single, 'Eight Miles High'/'Why', produced by Columbia's West Coast Vice President, Allen Stanton, was finally issued at the end of March and a special press conference was held in which McGuinn and Crosby 'demonstrated' the use of the sitar to the expectant world. While the flip-side of the single appeared to include two spectacular sitar solos, McGuinn admits that this was not quite the truth . . .

Was there a sitar on 'Why'?

'No. It was not a sitar but a 12-string Rickenbacker. We used this special gadget I had made. It was an amplifier from a Philips portable record player and a two-and-a-half inch loudspeaker from a walkie-talkie placed in a wooden cigar box which ran on batteries, and it had such a tremendous sustain that it sounded very much like a sitar. When I plugged my guitar into it, it had a very thin and sustaining sound.'

Is it true then that the Byrds never used a sitar on any of their recordings?

'I don't think there's a sitar on anything the Byrds ever did.'

And yet you were hailed as one of the artistes responsible for bringing the sitar into rock music

'Well, we brought the concept of it into rock music. We were doing the same thing with John Coltrane. We weren't playing saxophone, we were playing 12-string Rickenbacker to sound like a saxophone, and the same goes for the sitar. It was our interpretation of those instruments and musical styles, and that was what we were doing. We were translating it into a rock form. We used backward tapes and gadgetry.'

What about all those press photos of you with a sitar? Was it all a hype?

'Well, we had a sitar that CBS rented for that particular photo session.'

So you're saying that none of you actually learned to play the instrument?

'That's right. I'm sorry. We were just synthesizing those instruments with other electronics.'

With or without a sitar, 'Why' was still an impressive Byrds rock number, with a rawer sound than had been heard on any of their discs so far. As the official Shankar-influenced raga side, it was complemented by the Coltrane-inspired jazz rock 'Eight Miles High'. At the press conference, however, the Byrds' explanations caused so much confusion that the critics subsequently bracketed both sides under the label 'raga rock'. Crosby's fears that the single might conceivably 'bomb completely' were not unwarranted, as several critics of the period complained about its 'lack of melody' and 'over-complex guitar work'. However, while its chart potential was debatable, it was undoubtedly one of the most sophisticated rock singles ever released. The unusual lyrics, that most famous of opening bass lines and McGuinn's Coltrane-inspired guitar work made it dangerously innovative, but also fresh and exciting. Its unusual qualities became even more discernible when played alongside other hit records of the period. Although the single smashed into the Top 20, its progress was dramatically halted when several major US radio stations banned it from the airwaves on the grounds of its 'drug connotations'.

Early 1966 revealed middle America in the grip of an 'anti-drugs' purge and several discs suffered, including 'Rainy Day Women Numbers 12 and 35', which was banned in the same week. The radio stations argued that Dylan's line, 'everybody must get stoned' was an open invitation to take drugs, while the Byrds' 'Eight Miles High' was a vivid description of an hallucinatory experience. While it was reasonable for Coleridge's opium-induced *Kubla Khan* to be read in schools, the moralists argued that the ears of impressionable adolescents should not be polluted by the subversive preachings of degenerate musicians. It was also suddenly revealed that 'Mr Tambourine Man' was a thinly disguised allegory about a drugs pusher and as such would receive a token ban, even though it had been played over a million times in 1965. The Byrds pleaded ignorance of any obscure drug references on 'Mr Tambourine Man' and argued convincingly that their latest single was not an account of an hallucinatory experience, but simply a vivid description of an aeroplane flight. McGuinn explained the genesis of the song:

'We started it out as six miles high – Gene Clark and I wrote the lyrics – because that's the approximate altitude that commercial airlines fly. 42 or 43,000 feet, or about eight miles high, is the altitude reserved for military aircraft only; commercial aircraft have to fly below that – and that was one discrepancy which led people to believe it was about drugs and not about aeroplanes. But Gene said eight miles sounded better than six, and it did sound more poetic, and it was also around the time of "Eight Days A Week" by the Beatles, so that was another hook or catch, if you like.'

According to McGuinn, the plane touching down was a reference to the Byrds' arrival in London in August 1965. London was as strange a place as they had ever seen and their cultural shock was described in the image of the street signs that seemed 'somewhere just being their own':

'You come over here and try to find the names of the streets and you find them tacked up on the sides of buildings if they haven't been torn down or fallen off. So that line refers to how difficult it is to find which street you're on. It's one of the things that strikes a visiting American.'

Crosby maintains that 'Eight Miles High' was ambiguous from start to finish:

'Of course it was a drug song. We were stoned when we wrote it. We can also justifiably say that it wasn't a drug song because it was written about the trip to London. I wrote that verse beginning "Rain grey town" and I think I contributed most of the last verse and some of the changes. It was a drug song and it wasn't a drug song at the same time.'

In spite of their pleas, however, the ban was not lifted until it was too late and the lack of airplay in certain states prevented the single from achieving its full potential. The refusal to accept the Byrds' explanation of the true theme of the song was hardly surprising. Since the early days at Ciro's, the Byrds had been associated with a bizarre and unconventional following, and it was assumed that drugs played an important part in the lives of the group and their entourage. As Dylan had been singled out for writing drug songs and the Byrds had been photographed with him on their first album, they too became implicated in the 'plot'. Finally, the Byrds' use of drugs had been known to many following rumours of the FBI's appearance at the *Turn! Turn! Turn!* sessions investigating some hash that had allegedly been left on their plane returning from England. So the Byrds' tenuous connections with drugs were enough to maintain the ban. In England, there were no such restrictions, but, due to an apathetic record-buying public, the disc was even less successful than it had been in the States, reaching only number

28 in the charts. In retrospect, 'Eight Miles High' has generally been acclaimed as one of the greatest singles in rock history which is no doubt some consolation.

The controversy surrounding the banning of 'Eight Miles High' may have made the Byrds seem momentarily like rebels *with* a cause, but their public image continued to be peculiarly paradoxical. While the Byrds were certainly one of the more adventurous groups of the era, they avoided the excessive political rantings of the emerging San Francisco movement. They were hip enough to deride the ludicrous demands of the pop press, and yet they were equally concerned with their own image. Derek Taylor recalls this concern with some amusement:

'Chris always used to wear a straightener in his hair and he hated it! I remember Gene returning from San Francisco and telling me, "Long hair is all right but they look like girls out there. I mean you don't even know if it's clean, man". The thing about Byrds long hair was that they were always washing and setting it.'

Although McGuinn was willing to get high on LSD with several Beatles in a bathtub, his lifestyle was also hardly that of a degenerate doper, as Taylor testifies:

'McGuinn got smashed with restraint. He was austere. His belongings were always in order and his electronics were always working. He had a very formal relationship with Dolores. I found him both exact and demanding. I was always surprised how easy he was to be with because he did have that fussy school-ma'am attitude.'

Even Chris Hillman is guarded, and stresses that the Byrds' use of drugs during this period was less frequent than many have supposed:

'We experimented with acid, but I don't think that we were heavily into it. Some of the other bands of the period were a lot weirder than us in that respect'.

While the Byrds negotiated that delicate balance between pop star and progressive musician they looked set to reach a further plateau. Still accepted by the teenyboppers, in spite of the growing competition, they also became the darlings of the underground and seemed capable of retaining their two different audiences. Obviously, the drug allegations and the banning of 'Eight Miles High' did little to help their 'teenzine' image, but they were still chart contenders with a string of hits behind them. The drugs controversy was swiftly rendered inconsequential when news leaked out of a far greater crisis – Gene Clark had left the Byrds.

8
The Leaving Of Gene Clark

In 1966, personnel changes in a popular group were regarded as the cardinal sin, and Gene's departure seemed clearly to signal the death-knell for the group. Although McGuinn was nominal leader, Clark was regarded by many as the central figure in the group. He was the singer who stood stage centre, the tambourine man and, apparently, the only member capable of writing an album's worth of songs. At first the public was informed that Gene had left the group 'for personal reasons' but it was not long before the press revealed to their readers the startling story of Clark's pathological fear of flying. McGuinn explained the neurosis:

'He reached the point of crisis, the mounting pressure of the whole gig, and, at that point, it was pretty intense. We had two number 1s, there was pressure from the press and we had to be good. We were shuffled around like cattle and you get that boxed-in feeling. And this is what ganged up on Gene. He's a country boy from Missouri, a farm boy who got into this high intensity thing, and the aeroplanes got to him.'

According to numerous accounts, the fear of flight was the crucial factor in Gene's decision to quit. During his childhood, Gene had witnessed an air crash and had apparently never forgotten the incident. By 1966, the flight phobia was manifesting itself in extraordinary ways, as McGuinn remembers:

'Gene developed a tremendous fear of aeroplanes. One day we were going to New York from here (Los Angeles) to do a Murray the K Special and Gene was on the aeroplane. I got there late, just as the thing was closing up. I always do. Gene was already freaked out and they were holding his arms and he was saying: "I got to get off, I got to get off, I can't stand this thing!,, And he was vibrating with fear, it was like nine foot in diameter fear vibrations, very heavy panic. And I got into it and cold sweat came over me, you know, "Wow! Maybe he's right. Maybe he's psychic and knows something I don't know". But we stayed on and he got off. I said: "Hey, man, if you get off it's going to blow it for you". And he said: "If I stay I'm going to blow it too". So he got off and that was it, more or less. We worked a couple of more gigs with him but we couldn't hold together. He went on his own.'

After leaving the group, Gene was dubbed 'The Byrd Who Could Not Fly' but the traditional explanation for his departure seems remarkably inadequate. Most commentators assume that the fear of flying was ever present but neglect to consider that during this period the neurosis was aggravated by a series of more complex factors. Firstly there was the relationship between Clark and his colleagues. While McGuinn was befriending jet-plane manufacturer John Lear, and encouraging the Byrds, quite literally, to fly high, Clark became increasingly suspicious that his fellow member was attempting to oust him by playing on his flight phobia. The fears reached their climax on that aircraft bound for New York when, according to McGuinn, Clark became paranoid to such an extent that he believed Jim had planted a bomb on the plane! It was probably part of the panic attack for Clark and McGuinn had no history of conflict in the group. While searching for an additional explanation, however, McGuinn made an intriguing Freudian slip: 'Maybe the guilt factor was there because he was in Ferraris and things and we were still starving. He was making thousands and we weren't making anything yet'. But why should Clark feel 'guilty' about this? McGuinn appears to be suggesting that Clark felt 'guilty' because he was the major songwriter in the group, yet this is hardly something which warrants shame. Gene was never a dictator when it came to including his songs on albums. Indeed, he had a bulging back catalogue of songs that had already been rejected by Dickson and Melcher. He had even allowed 'She Don't Care About Time' to be excluded from the second album in the face of inferior material without a word of complaint. Clark's passivity is best expressed in his willingness to sacrifice his rhythm guitar to David Crosby without a fight. McGuinn himself admits that the Clark songwriting monopoly was as much to do with the lackadaisical attitude of his fellow members: 'Gene was so prolific that there didn't seem to be any point in trying to compete with him'. The 'guilt' factor, then, seems hardly applicable, but McGuinn's other comment, 'we were still starving' reveals undertones of mild resentment, even jealousy, on the part of the other Byrds.

Derek Taylor believed that the Byrds' attitude towards Clark was at fault: 'I got the impression that Gene was not regarded as a first-class Byrd. I don't think it was the flying. He was not taken seriously enough'. Certainly, some of the Byrds' later comments support this supposition.

Chris Hillman's description of Clark's original role in the group was decidedly unenthusiastic:

'The five of us started out from scratch, you know, like playing on nothing. Michael Clarke was hitting cardboard boxes, I was playing a $20.00 Japanese bass, and McGuinn had an acoustic 12-string. That was the real Byrds. Gene didn't really add that much.'

McGuinn has occasionally criticized Clark for retaining the overt Beatle influence on such songs as 'I Knew I'd Want You' and in off-hand moments has sounded coolly dismissive:

'Gene Clark didn't really know how to keep time at all, at all. He was playing tambourine: Cah, Cah, Taw! He was just spastic on the tambourine. I'm glad he left, actually'.

If McGuinn's attitude to Clark was blase during this period, then Crosby's was aggressive. Eddie Tickner feels that Crosby was Gene Clark's greatest tormentor:

'I don't believe there was a conspiracy against Clark, at least not an overt conspiracy. I think the feeling was that it was Crosby who was tantalizing Gene. He was making Gene Clark feel insecure and criticizing him. He had already taken the guitar out of his hands.'

Crosby does not dispute Tickner's appraisal of the situation:

'I intimidated Gene, I'm sure. I am aggressive. But I've got an enormous affection for Gene Clark. I think the guy's a real good guy. What happened was over and over again he would be behind the beat, slow and awkward. He has no sense of time on stage. It would be really awkward. He'd come in a quarter of a beat late with the tambourine, playing it real loud behind the beat, which was wrong. It would drive me nuts.'

Clark was clearly disappointed by the group's lack of interest and encouragement particularly after composing such songs as 'Set You Free This Time'. There were a cache of others hitting Dickson's desk during and after this period including 'Translations', 'Don't Let It Fall Through', 'I Am Without You', 'It's Easy Now', 'Don't Know What You Want', 'So Much More' and 'Along The Way'. Some were fair, others very good to excellent, but the Byrds could never have included them all on albums. Perhaps the sheer bulk of songs convinced his fellow Byrds that the material could not have been that great. Dickson explained the problems they all faced in selecting appropriate material:

'Gene could write 15-20 songs a week and you had to find a good one whenever it came along because there were lots of them that you couldn't make head or tail of. They didn't mean anything. We all knew that. Gene would write a good one at a rate of just about one per girlfriend.'

Over the years, Clark has always been able to live with his massive backlog of unrecorded songs and would probably have remained in the Byrds had he been able to win their full attention and respect as a singer-songwriter. At this point, however, the rivalry between McGuinn and Crosby was continuing to grow, and the Clark problem was thrust into the background. Taylor even recalls moments when Crosby looked set to depart:

'In early 1966 there was a lot of chat about Crosby leaving. Dickson, Tickner and I were having endless discussions about whether he should stay or go'.

Tickner explained the reasons for these discussions:

'There was a point when if Crosby didn't get his own way he would be very brought down and his guitar playing would be affected. If he wasn't pleased, he would not play well on stage.'

While the management were discussing the Crosby question, however, the pressures upon Clark were becoming intolerable. The fear of flying, the continual bickering, the apathetic attitude of the other Byrds towards his own material, the problems with Crosby and the niggling pressures of deciding whether to remain in the group or pursue a solo career, had each taken their toll. Gene was unable to surmount these pressures and, as Taylor remembers, his lifestyle was such that matters only became worse:

'I always thought that David got smashed with a little abandon, but, as for Gene, he would do *anything*. He'd have a glass in one hand and a pill in another. He was an excessive.'

It seemed that the greater the pressures became, the greater became Gene's fear of flying. And the greater his fear of flight, the more he drank. And when drink was not enough he would resort to drugs in order to deaden his fear. Taylor vividly recalls one such incident when Clark, flying under the influence of LSD, mistook a ray of sunlight on the wing of their plane for a raging fire. The results were predictably traumatic. Patti McCormick, a friend of Gene's from the Ciro's days, feels that his use of LSD was ill-advised:

'Gene warned me against taking LSD because when he'd taken it he stared out of a window for two hours. But the thing was, I could take LSD and Gene couldn't.'

By the end of March, Gene was in no fit condition to remain a high-flying Byrd. Taylor revealed all in a surprisingly frank and poignant press statement:

'He left not because of a row, and not because he was fired. He left because he was tired of the multitude of obligations facing successful rock 'n' roll groups. Tired of the travel, the hotels and the food. Tired of the pursuit of the most relentless autograph hunters, weary of the constant screaming. Bothered by the photographs and interviews, and exhausted by the whole punishing scene.'

The final decision to quit, then, was not simply the result of a fear of flight, but a combination of pressures that aggravated each other. Nor was the decision a sudden one, as Clark explained:

'I had been thinking about it for some time. I finally made the decision that I wanted to leave and go solo. We sat down as a group and talked it over. We all agreed that it could be worked out and that the Byrds would continue as a group of four.'

There was no doubt that since 1964 there had been a gradual move away from Gene Clark songs, as Crosby confesses:

'That was true. I didn't think the lyrics were that good. But all our songs were juvenile at that stage. Listen to the words. We were all kids. As we became more aware of Dylan and other sophisticated writers, we obviously pulled for the best we could. This upset Gene a little, but not much. Gene's smarter than he can articulate, and a lot smarter than most people give him credit for being.'

While Gene left by mutual consent of the Byrds, Eddie Tickner recalls that one member of the group was particularly upset by Clark's decision. Ironically, that person was his chief tormentor, David Crosby:

'Although David did tantalize Gene, when he finally quit Crosby was the first to demand that he not leave. He would not hear of it. He couldn't see the Byrds without Gene. As far as he was concerned, Gene Clark was Mr Tambourine Man.'

There was an attempt by Tickner to dissuade Gene, but it came to nothing. Dickson maintains that Clark's departure damaged the group's credibility at CBS, but he has no memory of any fear or regret expressed by the other Byrds:

'I suspect Crosby probably saw it as an opportunity and McGuinn felt it would bring the focus towards him. I don't think they saw the gravity of it. I don't remember any of them coming and saying: "Man, why can't you do something about Gene?"'

Having discussed their respective futures, Gene and the Byrds parted amicably. Even after returning to Los Angeles from his home town of Kansas, Clark was still noticeably shaken as the press observed:

'It was a new Gene Clark that walked through the door. Still recovering from his state of physical exhaustion he seemed quite pale and walked at a much slower pace. It was now even more apparent that he had been quite ill.'

Although Clark's exit was accepted by the public in 1966, there were many who felt that the original spirit of the group had been irrevocably lost as a result of his departure. Dickson was not unsympathetic to such a view:

'To each person the Byrds began when they arrived and ended when they left. David's no different. Chris is no different. McGuinn is the only one that didn't leave so there's no Byrds without him. To hear Gene Clark tell it there's no Byrds without him. I'm the same. There's no right or wrong.'

9
Beyond The Fifth Dimension

The shock departure of Gene Clark from the group at least had one positive short-term effect – it quietened down David Crosby. The Byrds briefly became a united unit once more. However, certain members of the press, not to mention a large proportion of the fans, were beginning to wonder whether the Byrds could survive without Gene. The group answered this question by immediately setting to work on their third album. In July a pilot single, '5-D (Fifth Dimension)', was released but it seemed a little too obscure to be a commercial success. McGuinn explained how the song came to be written:

'"5-D" is a poem in 3/4 about a book I read *1-2-3-4, More, More, More, More* written by Don Landis and published by Dylart. If you can get your hands on a copy, you'll understand what I did in the song. If you don't it's sort of vague and philosophical. It's sort of weird but . . . what I'm talking about is the whole universe, the Fifth Dimension which is height, width, depth, time and something else. But there definitely are more dimensions than five. It's infinite. The Fifth Dimension is the threshold of scientific knowledge. See, there are people walking around practising fifth dimensional ways of life and the scientists are still on two or three dimensional levels. There's a conflict there. A lot of our world is very materialistic and scientific. It overlooks the beauty of the universe. That's what the song is about. Maybe it'll tell a few people what's going on in life. The organ player on it is Van Dyke Parks from Los Angeles. When he came into the studio I told him to think Bach. He was already thinking Bach before that anyway. I wrote that song but the arrangement just came out the way it did. We just sat down and did it.'

Predictably, '5-D' failed to break into the charts. In fact, its release led to further accusations that the Byrds were propagating the use of drugs. McGuinn defended the song with great eloquence, and in later interviews expressed despondency that the true message he was attempting to convey had been misinterpreted:

'I was talking about something philosophical and very light and airy with that song, and everyone took it down... they took it down to drugs. They said it was a dope song and that I was on LSD, and it wasn't any of that, in fact. I was dealing with Einstein's theory of relativity, the fourth dimension being time and the fifth dimension not being specified . . . so it's open, channel five, the next step. I saw it to be a timelessness, a sort of void in space where time has no meaning. All I did was perceive something that was there. The catalyst to the whole idea was a booklet someone sent me called *1-2-3-4, More, More, More, More* which was about dimensions but explained in a cartoon way. It gave me the premise for the song, but I think that the booklet should've been issued with the song so people would have been able to understand. I gave the copy I had to Allen Stanton (the producer) who read it and gave it to his kid because he thought it was a comic.'

The song was the culmination of McGuinn's experiences in the religious sect known as Subud, in which he had been initiated as early as 10 January 1965, only days before recording 'Mr Tambourine Man'. In later interviews McGuinn described the lyrics of 'Mr Tambourine Man' as a surrender to Allah, and the closeness of the Subud initiation to that crucial first Columbia audition suggests that such an interpretation was in his mind when he sang the song. For all his arguments, however, McGuinn could only watch in frustration as the media, unaware of his spiritual leanings, perceived '5-D' as an unambiguous 'drug song'.

Although '5-D' appeared to be breaking new ground in its lyrical content, the flip side, 'Captain Soul', was a disappointment to some reviewers who regarded it as something of a filler. The instrumental was recorded during a short break between sessions when the Byrds began improvising the riff of Lee Dorsey's 'Get Out Of My Life Woman'. Originally, the number was to be titled 'Thirty Minute Break' until Chris Hillman came up with 'Captain Soul'. McGuinn, in retrospect, feels that the instrumental was not a complete write-off: 'It wasn't really funky but it was interesting. Essentially, it was Mike Clarke's trip. He wanted us to do something soul-oriented so we did that for him'.

Fifth Dimension was finally released in the summer and met with a mixed reception from the critics. On the credit side, the album showed that the Byrds were beginning to move away from their folk rock image and were thinking more in terms of an 'album concept' rather than a collection of songs. The album was not without its flaws, however. Several songs seemed to lack the familiar harmonic blend that was so evident on the first two albums. Moreover, much of the material had an unusually raw, metallic-guitar sound, unfamiliar to pop audiences in 1966. The Byrds were experimenting in order to produce a new sound, but the results seemed slightly erratic. The songwriting and melodies were sometimes intriguing, sometimes unmemorable. The entire album appeared to have been put together hurriedly, under great pressure. With eleven tracks instead of the usual twelve, several of which had appeared on singles, the album hardly seemed a bargain in strictly economic terms. Such factors may seem trivial today, but at the time they were important and disconcerting. It is easy to assume that pop critics applauded the Byrds in the mid-60's, but all too often the group was ignored. Even a respected underground rock writer such as Jon Landau was capable of underestimating the Byrds' innovative qualities and expressing a preference for the more commercially acceptable jingle-jangle sound of the earlier albums: 'This album, then, cannot be considered up to the standards set by the Byrds' first two and basically demonstrates that they should be thinking in terms of replacing Gene Clark, instead of just carrying on without him'.

In effect, *Fifth Dimension* was a transitional album, which showed that the Byrds were still capable of forging ahead into new musical territories, with or without Gene Clark. The most interesting feature of the album is its exploration of a variety of musical styles. Folk rock, raga rock, jazz rock, blues and space rock are all represented and effortlessly assimilated into the Byrds songbook. 'Wild Mountain Thyme' and 'John Riley' represent Byrds folk rock but on this occasion their borrowings are traditional. Was the lack of Dylan songs on *Fifth Dimension* a deliberate move? McGuinn felt this might have been the case:

'Well, perhaps we were consciously trying to get away from it. I guess we were trying to show Dylan we didn't need him. But that was a mistake because his songs were good for us'.

When I suggested the alternative theory that the Byrds' recordings of these traditional songs was merely an attempt to perpetuate their secure folk rock image, McGuinn reacted angrily: 'I wasn't trying to perpetuate anything except my love of folk music'.

The *Fifth Dimension* folk songs were noticeable for another new feature, the introduction of orchestration. The use of strings was tasteful enough not to over-sentimentalize these romantic songs and served as an effective contrast to the heavier numbers on the album. McGuinn credits his producer for suggesting the use of strings:

'The orchestration was Allen Stanton's idea. He was always into the idea of using strings. I went along with it because I liked the idea of orchestration on those folky things'.

The Byrds' first excursion into the realms of science-fiction was to be heard on 'Mr Spaceman', which provided their music with the tag 'space rock'. Apparently, McGuinn's idea was to write a serious dramatic song about a trip into outer space, but, as the theme developed, it became gradually more whimsical. McGuinn explained the message of 'Mr Spaceman':

'I'm interested in astronomy and the possibility of connecting with extra-terrestrial life and I thought that it might work the other way round, if we tried to contact them. I thought that the song being played on the air might be a way of getting through to them. But even if there had been anybody up there listening, they wouldn't have heard because I found out later that AM airwaves diffuse in space too rapidly.'

'Mr Spaceman' was lighter in mood than the other songs on the album and revealed closer affinities with their earlier work. Michael Clarke plays Gene's tambourine, and McGuinn's confident vocal and occasional duet with Crosby creates an effective harmonic blend. Lastly, the title 'Mr' cleverly echoed their first worldwide hit.

In complete contrast, 'I See You', with its intricate, jagged guitar work, veered towards psychedelia. Musically and lyrically, it lacked the power of 'Eight Miles High' but it provided us with a clear signpost for what would be happening in rock music in 1967. The lyrics were almost deliberately obscure, and sung so fast that they were difficult to decipher. It might be said that the Byrds were attempting to imitate Dylan's writing here, but this is hardly the truth. Rather, 'I See You' seemed a development from the kind of songs that Gene Clark had been writing while he was in the group. Essentially, the Byrds were still writing love songs, but not in the old Beatles tradition. 'I See You' marked a turning point and showed the group gradually becoming more concerned with analysing psychological states than documenting love stories.

David Crosby's growing influence on the Byrds was effectively demonstrated on his first solo contribution, 'What's Happening?!?!', a song dealing with the problem of emotional confusion. It was certainly the most unusual song that the Byrds had recorded up to this point in their career. Crosby chose not to create a dramatic situation as a vehicle for the theme, but rather to deal directly with the emotional experience. Crosby clearly regarded it as his most intriguing song to date: 'It's a very strange song, it asks questions. Why is it all going on? I just ask the questions, I really don't know the answers. Each time I ask a question McGuinn answers it with his 12 string'. An effective and ambitious work, 'What's Happening?!?!' continued the raga rock experiment begun on 'Why' with the addition of a droning guitar.

No less unusual was the closing cut on side one,'I Come And Stand At Every Door', which must qualify as the most morbid song the Byrds ever recorded. The narrator relates the story of a seven-year-old child, the victim of radiation fall-out following the bombing of Hiroshima, whose spirit walks the earth in search of peace. The sentiments are essentially the same as 'Turn! Turn! Turn!', though the point of view is somewhat less optimistic. The song itself is an adaptation of a poem written by Nazim Hikmet. The melody was adapted from the traditional ballad 'Great Selchie Of Shule Skerry' which had appeared on the second Judy Collins album, *The Golden Apples Of The Sun*. Surprisingly, that great critic of negative lyrics, Jim Dickson, applauded the song:

'"I Come And Stand At Every Door" was fine for McGuinn to do. It was depressing, but it was classy. It had more scope. I couldn't argue with it. McGuinn certainly should have been allowed to do it'.

Crosby's second solo offering on the album was a fast arrangement of Dino Valenti's 'Hey Joe'. Rival West Coast group Love, which featured ex-Byrds roadie, Bryan MacLean, had already recorded the song, but Crosby could not resist a reply. His recording was not exactly a favourite of the other Byrds, as McGuinn remembers:

'The reason Crosby did lead on "Hey Joe" was because it was *his* song. He didn't write it but he was responsible for finding it. He'd wanted to do it for years but we would never let him. Then both Love and the Leaves had a minor hit with it and David got so angry that we had to let him do it. His version wasn't that hot because he wasn't a strong lead vocalist.'

Even Crosby later came to realize that the song did not deserve a place on the album and admitted that the recording was a blatant error on his part.

The final track on the album, '2-4-2 Fox Trot (The Lear Jet Song)' seemed little more than a throwaway. Another example of Byrds humour, but it is hardly sufficient to stand in its own right as an album track. The bracketed title is a tribute to jet manufacturer John Lear, who was a friend of the Byrds during this period. For years this number had been a joke among Byrds fans, some of whom suspected that the sound of the Lear jet was probably caused by a vacuum cleaner. One person who failed to appreciate that joke was McGuinn:

'It was not a vacuum cleaner, it was a Lear jet. We went out to the airport with an Ampex tape recorder and recorded the jet starting up. I really resent the fact that some people think it's a vacuum cleaner. But, then again, I guess they sound pretty much the same on record.'

Crosby was also defensive about the song at the time, feeling that the use of mechanical effects on records, in place of instruments, was very innovative and would be employed by other artistes. When the Beatles released 'Yellow Submarine' during the summer, Crosby was delighted to discover that his prediction had been partly fulfilled.

Although a substantial step forward, *Fifth Dimension* was not a great commercial success and within the Byrds line-up insecurity was once more rife. To make matters worse, the Byrds were being seriously challenged by other acts, including the Lovin' Spoonful and the Mamas and the Papas. Although both of these groups had gained their popularity by incorporating the folk rock elements pioneered by the Byrds, there was no sense of jealousy or rivalry between the groups, as Michelle Phillips remembers:

'There was never any sense of competition because we were all friends. I'd known David Crosby long before the Byrds, and McGuinn too. It was the same with John Sebastian and the Spoonful. We'd all come from the same place really. I think the fact that we were politically of the same mind helped to unify us.'

Although the Byrds could be greatly competitive amid their own ranks, they were also capable of magnanimity towards others. Stephen Stills recalls Chris Hillman in the surprising role as a patron of the arts to the emerging Buffalo Springfield:

'Ironically enough, it was Chris who got us off the ground to begin with. He was in the Byrds, who were really successful at the time, and he happened to come and see us rehearsing on what little equipment we had. He really dug us and literally got us off the street, borrowed equipment from his friends and really got us going.'

Hillman remembers his increasing involvement in the early days of the Buffalo Springfield:

'I was involved as an adviser and got them their first job at the Whisky-A-Go-Go. The owner of the Whisky loved me for that because they were great. For a while I considered managing them.'

Although Hillman was excited by the idea of becoming a manager he was wary of taking full responsibility and so attempted to persuade McGuinn to become co-manager. McGuinn was less impressed with the group, however, and declined the offer, upon which Hillman also withdrew his services. Crosby also attended the Whisky gigs and, before long, became friends with Stephen Stills. That, in itself, was to have repercussions for the Byrds the following year. In the meantime, the Buffalo Springfield were given a support spot with the Byrds and performed well enough to suggest that they could become strong competition.

During July 1966, the Byrds entered the studio and attempted to record a new single 'I Know You Rider' b/w 'Psychodrama City'. The news even filtered through to the British music press, but sadly the single failed to appear. Dickson recalls the Byrds' failure to cut a suitable version of this traditional folk tune:

'They recorded "I Know You Rider" on three separate occasions and worked hard on it. In every case, it was rejected. I think McGuinn was hoping for a single. There's a great danger in telling people your plans. They were never satisfied that the song was good enough. My import wasn't asked for but it would certainly have been not to do the song.'

Crosby's 'Psychodrama City', complete with a controversial verse about Gene Clark's fear of flying, was also consigned to the vaults where it remained for over 20 years.

The aborted final attempt to record 'I Know You Rider' was also the last session on which Allen Stanton appeared as Byrds producer. Shortly after this, he left Columbia to join A&M, but the blow was not as serious as it appeared, as McGuinn explained:

'Allen Stanton was always difficult to work with. He used to keep me after class as though we were at school and ask me, "Why is David so hard to understand? Why can't this go this way? Why can't we do that?" It was ridiculous!'

Observing the internal pressures, Eddie Tickner decided that it was time to take some strong measures in order to ensure that a Byrds dissolution was not a financial disaster:

'There was a separation at the time. Dickson had left, creatively, and Gene Clark had gone. The guys weren't very close. I said to them: "Let's put our shoulders to the wheel, make another record, push it and I'll re-negotiate your contract and get $1,000,000. We'll take $200,000 and call it a day". The idea was "Let's rob a bank", but in order to rob a bank you have to plan it. So the idea was spend a month writing, collecting material, spend a month rehearsing it, go into a studio, record and release a single. Then we'll all go to Europe, promote the single and then re-negotiate our contract. I wasn't too sure that there would be another album.'

For the remainder of the year, Tickner's master-plan was adhered to very closely. Although the Byrds seldom rehearsed, they spent more time than usual in the offices of 9,000 Sunset Boulevard. They continued performing infrequently at venues such as the Fillmore East and Village Gate, while gradually writing and preparing material for another album. In October, 'Mr Spaceman' was issued as a single, complete with a spoof claim that the Byrds had been insured against abduction by space aliens. A poker-faced Eddie Tickner was quoted in the publicity memos as saying: 'We live in weird times, and it would be foolish not to take seriously the possibility that there may be a response from outer space'. Not surprisingly, the joke did not extend as far as actually forking out any money to protect the Byrds from this unlikely occurrence. However, thanks to some television promotion by the group, the single became a minor hit, climbing as high as number 36 on the *Billboard* charts. Its progress was also helped by some personal promotion by Michael Clarke, who was sent out on the road in order to make guest appearances at various radio stations. Characteristically, Clarke's promotional work ended in a vacation, as Tickner smilingly revealed: 'Michael went out on the road. He got as far as Dallas. He was put on a plane for New Orleans but never arrived. He went to Canada instead'.

While the minimal success of 'Mr Spaceman' was sufficient to keep the Byrds in the public eye, it was clear that they were becoming jaded with live performances. Anxious to progress in their studio work and aware of the growing competition from other underground groups, the Byrds temporarily retired from public appearances.

10
Younger Than Yesterday

By early 1967, rumours began to circulate that the Byrds were on the brink of folding. Although the group had recently entered the studio and recorded an album's worth of material their lengthy hiatus suggested that something must be amiss. Jim Dickson, though still manager and publisher, had long been relieved of any constructive, creative input. Watching from the sidelines, even he feared the worst:

'By that time, the future of the Byrds was up for new interpretation daily. KRLA, the station that broke them, published in their paper that the Byrds were finished and they didn't expect them to last the year. The Byrds had died and died, and they were still there! People weren't on their side the way they were before. When the Byrds first broke onto the scene in Hollywood just about everybody was on their side. They were the only game in town. By 1967, they couldn't draw flies. A lot of that had to do with the bad performances that disappointed people and a lot had to do with who they turned out to be. Look at who David Crosby turned out to be. Loads of people in Hollywood have egos that they mostly try to control and be civilized about. There's a guy in the Byrds who's got a bigger ego than any movie star, than any musician, than *anybody*. People got soured. It's not important enough for them to put up with. I put up with a lot and the group put up with a lot from David Crosby, but people outside got tired of putting up with David Crosby. He's great when he's up, but when he's down he can ruin your day, your week, your month! The glitz was off, there were other bands. They weren't the only game in town anymore. There were people that came along who were prepared to be a whole lot more fun to be around.'

The Byrds' reaction to the less illustrious peers that were not deemed part of their circle was characteristically caustic. Their feelings were neatly summed up in the title of their new single, 'So You Want To Be A Rock 'n' Roll Star', released in February 1967. The mood of the song was almost Dylanesque in tone, with a heavy dose of sarcasm which McGuinn felt was justified:

'Some people have accused us of being bitter for writing that song, but it's no more bitter than "Positively 4th Street". In fact, it isn't as bitter as that. We were thumbing through a teen magazine and looking at all the unfamiliar faces and we couldn't help thinking: "Wow, what's happening . . . all of a sudden here is everyone and his brother and his sister-in-law and his mother and even his pet bullfrog singing rock 'n' roll." So we wrote 'So You Want To Be A Rock 'n' Roll Star' to the audience of potential rock stars, those who were going to be, or who wanted to be, and those who actually did go on and realize their goals.'

Although it has often been fancifully assumed that 'So You Want To Be A Rock 'n' Roll Star' was autobiographical, Chris Hillman insists that the song was written primarily as a reaction against the production of manufactured groups such as the Monkees. A strong single, it was given even greater momentum by the addition of brass. Apart from Hugh Masekela's trumpet, the song was also memorable for another surprise feature: screaming girls. Their inclusion was courtesy of Derek Taylor who claims: 'They were good British screams. I taped them from a show at Bournemouth during the 1965 English tour'.

In spite of the gimmicks and originality the song was not a massive hit, although it did restore the Byrds to the coveted US Top 30 after an absence of almost a year. The new album, *Younger Than Yesterday* followed the same pattern, achieving only moderate success, which was a terrible injustice, for it was not only a major progression for the Byrds but also a giant step forward for rock music, predating *Sgt Pepper's Lonely Hearts Club Band* by several months. In short, it proved conclusively that the Byrds were light years ahead of their nearest rivals.

Perhaps the most surprising feature of the new album was the sudden emergence of Chris Hillman as both a singer and songwriter of great charm and wit. His contributions to *Younger Than Yesterday* had a distinct McCartneyesque flavour, which served as an effective contrast to the more ambitious work of McGuinn and Crosby. What was more amazing, however, was the fact that Hillman wrote more songs on this album than either of his partners. Although, in retrospect, many critics refer to Chris' contributions to this album as essentially 'country-flavoured', this was far from the entire truth. 'Have You Seen Her Face', for example, is mostly memorable for McGuinn's intricate guitar work, which would have been totally out of place in a country idiom. Here, the unusual juxtaposition amplifies the emotive effect of this essentially simple song. Hillman explained his sudden interest in songwriting as a result of recent session work with Hugh Masekela.

'CTA 102', like its predecessor, 'Mr Spaceman', again contained elements of whimsy, but this time the idea was a little more serious. McGuinn and Bob Hippard's science fiction concept for 'CTA 102' concerned a quaser that might be a source of intelligent radio signals from outer space. The song brought McGuinn fame in other circles when Dr Eugene Epstein at Jet Propulsion Laboratories included a reference to 'CTA 102' in *The Astrophysical Journal*. The track itself was full of puzzling gimmicks, strange sounds and unearthly voices. McGuinn explains how the special effects were achieved:

'We used earphones fed into microphones and talked into them, and then we speeded it up. It was just nonsense but we deliberately tried to make it sound like a backward tape so people would try and reverse it . . . we were playing a joke really because it was a big fad at the time to play things backwards. We used an oscillator with a telegraph key, and that booming bang that you hear is the sustain pedal of a piano being held down and banged with our fists . . . a sort of Stockhausen idea.'

The Byrds' versatility on *Younger Than Yesterday* is clearly shown by the way they can effortlessly move from a futuristic song such as 'CTA 102' to the medieval atmosphere of 'Renaissance Fair'. This song, written by McGuinn and Crosby, again explores the symptoms of confusion, a theme developed from 'What's Happening?!?!' on the previous album. The narrative deals with the Renaissance Fair, a mock medieval festival, sponsored by one of the Los Angeles radio stations, in which the participants dressed themselves in twelfth century costume. However, this account is not so much a physical description of the event as an exploration into the feelings of the narrator. The real theme is not the event itself but the state of confusion it produces in the participant. Crosby seems to be relating the acid/dream experience through a continual concentration on the individual senses of hearing, smell and sight. The images pass in dream-like sequence, fully capturing the sense of wonder and awe produced by the event. This is definitely one of the most evocative songs in the Byrds canon; the bass work is excellent, and note the subtle way each layer of instrumentation is carefully added.

For 'Time Between' Chris Hillman introduced the Byrds to an old friend of his, Clarence White, who contributed the lead guitar break. The country influence was once more subtle enough to go unnoticed, especially with the added accompaniment of marraccas. The song was commercial enough to have made a reasonable latter-day Byrds single. At such an early stage in his songwriting career it was pleasing to see Chris having fun experimenting with elongated rhymes: '"Time Between" was the first song I ever wrote, so God knows what I was trying to do'.

The final track on side one, 'Everybody's Been Burned', quietly threatened to dwarf everything else on the album. A magnificent vocal from Crosby, and one of the most beautifully moving guitar solos of all time from McGuinn. Full marks too to Chris Hillman, whose jazz-influenced bass work reached unforeseen heights here. Crosby once said that Hillman's work on this track was unsurpassed by any rock bassist. The song itself was written by Crosby back in 1962, which must make it the oldest Byrds song of all. Though less ambitious than either 'Renaissance Fair' or 'What's Happening?!?!' it was clearly superior, and remains one of my favourite all time tracks. The song attempts a subtle balance between disillusionment, with the image of the door closing on the dream, and the determination to continue with a relationship: 'But you die inside, if you choose to hide/So I guess, instead, I'll love you'.

A candidate for the best ever Chris Hillman song opens side two: 'Thoughts And Words'. The duet is so perfectly synchronized that one is inclined to suspect that this is double tracking. The melody, possibly influenced by the Beatles, is broken up twice by the sitar-like sound of guitars taped backwards. Another gimmick, perhaps, but it fits perfectly into this unusual love song. 'Thoughts And Words' has a slight metaphysical air with its reference to 'mind', and the raga rock effect of those guitars makes an apparently simple song seem unusually profound. Hillman explained the song's construction: 'The backwards guitar insert was McGuinn and Gary Usher's idea. I didn't consciously borrow the melody from the Beatles. Any similarities are purely coincidental'.

An attempt at profundity of a different kind followed with 'Mind Gardens', in which Crosby consciously took his notions about raga rock to their furthest extremes. His writing seemed almost to have reached its frightening limits with this dangerously ambitious song. The title, 'Mind Gardens', and the content of the song, deliberately invite us to see the composition as allegory. The garden, overprotected and free from harm, will be suffocated by its own security, unless it is allowed to feel pain as well as pleasure. In this sense, the song seems not simply a direct allegory between garden and mind but gains symbolic force through its various associations. We may see the garden as representative of woman, knowledge, truth or anything else that may suffer from being locked away or overprotected. Whether the song is a success or not is still a matter of burning controversy among the Byrds public. Many felt that it worked as a unique example of Crosby's venture into psychedelia, whereas others, including the remaining Byrds, complained of its excess. Certainly, the self-indulgence is there, from the over use of those droning sitar-like guitars to Crosby's insistence on showing us he has read some Shakespeare, or at least is familiar with one of his most famous lines: 'The slings and arrows of outrageous fortune' (*Hamlet* III, i, 58). Moreover, the loose connection between 'mind' and 'gardens' makes it too vague to stand as allegory. Yet, the song still holds interest, perhaps because it is so unusual. Crosby later admitted that the song was not a success and never again attempted to write such a composition. Sadly, even the sitar-like guitar sound, which had previously been used to such effect on 'Why', was never employed on any subsequent Byrds number. The raga rock dream ended here.

Crosby appears to agree with most of the above points, although he retains a distinct distaste for genre classifications such as 'raga rock':

'"Mind Gardens" had nothing to do with ragas or rock. It had to do with the words. And they're good. It wasn't excessive. They're just good words. However, it was unusual and not everybody could understand it because they'd never heard anything like it before. At that time everything was supposed to have rhyme and have rhythm. And it neither rhymed nor had rhythm so it was outside of their experience, and they weren't able to get into it.'

Crosby's defence is persuasive, but even he realizes that a song cannot survive on its lyrics alone, and requires a complementary melody. Whether the 'backward guitar' tape compensates for the lack of melody in 'Mind Gardens' remains the debatable point. Crosby's objection to the term raga rock is also inadequate. As a blanket term to cover all rock songs in which Indian instruments are played or imitated, it is an effective genre classification. Certainly, raga rock has a far more comprehensible meaning than other vague labels such as folk rock. Although Crosby denies that the playing on 'Mind Gardens' had anything to do with ragas, he neglects the main point that the use of a 'backward guitar' tape is part of the raga-rock tradition since it was one of the ways in which rock musicians effectively imitated the sound of a sitar.

While controversy surrounded 'Mind Gardens', the next cut 'My Back Pages' was another source of minor disagreement. The placing of the two tracks side by side clearly underlined the division between Crosby and the other Byrds at this point. McGuinn, ready to record a Dylan number once more and anxious to use the theme for the title of the album, felt that 'My Back Pages' was a good choice. Crosby, on the other hand, argued that it was a formula record, a backward step to the days before *Fifth Dimension*. Crosby lost the argument, not only to the Byrds, but also to the general populace, who felt the song was both tasteful and progressive. While Crosby shouted 'sell-out' the critics praised McGuinn, and the fans warmed to that classic Rickenbacker solo. In retrospect, Crosby is not too upset by the Byrds' version of the song:

'There wasn't really a dispute over it. I did think if there was a Dylan song that we really wanted to do, then we should do it. But I thought that putting a Dylan song in as a formula was dumb. "My Back Pages" wasn't the best Dylan song, but it was OK. It didn't hurt.'

Clarence White's second uncredited appearance can be heard on the penultimate track, 'Girl With No Name'. Again, Chris shows his ability to write a commercial song and one cannot help wondering how the previous albums might have sounded were he more actively involved. The anonymous girl in the title of the song was actually a name borrowed from a real person: Girl Freiberg. Dickson was pleased enough to see Hillman finally emerge as a songwriting contributor:

'I thought his stuff on *Younger Than Yesterday* was OK and I was glad to see him do it. It was better that there were more contributors from within the group. There were a lot of plusses with Chris writing. I thought the songs were OK. They weren't astounding, but they were good. They weren't as bad as their bad stuff or as good as their best stuff. I would have been happy to have had a couple of Hillman's songs at any time. I particularly liked them because of the country flavour. McGuinn, in spite of the later *Sweetheart Of The Rodeo*, has no sensitivity towards country music.'

The final track on *Younger Than Yesterday*, 'Why', broke the tradition of joke endings to Byrds albums, or did it? The song was already a year old, and the raga version that appeared on the b-side of 'Eight Miles High' was infinitely superior to this watered down copy. Why the Byrds bothered to issue an inferior version at so late a date remains a mystery. Jim Seiter, the Byrds' road manager at the time, maintains that it was Crosby's idea: 'They weren't satisfied with what they had and David wanted equal time. "Why" was a song that Crosby had written, so "Why" was done as a stroke for David'.

Dickson concurs with Seiter's theory:

'When something's on a b-side to us, it was as if it never existed. B-sides of singles not getting on albums was CBS policy, so it took extra effort to get them on there. By the time *Younger Than Yesterday* emerged, you'll notice there's more Crosby and Hillman songs. That reflects how David's power in the group had increased. The attitude may have been: "We'll do a better version". Who says it's better? Gary Usher! David Crosby! If they say it's better, it's better. Who cares, but David? McGuinn's always prepared to believe that he can do a better solo.'

In retrospect, Crosby admitted: 'The version of "Why" we did at RCA with Jim Dickson was the best one of all'. Certainly, those stunning sitar-like breaks on the RCA and original CBS b-side takes seem far superior to the standard breaks on the *Younger Than Yesterday* track, though Dickson remains far from convinced:

'I wouldn't say the solo wasn't as good. I was later able to make what I thought was a stunning solo, a one that made me question whether I should put out the RCA version on *Never Before*. I left it up to McGuinn. It was *his* solo. McGuinn agonized over it and said: "I guess we should use the RCA version, though it's a lot rougher in some ways". So it was not an easy decision to choose the best version, even recently.'

While *Younger Than Yesterday* failed to sell a million, it attracted the attention of various members of the US underground and helped to establish the Byrds as an albums band. Although the tensions in the group continued to grow, the Byrds were now working at white heat. With three singer songwriters, each growing more powerful with every succeeding song, the Byrds were once again in a position to challenge, and even topple, the Beatles as the world's finest rock group. With Hillman having already outshone McCartney as a bassist, and now threatening to emerge as an extremely competent singer songwriter, everything seemed possible. In addition, the songwriting talents of McGuinn and Crosby had finally proven sufficient to compensate for the loss of Gene Clark. Akin to the emerging underground, Crosby looked forward to further revolutionary musical changes. Meanwhile, McGuinn was also concerned with re-establishing the Byrds as a Top 40 group and seemed optimistic about the hit potential of 'My Back Pages'. As with 'So You Want To Be A Rock 'n' Roll Star', it was a minor hit in the USA but failed to crack the Top 20. Undaunted, the Byrds took a holiday in the form of a promotional visit to Europe. The highlight of the visit was a Byrds fan-club gathering at Chalk Farm Roundhouse which was a tribute to the 1,700 young people who signed a petition begging the group to return to England, following the disastrous 1965 tour. The Byrds travelled on to Denmark, Sweden and Italy and, although they played no concerts, they made frequent appearances on television and radio. The lack of public performances made Crosby even more irritable, and it was now over eight months since the Byrds' last concert tour. On the horizon though was one scheduled appearance at the Monterey Pop Festival at which the growing conflict between Crosby and the other Byrds would come to a head.

Although the Byrds had survived the traumas of the past year, and had partly fulfilled Tickner's promotional plans, the relationship between management and group was far from secure. By the summer, Tickner and Dickson departed, to be replaced by Crosby's new find, Larry Spector. Although Crosby had a tremendous respect for Dickson's work, he was instrumental in encouraging the group to break away from their management. Eddie Tickner recalls his final days with the Byrds:

'Larry Spector was a business manager for a lot of the young guys around Peter Fonda and Dennis Hopper, who were all friends with David Crosby. So David came in one day and said: "I've found a business manager who'll do really well". Then some undercover things went on, a conspiracy to leave Tickner/Dickson and go with Larry as personal and business manager. Actually, I'd called it a day after Europe. Dickson came down from the hills and took over for the remaining period. We negotiated a settlement and we officially left on 30 June 1967. I still get a royalty cheque!'

11
Mutiny From Stern To Bow

By mid-1967 Crosby's rise to power had become more noticeable. He was suddenly the central figure in the group, both visually and musically. The green suede cape was replaced by a wardrobe of flamboyant velvet shirts and a broad-brimmed hat. An innocent reviewer of the time summed up the situation without even realizing it:

'David Crosby is evidently the lead singer, as Jim McGuinn had only one solo in two sets. David has a lovely tenor folk voice which comes across very well on record, but in person he tries too hard to sound bluesy and loses the "sweet" quality of his voice.'

Crosby's desire to become leader and lead singer of the group went hand in hand with his frustrated ambition to become a blues singer. However, his dream would not be realized until two years later when he found the necessary aggression in his voice to sing 'Long Time Gone'. In the meantime, Crosby continued to isolate himself from the rest of the group through his outspokenness on political matters and his fraternization with rivals such as the Buffalo Springfield and the Jefferson Airplane. Crosby loved an audience and enjoyed being controversial, especially on important television shows. McGuinn recalls one such incident:

'We were on *The Dick Cavett Show* once and at the end of the programme Cavett said: "There are a few minutes left, do any of you guys want to say anything?" And he came to Crosby and Crosby said, "Yeah. I'd like to say that I don't like what General Motors are doing polluting the atmosphere!" And Dick said, "But David! General Motors are sponsoring the show". Crosby hasn't got a lot of tact, I guess'.

The Crosby problem became more acute following the Byrds' appearance at the Monterey Pop Festival in June. Musically, the group were tighter than in recent months and had spent weeks in the rehearsal room in a determined effort to prove to the critics that they could reproduce their studio sound on the concert platform. They were at least given a chance to show their humour and versatility when, during their set, a Boeing 707 came soaring over the festival site. The Byrds continued playing above the noise of the jet, adjusting the tempo to simulate the sound of the aircraft as it landed at a nearby aerodrome. The incident was a whimsical justification of McGuinn's concept of the Byrds as the first group of the jet age. Although the music was good, the Byrds received mixed reviews, mainly due to Crosby's tirade about LSD and the Warren Report. The remarks concerning the Warren Report were part of the standard introduction to 'He Was A Friend Of Mine', but recently Crosby's preamble had become a little too controversial for McGuinn, who felt such comments were unnecessary:

'I respected Pete Seeger more for what he said than Crosby. I think he believed what he said, but many of the comments were outrageous, and not necessarily valid. He was speculating about the Warren Report onstage but he really didn't have anything to say beyond what we all knew. At the time he said that Paul McCartney had said, "Everyone should take acid", which was unnecessary. I think he was just trying to be hip and I felt he should have been more discreet.'

Crosby does not feel that his comments were particularly outrageous:

'I probably did encourage people to drop acid because I thought it was a good idea. It did sort of blow us loose from the 50's. And at the time, it seemed a great idea. I did say something about the Warren Report as an introduction to 'He Was A Friend Of Mine'. That's why I said it. It was pretty relevant, I thought.'

McGuinn clearly preferred tact and discretion to sermonizing. Discretion, however, was not a noticeable trait in Crosby's personality during the latter half of 1967. While advocating LSD, he continued to wear the STP sticker on his guitar which hardly endeared him to the makers of Specially Treated Petroleum. If his words at Monterey embarrassed McGuinn, his actions seemed even less justifiable. For Crosby, it was a pleasure to get up and play alongside the Buffalo Springfield, but to the other Byrds it seemed like an act of open defiance. Jim Seiter recalls Crosby's attitude:

'At Monterey he showed to the world that he'd rather play with the Buffalo Springfield. When he appeared with them he was God's gift to the harmony voice but he was terrible with us. David hated being a Byrd. He didn't consider it hip for some reason. He wanted to be a Buffalo Springfield, a Jefferson Airplane or a Door. David's a groupie, always was and always will be.'

By the close of the Monterey Pop Festival, the Byrds had effectively split into two factions and it was clear that the months ahead would indeed be stormy.

Meanwhile, McGuinn, continuing his interest in the spiritual organization, Subud, had changed his name from Jim to Roger:

'When we had our son I named him James IV. Then we decided to send to Indonesia to find out what his name was, and it came back Patrick McGuinn. I thought, "Wow, what a groovy name". That's a better name than I would have thought of. So I was curious to see what mine was, and my wife and I both sent for our names. We got them, and she was Ianthe and I was Roger . . . you get a letter back that suggests the first letter of your name and suggests that you make up 10 names that you might like to have. So I made up weird names like Retro and Rex and others. I sort of put down nine ridiculous ones and Roger, sort of picking my own. I liked it because it was aeroplane talk, you know, "Roger". It had a very right, positive sound.'

Crosby, however, was less than impressed with McGuinn's spirituality and openly derided Subud as the oriental conspiracy to overcome the rock 'n' roll world'.

On 7 August, Columbia released *The Byrds' Greatest Hits* which, ironically, sold more copies than any of their regularly released albums. Strangely enough, the underground press, traditionally wary of blatantly commercial products such as compilation albums, greeted the Byrds release with warm compliments. Paul Williams waxed eloquently on the compilation, as though it were a major artistic work:

'Any greatest hits album is insignificant. By definition it contains nothing unfamiliar; and yet this very fact offers great potential beauty, for a well-made greatest hits LP might then unleash the emotion of familiarity in an artistic context. The Byrds have achieved that goal; always masters of the form, they have now taken the concept of a great hits anthology and created from it an essay into rediscovery.'

As a performing group, however, the Byrds were showing few signs of any 'rediscovery'. Since Monterey the group's live shows had become less and less memorable. They seemed content to play their 'greatest hits' in a mechanical manner, and the animosity between Crosby and the others was now plainly evident to the audience, as Seiter remembers: 'It was Crosby versus the rest onstage. It was a joke. At times the audiences loved it. But back in LA it was dreadful'.

For most gigs, the Byrds played a mere 40-45 minute set and, according to Crosby, McGuinn would frequently refer to his watch, impatient to return to the dressing-room. The once stage shy Chris Hillman had also developed a new brand of cool arrogance and was not beyond missing a few notes in order to take a drag from his cigarette. While Crosby complained of the other Byrds' boredom and lack of commitment, McGuinn replied in equally derogatory terms: 'He'd be off, off out of tune. But when it came to one of his songs, he'd shine, man'.

Seiter concurred with McGuinn's opinion:

'David did some of the most unprofessional things ever onstage. He'd start a song, play a couple of bars, and then insist upon a five minute tuning interlude. It was on a night like this that Hillman went up to the microphone and announced, "Ladies and gentlemen – the David Crosby Show". And Hillman never said much, but he'd sneak around and get his digs in.'

The Byrds' live shows were swiftly becoming a battleground. By September, Crosby still held sway, and had even achieved the rare distinction of including one of his songs, 'Lady Friend', on the a-side of a new Byrds single. The song was equally as interesting as anything the Byrds had ever produced in single form and considerably outshone the McGuinn-Hillman film theme flip-side, 'Don't Make Waves', which Roger later dismissed as 'embarrassing'. Moreover, 'Lady Friend' was undoubtedly the loudest, fastest and rockiest Byrds single to date. The theme, concerning the fragmentation of a personal relationship, was typical of 1967 Crosby but the inclusion of brass gave the song even greater momentum than David's earlier efforts. The other Byrds, however, were less than enthusiastic about 'Lady Friend'. Crosby was very bitter about their attitude to the song, which failed to appear on the next album:

'I thought up the brass parts and they all played on it, but the song never got put on a fucking record. Now, do you think I'm kidding you about not being able to get my stuff on a record? Was "Lady Friend" good, did you like it? I couldn't get it on the record. They wouldn't put it on the record because it was mine, and not theirs. It never got a chance, man, they wouldn't put it on a record. That's one of the reasons why there was a lot of bitterness on my part. It wasn't a joke, it was a very real problem I was up against. Do you understand that?'

Unfortunately, Crosby failed to prove his point in commercial terms and the single flopped, receiving little or no airplay.

Crosby was still determined to include his best material on Byrds albums but ran into more difficulties over the controversial 'Triad'. McGuinn felt that Crosby's account of this unusual relationship was not in the best of taste, and promptly vetoed the song. Crosby's final days with the Byrds were noticeably traumatic, as Seiter revealed:

'David got real uptight with me during his last days with the group. One night I received a call from a girl who lived in a house below his, and she asked me to come up there and keep him awake because he'd taken an overdose of something weird. He was passing out and she wanted to keep him together. So I went up to his house to keep him alive. He was in a sad shape. The next day I talked to Larry Spector and told him David was depressed. We went to San Francisco. The group stayed in one place and David stayed in another hotel, with me next door to him. That night Bill Graham asked us to play a slightly longer show. The first night they played 55 minutes instead of the usual 45 minutes. When they came offstage David was furious. He threw his guitar on the floor and yelled at me, saying that I'd better not ever let him play 55 minutes again. The next night I had a great big stopwatch onstage and I pushed it as soon as they started. They were offstage to the second at 45 minutes, which annoyed Bill Graham. While I was putting some equipment away, David bursts into my room, throws his guitar down, again, runs over and starts punching me in the head. As far as he was concerned, I'd left them onstage too long again. He wasn't in good shape, mentally. That night he called me up a hundred times, crying and apologising over and over again.'

David's last performance as a Byrd took place the evening after his clash with Seiter and, ironically, it was all smiles and good vibes. The trauma had temporarily passed, but for the Byrds a decision had already been reached.

On a fateful day in October, McGuinn and Hillman drove over to Crosby's house to inform him that his days as a Byrd had ended. Crosby recalls the final confrontation:

'They came over and said they wanted to throw me out, and they would do much better without me. They came zooming up my driveway in their Porsches and said that I was impossible to work with and I wasn't very good anyway and they'd do much better without me. It hurt like hell. I didn't try to reason with them. I just said: "It's a shameful waste, goodbye".

The precise reasons for Crosby's dismissal were unpublished in 1967 and, strangely enough, even David himself has often appeared unsure of what prompted the final move. Even seven years later, he was addressing audiences with new interpretations of his firing:

'This is a song ("Triad") that I usually, well, for a long time I introduced it as being one of the main reasons they threw me out of the Byrds. But, actually, I went back and checked with them recently, and they said: "No, I was just being an asshole, it was just me".

Crosby's final appraisal of the situation seems close to the truth, as McGuinn confirms:

'"Triad" wasn't the crux of it. That was nothing really. It was just a song I didn't think was in particularly good taste. No, he was just trying to dictate what our policies should be, which songs we shouldn't do. I think one of our big disagreements was over a song called "Goin' Back". He didn't like that at all. So I thought, well his heart wasn't in it. At this point he was hanging out with the Buffalo Springfield a lot, playing around town with other groups, sort of shopping for a new position. I figured that he wanted to get out of it, and we did him a service. We bought him a ketch which he still has, and he's sailed around on it a lot, brought it from the East Coast to the West Coast via the Panama Canal.'

Clearly, it was the culmination of a series of clashes throughout the turbulent year of 1967 which finally ended Crosby's reign. Remembering the traumas of those months, McGuinn recounts the factors leading up to the final decision:

'Even though I didn't agree with David on certain issues – and he said things onstage which made me say them by proxy since we were a group – we always had this policy where you could wear what you liked, do anything you wanted to onstage or off, and the fact that he was outspoken onstage wasn't the reason he was fired or asked to leave. It was merely that he was becoming a dictator and was trying to dominate the present and the future of the Byrds.'

Crosby maintains that at the time of his dismissal he was at a creative peak and was not given sufficient opportunity or encouragement to develop as a songwriter:

'I'm a very opinionated person and I know that doesn't make it easy. But Spector had those guys pretty well fooled. It was a big mistake on my part getting him, but I'd already figured him out. He knew this, so he did his level best to set McGuinn and Hillman against me all the time. But, mainly, it was just ego on their part. They felt me getting stronger. I think they either resented it or were worried by it. The resistance to my material was like the resistance of the Hollies to Nash's material. It was just dumb. And I kept writing better and better songs. When they threw me out I had just written "Guinevere", "Wooden Ships" and "Laughing". Now, who the hell do you think is the best writer there? They can't fight it, man. There isn't one of them can write as good as me, and you know it. I'm better than they are. I'm a better writer. And they can't touch it. None of them has ever written anything as good as that.'

In retrospect, McGuinn admits that the sacking may have been an error, though he also hints at its inevitability: 'Maybe it was a rash decision. I thought that afterwards at times. But he was impossible to work with and I felt that firing him was the only solution'. Although it has generally been accepted that McGuinn was responsible for firing Crosby, Hillman's involvement in the affair should not be underestimated: 'Chris was always the catalyst to these departures. Everyone blames me because I was the figurehead, but Chris was always there in the background saying, "Get rid of him".'

Crosby's departure was a serious blow to the Byrds, but an immediate replacement was found when former Byrd, Gene Clark, made his comeback. Gene's much vaunted solo career had failed to bring any critical or public acclaim, in spite of the release of an excellent album with the Gosdin Brothers titled *Echoes*. Producer Jim Dickson vainly hoped that the title track might chart but its failure effectively blighted the album's success. With only one recording in 19 months, and little or no publicity, it was evident that Gene's solo career had failed to reach fruition. Like his fellow Byrds, Gene had decided to leave Tickner/ Dickson Management and throw in his lot with Larry Spector. It was anticipated that Clark's return would benefit both his own career and that of the Byrds. Jim Seiter explained the reasons for Spector's returning Gene Clark to the fold:

'Larry was an opportunist. He was a great business manager. His supposed forte was dealing with funds. He couldn't get a deal for Gene Clark, so he decided to get him back in the Byrds. Gene had no money in the bank but he owned two $35,000 Ferraris. That was Gene. We'd already done most of the album when he arrived. We were just about to set out on tour.'

The intense pressures that forced Gene to leave the group in 1966 seemed less threatening now that the Byrds had fallen from commercial grace. Determined to re-establish his rightful place in the rock world, Gene expressed confidence in his ability to overcome his fear of flying, believing that the absence of screaming female hordes, relentless autograph hunters and scoop-seeking reporters would enable him to function adequately in the new line up. Meanwhile, McGuinn and Hillman were confident that the departure of Crosby would be alleviated by the return of the Byrds' former, foremost singer-songwriter. Clark returned to the group clutching not a tambourine but a rhythm guitar and promising to stop the instrumental gap resulting from Crosby's dismissal. It seemed a perfect solution from the point of view of both Clark and the Byrds, but nobody could have foreseen the calamitous weeks ahead.

Jim Seiter remembers Clark's failed attempt to re-establish himself as a Byrd:

'We were booked for three days in Minneapolis and then New York. The first night was weird. He was so scared. He kept asking everybody, "Did I play good? Was I OK?" He was so insecure. I turned his rhythm guitar off. We weren't using it. He was singing flat. I turned his mike off. His own songs weren't that bad except that he'd get paranoid halfway through them. They couldn't believe what they'd got themselves in for. They were going to New York where they had a real big following, and they were really dreading it because Gene had been so bad.'

Gene was determined to fly at all costs, even if he had to be drugged to the eyeballs with tranquilisers. After the final Minneapolis gig, however, he stayed up all night in a cold sweat and early the next morning announced that he would not travel by plane. While McGuinn suggested that they knock him out with pills, one person in the Byrds camp had the insensitivity to taunt Gene. McGuinn described the ensuing argument as a melodramatic soap opera as Gene screamed back at his tormentor and concluded his second coming by taking a train back to Los Angeles. Even after returning safely, Gene was to discover that the nightmare of the last three weeks had not quite ended, as Seiter revealed:

'We did a gig as a trio and it was even easier. The next day Larry asked me to go to the station and meet Gene as he'd only just arrived by train. When I got there and met him at the train, he just walked past me at a fast pace, and didn't say a word, got in a yellow cab and split to the office. Now, Gene was always afraid of small closed spaces. He never took elevators. We had this old-fashioned elevator in the office building and Gene never took it. But for some reason he did that day. When I arrived at the office the police are there and the Fire Department – someone is stuck in the lift. Gene is stuck in the lift for two-and-a-half hours. When they finally opened it he ran out, soaking with sweat, and split. I didn't see him for six or eight months after that. The inside of the elevator was totally scratched up where he'd tried to get out. You should have heard him screaming. Unbelievable. He was going crazy in that elevator. He screamed at the top of his lungs for almost an hour. Bad time for Gene.'

With no suitable candidate available as a replacement for Clark, the Byrds determined to continue as a trio. However, the morale of the trio was so low that Michael Clarke found himself an ex-Byrd at the end of the year. Tired of the group traumas and the continual pressures of life in LA, Clarke moved to Hawaii and temporarily left the music business altogether, securing a mundane job in an hotel. McGuinn reveals the reasons behind Michael's sudden disenchantment:

'I think he was on the point of quitting when we suggested that he should leave. He seemed to be depressed at the time and didn't want the responsibility of being a Byrd, although he didn't really have to do that much. Another factor was our audience which was changing. We weren't really pulling in any teenage girls and Michael missed that. He liked the idea of being a sex symbol.'

David Crosby provided an assessment of Michael Clarke's contribution to the group:

'Michael would turn the time round two or three times in a song back to front. But he improved steadily and he tried very hard to get better. He surprised me because he got better and better after he left the Byrds. He can play a groove quite well'.

The comings and goings at the end of 1967 threatened the completion of their next album but McGuinn and Hillman were determined to finish the project and succeeded with the help of some notable session players including Jim Gordon, Red Rhodes and Clarence White. In England, a new single, 'Goin'Back'/'Change Is Now' was released in Christmas week as a festive treat for British Byrd followers. Ironically, much publicity was given to the fact that the Byrds were now reduced to a trio, nobody realizing that the situation had worsened and was now critical.

12
Wanted: The Notorious Byrd Brothers

At the close of 1967, the critics were asking whether McGuinn and Hillman were poised to become a West Coast Simon and Garfunkel-type act. By the first week of January 1968, however, reports filtered through that the Byrds had found a new drummer, Kevin Kelley. As the first non-original Byrd, Kevin had one particularly distinctive quality; he was cousin to Chris Hillman. Kelley's musical background was far from unimpressive. He had studied music and specialized in composing at both Santa Monica and Los Angeles City colleges. Following high school, he entered what he refers to as a state of confusion and enlisted in the marines for three years. Strangely enough, throughout this period, Kelley gave up music completely. Returning to civilian life, Kelley joined Taj Mahal and Ry Cooder in the Rising Sons, replacing Ed Cassidy as drummer. Somewhere along the way he taught himself guitar and piano, but remained essentially a drummer. By the time Chris Hillman reached his cousin it seemed that the latter was entering another period of musical lethargy and was gainfully employed in a men's clothing shop. Like Michael Clarke, his entry to the Byrds was sudden, unexpected and welcomed.

During the same month everyone was amazed by the sudden American release of *The Notorious Byrd Brothers*, which many had felt was merely at the planning stage. However, the intense pressure of three departures in as many months had acted as a catalyst in getting the album completed, and McGuinn and Hillman had worked extensively throughout the early weeks of December in order to meet their proposed deadline. The album was a surprise commercial success at that time, and the Byrds had done it again. Lyrically, musically and production-wise, they were pushing forward to new musical horizons, even as their ranks were diminishing to an alarming extent.

'Artificial Energy', revealed the first signs of a new Byrds sound with its extensive use of brass. Crosby had previously persuaded the Byrds to use the trumpet of Hugh Masekela on 'So You Want To Be A Rock 'n' Roll Star' and 'Lady Friend', but McGuinn denies that the employment of brass was inspired by David:

'No, the brass was Gary Usher's idea. I remember we had a really "square" brass section. So I took this electronic device and made them boogie. They were doing Harry James-type swing music and I electronically modified an entire brass section by myself, with my right hand, and made it come out as it did.'

The track is full of subtleties, with its barely audible piano, and the humorous steal from the Beatles' 'Ticket To Ride' (sung 'ticket to ri-hi-hide'), another example of McGuinn using the media as a private communications device. Lyrically, the song is full of fascination, from its Frankensteinian reference to the effects of amphetamine ('powerful things are brewing inside') to the final horrific image of the drug taker imprisoned for murdering a homosexual ('I'm in jail 'cos I killed a queen'). McGuinn gives Hillman much credit for the conception of this famous anti-drug song: 'It was a collaboration on the lyrics though it was mainly Chris' idea. He said, "Let's write a song about speed".'

The unearthly sounds that end 'Artificial Energy' abruptly metamorphose into the opening strains of 'Goin' Back', a poignant song of nostalgia and lost innocence, in complete contrast to the grim realism of the first cut. Written by Gerry Goffin and Carole King, the song was already well known in Britain, having been a hit for Dusty Springfield in the summer of 1966. In spite of that association, nobody could argue with the fact that the Byrds had made the song their own. The theme of thinking young and growing older recalled the title of their last album, *Younger Than Yesterday*, while the distinctive 'ahhs' immediately placed the song in a Byrds context. Another notable feature of the song was the superb drumming, apparently the work of Jim Gordon, and Red Rhodes' pedal-steel fade-out, which echoed the unusual ending of 'Artificial Energy'. Although 'Goin' Back' was recorded early in the sessions, Jim Seiter remembers that Crosby did not appear on the track:

'During the session for "Goin'Back", David sat on a couch for three days with his hat over his eyes and didn't do a thing. "Goin' Back" was in direct competition to "Triad" for a place on the album and David had really wanted to do "Triad". He eventually went off to a Jefferson Airplane session and made them stop to listen to "Dolphin's Smile".'

The Airplane did not record 'Dolphin's Smile' but included 'Triad' on their 1968 album *Crown Of Creation*.

The other-worldly sounds continued on Chris' solo contribution, 'Natural Harmony', a song which actually enacts the freedom longed for in 'Goin' Back'. Having asked us in 'Goin' Back' to return to the days when we were young enough to know the truth, the narrator of 'Natural Harmony' actually does describe a feeling similar to the day of birth, 'our first awakening to this earth'. It is easy to dismiss the 'merging with a grain of sand' lyrics as the expression of a drug-related experience but, in doing so, we may be as myopic as those misguided commentators on 'Eight Miles High' and '5-D'. The important point is that the song, like 'Goin' Back', is a vivid impression of freedom and innocence. Someone once asked why the Byrds used the word 'graciously' and not, for example, 'gratefully'. The answer is, of course, that 'graciously' is a far more evocative term, close in association to the orderly concept of natural harmony. The word also more effectively describes the dream-like atmosphere, which is reminiscent of the medieval-tinged 'Renaissance Fair' on the last album. Paul Beaver's moog and Red Rhodes' steel guitar merge wonderfully to enhance the eerie musical effects.

Having already dealt with the subject of drugs, innocence and freedom, the Byrds next turn their attention to war with 'Draft Morning'. The song remains one of their finest, an example of the Byrds at their creative peak. Although Crosby received a composing credit and was mainly responsible for the idea of writing the song, he does not, according to Hillman, appear on the recording:

'Crosby had written the basic song but we had to rewrite some of the words because he had left right after introducing the song to us and we could hardly remember the lyrics.'

Much credit must also be given to producer Gary Usher who recruited the Firesign Theater to add the stunning special effects of gunfire to the track. Lyrically and musically, the song builds layer upon layer until we reach the dramatic introduction of the gunfire. The first verse introduces the narrator, awakening to feel the warmth of the sun on his face and hearing a figure, presumably his loved one, moving below stairs. The homely atmosphere of this scene is negated in the second stanza when we learn that this is the morning of the draft and the time approaches when the narrator must unwillingly be taught how to kill. The introduction of brass, and the gradually increasing volume of gunfire that follows, creates a startling effect, resulting in a shift of temporal distance. For when we next return to the narrator in the final few lines, he is no longer uneasily contemplating his approaching induction into the army but is already an active soldier. Note the move from the present to the past tense in the phrase 'today *was* the day for action' (as opposed to 'today *is* the day for action') indicating that military service has already taken place and implying, perhaps, that the gunfire we have heard was his own. Lyrically and musically, 'Draft Morning' must be ranked alongside the most brilliant of Byrds songs. The bass work of Chris Hillman was nothing short of superb and established his reputation as one of the finest players ever to grace rock music. One person who did not appreciate the quality of the Byrds' interpretation was David Crosby. He maintained that the Byrds' recording of the song was an unethical act on their part:

'It was one of the sleaziest things they ever did. I had an entire song finished. They just casually rewrote it and decided to take half the credit. How's that? Without even asking me!'

Although one might argue that the Byrds at least realized the value of the song, this is hardly sufficient compensation for Crosby:

'Man, they used it after they changed it, and took it for themselves without even asking me. That's theft! Do you understand? How would you feel? Suppose we were co-writing a book together, man, and you had just finished doing something with it and we split up. Then I rewrote all of your stuff in it and claimed that I had written the book. How would you feel? You'd be pissed off, wouldn't you? Well, I was pissed off'.'

In spite of Crosby's indignant words, the song, on which he received a co-writing credit, remains one of the Byrds finest, which is at least a tribute to his original idea.

The importance of *The Notorious Byrd Brothers* as a document of the 60's is reflected in these songs of innocence, freedom, rejection of war and, more generally, the desire to escape the restrictive values of conventional society, as expressed in the next track, 'Wasn't Born To Follow'. Significantly, the song was later chosen as the most suitable piece of music to express 'the search for America' in the motion picture *Easy Rider*. With its assertion of personal freedom and refusal to conform, the theme may serve as an effective answer to the problems presented in 'Draft Morning'. As another Goffin and King song, it appears to reveal the Byrds' great talent for discovering and adapting suitable extraneous material. However, McGuinn reveals that the real credit belongs to his producer: 'Gary Usher knew Carole King and he was responsible for getting those songs for us. We felt they were suitable choices for inclusion on the album'. Certainly, the Byrds were not content to produce a carbon copy of the song. They completely restructured the original melody, so that their version of the song was totally different from that of Carole King. Again, it is noticeable the way in which different instruments are juxtaposed for effect and, strangely enough, there is nothing disjointed about hearing Clarence White's guitar alongside all the phasing.

At the end of 'Wasn't Born To Follow' we hear the sound of what appears to be a door slamming. The Mamas and the Papas first used this technique on 'John's Music Box' (from *Deliver*) to announce the end of the album side, but here we still have one track remaining, 'Get To You'. While the composing credits are given as Hillman-McGuinn, Chris admits that the lyrics were almost entirely the work of his colleague. Although the song seems simple enough, documenting an aeroplane trip to London just prior to the advent of autumn, it leaves us with a single puzzle: who is the 'you' of the title? If we assume the speaker to be McGuinn, then it seems logical that the 'you' is London itself, which Roger did indeed wait some 20 years to see. In this sense, the phrase 'run my way' would have to be interpreted as simply a play on words, actually meaning 'runway' and indicating the arrival of the plane at London Airport! All this is complicated by the fact that in the second line McGuinn wants to be back there 'again' which clearly suggests that he has been there before, presumably at a very early age! Perhaps it is safer to assume that the narrator is purely fictitious, in which case the 'you' becomes simply some extremely patient woman in the mould of John Riley's 'fair young maid'. Another puzzle, which seems to have bothered a considerable number of Byrds persons, concerns the chorus of 'Get To You'. Never can a rock lyric have caused such widespread disagreement and resulted in such multitudinous interpretations as 'Back To America', 'Back To Roberta' and even 'Hansel and Gretel'! At least McGuinn can put that problem to rest for us: 'Actually, it's "Oh that's a little better". I never realized how difficult that line was to decipher'.

The most obvious difference that we discover upon listening to side two is the presence of David Crosby. He first appears singing harmony and playing on 'Change Is Now', one of the earliest cuts to be recorded for the album. The track also features Clarence White, appearing just prior to McGuinn's intriguing extended guitar solo. That supremely effective cymbal-crashing turns out to be the work of Michael Clarke, providing a final flourish before his departure. Once more, the lyrics are intriguing, celebrating a *carpe diem* philosophy, advising us to live life to the full. The underlying philosophical speculations ('that which is not real does not exist') are subtle enough to pass almost unnoticed and serve as an excellent example of the Byrds' concern to avoid overstatement. Much of 'Change Is Now' reflects the mood of the first side and contains many subtle echoes from 'Natural Harmony'. We are told to keep in 'harmony' with love's sweet plan, and the 'dancing through the streets side by side' of 'Natural Harmony' becomes an admonition to 'dance to the day when fear is gone'. It is no wonder that the album is so consistently described in terms of its 'total evocative experience'.

The mood of the album is constantly shifting, as we observe through the references to age, youth, childhood, death, laughter and tears in 'Old John Robertson', a song based on Hillman's memory of a childhood experience:

'I grew up in a small town of about 1,000 people (Rancho Santa Fe, San Diego County). There was an old man named John Robertson who retired there. He had been a movie director in the 20's. He wore a stetson hat and had this long, white handlebar moustache; quite an old cowboy character, but he was really nice to us kids.'

Like 'Wasn't Born To Follow', 'Old John Robertson' is broken up dramatically in the middle, this time by the intervention of orchestration. According to McGuinn, the song began as a country tune, until a harpsichord and baroque section entered the studio, played the break, and abruptly departed. Impressed by the unusual sound of the end product, the Byrds decided to allow the orchestration to remain. Although 'Old John Robertson' was essentially Hillman's composition, he did not contribute the bass-playing, which was the work of David Crosby:

'I played the bass on "Old John Robertson". What I did was a very simple thing. It was a picking pattern, an octave. It's the only time I ever played bass on anything. I wasn't any good at bass and the only time I could get away with it was on that particular tune, because it was suited to it. Also, Chris really wanted to play guitar. He was turning into a damn good guitar-player by that time. That's the main reason why I was allowed to do it.'

'Tribal Gathering' was primarily the work of Crosby, though Hillman also receives a composing credit. Like 'Renaissance Fair', the song evokes the atmosphere of a public event as though it were a dream-like experience, as McGuinn explained:

'"Tribal Gathering" was about the feeling that what we were witnessing was a strange gathering of tribes – the Hell's Angels, the hippies, the straight people and the police, all getting together for a musical event that made everybody feel wonderful. I think it was Monterey. I remember the cops had flowers in their antennae.'

Crosby corrects McGuinn and reveals that the song had nothing to do with Monterey:

'I wrote it entirely. It was about the first of the love-ins that I went to. It seemed like a tribal gathering to me. I liked it. It wasn't Monterey. It was a love-in in a park, somewhere in LA. It was called the Gathering of Tribes.'

Crosby's first song of the sea, 'Dolphin's Smile', concluded the many references to childhood, innocence and freedom that make up the main body of the album. This track gives us a final glimpse of the effectiveness of the Crosby/McGuinn partnership. With Crosby writing at his best, and Hillman contributing musical suggestions, McGuinn was free to develop the special effects:

'It was my idea to do the "be-de-lum" introduction. That was my fingernails on the neck of the Rickenbacker with a lot of echo. I was heavily involved in all the effects'. Crosby concluded that McGuinn should not have received a co-writing credit for the song: 'It was my idea, my music and my lyrics. I gave McGuinn half the credit to get it on a record. It was a political situation and very often I had to do that to get material recorded'.

The Sentinel, a short story by Arthur C. Clarke, on which he based the motion picture *2001: A Space Odyssey*, was the original inspiration for the Byrds' closing number. Although a long-time favourite of McGuinn's, the song is rather too monotonous to be of anything more than passing interest. The lyric is intriguing, however, with its speculation on the role of extra-terrestrial life in the evolution of man. Although it is generally accepted that one of the most important features of the album is the apparent musical continuity, McGuinn reveals that, like many great works, much of the ordering was fortuitous:

'It was purely accidental. We didn't plan it that way. It was natural. I think the only continuity occurred in the editing, the placement and the lead-in from one song to another. We sort of did it arbitrarily in about 35 seconds. Gary Usher said: "Let's work on that order". He took a piece of paper and he said, "Let's start off with 'Artificial Energy' and then end up with, um, 'Space Odyssey', OK?" And then he said, "Let's see, side one, what do you want to do? OK, the last cut on side one, 'Get To You'." Then he said, "Goin' Back", then he had it all like that. And I looked at it and said, "Man!" And I'm sure that he had no idea when he did it that it would come out the way it did. So it was a happy accident.'

At the time of the album's release, McGuinn revealed that he was disappointed with the finished product, and it was only in later years that he came to recognize the importance of the work. Along with *Younger Than Yesterday*, the album reveals the Byrds at the height of their creative powers, a fact which even McGuinn cannot dispute: 'Yes, I agree with you. I feel that was the best stage we ever reached'.

Crosby, while not denying that the 1967 period was the Byrds' finest, is a little more critical:

I thought *Younger Than Yesterday* was real good.'I thought *The Notorious Byrd Brothers* was considerably less good, and from there it went steadily downhill. I don't think it ever touched the stuff I did with them again'.

McGuinn maintains that *The Notorious Byrd Brothers* was essentially the work of himself and Chris Hillman, in collaboration with Gary Usher. Crosby, however, feels that such an opinion devalues his own contribution:

'That's dumb. I'm all over that album, they just didn't give me credit. I played , I sang, I wrote, I even played bass on one track, and they tried to make out that I wasn't even on it, that they could be that good without me. And that was bullshit because I was there. You can tell from the bitterness in my voice that it was a strongly emotional problem. It hurt me a lot. McGuinn used to do that stuff regularly. He wanted to stay on top. He wanted to be the boss of that band. And I don't really allow anyone to be my boss. I won't have any bosses. I have partners, but nobody is my boss, ever.'

Crosby's final comments on the situation provide us with an interesting question about the respective merits of the individual members of the Byrds:

'Do you understand what happened? Excuse me for being angry, but it was unjust what did happen. They didn't mean to do it. They didn't consciously set out to fuck me over and they're OK guys. I don't hate them. But it hurt, and it was so frustrating that you couldn't believe it. I was writing good stuff and I wasn't getting credit for it, and I was doing good work and I wasn't getting allowed to grow. And I was growing. Look what happened next. What did they do next, man. Compare them. What's the lasting worth of what they did next, in comparison to what I did next?'

One cannot help wondering what might have been achieved had Crosby remained or had Gene Clark not been forced to leave after only three weeks. Perhaps the quality of the album is a reflection of the tensions and pressures that forced McGuinn and Hillman to extend their creative abilities to even greater heights. On the other hand, it is quite conceivable that an album of greater stature than *The Notorious Byrd Brothers* might have been achieved if the final breakdown towards the end of 1967 had been temporarily averted.

13
Gram Parsons – The Struggle For Supremacy

Following the success of *The Notorious Byrd Brothers*, the Byrds began touring as a trio. It was a gratifying period, for they had begun playing the college circuit for the first time. Crosby had always been against the idea because it seemed to conflict with his philosophy that rock should not be intellectualized. Although the gigs were reasonably successful, it was clear that a trio would be insufficient to realize the Byrds' musical ambitions, so the group began to consider introducing a fourth member. In deciding upon the right person, much thought would have to go into the subject of where the Byrds' music was to progress after the stupendous *The Notorious Byrd Brothers*. Always ambitious, McGuinn felt that they should either develop their electronic concepts, or perhaps continue the jazz rock dream begun on 'Eight Miles High'. By this time, McGuinn had finally come to accept that the Byrds were no longer a singles group and he saw their future primarily as an albums band. Always receptive to new ideas, and a well known jazz buff himself, Hillman had no cause to disagree with McGuinn's latest ambitions. In order to pursue his purpose, Roger decided that the group would need a keyboard player.

While the Byrds were considering their musical future, their business manager had recently discovered a new talent known as Gram Parsons. Parsons was well known in Los Angeles as a group singer and songwriter, and had recently seen one of his songs, 'November Night', recorded as a single by Peter Fonda. Gram had gained considerable regional acclaim during the early 60's playing in a folk group known as the Shilos. He moved closer to the rock scene with the formation of the International Submarine Band at Harvard in 1965. Having issued two unsuccessful singles, 'The Russians Are Coming' and 'Truck Driving Man', in 1966, his group moved to Lee Hazelwood's LHI label and released what is generally regarded as the first country rock album, *Safe At Home*, towards the end of 1967. Following the commercial failure of the album, the group had degenerated into a bunch of jamming musicians loosely known as the Flying Burrito Brothers. While playing the bars of Southern California, in early 1968, Gram had crossed paths with enough influential people to become a candidate for the vacant position in the Byrds. He even remembered appearing at an early session for *The Notorious Byrd Brothers* at which, he claimed, the Byrds considered titling the album, *The Flying Burrito Brothers*.

Still intent on projecting the Byrds into the area of future electronics and jazz, McGuinn, while ignoring Parsons' other qualities, hired him on the strength of his keyboard abilities: 'When I hired Gram Parsons, it was as a jazz pianist. I had no idea that he was a Hank Williams character. He pretended to be a jazz player too'.

The recruiting of Parsons to the group, in March, was to result in drastic changes to the Byrds' musical policy. Firstly, Hillman was lured away from McGuinn's jazz dream when he discovered Parsons' irresistible enthusiasm to play country music. Singing along with Gram on tunes he had himself played during his period with the Hillmen, Chris became convinced that Parsons' dream of a country Byrds was feasible. The problem lay in persuading McGuinn to take the country route which would, presumably, mean sacrificing his twin dream of the electronic-jazz Byrds. While Roger, with his folk background, would be capable of functioning in a country-orientated band, there seemed little likelihood that he would agree to such a fundamental change of his professed musical direction. Unbelievably, however, McGuinn not only agreed to the idea but seemed fully to support it, and within a couple of weeks the Byrds' set was interspersed with old and new country tunes. McGuinn had not surrendered his ambition, however, but had merely substituted one dream for another. Country, folk, jazz, electronic music, they were all contained within McGuinn's scheme of things. It now occurred to him that even jazz and electronics were no longer adequate. What he desired was an even greater challenge and, unwittingly, Parsons had brought it to his attention. McGuinn now conceived of a gargantuan concept which was so immense that it would indisputably elevate the Byrds to a level alongside the Beatles as the world's most innovative rock group. McGuinn's concept was a veritable history of twentieth-century music, beginning with traditional country and ending with the most advanced form of electronic wizardry. Even today, McGuinn remembers the project with a glint in his eye: 'It was going to be a chronological thing. Like old-time bluegrass, modern country music, rock 'n' roll, then space music. It was meant to be a five-stage chronology.' It is difficult to imagine Parsons ever accepting the notion of 'space music' but , at the time, McGuinn spoke as if he had the full consent of the other members. They planned to cut 25 or 30 tracks in the spring and a final selection would be made, culminating in a double album which would be in the shops by early summer.

While McGuinn continued to dream and formulate vague plans for executing his grand design, Parsons was gradually asserting his own independence. Within a couple of weeks, the Byrds were performing with a mystery steel guitarist, cryptically referred to as 'J.D.' This was, in fact, Jay Dee Manness, one of the session musicians who had assisted in the recording of the International Submarine Band's *Safe At Home*. One of the first gigs featuring the quintet took place at Derek Taylor's farewell party, in mid-March. Rather fittingly, Taylor had chosen Ciro's, the venue at which the Byrds first received critical acclaim, as the site for his final night in Hollywood. It was a unique gathering of friends, old and new, and among the guests were many of the dance troupe who had religiously followed the Byrds back in 1965. When their time came to take the stage, the Byrds delighted the audience by combining their country 'n' western style numbers with a series of hits from their illustrious past, including 'Chimes Of Freedom', 'Mr Tambourine Man', 'Eight Miles High' and 'He Was A Friend Of Mine'. During the festivities, they were joined onstage by Gene Clark but it was not exactly a glorious reunion, as Derek Taylor remembers: 'Gene was drunk. He sang a few songs with them but stayed up there too long. There was mild irritation. The Byrds never really got on. They were always marvellously dangerous.'

Jim Seiter vividly recalled Gene's exit:

'He fell flat on his back at my feet. I was standing behind the amps. McGuinn's old lady was tugging on him, trying to get him offstage. Then she lost hold of him. He slipped, fell backwards, fell over an amplifier and his head hit hard on the stage at my feet. And I looked up at him and the look in his eyes was incredible. He jumped up, almost superhumanly, and he ran off the stage , straight through the people and gone. We didn't see him for months after that. It was terrible. He did that many times. Gene's whole life got shattered when he left the group. All of a sudden he was walking around Hollywood and he wasn't a Byrd anymore. That hit him hard, man. He came to many gigs, drunk as a skunk. He was just a mess and I had to deal with him and keep him away from the band when they were onstage, because he'd try and get up there.'

Throughout April, McGuinn was continually pressurized by Parsons to accept Jay Dee Manness as a permanent member. McGuinn held out, however, and refused to acknowledge Manness as anything other than a 'temporary' Byrd, at least for the present. While Roger's plans to record the electronic part of the double album were still unfulfilled, the country section was progressing in leaps and bounds. Parsons even managed to persuade the Byrds to leave Los Angeles and record over half of the album in Nashville. By this time, several of Parsons' former side-men began appearing at the sessions, including Jon Corneal and Earl P. Ball. It was also rumoured that Parsons had taken over lead vocal from McGuinn on virtually all the cuts. Between sessions, the Byrds amazed and confused their followers back in LA by performing at the Grand Old Opry before a staunch redneck audience. It was here that Parsons' overwhelming influence was most visually apparent, for both Hillman and McGuinn were sporting new, short haircuts. McGuinn had even shaved his moustache, and appeared unimaginably conservative. If the Byrds were attempting to win a new country following, however, their efforts proved unsuccessful, for the partisan Nashville audience were unlikely to accept the idea of Los Angeles hippies playing their music.

Undaunted, the Byrds swiftly arranged a visit to Europe, in order to demonstrate their new sound to a more appreciative audience. Having failed to recruit Manness as a Byrd, Parsons now recommended another steel player, Sneaky Pete Kleinow. Hillman also supported Kleinow, and McGuinn suddenly found himself under tremendous pressure from all sides. Even Crosby had never challenged his leadership so effectively, and though McGuinn still wished to control the musical direction of the Byrds, his influence was almost non-existent:

'Gram and Chris took over at that stage of the game. They really brought it into the country thing. That wasn't my idea but I went along with it because it sounded fun. It was totally their trip. They actually wanted to fire me and get Sneaky Pete in my place. In essence, they later did this by getting the Flying Burrito Brothers together.'

The European tour served as a respite from the power struggle and allowed McGuinn to demonstrate the importance of his role in the new line-up. Kleinow was unable to tour with the group so his status as a Byrd remained unclear. However, banjoist Doug Dillard was invited along as a guest in order that the country tunes would sound sufficiently authentic.

A new single, 'You Ain't Going Nowhere', was released to coincide with the tour, and it did no damage to McGuinn's reputation. It was very much in the old Byrds tradition, being an unreleased Dylan song and featuring McGuinn on lead vocal. Parsons' influence was minimal and it appeared that McGuinn was very much in control of proceedings. The interviewers of the time flocked to McGuinn and Hillman for comments on the 'new' Byrds, and Parsons suddenly discovered that his domination of the group was far from complete. McGuinn spoke frankly to the press, providing them with such shock revelations as the fact that he was the only Byrd to have played on the million-selling 'Mr Tambourine Man'. In this way, McGuinn asserted his importance as the man who had formulated the group's sound, and nobody could doubt that he was still King Byrd. The concerts also boosted McGuinn's confidence, as the Italian and British fans warmed to the old hits, while politely acknowledging the new country numbers. The Byrds included a variety of songs from every one of their previous albums and, in this way, asserted their historical importance. Parsons' influence once more seemed merely relative, for the gigs had effectively demonstrated that Roger McGuinn was the Byrds. While in England, the group were entertained by Mick Jagger, who showed some concern about McGuinn's plan to tour South Africa during the early summer. McGuinn was undaunted, however, and had already convinced the other Byrds that it would be an interesting experience: 'It was to be an experiment. I'd known Miriam Makeba, who'd grown up there and was aware of the situation. I wanted to see it for myself'. Following their lightning visit to Europe, the Byrds returned to California, promising to return to London, Rome and Majorca in the early summer.

In spite of McGuinn's effective assertion of independence, it was clear that Parsons still controlled the Byrds in the studio. Although McGuinn once more stressed his desire to record a double album, with country and electronic music, the plan was totally dismissed:

'We split into two different camps at that stage and the country thing won. Chris, Gram and Gary Usher just didn't want to go along with the electronic music idea, so I was outvoted'.

Accepting the decision for the moment, McGuinn contented himself with the realization that country music was at least a healthy reaction against the spate of psychedelic groups that had followed in the wake of the Byrds. The Byrds had pioneered jazz rock, raga rock and psychedelia, so it would be fitting that they should be the first to react to the overkill. Once the country album had been completed, McGuinn felt that the quartet would be ready and willing to move into the field of electronic music. For the present, McGuinn committed himself to Parsons' professed project.

While it seemed that Parsons had succeeded in recording a complete album of his own, under the guise of the Byrds, his fortunes suddenly reversed when Columbia threatened to undo all his work. Apparently, Parsons' release from the LHI label was not legal, for he still had contractual obligations. Rather than being the recipients of a law suit from Lee Hazelwood, Columbia Records insisted that the completed album be re-recorded. According to Terry Melcher, Gram became paranoid when McGuinn announced that all the lead vocal work was to be erased:

'Parsons got really mad because Roger told him CBS insisted on that, but he didn't believe it. He thought it was Roger's own idea. But Parsons had a lot of things in life distorted. He and McGuinn were not friends for a while because of this.'

According to Parsons, Columbia took complete control and began to overdub and delete all his contributions. Meanwhile, McGuinn had begun re-recording some of the songs, and actually imitated Parsons' voice in an attempt to maintain the country effect. By the time Gram's release had been confirmed, only 'Hickory Wind' remained in its original state. Columbia further complicated matters by arbitrarily inserting some cuts from an earlier warm-up session, on which Parsons' lead vocal was included. According to Gram, these cuts, including 'Life In Prison' and 'You're Still On My Mind', were never intended for inclusion on the album and, if they had been, the recordings would have been taken more seriously.

With extensive tour commitments looming, and pressure from Columbia to complete the record, there was no time to re-record the album. While Parsons was upset, McGuinn was less concerned about the state of the overdubbed album, especially as it now included some of his lead vocal work. Parsons was further disappointed by McGuinn's continued reluctance to enlist a permanent steel guitarist. Sneaky Pete appeared with the Byrds on several dates throughout June, but it was clear that he was no closer to becoming a full-time member of the group. In addition, Gram had become alienated from Chris, to a certain degree, due to his excessive ego. During the later stages of his attempt to gain domination of the Byrds, Parsons began to push for a higher salary, and at one point actually demanded individual billing. It was these excessive demands which lost him the full support of Hillman during the struggle for power. For a short time, Parsons had all but ousted McGuinn as leader but, at the last, his supremacy was severely qualified.

The Byrds returned to England in July and played a charity concert, along with seven other artistes, at the Royal Albert Hall. The Byrds closed the first half of the evening, and the Move, who were joint bill-toppers, were the last act to appear. It was the Byrds, however, who stole the headlines, and it was evident from the cry 'bring back the Byrds' throughout the second half of the show that they were the real stars of the evening. Commencing with a stunning 'So You Want To Be A Rock 'n' Roll Star', the group moved through a series of hits and country songs and astounded the star-studded audience with an excellent version of 'Eight Miles High'. The following day, the Byrds prepared to leave for their extensive tour of South Africa. As the bags were being removed from the hotel, Gram informed Roger that he would not be accompanying the Byrds on tour. After less than five months, the Parsons domination of the Byrds had ended with the most dramatic of exits.

14
The Great South African Disaster And Its Aftermath

Although the suddenness of Gram's departure was a shock, McGuinn appeared unconcerned. By contrast, Chris Hillman was extremely angry and frustrated, and vented his feelings to the press, denouncing Parsons as a sensation-seeking egotist. Parsons' reasons for leaving the Byrds seemed suspect. The official explanation for Gram's refusal to tour South Africa centred on his bitter opposition to the apartheid laws. Yet, less than two months before, Gram had agreed to the proposed tour. What appears to have happened is that, following the announcement of the tour, Gram began to conduct his own investigation of the South African situation and was duly horrified by the racist policies. His abrupt and calculated departure, however, seemed designed to give him maximum publicity and, apart from his racial conscience, it seems safe to assume that his many other squabbles with the Byrds played an equally important part in formulating his final decision. Parsons had recently become fascinated with the Rolling Stones and was, no doubt, heavily influenced by Mick Jagger, who had already voiced his objection to the tour.

Although they were ill-equipped to compensate for the loss of Parsons, the Byrds decided to continue with the tour schedule and boarded the plane to South Africa. It was a disastrous decision. McGuinn persuaded the Byrds' roadie, Carlos Bernal, to play rhythm guitar, and the unit were reduced to such absurdities as rehearsing their repertoire for the first time during the flight to Johannesburg. With Bernal masquerading as Parsons, the Byrds struggled through a gruelling series of concerts and during those ten days gave what were probably the most unprofessional performances of their entire career. Bernal recalled the chaotic schedule:

'Roger asked me if I could do the tour so I said, "Sure, if you could run down some of the things for me". We had 16 or 17 concerts throughout South Africa. We hired another fellow to take care of the sound, and I'd take care of all the gear at the concert before the show, dash back to the hotel and bring everybody, and then change into Gram. Then, after awhile, I changed into a combination of him and me, and then I finally became just me, at our last gigs in Rhodesia.'

The Byrds could hardly have expected a rougher passage and, in retrospect, it seems remarkable that the tour was even undertaken. Chris Hillman remembered one night when the pressure apparently became too much for his partner:

'We got to the third song and Roger said, "I got to get out of here!" and literally runs off the stage. It was a full house, and there's me having to take leads on the bass. He left me hanging in South Africa with a bunch of angry Afrikaaners. Jesus Christ! That was a dumb tour to begin with. We should never have gone.'

McGuinn provides a more accurate account of the reasons for his apparent breakdown:

'I did have a nervous reaction, it's true. For the whole tour I had a 102 temperature. We were under a lot of pressure because of the political statements we'd been making about apartheid. The people were against us and there was blatant hatred emanating from the audience. I'm very sensitive, but I didn't desert under fire. I was very polite about the whole thing. I walked up to the microphone and said: "Ladies and Gentlemen, I've a touch of influenza and if you'd excuse me for 10 minutes we'll be back". We retired to the dressing room. I'd been trying to kick cigarettes at the time, so I had a cigarette, then recovered, went back onstage and finished the set. I didn't just run off leaving them onstage. That was an untrue accusation by Chris Hillman. I've had similar feelings to that since then and I haven't left the stage, but just gone right through. I've learned to cope with that feeling of nervousness. It happens now and again for no apparent reason. It's like stage fright. It gets so intense you think you're going to die. You can't feel your hands, but you have to keep going and I've learned to function as though my body were a spaceship and I was the pilot. I think I've learned my lesson and can deal with that phenomenon.'

While newspaper reports indicate that this particular audience was a little more sympathetic than Roger suggests, his account of the general reaction seems accurate enough. It was the Byrds' attitude to South

Africa, however, which caused most of the publicity and bitter antagonism. Exaggerating some of their statements, the newspapers were running headlines such as 'Byrds Say South Africa Is Sick, Backwards And Rude'. As a result, the Byrds were heckled at some shows. McGuinn became the victim of several abusive telephone calls, while Hillman even received an assassination threat.

Apart from the musical deficiencies and the controversial press reports, the Byrds were also the victim of financial exploitation. To make matters worse, false rumours were spread that the group were certified drug addicts. This fabrication, claims McGuinn, was corroborated by false statements from hotel bell boys, who had been bribed. Even the terms of their contract had been altered so that they were forced to play before segregated audiences until their arrival in Rhodesia at the end of the tour. Defeated, exhausted and morose, the Byrds returned to California and rested for a few days before making a scheduled appearance at the Newport Pop Festival towards the end of July. Many fans were surprised to discover that a replacement had already been found for Gram Parsons in the form of a country guitarist and banjoist named Clarence J. White.

While the induction of White suggested that the Byrds were stabilizing themselves once more, this was not the entire truth. Following the South Africa fiasco, Chris Hillman had become increasingly disenchanted with the Byrds and was seeking employment elsewhere. Although Hillman had severely criticized Gram Parsons for leaving the Byrds in the face of disaster, the two musicians quickly reconciled their differences following Chris' return to California. Informally, Chris and Gram continued to discuss the possibility of forming a group called the Flying Burrito Brothers. Apparently, this idea had been a serious consideration even before Gram Parsons had left the Byrds and, according to drummer Gene Parsons, he and Clarence White were initially invited to join the fledgling Flying Burrito Brothers. The discussions about this new group had actually led to some serious recording and, financed by Eddie Tickner, three tunes were cut by a line-up comprising Chris Hillman, Gram Parsons, Clarence White and Gene Parsons. Gene remembers Clarence choosing between the Byrds and the Burritos:

'The group was a prototype Burritos. Chris had asked Clarence to join the Byrds temporarily and later become a Burrito, but Clarence decided to stay with the Byrds because he felt it would be a safer bet.'

While White had committed himself to the Byrds, it was clear that Chris Hillman's departure was not far away.

Clarence White was, of course, the obvious choice as successor to Gram, since he had already played on both *Younger Than Yesterday* and *The Notorious Byrd Brothers*. As a session musician, White was well respected and as a player his experience was vast. White had begun playing professionally, with his father and brothers, atthe age of 10, in a group known as the Country Boys, which later metamorphosed into possibly the finest urban bluegrass band of the 60's, the Kentucky Colonels. Coincidentally, White had been approached in 1964 by Byrds manager, Jim Dickson, with a view to recording an electric version of 'Mr Tambourine Man', a demo of which Dickson had recently received. Unfortunately, White could convince nobody of the validity of electric folk rock and so he missed the opportunity of pioneering a new musical form. Clarence's desire to play electric folk music resulted in his departure from the Kentucky Colonels in 1965 and a move into the lucrative world of session work. Having established his reputation working with acts as diverse as Pat Boone, Ricky Nelson, and the Monkees, White eventually met up with Gene Parsons, Gib Guilbeau and Wayne Moore and formed the country rock group Nashville West in 1966. Parsons and Guilbeau had previously attained local popularity as Cajun Gib and Gene and, originally, the Castaways. Although satisfied with Nashville West, White could hardly resist the challenge of joining a group with the reputation of the Byrds. McGuinn gave his full support to White, recognizing his ability as a player and aware that he was a less dominant personality than Gram Parsons.

In August, *Sweetheart Of The Rodeo* finally received its American release and met with a reasonable reception from the critics. It was such a drastic change from their previous album, however, that some fans were disturbed. Evaluating the importance of the album is made doubly difficult by the erratic quality of the work, no doubt due to the many overdubs and re-recordings.

'You Ain't Going Nowhere' (already issued as a single) was probably the most Byrdsy sounding track on the album, mainly due to McGuinn's Dylanesque vocal and the familiar harmonies. The steel guitar work is exceptional, blending perfectly with McGuinn's Rickenbacker and providing a country feel which is subtle but not pervasive. McGuinn took some poetic licence with the song, altering the lyric from 'pick up your money, pack up your tent' to 'pack up your money, pick up your tent'. Annoyed by McGuinn's presumptuousness in interfering with his work, Dylan exclaimed in a later version of the song: 'McGuinn, you ain't going nowhere'.

'I Am A Pilgrim', arranged by Hillman and McGuinn, and featuring the former on lead vocal, was the group's first straight country 'n' western outing. There are no complementary rock instruments to be heard, simply McGuinn on banjo and John Hartford on fiddle. At the time, it seemed rather strange to hear the Byrds singing a religious song, even though they had used biblical imagery previously on 'Turn! Turn! Turn!'. For Hillman, the song was an excellent opportunity to re-live his past: 'It was my idea to do "I Am A Pilgrim". I used to play that song with Clarence White during the bluegrass days'.

'The Christian Life' continued to stress the religious theme, and to hear the Byrds celebrating the virtues of godliness seemed, to many listeners, almost ironic. This was one of the tracks that had to be re-recorded with McGuinn replacing Parsons on lead vocal. Roger clearly attempts to imitate Parsons' vocal style and the entire effect is bizarre. What is, presumably, meant to be a serious song, in celebration of the Christian faith, comes across as unintentionally parodic, with McGuinn sounding as though he is mimicking rather than imitating Parsons' vocal phrasing.

On William Bell's 'You Don't Miss Your Water', McGuinn reverts to his familiar vocal style, which is juxtaposed alongside the sound of a steel guitar and Earl P. Ball's honky tonk piano. The harmonies are well executed and the slowed-down ending gives the song an authentic, countrified conclusion.

'You're Still On My Mind' was one of the songs that Columbia retrieved from an earlier session and, thus, it should be stressed that this was not originally intended for inclusion on *Sweetheart Of The Rodeo*. Gram's Southern drawl is well-suited to the sentiments of this song, which reflects the country 'n' western obsession with the melancholic alcoholic and his lost love.

'Pretty Boy Floyd' ends side one on a high note, with the return of the bass guitar, even though it may be Roy Huskey rather than Chris Hillman. Much credit should be given to John Hartford, who played the exceptional banjo and fiddle parts. Hillman's mandolin fuses effectively with the other instruments to create a powerful backing for McGuinn's deliberate folky vocal style on this Woody Guthrie classic.

'Hickory Wind' represents one of Parsons' finest recordings and reveals how stupendous this album would have been if more care had been taken over the track selection. As it is, we are fortunate that this excellent vocal performance was saved from imminent erasure, as Parsons recalled: 'They were just about to scrap the last one of mine that they'd saved, "Hickory Wind", when the lawyer came in waving the piece of paper confirming my release.'

'One Hundred Years From Now', with its noticeable percussion, seems closer to country rock than the more traditional numbers on the album. The harmonies, which were substituted for Parsons' solo lead vocal, work very well and the song remains an interesting example of Gram's pre-Burrito style.

'Blue Canadian Rockies', which does feature Parsons on lead vocal, would seem to be merely another warm-up song that was included at the last minute, yet there is good reason for suspecting otherwise. The arrangement and execution are both precise and confident, and it is difficult to imagine the Byrds coming up with something quite as good as this at the rehearsal stage. Certainly, the song is enough to make us ponder upon Parsons' testimony that, of all his vocal contributions, only 'Hickory Wind' remained in its original pristine state.

'Life In Prison', in spite of its intriguing introduction, was definitely a warm-up number and Parsons was bitterly disappointed that the group did not record a more competent version. The mystery surrounding the re-recording of *Sweetheart Of The Rodeo* will probably never be resolved to everybody's satisfaction. Some commentators, possibly confused by the many vague and complicated accounts of deleted tracks and re-recordings, have hinted that two tapes of several songs were in existence simultaneously at one point and instructions were issued to use Parsons' vocals. However, Parsons himself never claimed this to be the case, even though his criticisms of the album were well documented. What does seem doubly odd is that if the material included was not quite what they originally intended, why did they not choose to include several of the other songs recorded at the sessions, including 'Reputation', 'Lazy Days' and 'Pretty Polly'? All these recordings are still available in the Columbia vaults so perhaps one day we will sample the remaining fragments of the *Sweetheart* experiment.

The closing cut on the album, 'Nothing Was Delivered', was a surprise highlight with a brilliant vocal from McGuinn in his best Dylan imitation voice. Hillman recalls the Byrds specifically selecting unreleased material from their immemorial mentor: 'Roger and I had access to Dylan's tapes through Columbia and we chose "Nothing Was Delivered" and "You Ain't Going Nowhere" as the most appropriate songs for the album'.

In conclusion, we can see that the real problem with *Sweetheart Of The Rodeo* was that a handful of tracks were simply too traditional and hastily recorded to be totally convincing. Much of the album was not, as many have termed it, 'country rock', but rather far closer to traditional country 'n' western. Although there are some exceptionally strong cuts which stand alongside the Byrds' best work, especially 'You Ain't Going Nowhere', 'Pretty Boy Floyd', 'Hickory Wind' and 'nothing Was Delivered', these are marginally outweighed by some weaker cuts. Had the album not been tampered with, or had it been improved upon, then the Byrds might have released an album as impressive in its way as *Younger Than Yesterday* and *The Notorious Byrd Brothers*. As it stands, the album is a flawed meisterwerk, weakened by those warm-up songs which lack the necessary punch. One need only compare them to some of the cuts on the Flying Burrito Brothers' debut *The Gilded Palace Of Sin* to see what might have been achieved. While the rock audience finally caught up with the Byrds on *The Notorious Byrd Brothers*, the rift was created once more by the sudden shift in musical policy on this album.

For those who clung to McGuinn's ambition to extend the electronic dream begun on *The Notorious Byrd Brothers*, the country excursion was a completely unexpected trip. For the discerning listener, the album was probably both a shock and a pleasant surprise. It may not have been what they expected but it was gratifying to see the Byrds refusing to rest on their laurels. *Sweetheart Of The Rodeo*, released a full year ahead of Dylan's celebrated *Nashville Skyline*, was a healthy reaction against the excesses of psychedelia and spearheaded the interest in country rock which was to grow to suffocating levels during the mid-70's. It was probably the bravest move that the Byrds made in their entire career, risking everything in order to pursue a new musical goal. It effectively demonstrated how consistently ahead of their time the Byrds were and earned them that distinctive tag, 'always beyond today'.

Exhausted after the South African debacle, McGuinn went through a period of apparent apathy. Meanwhile, the Byrds' integrity had been seriously questioned in the liberal press because of their decision to tour South Africa. The English Musicians' Union had taken a stand and banned the Byrds from appearing in Britain in the future. Fortunately, that problem was resolved when reports began to filter through of the Byrds' controversial and derogatory remarks about the apartheid policies. In America, however, the press was less sympathetic, and in subsequent interviews McGuinn was always careful to exaggerate the reasons for the tour, even referring to it as a 'sacrificial missionary trip'. There may be much truth in these verbal defences, but the facts suggest that Roger's original motivation was simply curiosity, and that seemed an inadequate apology after the incident became blown into a full scale issue.

McGuinn contented himself briefly with the deceptively promising sales returns of *Sweetheart Of The Rodeo*. Soon, however, it became evident that the album was selling less copies than any previous Byrds record. At least Roger had a stable group and was free from the domineering tendencies of Gram Parsons; or was he? Within weeks, White began to criticize the drumming of Kevin Kelley, arguing that it was not suited to his style. At the same time, Clarence began to urge Chris and Roger to replace Kelley with Gene Parsons, who had recently dissolved Nashville West. In essence, White's motives were not far removed from those of Gram Parsons. As a renowned session musician, White could certainly have adapted to any style of playing, including the unorthodox drumming of Kelley. Like Gram Parsons, however, White was anxious to bring his former aides into the Byrds. Unknown to Kelley, Gene was auditioned and the drummers compared. Gene Parsons recalls the circumstances surrounding his introduction to the group:

'Clarence convinced them that they needed me. Kevin was Chris' cousin and he was not happy with him. I think they were looking for a heavier drummer. They auditioned me and had me play the same tunes as Kevin so that they could compare us. Strangely enough, I thought Kevin was a really good drummer. His work on *Sweetheart Of The Rodeo* was really good.'

Jim Seiter supports Parsons' contention that Hillman was also dissatisfied with his cousin's role in the group:

'You make a mistake when you play with relatives. Kevin was always treated as an outsider because he was Chris' cousin. Instead of dealing with Kevin directly, the other members of the band would complain to Chris. So Chris resented having that responsibility. They used an excuse that Kevin had got busted for something, but I think it was his playing that was the problem. He wasn't a rock drummer, he was more into jazz and country. On stage, he'd never start a song the same way twice. Every time they started "So You Want To Be A Rock 'n' Roll Star", Chris would look at me, as if to say, "What's he going to do this time?" The tempo and rhythm pattern would be totally different.'

Encouraged by White and Hillman, McGuinn lent his support to the new drummer and Chris was given the unenviable task of informing his cousin that he was no longer a member of the Byrds. Kevin left the Byrds with dignity but, sadly, never managed to aspire to any great heights in his subsequent musical career.

The new line-up of McGuinn, Hillman, White and Gene Parsons lasted less than a month, however, for in October, Chris Hillman departed in dramatic fashion. Roger's recent apathy concerning the state of the Byrds had become even more evident in his attitude towards the group's financial situation. By this time, Hillman and McGuinn had acquired joint ownership of the Byrds, while Parsons and White were paid a weekly salary. The two original Byrds each had $50,000 in their bank accounts but, as they had signed contracts naming Larry Spector as their legal representative, he effectively had power of attorney, which enabled him to withdraw their money at will. While Spector spoke of bills and expenses, McGuinn discovered that their bank balances had dwindled to $20,000. All the transactions were, it should be stressed, perfectly legal and valid under the terms of the contract they had signed.

It was at this point that Hillman could take no more. Prior to a gig, he erupted in a violent outrage and pinned Spector against the wall of their dressing room. Realizing the futility of threatening behaviour, Chris announced that this was his last night as a Byrd and, raising his prized Fender above his head, he smashed it against the dressing room wall. For Gene Parsons, it was not a very pleasant introduction to the Byrds: 'The first time I played was the night Chris quit. He left just before we were to go on. Shortly afterwards, we had a gig booked for Salt Lake City and were really hard pushed to find a bass player'.

THE GREAT SOUTH AFRICAN DISASTER

McGuinn remained characteristically cool in the crisis and argued that Chris' tantrum would be resolved in a matter of days. Hillman failed to return, however, but took the remainder of his money and bought some land in New Mexico, after which he resurfaced to form the Flying Burrito Brothers. Within a year, Spector decided to quit the management business. According to Dickson, Hillman was so bitter about the final days of the Byrds that he poured those feelings into that apocalyptical vision of Los Angeles, 'Sin City'. The line 'On the 31st floor a gold plated door won't keep out the Lord's burning rain' was allegedly inspired by the location of Larry Spector's office on Brighton Way, Beverly Hills.

While Spector's handling of the Byrds' financial affairs has been severely criticized by almost everybody connected with the group, Ed Tickner reminds us that this was a period when desperate measures were required:

'The game was pretty much over. It'd all fallen apart. In order for it to work with anybody, it had to be put together piece by piece. That means taking the Porsches and the houses on the hill away from everybody, and going back to Rice Krispies and hamburgers.'

Fortunately, Chris was immediately replaced by bassist John York, a former member of the Sir Douglas Quintet who had toured with the Mamas and the Papas and worked on sessions with Johnny Rivers. For York, it was a second chance to become a Byrd:

I was visited by Lawrence Spector, who was a friend of mine, and he asked me to join the group. I first met Lawrence a year earlier while playing some gigs with Gene Clark. I think he was managing Gene. He had approached me then because David Crosby had just left, but I said "no" to the offer. I'd hitchhiked out to New York and was flown back to join the Byrds. There was no audition because Clarence and I had already played together in that group with Gene Clark.'

York's arrival received little or no publicity, however, and the majority of the music press appeared to believe that the Byrds had folded following Hillman's departure. By the end of November, a confusing report reached Britain revealing that Roger McGuinn was the only surviving member of the group adding, somewhat cryptically, that the Byrds were now the Byrd. Amid the confusion, many depressed fans went through their second consecutive Christmas believing that the Byrds were dead.

15
A Period Of Reconstruction

The early months of 1969 saw the remnants of the Byrds coming to terms with their past. David Crosby was busy working on the first Crosby, Stills & Nash album; Hillman and Parsons were working on the celebrated *The Gilded Palace Of Sin*; Gene Clark was forging ahead with the memorable *Fantastic Expedition Of Dillard And Clark* and Michael Clarke was preparing to tour with the Expedition and would soon reunite with Chris as a Flying Burrito Brother. Meanwhile, McGuinn was desperately attempting to keep the Byrds together and effectively starting from scratch. He soon discovered how far the group had fallen from public favour. The once undisputed bill toppers were now playing second or third support to a host of mediocre, flash-in-the-pan nonentities. Even when the Byrds managed to headline a show, their profits were invariably low, and the lack of a successful album meant that they had to travel in order to maintain their existence. Close to bankruptcy, with money owing to the airlines, the Byrds were forced to accept bookings that they would not normally have considered. On one occasion, the Byrds found themselves in deepest Mexico, but even here all was far from well. They were booked to play on the bill of a rock concert at the Sports City Stadium before a sizeable audience of 42,000 people, but following some crowd disturbance, the event degenerated into a full-scale riot. Bravely, the Byrds completed their scheduled 10 song set amid a barrage of flying bottles and broken chairs. While desperately fighting their way back to the dressing room, the Byrds almost fell victim to the mania of souvenir-seeking rioters. McGuinn remembers the 'highlights' of the concert:

'We were surrounded by rioting people breaking up wooden chairs and slamming me over the head with them, and trying to strangle me with my guitar. They did manage to rip off our briefcase with our passports and all the money we'd made. Wonderful!'

While the Byrds were encountering problems restoring their reputation as a live act, work continued on their new album. Following Chris' departure, McGuinn had decided to pursue the electronic dream, but he soon realized that the desire was his alone:

'It was just a concept of mine. I did manage to record it after *Sweetheart Of The Rodeo*. I cut a number of hours of electronic stuff, but I didn't feel that the quality was sufficient to release it. It's still on tape though.'

Apart from the lack of support from his fellow Byrds, McGuinn was frustrated by his own ability to produce a worthwhile product:

'I couldn't really pursue the electronic thing on our next album because I hadn't mastered the keyboard. I didn't get my synthesizer until late 1968. I'd never been a keyboard player and they hadn't come up with a realistic neck that worked for the synthesizer. Ultimately, I think it would have been a Roger McGuinn album rather than a group work. It would have come out like Paul Beaver or Walter Carlos, one of those things.'

Abandoning his dream, McGuinn contented himself with the notion that the next Byrds album would be a mixture of country and electric rock music. At the end of February, a single, 'Bad Night At The Whiskey', co-written by Joey Richards, whom Roger had known through his association with Subud, remains of the great neglected Byrds songs. The title of the song seemed totally unrelated to the lyrics in the same way as Dylan's 'Positively 4th Street' and 'Rainy Day Women #'s 12 and 35'. According to Roger, Richards had first suggested writing lyrics to a McGuinn melody following a less than auspicious Byrds gig at the Whisky on Sunset Strip. When it came to decide upon a title they immediately associated the two incidents and 'Bad Night At The Whiskey' was born. Musically, the song suggested that the Byrds might be moving towards a heavier, more intricate, guitar sound but the idea was undeveloped. The contrasting flip-side, 'Drug Store Truck Driving Man', was equally intriguing, outshining many of the tracks on *Sweetheart Of The Rodeo*. Co-written with Gram Parsons in London, just prior to the South African disaster, it was a satiric riposte to the Nashville audience who had rejected the Byrds. More specifically, the song was directed against Ralph ('This one's for you') Emery, the country music disc jockey who had denounced the Byrds as hippies on his radio show. Between record plays and right-wing comments about the Byrds, Ralph would announce commercials for various items such as truck components, and it was from this that McGuinn developed the image of the drug store truck driving man who was so reactionary that he might as well be the head of the Ku Klux Klan. The lyrics were undoubtedly the wittiest that the Byrds had ever produced. Musically, the song was equally flawless, with a striking steel guitar by Lloyd Green and some excellent harmonies. Very much in the Byrds traditon of 'You Ain't Going Nowhere', this song showed that the group were the true precursors of country rock.

The new album, *Dr Byrds And Mr Hyde*, released some weeks later, lacked the consistent excellence of the single cuts but showed great promise for the future. The cover design, with its portrayal of spacemen as cowboys, was McGuinn's idea, and partly commented on the music, which veered between country and rock. Having lost their previous producer, Gary Usher, who left Columbia after spending too much money on a Chad and Jeremy album, the Byrds chose Bob Johnston as a replacement. Johnston had impressive credentials, and his work with Bob Dylan and Johnny Cash had been highly commended. Initially, McGuinn praised his production on *Dr Byrds And Mr Hyde*, but later reversed his opinion. It seems safe to say that the remaining Byrds were disappointed from the outset. White and Parsons criticized the mixing of the album and accused Johnston of playing a passive role as producer. John York concurs with this viewpoint:

'Bob was a joy to work with. He was very patient and kept us amused. But sometimes it went too far in that direction in the sense that there was not always the feeling that work was being done. He didn't really understand what we were doing.'

The main contention was that Johnston had mixed the album so badly that no vestige of the Byrds sound remained. However, while it is true that the familiar jingle-jangle sound is inaudible, the same cannot be said of McGuinn's vocal, which gives the album a distinctive Byrds sound texture. Johnston may have been guilty of burying the instruments at times but the overall result is not great enough to spoil the album. Perhaps this is due to McGuinn's determination to take control of proceedings. *Dr Byrds And Mr Hyde* remains the only Byrds album on which McGuinn takes the lead vocal on every cut.

Characteristically, the Byrds opened their new work with an unreleased Dylan song, 'This Wheel's On Fire'. As usual, McGuinn's vocal is good and ironically highlighted by Johnston's decision to bury the instrumentation. Gene Parsons' drumming sounds very strange, which is hardly surprising when we consider that Johnston had made him tune his snare drum so loose that it was almost impossible to play. Parsons admitted that he felt as though he were hitting a paper towel. The fuzz guitar work of White was passable, though he later confessed that he felt it to be the worst track he had ever recorded. It was certainly a departure from the familiar country sound of White, who felt that someone else should have been brought in to play the lead guitar:

'I felt I was faking it. In bluegrass music there is a lot of gospel and blues influences and flavouring. So the blues part was in me, but there were so many people playing blues that I didn't ever feel that I could catch up with them. So I just wanted to play honest music in an honest style that I believed in and felt at ease with. It's funny you should mention "This Wheel's On Fire" because that's the most embarrassing thing I've ever done. It's horrible.'

'Old Blue' was deliberately placed in stark contrast to the electronic fade-out of 'This Wheel's On Fire' and provides welcome relief. With McGuinn on vocals once more, it reveals a more identifiable Byrds sound than much of the material on *Sweetheart Of The Rodeo*. The track also features Clarence White playing the famous Parsons/White string bender, an invention by the Byrds duo that effectively duplicated the sound of a steel guitar.

Although 'Your Gentle Ways Of Loving Me' was introduced to the Byrds by Gene Parsons, Roger again takes the lead vocal credit, clearly demonstrating his dominance over the rest of the group. One feels that McGuinn was unwilling to take any chances in allowing the other members too much freedom on the vocals. This song seems to be approaching a 'Gentle On My Mind' type of country standard, though the material is not quite strong enough. The homely harmonica, contrasting strongly with the surprise reverberating conclusion suggests that the 'Dr Byrds versus Mr Hyde' concept was very much in McGuinn's mind during the recording of the album.

'Child Of The Universe' was actually mixed twice, once for the film soundtrack *Candy*, and once for this album. Whereas the soundtrack version featured added brass and orchestration, this is a less ambitious interpretation. Although the song is far from brilliant, McGuinn's vocal is impressive and the harmonies are well executed. In retrospect, McGuinn is not overly critical of the track: 'It was an attempt to write a song for a movie. I thought the song was appropriate for the movie the way it turned out.'

The square dance music of 'Nashville West' closes the first side, ending with a drunken free-for-all in the studio in which everyone contributed to the inaudible mumblings. White and Parsons were unimpressed with this new arrangement, however, preferring the version they had performed during the Bakersfield International days.

Following 'Drug Store Truck Driving Man' on side two is the excellent 'King Apathy III'. The guitar work is intriguing and the lyrics have a distinctive Dylanesque quality rare in McGuinn's writing:

'I guess I was imitating Dylan's style. I was just commenting on apathy in general. I was very disturbed by the fact that there was so much apathy in the world. That was just my comment on it.'

In the song, Roger appears to be defending his move to country music on the grounds that he needs to rest from the excesses of rock 'n' roll. There is also the hint that had he continued to play the predictable music of the current rock world and 'hung round that scene', he would by now be, artistically, 'dead'.

John York receives his first co-writing credit on 'Candy', although McGuinn once more insists on taking lead vocal. The guitar work is again notable, the singing high, and the song, though generally disregarded by everybody, has a strong period charm. Unfortunately, 'Candy' did not impress the movie producer, as John York remembers: 'Roger and I wrote "Candy" for the film and they rejected it. They felt we needed a known writer, so they brought in Dave Grusin. The rest of us didn't think much of his song'.

The closing medley was as unusual and unexpected in its own way as 'We'll Meet Again' or 'Oh Susannah'. The snatch of 'My Back Pages' is so paltry as to be almost irrelevant. 'B.J. Blues', with its harmonica break, is totally unlike any previous Byrds cut. Finally, the foursome reveal their own back pages with 'Baby, What Do You Want Me To Do', which seems to serve as a tribute to rock 'n' roll. The Byrds' signature tune of the period, 'Hold It', already familiar to their new audiences, closes the album, while McGuinn signs off with a warning that he will return. According to John York, the medley was an attempt at spontaneity: 'It was a spur of the moment thing. Roger was willing to try anything at that point. It was a theatrical touch to remind the people of the live band. We decided to leave the ending in'.

The album as a whole showed McGuinn's determination to continue using the Byrds name and his growing insistence that country material be placed in a rock framework. Essentially, then, the album was more 'Dr Byrds than 'Mr Hyde'.

Perhaps the greatest criticism of the album came not from the press but rather McGuinn's former colleagues, Chris Hillman and Gram Parsons. They publicly denounced McGuinn, while Parsons stressed that Roger was totally uninterested in rock music and seldom bought records or listened to the radio. Hillman was particularly angry about the *Dr Byrds And Mr Hyde* recording and accused McGuinn of carrying on for the sake of the money. According to Hillman, the Byrds no longer existed, it was simply McGuinn supported by hired musicians. While Hillman's comments were undoubtedly unwarranted and short-sighted, there was more than a grain of truth in them. Financially crippled at the end of 1968, McGuinn may well have decided to continue for economic reasons, rather than any aesthetic motives. But while the early gigs of 1969 were an uphill struggle, it was clear that McGuinn was fronting a more than competent group. The other Byrds remained optimistic, as John York recalls:

'I had the same voice as David, the high voice that had been missing for a long time. I think Roger felt he finally had the band he wanted for the road. I thought of it as a period of reconstruction after a great battle.'

Hillman's accusation of 'hired musicians' was true inasmuch as the rest of the group were paid on a weekly basis by McGuinn. However, similar conditions of employment had been enforced when Chris had joint ownership of the Byrds, so, in a sense, little had changed.

In spite of the Byrds' dissatisfaction with the mixing of *Dr Byrds And Mr Hyde*, another Bob Johnston production appeared as the new Byrds single, 'Lay Lady Lay'. The song fared badly in the States and was later heavily criticized by many, not least the Byrds themselves. It was Johnston's last production of a Byrds disc, mainly because they became incensed with his decision to back them with a choir. According to York, and his account is corroborated by his fellow members, the Byrds had no say in the final product:

'We loved "Lay Lady Lay". After *Nashville Skyline* Bob played us that cut at Roger's house and we decided to do it. But then, unknown to us, he overdubbed the girls' voices and it became an embarrassment. We even stopped doing it in concert.'

In Britain, however, the critics were far more tolerant and clearly supported Bob Johnston's decision all the way. One review proclaimed:

'A great version of one of the strongest numbers on Bob Dylan's LP. The harmonic support behind the solo vocal is really outstanding, largely because the Byrds have been augmented by a girl chorus. This, plus the familiar acoustic guitars, the attractive melody and the obstructive beat, makes it one of the group's best discs in ages.'

The single even received a fair amount of airplay and became yet another in a series of Byrds near misses. One wonders what the Byrds might have thought of Bob Johnston's decision had the single become a hit. Ironically, Dylan's own version of the song was released shortly afterwards and reached the Top 10.

Following Bob Johnston's exit from the Byrds' camp, the group were left to seek another producer. In the meantime, they were to be heard on their third soundtrack album *Easy Rider*. Bob Dylan had refused to allow his song, 'It's All Right Ma (I'm Only Bleeding)' to be included in the film and so Peter Fonda approached Roger McGuinn, who agreed to record it. In addition, McGuinn is credited with the title track, which closed the film. Both songs sound quite unusual when compared to the material that the current Byrds line-up were in the process of recording. McGuinn adopts his Dylan imitation voice and sounds like an ex-Greenwich Village folkie revisiting old memories. Gene Parsons adds to the effect by playing bluesy harmonica on both tracks. '(I) Wasn't Born To Follow' (from *The Notorious Byrd Brothers*) was also included in the film, which no doubt prompted CBS to issue it as a single. It is difficult to estimate the effect that the film had on the popularity of the Byrds. It certainly put their names back in the limelight and no doubt attracted people towards their latest album, which was due to be released some months later. But if that public looked to McGuinn for songs about freedom, motorbikes or revolution, then they would be bitterly disappointed.

On 29 July the Byrds received more publicity when Together Records issued *Preflyte* (discussed in Chapter Two). As with *Easy Rider*, this release reminded the rock world that the Byrds were a group with a long and important history. During the summer, the Byrds toured extensively, strengthening their live performance at each successive gig. The highlight of the tour was at the Boston Tea Party (August 11-13) where they shared the bill with the Flying Burrito Brothers. While Chris and Gram had verbally attacked McGuinn earlier in the year, all such differences were now forgotten. On the first night of that particular booking, both groups took the stage together and produced one of those legendary moments in rock music. Their repertoire extended to include old and new songs; three superb Dylan renditions: 'You Ain't Going Nowhere', 'My Back Pages' and 'It's All Over Now, Baby Blue'; a stunning Gram Parsons solo set, including the haunting 'Hickory Wind', and Hillman reaching back to *Younger Than Yesterday* for 'Time Between'. Even McGuinn acknowledged the sense of occasion and included 'Pretty Boy Floyd' and 'The Christian Life' from the one album that the three had recorded together. The highlight of the evening, however, was a stunning rendition of 'You Don't Miss Your Water' which Gram had originally sung on the *Sweetheart Of The Rodeo* sessions, only to see it replaced by McGuinn's version. Parsons' rendition, backed by McGuinn on harmony, placed the song in a new perspective. Another interesting facet of this set was that three of the songs performed were never recorded by the Byrds. The first was a new Gene Parsons song, entitled 'Take A City Bride' (later to be recorded on his solo album *Kindling*) composed by Gib Guilbeau of Nashville West fame. John York contributed 'Long Black Veil' (an old country standard) and duetted with McGuinn on 'Get Out Of My Life Woman' (the old Lee Dorsey hit that the Byrds had re-arranged into 'Captain Soul'). After the gig, McGuinn revealed to the press that the next album would be called 'Captain America' after the central character in *Easy Rider*. Needless to say, things turned out differently.

Due to the success of the gig, the Byrds again performed with the Burritos, and rumours began to spread through the music industry that a joint album was more than a distinct possibility. Nothing came of it, however, and their gigs ceased to coincide regularly in the future. In retrospect, John York feels that the collaboration should have been continued: 'Those gigs were really magic. Something more could have come from it. Someone should have booked a tour because, organically, it was already alive.'

The Byrds appeared with the Burritos on three separate occasions, with Gram and Roger alternating vocals and Sneaky Pete Kleinow and Clarence White exchanging leads. According to McGuinn, all three gigs were more successful than the usual Burritos and Byrds sets of the period.

As the Byrds completed their successful summer tour, it became increasingly evident that all was not well with John York:

'I was very unhappy. I began to realize that what they wanted from me was pretty small in terms of what I could give them. I sing, play the piano, bass and write. Roger wanted to encourage those things in me, but he didn't want another Gram Parsons on his hands.'

Having considered leaving, York realized that his status as a Byrd might be increased by contributing to the new album, so he decided to remain.

16
The Easy Riding Byrds

With the completion of both a summer tour and a new album, the Byrds once more seemed a relatively stable unit. However, at the end of September, John York was officially asked to leave:

'I was very depressed. I told Clarence and Gene that I planned to stay for three months more. I figured that would give them time to find a new bassist and get me some money to survive. Little did I know that they'd been monitoring me and had someone who was willing to join immediately. I didn't quit. I said I was going to quit, then the next day they phoned me and told me they wanted Skip. They said as far as they were concerned I was out of the band. Well, I was glad they'd found somebody, and there were no bad feelings. It was just that I was unhappy.'

According to McGuinn, York had difficulty coming to terms with the group's image stemming from an infatuation with the group in 1965. The transition from Byrd fan to Byrd was, claims McGuinn, too overwhelming for the impressionable York. The pressure of living up to the image of a Byrd was, supposedly, intolerable and McGuinn believed York felt it was 'like being a Beatle'. York, while not entirely agreeing with McGuinn's analysis, admits that there were problems:

'I was not a Byrds freak. I did really love "Mr Tambourine Man" and the early songs, but after the second album I completely lost touch with their music. However, there is an element of truth in Roger's statement. I was beginning to feel like a computer part. On stage, people would go bananas before we even played a note. I felt almost like a liar. What I had to give could never come across because it didn't seem to matter who the

Byrds were. The people in the audience had this idea in mind and it didn't seem to matter who was there, as long as it was McGuinn and some other guys. I felt I was not giving. It was like living a lie. I felt that leaving was a matter of integrity.'

What York saw as integrity, however, was interpreted by the other Byrds as an example of naivety and unprofessionalism. In retrospect, York feels that his inexperience may have alienated him from the other Byrds:

'I'd always known how to perform but I never really knew the business. Once we played somewhere and were two-and-a-half hours late. But the people were so patient; no stamping or anything. We went out and did a 35 minute set. I wanted to play all night. I felt we owed them more. I wanted to give them something they'd never forget. But I was embarrassing everyone by getting so upset. The other guys were saying, "Cool it, man". Had I been more professional, I would have said, "We'll get them next time around", or realized that Roger knew what he was doing'.'

The dismissal of York was seen by some critics as a further example of McGuinn's dominance over the Byrds and refusal to compromise. According to York, however, Roger was not a heartless hirer/firer but a leader who took a sympathetic interest in John's musical development. York's account of his relationship with McGuinn presents an aspect of Roger's character seldom seen in print:

'People always say Roger is cold but I used to tell him exactly how I felt. I remember I went through a period when I was very unhappy and used to tell Roger what I thought was wrong with the group. He would say, "This will be a good stepping stone for you when you leave". But I would say, "How can you talk about leaving?" I wanted to put energy into it. Roger advised me to leave if I didn't like the band. But I didn't want to split. I wanted to be part of it. But the part was so small. I used to think Roger was pushing me forward with one hand and holding me back with the other. But, essentially, I was doing it to myself. Roger was right, but at the time it seemed utter nonsense to me.'

The new Byrd, Skip Battin, was, at 35, the oldest member, and also the one with the longest musical history. Skip discovered the electric bass in 1951, moved to Tucson, having gained admittance to the University of Arizona, and there met Gary Paxton, with whom he formed the Pledges, then Clyde and Gary, and, finally, Skip and Flip. With Gary on guitar and Skip on bass, they took a demo of original songs to Floyd Ramsey (Duane Eddy's producer) at his Phoenix studio, recorded four songs, and were signed to Bobby Shand's Brent label. Between 1959 and 1961, they notched up several hits including 'It Was I', 'Cherry Pie' and 'Fancy Nancy'. Abandoning the prospect of a potential career as a Physical Education teacher, and the chance to go to theatre college, Battin moved to Los Angeles, appeared in several films and television shows, and finally formed a 'twist band' which gigged around Hollywood until its demise in 1963. Reverting to studio work, Battin later formed Evergreen Blueshoes in 1966. They lasted two years, during which time they played the Hollywood club circuit, worked for nine months at the Corral in Topanga Canyon, and released one album, a not particularly auspicious work, on Amos Records. The most notable feature of the album was the sleeve, which included nude photographs, carefully out of focus. Following the disbandment of the group, Battin continued with his studio work and jammed for a few months with Art Johnson, a jazz guitarist. During this period, Battin met Gene Parsons at a recording session, reunited with Clarence White, whom he had known a couple of years earlier, and within two months had replaced John York in the Byrds.

Towards the end of 1969, the Byrds found themselves back in the news. Apart from Battin's arrival, and all the publicity surrounding the *Easy Rider* soundtrack, news had leaked out of a musical McGuinn had co-written with Jacques Levy, a former practising psychologist who later became director of the New York productions of *Oh Calcutta* and *Scuba Duba*. Titled *Gene Tryp* (an anagram of *Peer Gynt*) the musical was apparently destined for Broadway, with McGuinn boasting of an opening night as early as the autumn. McGuinn's flurry of activity was supposedly only a prelude to even loftier ambitions involving Gram Parsons and Michelle Phillips (as two intergalactic flower children!) in a science fiction movie to be entitled *Ecology 70*. As the interviews multiplied, McGuinn even found himself denying rumours that he was abandoning rock 'n' roll to become a Broadway star. The great contemporaneous interest in rock as theatre had attracted the press back to McGuinn and helped to defuse the recent criticism of his supposed dictatorial tendencies.

On 10 November, the new Byrds album, *Ballad Of Easy Rider*, was issued, with the return of Terry Melcher as producer: 'Roger and Clarence came down to my house on the beach, and I agreed to become producer and personal manager, not wishing for a repetition of the Dickson affair'.

Many people will probably still sneer at the abominable sleeve of *Ballad Of Easy Rider* which was even condemned by McGuinn as the worst Byrds cover. One might be excused for assuming that the cover was designed as a parody of *Easy Rider*. Instead of the drug-taking, freedom-loving, easy-riding hippies that were portrayed in the film, we were confronted with a feeble-looking individual, weakly clutching a rifle and smiling inanely, as he sat, rather uncomfortably, on an archaic motorbike. The advertising department at CBS obviously did not agree with this interpretation and insisted upon equating the album with 'a generation's search for freedom and expression'. The implications of that phrase was that the album contained songs in the vein of 'The Pusher' or 'Born To Be Wild', which were included on the soundtrack album. *Ballad Of Easy Rider* no doubt attracted great public interest and enticed many old Byrds fans back in search of such songs as 'Eight Miles High', '5-D' or 'So You Want To Be A Rock 'n' Roll Star'. Perhaps others were simply curious to discover what McGuinn was into these days. The advance publicity only served to dampen people's expectations and the absurd cover was a truer reflection of the music than might have been supposed. Apart from the title track, the theme of *Easy Rider* is nowhere to be seen, and neither is the songwriting McGuinn. The promotion of the album was totally inappropriate, for the Byrds were not ready for any revolutionary changes on this occasion, but seemed to be pacing themselves in preparation for a greater work. As a transitional work, however, the album was impressive and worthy of some discussion.

'Ballad Of Easy Rider' begins the album on a strong note, like the opening cuts on many of their earlier works. Whereas the original soundtrack version introduced us to the solo 'folk singing' McGuinn, complete with acoustic guitar and accompanying harp, this later arrangement shows a lot more depth. The song itself had been lengthened by grafting the first verse on to the end of the second. Meanwhile, the pace was quickened, with Roger reverting to his more usual vocal style for a perfect delivery. The most striking alteration, however, was Terry Melcher's tasteful and unobtrusive introduction of orchestration. As he recalled: 'It was my idea to add the strings. I was trying to make the song into a "Gentle On My Mind" or "Everybody's Talking".' Although the song is credited to Roger McGuinn, it is generally accepted that Bob Dylan was at least partially involved in its composition. In August 1971, McGuinn revealed:

'When I wrote that track for the film, Dylan had something to do with it and so his name came up in the credits. He called me and said, "Take that off, I told you not to give me any credit. I do things like that for people every day. I just gave you a line that's all". Which actually was true, we hadn't really got deeply involved together over the song.'

Gene Parsons later complicated matters by suggesting that Dylan had written the lyrics, while McGuinn was only responsible for the melody. In a later interview, McGuinn again stressed that Dylan was responsible only for composing a couple of lines, and by the time I caught up with him, he revealed:

'Dylan did write half the lyrics, and I wrote the other half. Then the screen credit said, "'Ballad Of Easy Rider' by Roger McGuinn and Bob Dylan." He said, "Take it off!" because he didn't like the movie that much. He didn't like the ending. He wanted to see the truck blow up in order to get poetic justice. He didn't seem to understand Peter Fonda's anti-hero concept.'

The second track, 'Fido', was John York's first and last solo for the Byrds. York was not entirely satisfied with the production: 'I didn't like Melcher double-tracking my voice. The original idea was that Gene should have a drum solo, and at least he did get that opportunity'. Terry Melcher indicates that the remaining Byrds were also dissatisfied with the song: '"Fido" was a problem with Roger. The guys didn't like it too much. But York was a pro and a nice guy. He never showed up loaded and he worked hard'. The song was really only memorable for the Gene Parsons drum solo and the fact that it continued the illustrious tradition of Byrds dog songs begun on 'Old Blue' on the last album.

According to White, 'Oil In My Lamp' was the first time he had sung lead on a song since the days of the Kentucky Colonels. Not a particularly impressive song on which to make a comeback, I fear. This was another example of the Byrds unnecessarily digging up a traditional old chestnut which ends up sounding like an unimpressive filler.

For 'Tulsa County Blue', White introduced the Byrds to world champion fiddle player Byron Berline, who had recently begun working as a session player. The song was impressive but once more it came from outside the group, as Terry Melcher explained:

'"Tulsa County Blue" was a copyright I'd owned for a long time. It was a country hit for June Carter, written by Pam Polland who had a group called Gentle Soul who I cut an album with for Epic with Ry Cooder, Van Dyke Parks and Larry Knechtel. It was John York's idea to cover the song and I was obviously very pleased because it was my copyright.'

Another traditional song, 'Jack Tarr The Sailor', closes side one. At least on this occasion the Byrds show that they have a variety of sources by adapting an Old English folk tune. Gene Parsons vividly recalls Roger getting drunk one night and convincing himself that he was a sailor, after which the song was recorded. In many ways, this number is the precursor of such songs as 'Heave Away' and 'Jolly Roger'. McGuinn delivers the song in best British folk-cellar nasal style. The only other Byrds songs resembling this arrangement are 'I Come And Stand At Every Door' and 'Space Odyssey'.

On 'Jesus Is Just Alright', the Byrds turned their attention to gospel music. I used to be irritated by the repetitiveness of this song, until I heard the Byrds perform it in concert. It remained one of the best numbers in their 70's sets. The song retains that distinctive Byrds sound and includes some solid bass playing as well as the return of the tambourine. Parsons introduced the group to the song, having attended the original recording by the Art Reynolds Singers, who were produced by his former partner, Gib Guilbeau. Terry Melcher added to the effects by remembering an old trick borrowed from the days of *Turn! Turn! Turn!*:

'I had a whole string section on "Jesus Is Just Alright" that you

Clean-cut: Crosby, McGuinn and Clark.

The Jet Set in 1964. Crosby, Clark and McGuinn.

Jim McGuinn. The first fruits of Beatledom.

A smiling David Crosby poses with McGuinn's Rickenbacker.

Gene Clark, the most prolific writing talent in the Byrds.

Chris Hillman displaying his torturously straightened Beatle-cut.

Michael Clarke masters the Brian Jones look.

Gene Clark and Jim McGuinn onstage at Ciro's.

Clark, Crosby and McGuinn at an early Columbia recording session.

The semi-naked David Crosby with a bevy of fawning female fans.

Terry Melcher (left), the Byrds' first producer at CBS.

McGuinn with his trademark granny glasses.

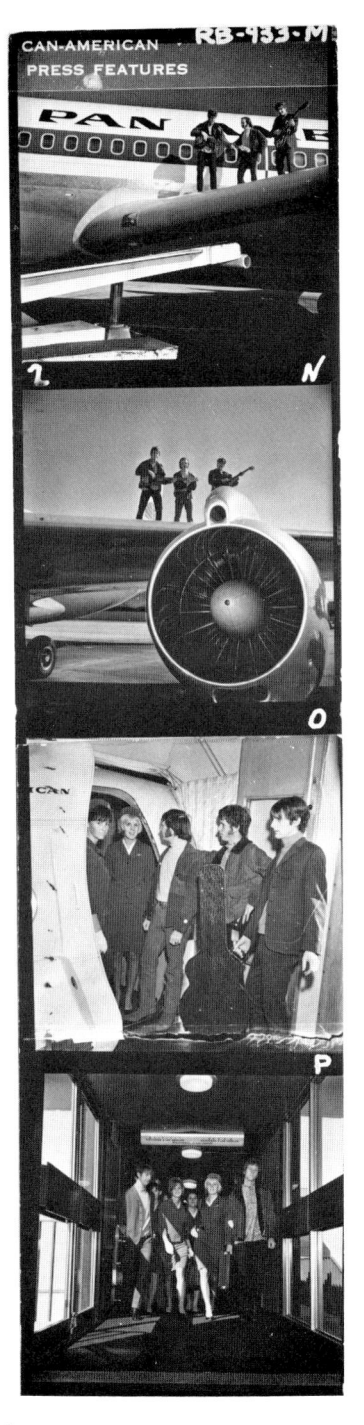

January 1968. Kevin Kelley joins the struggling duo.

The youthful Gram Parsons, before money and drugs insidiously killed his promise.

Early 1968. Parsons, Kelley, Hillman and McGuinn.

Onstage at The Piper Club, Italy (1968).

Kentucky Colonels. A rare shot from the archives.

Nashville West, (l. to r.) Gib Guilbeau, Clarence White, Wayne Moore, Gene Parsons.

Line-up changes. Clarence White (far left) joins. July 1968.

Clockwise: White, McGuinn, Parsons and York.

Autumn 1968, (l. to r.) McGuinn, White, Hillman, Gene Parsons.

John York (far left) joins the group (November 1968).

(l. to r.) McGuinn, White, Battin and Parsons.

The most stable Byrds line-up, (l. to. r.) White, Parsons, McGuinn, Skip Battin.

A sinister looking McGuinn ponders the future.

McGuinn visiting the Byrds Appreciation Society in 1971.

Smiling and sombre at the grand reunion. (l. to r.) McGuinn, Hillman, Crosby, Clarke and Clark.

Clarence plays the prototype Parsons/White stringbender.

Jim Seiter-The Byrds longest serving road-manager.

John Guerin replaces Gene Parsons.

The final Byrds gig, (l. to r.) White, Joe Lala, Hillman, McGuinn.

Clarence White, 1944-1973.

C. S. & N. during the 1977 reformation tour.

David Crosby onstage with McGuinn, Clark & Hillman.

Gene Clark onstage at Hammersmith Odeon (1977).

The first publicity shot of McGuinn, Clark & Hillman standing in the wrong order.

Gene Clark continued to record for small labels after leaving McGuinn and Hillman.

McGuinn, the beautific troubadour of the '80s.

probably never heard. I had them drone two notes through the entire record and I ran it through a tape phaser. The idea was an adaptation of McGuinn's drone concept on "If You're Gone".'

Having attempted to record 'It's All Over Now, Baby Blue' in 1965 and 1967, the Byrds eventually cut an adequate version in 1969, though McGuinn claims that he was still dissatisfied with the end product. His criticism seems perceptive, for this new treatment of the song seems neither original nor striking. The tempo is deliberately slowed down, in marked contrast to the 1965 version, and Roger drags the syllables out of each word in order to provide it with the obligatory Dylanesque flavour. John York's vocal is nowhere to be heard on the recording, as he reveals:

'That was a time of turmoil. I walked out of that session. I played the bass on it, but I got the feeling that Terry Melcher wanted to be a rock 'n' roll singer so badly and there was only room for four voices at the time. I began to feel I was in the wrong place. I went into another room and played the piano while they did the vocals.'

The decision to cover Vern Gosdin's 'There Must Be Someone' was primarily instigated by Gene Parsons. Unfortunately, this particular arrangement is pretty average. Parsons' solo is set against a virtually non-existent backing and seems totally out of place on what is, after all, a Byrds album. Parsons implies that McGuinn was unsure about including the song on the album: 'I think Roger might have questioned whether it was sufficiently Byrds-sounding, but he was very open to new musical ideas at the time, so he allowed it to be included'.

By contrast, 'Gunga Din' is possibly the best song Parsons ever wrote, and remains one of the highlights of the album. The intriguing lyrics were inspired by an actual incident, as Gene explains:

'The song was based on a series of events that happened on our visit to New York. Part of it was written about John York and his mother. We always used to stay at the Gramercy Park Hotel and we spent hundreds of dollars there. On one occasion, John wanted to take his mother to dinner but they wouldn't let him in the restaurant because he had a leather jacket on. It was very upsetting and insulting. The song also documents a gig we played at Central Park, where Chuck Berry, "Mr Rock 'n' Roll", failed to appear, and the crowd were really angry. Part of the song was written on the plane when we really were chasing the sun back to LA. I threw in the "Gunga Din" part to make up the rhyme.'

'Deportee (Plane Wreck At Los Gatos)' was the second Woody Guthrie song recorded by the Byrds, 'Pretty Boy Floyd' being the first. Like 'Turn! Turn! Turn!', this was another song McGuinn borrowed from the third Judy Collins album. Woody had put the music to a poem about the California tradition of employing cheap labour to pick the fruit. As an isolated track, the Byrds interpretation of the song seems reasonable, but on an album already glutted with unoriginal material its inclusion is questionable.

'Armstrong, Aldrin And Collins' continues the Byrds tradition of ending their albums with an unusual track. Terry Melcher points out the analogy: 'The Zeke Manners song was our joke, our "We'll Meet Again". We were trying to get back to the feel of the first album. The song was originally very long when Zeke gave it to us, so we cut it down'. The contrast between the folky delivery and the electronic wizardry is supposedly designed to illustrate the importance of commonplace truths in the search for universal wisdom (i.e. they were launched into space, but they had God's helping hand). If McGuinn's arrangement helps to qualify the moral, it does not drastically improve the song. His folky style and the use of synthesizer do not complement each other on this occasion, for the one negates the other. We had to wait till 'Time Cube' (on McGuinn's debut solo album) before learning how such a fusion could be demonstrated effectively.

Commenting on the album, Gene Parsons revealed that there was conflict with John York throughout the recording and expressed surprise that *Ballad Of Easy Rider* actually emerged as an acceptable piece of work. Although the album still sounds reasonable, however, it had several faults. Firstly, it should be noted that, apart from the title track, the LP contained only two songs written solely by group members. Fortunately, one of these, 'Gunga Din', turned out to be excellent, while the other, 'Fido, may best be described as 'adequate'. Sadly, the remainder of the extraneous material, with the notable exception of the gloriously distinctive 'Tulsa County Blue', seems ill-chosen. The Byrds insist on reviving a Woody Guthrie standard that had already been recorded by scores of other artistes, and to which their interpretation adds little that could be described as innovatory. While a reworking of a current Dylan number might have been interesting, McGuinn insists on continuing the ill-fated attempt at recording 'It's All Over Now, Baby Blue', and allows it to be included on the album in spite of his dissatisfaction with the end product. Gene Parsons is given leave to include the lacklustre 'There Must Be Someone', and the pruned Zeke Manners composition becomes little more than a vehicle for McGuinn's wit. As if this extraneous material were not enough, they even insist on resurrecting another two traditional songs. Of all the foreign compositions, only 'Jesus Is Just Alright', with its strong gospel flavour, shows the Byrds attempting to reach any new musical horizons so far uncharted by them. And this from the group whose name became synonymous with the phrase, 'always beyond today'. However, it is McGuinn whose role in the album appears most perplexing. Although *Ballad Of Easy Rider* still sounds fresh and eminently listenable, this is due far more to Melcher's production than any effort by McGuinn. With the title song having already appeared on the *Easy Rider* soundtrack (albeit in a different form) we were left with a Byrds album that contained not even a single *new* Roger McGuinn composition. Rather than suggesting that McGuinn had simply dried up, it seems far more logical to suppose that his attention was being distracted by another project.

It should be noted that during the lead-up to the recording of *Ballad Of Easy Rider*, McGuinn was heavily involved in the *Gene Tryp* musical. No doubt it was those commitments that accounted for the apparent exhaustion of his creative energies. What we were left with on *Ballad Of Easy Rider* was a sprinkling of excellent Byrds songs amid a glut of unoriginal material. All things considered, it is remarkable that the album sounded as good as it did. Thankfully, though, the songs that resulted from McGuinn's extra-mural activities were destined for release in the New Year and they would certainly be worth the wait.

17
The Byrds Enter The 70's

As a result of the criticism McGuinn had been receiving the previous year, he made a firm decision to re-establish the Byrds as a major musical force. At this point, such a move was an ambitious one. The Byrds were in a chronic financial state and were still feeling the repercussions of their massive split in 1968. Moreover, the group still had a long road to travel in terms of critical acceptance. Although the involvement in *Easy Rider* had resulted in a resurgence of critical interest, many still regarded the Byrds as a dead group. The critics' complained about McGuinn's continued dominance of the group, and many still accepted the myth that the Byrds were unable to perform live. Perhaps, in desperation, McGuinn saw the need to re-think his future, and concluded that a Byrds revival could only be effected through an intensive work schedule.

Throughout 1970, then, the Byrds concentrated all their efforts on perfecting the musicianship which would be necessary if they were to make the classic album that would restore them to the premier league of 70's US rock acts. More importantly, the Byrds realized that, if they were to be a successful 70's act, they would need to recruit a new, younger audience to supplement their die-hard followers from the 60's. The only way to recruit new fans was literally to go out and play to them, in clubs, bars and, more especially, the seemingly endless college circuit. Within a year, the Byrds played a staggering 200 gigs, visiting countless colleges across the face of America. Roger recalls the exhausting work schedule: 'We were doing a lot of gigs, commuting from LA to New York every week, doing four days out and three days back. It was quite expensive but we had a lot of gigs booked on the East Coast'.

By the summer, a short tour of Europe had been added to the apparently inexhaustible itinerary, and continental fans were overjoyed to discover the Byrds playing at the Midnight Sun Festival in Ludkopping, Sweden (June 19), Frankfurt (June 20) and Rotterdam (June 26). The tour culminated in a memorable appearance at the Bath Festival on 28 June. The Byrds appeared towards dawn, but the thunder, lightning and torrential downpour prevented them from playing an electric set. Undaunted, they emerged with acoustic guitars to play all their old classics, even 'Eight Miles High'. The crowd was ecstatic, and McGuinn treasures the memory to this day. A fan of the time summed up the general feeling of the crowd:

'When the Airplane walked off the stage cursing the weather I was all set to turn my back on rock 'n' roll and all that it represented. But I stayed. I found the crowd fascinating. Half of them had already gone home, but those who remained were drenched through, miserable and defeated. It was pathetic. Like a refugee camp after the War. Then this solitary figure appeared on stage with an acoustic guitar and sang 'So You Want To Be A Rock 'n' Roll Star'. McGuinn summed it all up, just like that. The emotion of the moment was so great that I was not the only one of the crowd who cried for joy, I was so moved. The Byrds performed their entire repertoire and more, and saw us through that sad night. They gave us 'Mr Tambourine Man' just as the first ribbons of light appeared in the sky. They were magnificent.'

In effect, the Byrds had reversed the events of their British appearance five years earlier. This time, they had left England triumphantly.

With months of gigging experience behind them, the Byrds at last felt confident enough to take a unique step in their career by recording their first live album. At the same time, it was felt that each member had sufficiently impressive material to donate to a new studio album. The dilemma was solved when the Byrds determined to record a double album, half of which would be cut live and the other half recorded in the studio. The idea was apparently the brainchild of Terry Melcher:

'It was my idea to do a double album, half live and half studio, and sell it for the price of a single album. One record was to enable us to toss in a load of hits, with live excitement, in order to get us back into the charts.'

In the meantime, McGuinn ensured that they were receiving enough publicity to attract the interest of the public. Rumours began to circulate about a possible union of Bob Dylan and the Byrds on album, and in April, McGuinn revealed:

'We may be doing an album with Dylan soon, either here or in Nashville. Yes, it is great. We don't have any concept in mind. He just said to bring some of our stuff and he'd bring some of his. He said he hasn't been writing much lately and he needs his new songs for his own album, so he may even want to do some Byrds songs. Who knows what will happen?'

Needless to say, nothing did happen, and the project fell through. According to Clive Davis, McGuinn failed to attend the session, and by the time he was contacted it was discovered that the other Byrds had returned to Los Angeles. McGuinn, however, tells a different story and blames the failure of the project on the organizers, rather than the artistes. The Byrds had flown to New York for the weekend in order to perform two gigs at the Felt Forum and Queens College. These were the all-important concerts from which the live part of their album would be selected. At the same time, they expected to finalize the deal with Dylan but, according to McGuinn, the promised telephone call came too late:

'It wasn't our fault. Clive Davis was supposed to meet us after the gig at Queens College, the previous night, but he didn't show. I was expecting a call from Bob Johnston, whose job was to notify us of the time of the session, but he didn't call us either. Dylan was really mad about it.'

It seems likely that the mix-up resulted in a temporary rift between McGuinn and Dylan. The argument over the co-writing credit on 'Ballad Of Easy Rider' had angered Dylan, and this incident only served to increase his wrath. Certainly, McGuinn and Dylan lost contact with each other at this point though there was no argument or genuine bad feeling, just a lack of communication. However, in retrospect, it seems that McGuinn has no regrets about the failure of the project:

'What he wanted was us to back him. It wasn't our material, and from my point of view, it wasn't a very attractive project. It was like the Byrds being subservient to Dylan. It was just Clive Davis's idea to sell some records'.

So the Byrds kept their integrity but, temporarily, lost the chance to re-establish their name on the front pages of the music press.

The new album, *(Untitled)*, was released in the autumn to critical acclaim. The work revealed that McGuinn had at last found the stable line-up for which he had been searching since 1967. The evidence was fully demonstrated through the music, and suggested in the sleeve notes, with their discussion of discarded titles, such as 'Phoenix' and 'the first Byrds album'. This was, in effect, the first Byrds album since *Younger Than Yesterday* on which every member had an equal control in the group, both musically and politically. Although the members were new, and the music seemed innovative, the sound was distinctively the Byrds. McGuinn's Rickenbacker was still loud and clear; the live songs were former Byrds classics; and the production was controlled by the old firm of Terry Melcher and Jim Dickson. On this occasion, however, there was a shift in the balance of power, as Melcher explained:

'Getting Dickson was a magnanimous gesture on my part, almost revenge. I didn't co-produce it with Dickson. What I did was allow him to edit the live tapes while I was cutting the studio part of the album. On the live side, we came back with five hours of live music and I gave Dickson all the tapes. We got on well because he didn't have any power. One thing about Dickson though, he's got taste.'

Dickson disputes Melcher's suggestion that his involvement did not extend beyond editing the live tapes and cites Clarence White's commments on 'Take A Whiff' printed later in this chapter to prove his point.

The re-unification of Dickson and Melcher, however, proved an enormous asset in ensuring the album's quality. The intriguing idea behind the 'non-title' of the album was, according to Roger, an accident:

'Somebody from Columbia called up our manager and asked him what it was. He told them it was "as yet untitled" and so they went ahead and printed that. Before that we were considering "McGuinn, White, Parsons and Battin", but that would probably have been misinterpreted.'

Terry Melcher, however, tells a slightly different story:

'I'll tell you what really happened. It went from my office that way. On the label copy information, on which you list artiste, producer, song titles, writers, publishers and times, I put down "Untitled". "Phoenix" had been considered but at that time they were still unsure. Before I knew it, they'd pressed it up as *(Untitled).*'

The live segment of *(Untitled)* begins with 'Lover Of The Bayou', which served as the opening number at most subsequent Byrds concerts. The song remains a showcase for White's interweaving guitar work. Originally, the song was intended for inclusion in the *Gene Tryp* musical, but was later deleted from the score, as Roger remembers: 'The bayou scene was cut because the play was already running too long. The scene was set during the Civil War, and Gene Tryp was smuggling guns to the confederates. At the same time, he was selling drink and stuff to the bayou people'.

With 'Positively 4th Street', McGuinn regressed five years to borrow one of Dylan's most bitter put-down songs. The inclusion of this song might be construed as a subtle put-down of Dylan, though McGuinn denies this. Nevertheless, the rift between Dylan and McGuinn meant that the Byrds were receiving no new unreleased Dylan material at this point. In fact, this was the last Dylan song to appear on any Byrds album.

Though it could hardly be described as a Byrds classic, 'Nashville West', like many instrumentals, worked effectively in live performance. Gene Parsons, while preferring the live version to the studio cut that appeared on *Dr Byrds And Mr Hyde*, felt that both versions paled alongside the original recording by Nashville West.

Side one of the album ends with three of the most famous songs from the first two Byrds line-ups. 'So You Want To A Rock 'n' Roll Star', with its driving rhythm, is, undoubtedly, the tour de force of the set, and is taken at a faster pace than the original version. 'Mr Tambourine Man', the most famous of Byrds songs, returns to the set after several years' absence, indicating that McGuinn was placing the current group in an historical perspective. Roger was determined to demonstrate that the group was capable of performing the old songs as well as the new. The inclusion of these songs was a deliberate attempt to show that the new group was not simply Roger McGuinn and three hired musicians, but rather four individuals who collectively embodied the spirit of the original Byrds. The quality of the live material was evident enough, though, in retrospect, McGuinn and Dickson may have overstated the case by allowing the first side to end with an unspectacular version of 'Mr Spaceman'.

The restructuring of 'Eight Miles High' represented nothing less than the ultimate fusion of the old Byrds and the new. While the familiar old Byrds songs on side one were faithful to their prototypes, the extended 'Eight Miles High' took the group into a new dimension. Originally, the live version of 'Eight Miles High' was part of a medley with 'Turn! Turn! Turn!' and 'Mr Tambourine Man'. During rehearsals, however, the Byrds began jamming on the song and the extended version gradually evolved. The distinctive riff was transformed into a vehicle to demonstrate the individual rapport between the bass work of Skip Battin and the drumming of Gene Parsons. The track is a concrete realization of that perfect balance McGuinn sought between a desire to sustain the spirit of the old Byrds, while moving into new directions with this latest line-up. As a result, the 'Eight Miles High' riff fades into the background soon after the opening of the song, only to re-emerge towards the end, along with the first verse of the song. Here McGuinn is careful not to overdo the nostalgia and the curtailing of the song after the first stanza prevents the emotional climax from becoming overtly sentimental. Although side long instrumentals were one of the more self indulgent exercises of late 60's/early 70's groups, this stands up to the test of time a little better than most. While it is still dwarfed by the classic original, the live 'Eight Miles High' is a pleasing reminder of what the Byrds sounded like in concert during their most well-travelled period.

The live concert ends with the Byrds' signature tune, 'Hold It', which was first heard at the end of the medley on *Dr Byrds And Mr Hyde*. According to Gene Parsons, the idea of a signature tune began as a joke but the end result was so neat that the group decided to retain it as the closing chorus to each set, followed by McGuinn's grateful thanks to the audience for their patience and participation. The extent of the Byrds' pride in their live performance is emphasized in the words of McGuinn:

'I preferred the live segment of *(Untitled)*. I thought the Clarence White Byrds were a better live band while the original Byrds were a better studio band.'

Most people, however, would disagree with Roger's opinion concerning the superiority of the live album. Impressive as they are, these excerpts from the concert do not totally reflect the extent of the Byrds' musical and lyrical progression on this album. In order to understand the achievement that the album represents, we must take a closer look at the studio tracks.

'Chestnut Mare' was, undoubtedly, the most exciting thing that the Byrds had produced since their creative peak in 1967. The lyrical content alone eclipsed anything that had been written since Crosby left the group. Melodically, it was also the Byrds' most commercial song for many years, and an edited version gave the group their first UK Top 20 hit since 'All I Really Want To Do' in 1965. Musically, 'Chestnut Mare' contains everything that we associate with the term 'the Byrds sound'. McGuinn's piercing 12-string jingle jangle guitar work is complemented by the subtlety of White's underlying careful picking. The theme of an individual's struggle to capture and tame a wild horse conjures up visions of freedom, love, achievement and optimism – in fact, everything that the Byrds' music represents. Some commentators have suggested that the song should be treated allegorically, but no plausible suggestions have ever been put forward to support this theory. In essence, the song is a simple statement of man's desire to capture the beauties of nature for his own, but the concept is too general to be given any specific allegorical application. Moreover, as Roger reminds us, the song was primarily written for inclusion in *Gene Tryp*: 'We modified the story a little there. Peer Gynt was trying to catch a reindeer or some animal like that, but we changed it to a horse to bring it back to America'.

'Truck Stop Girl' was another showcase for White, who introduced this Little Fcat song to the Byrds: 'I used to run into Lowell George a lot in the studio and he gave me some material on tape, and that was one of the songs'. The nasal whining vocal is employed extremely effectively on this song about a tragic, violent death. The theme now takes on a sad irony when we consider the circumstances of White's death.

'All The Things', the third *Gene Tryp* song on the album, is concerned with self-revelation as expressed through an observation on the power of nature. The theme is almost pantheistic, stressing the disillusionment that results from a conscious decision to isolate oneself from the natural processes of life. At this point, we might question the extent to which these songs were merely composed to suit the *Peer Gynt* theme. One wonders whether McGuinn and Levy were using the theme as a vehicle to expostulate their own beliefs and ideas. The sleeve of the album suggests that Gram Parsons guested as harmony vocalist, and this is verified by Terry Melcher: 'I'd have loved to see Gram back in the Byrds. I think I was drunk that night and he came in and asked to do the harmony'.

Penned by the unlikely co-writing team of Parsons and Battin, 'Yesterday's Train' features Gene on vocals, acoustic guitar, harmonica and drums, with Sneaky Pete Kleinow on additional steel guitar. Skip Battin explained how the song was composed:

'We wrote it in a hotel. Gene and I were sharing a room at the time and he actually began it. I was involved in Buddhism, so I latched on to the idea of re-incarnation and the feeling you get when you feel you know somebody from a former life'.

'Hungry Planet' was one of the earliest songs written by the Battin/Fowley team. The inclusion of McGuinn in the writing credits was a result of a restructuring of the melody, as Battin explained:

'The original melody was completely different. On the *(Untitled)* version we tried to experiment. Roger wanted to do some work on the synthesizer, which he felt would be a good idea at the time. But none of us liked the way it turned out. It just fizzled. I intend to re-record it someday with the original melody.'

The final *Gene Tryp* song on the album, 'Just A Season', with its references to 'hills' and 'circles without reason'. corresponds to the episode in the musical in which the hero is forced to go round an immense circle in order to rediscover his loved one. In many respects, this song is equally as impressive as 'Chestnut Mare', and the jingle jangle guitar makes it sound like a conglomeration of several songs from the first three Byrds albums.

'Take A Whiff (On Me)' was originally slated for *Ballad Of Easy Rider*, but when White suggested the song there was a general lack of enthusiasm from the other Byrds. Coincidentally, when *(Untitled)* came to be recorded, Roger came up with the same suggestion. White vividly recalled the recording of the song:

'Roger said he'd like to do "Take A Whiff", and he didn't remember me talking about it earlier. But later, he said, "Yeah, seems I do remember you getting the lyrics to it". Well, we started cutting it and I guess it was more of my type of song, though Roger performs those old folk songs really well. I arranged it because his version was too like Leadbelly. Anyway, we laid down the track and he started putting the voice on, with me singing harmony. But Jim Dickson said, "Hold it, Roger, could I hear Clarence sing it by himself?" I used the words Roger had written down and not the ones I knew.'

The inclusion of an old traditional chestnut can often spoil an intensely lyrical album, but the humour of 'Take A Whiff' succeeds in alleviating, rather than impairing the mood of the entire work. The popularity of the song can be measured by its retention in the Byrds' live set, where the lyrics were altered in order to include a sarcastic gibe directed at the former mayor of Chicago, 'Come on Spiro, take a whiff on me'.

Byron Berline makes another guest appearance on a Byrds album playing some beautiful fiddle on the Battin/Fowley number, 'You All Look Alike'. The song sounds as though it might have been inspired by an actual incident, but, according to Battin, this was not the case:

'No, that was not a true story but a fantasy. At the time there was a newspaper report of a drummer who had been killed by his girlfriend. I was aware of that incident, but the song was not directly written about it.'

The closing cut, 'Well Come Back Home', was, in many respects, one of the most intriguing songs on the album. Unlike the many Battin/Fowley collaborations, this was not a novelty, but a political statement. Battin relates how he came to write the song:

'I was personally touched by the Vietnam situation, and my feelings about it came out in the song. I had a high school friend who died out there and I guess my thoughts were on him at the time. Roger heard me composing the song and he liked it. He suggested we record it. We were veering between the two titles "Well Come Back Home" and "Welcome Back Home". I used to be a practising Buddhist and that's how the chant got in there. "Nam Myoho Renge Kyo" is meant to be the highest sound in the universe. It was a one-take song and it really got loose at the end. It was probably the most serious song that I was ever involved in.'

The Battin chant maintained the Byrds tradition of closing their albums in a bizarre fashion.

Thankfully, all the work and energy that the group had put into re-establishing the Byrds' identity had paid dividends. McGuinn remembers 1970 as the year in which the Byrds achieved both satisfaction and security: 'We made a lot of money. That was a million dollar year for us, and it got us out of the red'.

18
Dares And Dreams And ...
Gene Tryp

By the end of 1970, the Byrds had a major-selling album on their hands and were at last being applauded as a successful live act. One idea that had failed to reach fruition, however, was the launching of *Gene Tryp* on Broadway. McGuinn explained that, though Jacques Levy remained confident that the play would be staged, there was some doubt about the efficiency of the business management. Already, there was some confusion as to precisely who would star in the play. Ideally, McGuinn wanted Dylan to play Gene Tryp but he also thought of auditioning himself. Other names were suggested, including Tim Buckley and Jon Voight, but nothing came of it. In spite of the apparent setbacks, Roger remained extremely enthusiastic about the play, and talked about the production at great length in several interviews of the period.

The plot of the play, though very much in the episodic form of a romance, had enough thrills and spills to keep a contemporary audience satisfied. The action was to be set in the Southwest of America during the 1880's. Originally, there was to be a wedding scene in which Gene Tryp entered and stole the bride away, *à la* Dustin Hoffmann in *The Graduate*. After escorting her to the High Country, Gene is abruptly smitten by a nubile young Indian who becomes his new woman. Incurring the wrath of the local tribe, Gene is forced to abandon her, and finally falls in love with a third girl, Kathleen. Together, they settle down and build a house on the prairie, but one evening, as Gene returns from chopping firewood, he discovers that his house has been surrounded by an impenetrable force-field. Unable to return to the house, Gene is forced to travel all the way round the world, which takes the remainder of his life. This leaves the producers free to include a variety of other scenes with Gene as an evangelist, a smuggler, a gun runner ('Lover Of The Bayou'), a presidential candidate ('I Wanna Grow Up To Be A Politician') and anything else that might later be adapted to the musical score. The play was to end on a dramatic note with Gene finally returning to the Penelope-like Kathleen, only to die in her arms.

As the script shows, the play was feasible enough and the many different scenes encouraged a variety of musical forms from country to bayou, to hard rock. However, the special effects were far too elaborate for a budget that had already been cut from $750,000 to $300,000. McGuinn spoke of rivers running on stage, a 23-piece pit band, tapes and liquid projections. Even the maximum $150,000 that Columbia had bid for the score was not enough to finance the project. Disturbed by the financial risks, the businessmen began to question the profitability of the venture. Millionaire David Merrick felt it would not last a year on Broadway, and bubblegum genius, Don Kirshner, after showing some initial interest, also withdrew his support.

While interest in the project continued to wane, McGuinn was firmly convinced that *Gene Tryp* was still a viable proposition. In 1971, McGuinn announced that Michael Butler, who had been involved in the staging of *Hair*, was showing some interest in the book, and the Byrds were awaiting his comments on the score. Assuming that Butler would support the project, McGuinn predicted that the play would be staged in 1972, three years after it had first been announced.

As time passed, however, everyone agreed that *Gene Tryp* was just a giant white elephant, and no reputable producer could afford to risk handling it. If the play had been staged, many believe that it might have vicariously projected the Byrds into superstardom. But it seemed that there was no real substitute for hard work, and the group were left to pay their own dues continuing their extensive touring schedule.

In spite of the continual setbacks, Roger's optimism about the *Gene Tryp* venture seemed unquenchable and as late as 1974 he was still toying with the idea, though in a somewhat modified form:

'I have considered reconstructing the play as an audio-musical, just doing a soundtrack album. I could have done it as a radio show where it would be narrated and say, "Now such and such is happening". You can get away with lots of flights of fantasy when you don't have actual sets to deal with. It would be a lot easier and a lot cheaper to do. It's a good idea for an album. I think Jacques Levy and I should adapt it for a radio show type of album. That's coming back into popularity, it would be a good country rock opera. Well, we have the book, we're sitting on it. We wrote it way back in 1968, it's been a long while.'

Unfortunately, neither the album nor the soundtrack ever appeared and by the time I reached him, Roger was willing to admit that the project had failed:

'It's *passé*. It wouldn't work today. It was good for 1968, but it wouldn't be good for 1978. I've had talks with Jacques Levy and he completely puts it down on the grounds that the novelty of country rock is over and the attitude of it is extremely male-chauvinistic, which just wouldn't go these days. Jacques is very cynical about the whole thing. He doesn't want to even think about it. I'd like to read the book again and check it out, but he's not interested, so it's just history. Too bad.'

Although the play never materialized, it would be a mistake to write off *Gene Tryp* as a complete failure. Even during the 80's, McGuinn continued to weave the songs from the musical into a rambling narrative, suitable for his solo concerts. Without the play, we would never have had such memorable Byrds songs as 'Lover Of The Bayou', 'Chestnut Mare', 'All The Things' and 'Just A Season'. It should be stressed that, without those tracks, *(Untitled)* would hardly have been such a commercial success. Moreover, it seems likely that without the critical acclaim bestowed on *(Untitled)*, McGuinn would have continued to change groups as frequently as he was to do in his subsequent solo career. More importantly, however, without *Gene Tryp*, Roger would not have established the successful co-writing team of McGuinn/Levy. Without the inspiration of Jacques Levy, who encouraged Roger to write a staggering 26 songs during one month, we would not have witnessed the resurgence of the Byrds at the turn of the 60's.

19
Melcher And Maniax

The Byrds continued their policy of touring and recording during the early part of 1971 and, in May, they returned to England for a series of sell-out concerts, beginning in Bristol on 3 May, and ending in a glorious night at the Royal Albert Hall, on 13 May. After exhausting their repertoire, the Byrds returned to rapturous encores and ended the evening with a moving version of 'Amazing Grace', which had originally been intended for inclusion on *(Untitled)*.

Following the gig, the Byrds discussed their latest and as yet unreleased album. From their defensive comments that night, it seemed clear that they were not entirely enthusiastic about every aspect of the album. McGuinn revealed that there had been problems with Terry Melcher during the recording of the new album and he had just resigned as Byrds producer.

A pilot single, 'I Trust'/'Is This My Destiny', was released to coincide with the tour, and the album, *Byrdmaniax*, reached the shops on 23 June. In spite of the Byrds' reservations about the new album, it received favourable reviews in the English press. Pleased by the critical response, the Byrds completed their tour, appearing on stage as a five-piece group. The fifth member was their irrepressible road manager, Jim Seiter, who had begun accompanying the Byrds in rehearsal, following which he decided to join them on stage.

While *Byrdmaniax* fared well in Britain, the response in America was scathing. McGuinn was particularly annoyed by one review which had described the album as 'excrements of pus'. In subsequent interviews, however, the Byrds severely criticized the album, while Gene Parsons totally disowned it. As far as the Byrds were concerned, the aesthetic and commercial failure of the album was entirely the responsibility of Terry Melcher. The comments of Clarence White typified the Byrds' opinion of the work:

'Terry Melcher put the strings on while we were on the road. We came back and we didn't even recognize it as our own album. It was like somebody else's work. Our instruments were buried. Melcher had produced some hits on the first two albums, then he almost got us hits with "Easy Rider" and "Chestnut Mare", so by the time of *Byrdmaniax*, Roger couldn't believe that Terry could do any wrong.'

The Byrds complained bitterly that Melcher had employed orchestration without their approval and had squandered over $100,000 on the project. Such criticism of Melcher's extravagance did not seem unwarranted, as Byron Berline was only too willing to testify:

'On the "Green Apple Quick Step" session I was there from 9 pm to 5 am. Terry would say, "We'll do this . . . ", and then he'd go off and drink coffee or something. But I didn't care. I got well paid for that.'

While the extent of Melcher's alleged extravagance has been duly noted, it does seem as though too many people were criticizing him solely for his introduction of strings and choruses. Few chose to remember that Melcher had employed strings effectively on *Ballad Of Easy Rider* and that his track record, up until this point, was impeccable.

When I spoke to Melcher, he agreed that his decision to continue recording *Byrdmaniax* was a fatal error on his part, but he added that the Byrds were in no fit state to cut the album during this traumatic period of their lives:

'My most vivid recollection of that album was catching McGuinn's wife, Ianthe, in mid-air as she was heading towards McGuinn's neck . . . Several members of the group were involved in divorces and they were hiding from their wives. It was complete bedlam in the studio. Everyone had too many problems.'

In answering the more controversial questions about the album, Melcher proved remarkably evasive, and later admitted that he felt like 'a worm squirming on the end of a hook'. It seemed only fair, however, to allow Melcher the full opportunity to defend himself against the castigating comments of the Byrds. The following snatches of interview, then, may serve as Melcher's defence plea.

'You claim that you weren't extravagant but how do you explain away the fact that you spent about $100,000 on the album?

'There were wasted weeks. McGuinn rented a Moog which was very expensive. I wasn't getting the guitar parts, so I added other instruments'.

Was the orchestration added without their approval?

'I think the orchestration was a big mistake, but the songs were weak'.

You're avoiding the question. Was the orchestration added with or without the Byrds' approval?

'I'm not a tyrant or anything. There was a lack of interest on everybody's part. With the divorces it was a problem. I was trying to save the album but it was a mistake. I should have called a halt'.

You still haven't answered my question. Do you admit that you did add the orchestration without their approval?

'No. Well, I mean I admit that I wasn't in consultation with them a lot and I didn't really deal with Clarence, Battin or Parsons on these matters. But I'm sure it was inconceivable that McGuinn did not know about the orchestration'.

Clarence said, 'Melcher buried our instruments'. Is that true?

'It's possible. If anything got buried it was because it was mediocre'.

Parsons described the album as 'Melcher's Folly'. How do you feel about that?

'I didn't get on too well with Gene Parsons. How does he describe *Ballad Of Easy Rider*? I used strings on that album too'.

Battin said that you didn't come to too many sessions.

'It's possible. I was having problems too. I should have never let it get past the first session'.

Is it true that you wanted to replace Battin and Parsons with session musicians?

'Probably. I thought Gene Parsons was a better guitar player than a drummer.'

McGuinn said that the album was taken out of your hands and remixed by an engineer in San Francisco. Were there any substantial differences in the final product?

'I can't remember the differences or even if there were any. All I can say is that my original couldn't have been any worse'.

A closer analysis of the album will reveal the extent of the supposed damage and the degree to which Melcher's erstwhile good name may be vindicated. The opening track on the album, 'Glory Glory', was another song that Gene Parsons borrowed from the Art Reynolds Singers. Melcher obviously felt that a strong vocal backing was required to bring out the gospel flavour and so he introduced a host of backing singers, including Merry Clayton. Unfortunately, this proved insufficient to save the song from mediocrity, as Melcher admitted: 'We were aiming to cut another "Jesus Is Just Alright", but we didn't make it. Larry Knechtel played piano on this cut but it was too fast. The whole thing was a mess'.

By contrast, 'Pale Blue', written by McGuinn, turned out to be one of the stronger cuts on the album. The theme, concerning the conflicting desires for freedom and security, is given great expression through Roger's sensitive handling of the vocal. Melcher's use of orchestration is fully justified here and strikingly enhances the romantic elements in the song. However, by allowing Parsons' harmonica breaks to remain, Melcher altered the whole effect of the song. The obvious juxtaposition of that most simple of instruments, the harmonica, with an elaborate string section, seems to have escaped the notice of everybody. When the Byrds' recut 'Ballad Of Easy Rider' for the CBS album, they wisely dropped the harmonica and allowed Melcher to embellish the song with some free-flowing orchestration. Here, however, they retain the bluesy harmonica, while adding the orchestration. The harmonica places the song in a folk genre and makes the theme a simple statement of love, unaffected by emotional complexities, while the orchestration provides an underlying pathos. Ironically, the song succeeds as a result of fusing these disparate elements and the harmonica and orchestration elucidate the conflicting feelings of domesticity and wanderlust to considerable effect. Here it seems 'Melcher's Folly' has been transformed into a success: 'The idea of orchestration came out of "Easy Rider". I like what you say about the harp and the orchestra working together as I've always liked to use strong contrasts. I thought "Pale Blue" was pretty close to what we wanted'.

It took McGuinn six years to compose a song around his famous catchphrase, 'I trust it will turn out alright'. Unfortunately, the song is one of Roger's poorer efforts. Melcher tries to give it greater significance by backing singers but the effect is detrimental. White's work is stifled and McGuinn's Rickenbacker is restrained to the point of frustration while the chorus is screamed out. All in all, an erratic song with some interesting moments that are never developed. In retrospect, Melcher recognizes the shortcomings of the song: 'I think you're right. Now you mention it, there wasn't really any distinctive jingle-jangle Byrds sound'.

The derivative Battin/Fowley composition, 'Tunnel Of Love', was memorable only for its lyrics. In the song, the guy sees a derelict Tunnel of Love and his mind commutes back into the past to conjure up a ghostly vision of his former self. The organ accompaniment, straight out of 'Blueberry Hill', is complemented by a saxophone backing. The other Byrds are virtually nowhere to be heard, and this sounds suspiciously like a completely solo outing from Battin. Although the diversity of material makes a pleasant change, McGuinn deserves censure for not taking a firmer stand and insisting that solo efforts be incorporated into a more unified group context. A classic case of group democracy gone wrong.

On the face of it, 'Citizen Kane' seems another example of McGuinn failing to curb the evil influence of the notorious Kim Fowley, whose work stands out like a gross aberration in the Byrds songbook. This song is partly rescued from the accusation of being a total novelty throwaway by McGuinn's lead guitar break. Battin stressed the autobiographical elements in the song: 'Kim wrote that incredibly quickly. It was novelty in one sense, but it was also true. Kim lived that Hollywood life and he saw a lot of that stuff as a kid'.

The *Gene Tryp* song, 'I Wanna Grow Up To Be A Politician', becomes, within the context of *Byrdmaniax*, another novelty, joke number. Yet, McGuinn's attitude to politics was quite serious at the time:

'Politically, I'm becoming much less apathetic. I've always been somewhat left of the centre, but now it's getting so that you have to take a stand. My writing is becoming more political. People have thought of us as representing a political viewpoint since the first album. "Chimes Of Freedom", even "The Bells Of Rhymney" were political songs.'

On the bootleg album *Live At Buddys*, McGuinn voiced a new political philosophy:

'Politics, something that must be dealt with. Some people contend that musicians and entertainers should not deal in politics. Others say that the musicians and entertainers of this era are the new clergy. I'm not sure what's happening, but I trust it'll turn out alright.'

Seven years later McGuinn, borrowing Lord Buckley's old catchphrase, confirmed: 'Entertainers are the new clergy'. All these expressions of commitment, however, do not alter the fact that during this period of avowed political interest, McGuinn was unwilling, or unable, to express any particular standpoint. Even Battin had indirectly commented upon the Vietnam War in 'Well Come Back Home', but McGuinn remained silent. The only comment we have in song is the unassuming 'I Wanna Grow Up To Be A Politician'. As McGuinn later admitted, his political expression was stifled by cynicism:

'I'm curious about politics. But I'm also very cynical because I came out of Chicago where Richard Daley had been mayor since I was a little kid. I knew the reason he was mayor was not because he was the best person for the job, but because he had the machine.'

'Absolute Happiness' proved to be Battin's most effective song on *Byrdmaniax*. The orchestration is negligible and has little or no marked effect on the mood of the piece. The song appears to begin with a dramatic situation, but later moves into a Buddhist speculation on the nature of absolute happiness. Battin recalled the track: 'It was a song about the Buddhist philosophy, as you say. We wrote it after a Buddhist meeting. Kim wasn't involved in Buddhism, but he absorbed the idea'.

The instrumental, 'Green Apple Quick Step', included White on mandolin and guitar, his father on harmonica, Parsons on banjo and Byron Berline on fiddle. The playing is so fast that it is difficult to believe that the tape has not been speeded up to produce the stunning effect. A track for which the Byrds ought to feel justly satisfied, but this is not the case. Parsons complained bitterly that Melcher destroyed all the supposed subtleties with Berline's fiddle part. Byron, himself, was unimpressed with the track:

'"Green Apple Quick Step" was a spur of the moment thing. They'd recorded that before the fiddle was overdubbed. I didn't record live with them. Terry wanted me to overdub three different fiddle parts. That was impossible! It didn't turn out as well as it should, the mixing was awful. One thing about the song; they put me up in a booth, way upstairs some place. I couldn't see anybody. They had a microphone way up in the ceiling, about six feet away from my fiddle in order to get that big hollow, echo feel. Terry Melcher is a very strange producer at times.'

When faced with this catalogue of criticisms, Melcher seemed to take the safest way out: 'I don't even remember how it goes'. In spite of what Melcher is supposed to have done with it, the end product is still a good cut. From Berline's comments, we can only conclude that the instrumental was not sufficiently traditional to satisfy Parsons and White.

'(Is This) My Destiny' was another song discovered by White. The whole approach is embarrassingly dated, and the steel guitar work and Floyd Cramer keyboards style fail to save the song from mediocrity. White often had good taste in his choice of material but this merely sounds like a bad outtake from *Sweetheart Of The Rodeo*.

'Kathleen's Song' was the last *Gene Tryp* composition that the Byrds recorded. The use of strings here is again justified, as the song is essentially a dramatic piece, with McGuinn singing the part of the long-suffering heroine. Full credit to Melcher for the tasteful orchestration, which is used in a similar way to 'Pale Blue'.

For most commentators, Jackson Browne's 'Jamaica Say You Will' remains the strongest cut on the album. The group, however, were far from satisfied with the version that appears on *Byrdmaniax*. Parsons recalls Melcher substituting a bad take of the song for a version on which White had apparently given his finest vocal performance. The Byrds insisted that Melcher added strings and horns to the alternate take, without their knowledge or approval. Clarence White's only comments were expressed in a tone of utter disappointment:

'On "Jamaica" I tried to do an excellent recording because I knew Jackson Browne was going to be known as a great singer and incredible songwriter. We did a good track underneath there, but when they added the strings there were almost 40 people in the studio, and they had to listen to the track because we don't always tune on pitch. So, instead of tuning to the piano, they had to tune from the earphones. So the whole orchestra is a little sharp and I'm singing flat. I was embarrassed when I heard it.'

There is no denying that it is a very strange mix. Parsons' drumming is, at times, inaudible, while the strings swirl round creating an unusual, though not unpleasing, effect. The lead guitar sounds very sharp, however, so perhaps the Byrds' criticisms are centred entirely on the weak vocal. Melcher maintained that his actions were not irrational:

'Clarence wasn't that great a singer in technical terms. I just chose the version that I thought was the best. Linda Carradine (formerly McGuinn) later told me that there was some friction in the group because Roger didn't like the idea of Clarence singing that song and wanted it for himself.'

Whatever our conclusion about the mix, and Melcher's decision to add orchestration, 'Jamaica Say You Will' remains one of the best songs on the album.

In conclusion, it seems too sweeping an assertion to dismiss *Byrdmaniax* as a failure on Melcher's part. Some of the material is reasonable and, though it lacks the consistent excellence of *(Untitled)*, the album still shows that the Byrds were capable of writing some good songs. Significantly, McGuinn voiced no great dissatisfaction with Melcher's production on 'Pale Blue' or 'Kathleen's Song', and the decision to employ orchestration on those songs proves an effective move. Moreover, even the severest criticisms of his production techniques on 'Green Apple Quick Step' and 'Jamaica Say You Will' seem unconvincing when we consider the quality of those cuts. Melcher's only real failure is his inability to cope with the Byrds' less impressive material. On weak songs, such as 'Glory Glory', he tries to compensate for the ineffective vocals by introducing backing singers, but, rather than succeeding, he only highlights the shortcomings of the Byrds in this respect. Instead of attempting to improve the instrumentation, Melcher occasionally decides to bury it, but such instances are the exception rather than the rule. His production on *Byrdmaniax* was a spurious controversy to my mind and though the results may have been unusual and disappointing to some purists, they were far from disastrous.

20
Farther Along The Road To Disunity

Having completed a successful tour of the UK in May 1971, the Byrds returned unexpectedly two months later to head the bill at the Lincoln Folk Festival on 24 July. Although billed as the 'acoustic Byrds', that did not prevent them from opening their performance with an electric 'So You Want To Be A Rock 'n' Roll Star'. The resulting set was half-electric and half-acoustic, and the crowd went away delighted. Instead of flying back to the States immediately, the Byrds chose to stay in London for a couple of weeks, during which they recorded a complete new album under the supervision of Mike Ross. It was a decisive move by the Byrds. Their dissatisfaction with *Byrdmaniax* had been voiced publicly, and they were anxious to rectify the damage as soon as possible. The recordings were brought back to the States and mixed by Eric Prestidge at Columbia Studios, Hollywood. It was another six months, however, before the album was released.

Meanwhile, the Byrds' hectic touring schedule was taking its toll and the group decided to take a vacation till January. During this period of silence, CBS (England) issued *Greatest Hits Volume 2*, a rather presumptuous title when we consider that of all the tracks listed only 'Chestnut Mare' could truly represent the album's title.

At the end of the year, it suddenly was announced that the Byrds were to embark on a European tour in January. Though nobody realized it at the time, this was to be, barring future reunions, the Byrds' last visit to

Europe with McGuinn at the helm. They played two nights at London's Rainbow Theatre (on 16-17 January) and were well received, in spite of persistent sound problems during the first performance. A gig at Midem, in Cannes, followed on 20 January, and the lightning tour ended with a remarkable concert at the Paris Olympia. The Byrds' contract had required that they finish by 8 pm but the show was such a success that the Parisians threatened to break up the theatre unless the group returned for more encores. Fortunately, the management persuaded the Byrds to pacify the crowd by extending their set by an extra quarter of an hour. The Byrds flew home from Europe leaving behind them a touch of old-fashioned, mid-60's Byrdmania.

To coincide with the European tour, CBS promptly issued the new album, *Farther Along*, which had been recorded the previous summer. The reviews were again reasonable and some commentators expressed pleasure that the group had reverted to a more austere production. If the album was acceptable, however, it revealed only glimpses of the Byrds' excellence. The new work seemed rushed, and much of the material was well below their usual standard. In their determination to compensate for *Byrdmaniax*, the group had haphazardly selected unsuitable material and recorded the new album in haste. It seemed more an emotive reaction directed against Melcher than an aesthetically pleasing venture. The whole album was structured in an almost identical fashion to *Byrdmaniax*, including the requisite number of Battin/Fowley songs, a new McGuinn composition, the latest Clarence White discovery and even another bluegrass instrumental. The Byrds were determined to prove that they could produce themselves far more effectively than Melcher, and the choice of material reflected this motive. Unfortunately, the experiment had failed, although they might have succeeded if they had taken more time.

If the Byrds had produced another *(Untitled)* then their point would have been proven, but the erratic *Farther Along*, rather than discrediting Melcher, showed that he was only trying to disguise the Byrds' own musical inadequacies. The most perceptive review of the album came from Bud Scoppa, whose diagnosis of the Byrds' current problems was to prove sadly correct:

'The Byrds recognized their failure on *Byrdmaniax*, but placed the blame on the lavish production job rather than their own disunity. So what we have on *Farther Along*, evidently rushed out to rectify the problems caused by the last LP, is more disunity, but this time in a basic unadorned state.'

Scoppa was right. The responsibility for the shortcomings of an album cannot be placed solely on the production, and people suddenly began to wonder why Melcher had seen a need to employ such drastic measures on *Byrdmaniax*. Was Melcher just an egocentric producer who had overstepped himself, or was he trying to save the Byrds from themselves by attempting to unify the work through orchestration? The question has no easy answer, of course, but a closer look at the album will show the extent of the disunity and the Byrds' unsuccessful attempt to discover a new direction.

'Tiffany Queen', the opening number, displays great enthusiasm, with its strident jingle-jangle guitar work. McGuinn seems to be attempting to re-introduce the old Byrds sound as an effective answer to Melcher's strings and girl choruses. Significantly, the arrangement is less cluttered than any track on *Byrdmaniax* and shows McGuinn's capacity to discover an excellent riff on which to build a song. Yet, 'Tiffany Queen' is more McGuinn's interpretation of 50's rock 'n' roll than a re-iteration of the Byrds sound. The amusing nonsensical lyrics and the deliberate imitation Chuck Berry riff in the middle of the song suggests that this is a rather self-conscious attempt at 50's rock 'n' roll. In fact, it is only McGuinn's occasional Rickenbacker work that prevents the song from becoming a pure parody rather than an interpretative work. The Byrds' great strength always lay in their ability to convert any musical style into their own unique sound. Here, McGuinn almost succeeds, but the synthesis of 50's rock 'n' roll and 70's Byrd rock was not an easy task. When we consider Battin's comment on the short duration between the composing and recording of the song, it is amazing that it worked at all: 'The whole thing was completed in a 24-hour cycle. It was written during the morning, rehearsed and recorded the same night'.

The next track, 'Get Down Your Line', shows the competence of the Byrds as producers and the mix is reasonable. Gene Parsons' echoed vocal is effective, but the material is sadly lacklustre. The song pales embarrassingly when placed alongside Parsons' earlier efforts, 'Yesterday's Train' and 'Gunga Din' and its validity as a Byrds album track is more than questionable.

'Farther Along', with its traditional origin, is, no doubt, the Byrds' answer to 'Glory Glory' on *Byrdmaniax*. The group took care to expand the arrangement but, despite all the work, the song still sounds terribly out of place. It is so obviously inspired by White that it seems a solo venture rather than a group effort. McGuinn's influence is undetectable, and his involvement here seems even more passive than on the *Sweetheart Of The Rodeo* cuts.

'B.B. Class Road', another below average track, was sung by the Byrds' roadie, Stuart 'Dinkie' Dawson. Dawson had the basic idea for the song and Gene Parsons added the melody. Unfortunately, the end result contained no distinguishable Byrds sound whatsoever. Literally, it could be anyone singing and playing. That a mere roadie could be given leave to appear on an album as easily as this is a testament to McGuinn's loss of control and general lack of interest in the group.

'Buglar', by contrast, proved surprisingly excellent. Among the other tracks on the album, it stood out like a diamond in the rough. Probably as a reaction against the disappointing vocal on 'Jamaica Say You Will', White invested all his efforts into this song. The result is nothing less than the best vocal performance of his Byrds career. Lyrically and melodically, the song deservedly stands beside both 'Truck Stop Girl' and 'Jamaica Say You Will'. Although Larry Murray, formerly of Chris Hillman's group the Scottsville Squirrel Barkers, never received the public recognition of either Lowell George or Jackson Browne, there can be little doubt about his excellence as a songwriter. 'Buglar' is so obviously superior to any other track on *Farther Along* that the remainder of the album becomes almost embarrassing. We should be thankful that, at a crucial point in its recording, White saved the song from a disastrous end:

'Because of *Byrdmaniax* we felt, "Let's see what we can do". We made our mistakes on *Farther Along* because we did it too fast – completed it and mixed it within five days. "Buglar" was one of the last songs we did and I could see by the way we were rushing through the album that we weren't getting the mixes right, so I purposely messed up my vocal on 'Buglar' and took it back to Hollywood CBS and dubbed on a bit of mandolin. Then we, just me and the engineer, spent a whole lot of time mixing it.'

As the last official recording released by White, this song remains a tribute to his musicianship and profound influence on the Byrds.

'America's Great National Pastime' indicated the strong influence that Kim Fowley had over Battin and the rest of the group at this point. Though the misguided might say that the lyrics are mildly amusing, the idea is pure novelty. While 'Citizen Kane' retained a vestige of distinctive Rickenbacker work, even that had disappeared on this song. 'America's Great National Pastime' represents the severest loss of musical identity that the Byrds suffered, and McGuinn's decision to include it on the album is inexcusable.

'Antique Sandy', written by all four Byrds, plus Jim Seiter, seems to have a close thematic link with the *Gene Tryp* number, 'Kathleen's Song'. Whether the Byrds deliberately sought to invite comparison between the folk-flavoured 'Antique Sandy' and the orchestrated 'Kathleen's Song' remains an interesting question. Skip Battin recalls that 'Antique Sandy' was essentially autobiographical:

'It was an experiment. The four of us had never written a song before. It was about Jimmi Seiter's girlfriend, Sandy. She lived in the woods and had a lot of antiques, but she wasn't particularly afraid of getting eaten by the bear.'

The effects used on the song, including double-tracked harmonies and electric piano, suggest that the Byrds took some concern over the track, which stands above much of the material on the album.

'Precious Kate' revealed the Battin/Fowley team at work again on another unimpressive cut. The highly derivative structure and arrangement is so ordinary that the composition can hardly be classified as anything other than mediocre. According to Battin, the song was written in five minutes, and the theme was inspired by an actual incident: 'It was an attempt to write a love song based on a true story about Kim and Kate. The "California Earthquake" line was the only memorable part of the song'.

The inclusion of the Fiestas' 'So Fine' was apparently suggested by White, who had long regarded the song as one of his favourites. Unfortunately, the song merely underlined how derivative most of the material was on this album. The guitar work on this track seems so contrived and uninteresting that you wonder why they bothered. If the Byrds were hoping to create a spark of spontaneity by bursting into an old rock number, such as this, then the result was a complete failure. The performance lacks any enthusiasm whatsoever, and no thought has gone into the arrangement or structure of the song. It sounds very much like a warm-up number or, at best, a bad outtake.

While the arrangement of 'Lazy Waters' sounds better than many of the other tracks, and the harmonies work well, the performance remains unconvincing. Battin appears to be looking for a serious song to match the power of 'Absolute Happiness' or 'Well Come Back Home', but this is not the one. His vocal is too self-consciously melodramatic to allow the sentiments to come across convincingly, which perhaps suggests that he had already become stylized as a purveyor of humorous novelty songs. For Battin, this condemnation is not valid:

'"Lazy Waters" was a serious song. I was living in the Mendocino woods and working on the road. I'd known the song a long time. It expressed my feelings about life in the country and life on the road.'

'Bristol Steam Convention Blues' was presumably meant to stand as the Byrds' reply to Melcher's treatment of their 'Green Apple Quick Step'. The picking sounds good, and it seemed that the Byrds were now replacing their mysterious novelty endings of old with bluegrass instrumentals. Despite the clarity of the production, however, it must be admitted that this number lacks the energy and enthusiasm of 'Green Apple Quick Step'. Moreover, the Byrds' attempt to compensate for Byron Berline's fiddle through the excellence of their performance ultimately proves inadequate. If we forget the comparisons, then the instrumental stands as a reasonable number in its own right. The inspiration for the song came as a result of Gene Parsons missing the Bristol Steam Convention twice in a row during the Byrds' visits to England.

What conclusions, then, can we make about *Farther Along*? The work as a whole seemed almost totally diffused, and although several of the tracks were individually effective, they contributed little or nothing to the unity of the piece. Each member of the group appeared to be moving away from the familiar Byrds sound into individual territories. At this point, the Byrds were failing to work in the studio as an effective unit and McGuinn still had firm plans for a long-overdue solo album. The prolific Battin/Fowley team had so many new songs that Skip felt the need to release them in a separate form from the Byrds. Clarence White had strong desires to record a country album and the multi-instrumentalist, Gene Parsons, was negotiating for a solo deal with Warner Brothers. It seemed as though there was a gradual polarization between the Byrds as four individuals and the Byrds as a group. While *(Untitled)* had redefined the Byrds' identity, the boundaries were now extending so far that nobody could say what differentiated a Byrds song from a solo work.

However, while we admit that the Byrds had split into four separate camps, there were elements in *Farther Along* which suggested that the group were desperately attempting to rediscover some common ground. In effect, they had to regress in order to maintain their aural unity. The influence of Kim Fowley on Skip Battin meant that their music was uncompromisingly grounded in the 50's.

Battin was being drawn away from his spiritual leanings into the realm of social satire and the glorification of American trivia. Any attempt to create a unified Byrds meant that it was necessary to regress into Battin's territory in order to search for a starting point. McGuinn attempted to bridge that gap by recording the 50's flavoured 'Tiffany Queen'. The experiment was almost a success, but it was clearly difficult, and McGuinn could hardly be expected to compose a series of songs in the same vein. White simply presented 'So Fine', which was, in effect, an admission that he could not create a nouveau-styled 50's rocker.

The four Byrds were hopelessly adrift from one another, and the results were agonisingly apparent on *Farther Along*. The album was not, it should be noted, an unlistenable disaster of unparalleled mediocrity though it had few saving graces. It was simply painfully uninspired and that was the most depressing conclusion of all. At this point in their career, the Byrds were still too alive to create a totally disastrous album, but *Farther Along* brought only unenthusiastic acceptance from their followers. There was hope that they might yet climb back to the heights of *(Untitled)* if they worked at their craft, so the critical reaction was tolerant rather than condemnatory. Yet, the very idea of an 'ordinary' Byrds album seemed a sad conceit. The Byrds were the musical pioneers of the 60's, and if their exploratory nature was to be replaced by laurel-resting works of questionable significance, then the spirit of the Byrds was already well and truly dead. It was obvious from their live performances that the Byrds could produce unspectacular but competent works such as *Farther Along* for several years yet before the formula finally exhausted itself. However, the ever-restless Byrds were not content to do this, and the fleeting revisits to rock 'n' roll music on the album reflected the pathetic futility of their search for new unexplored musical territories. The ideas were interesting but on the album as a whole they remained undeveloped. The Byrds needed to convert rock 'n' roll to Rickenbacker, and this could not be achieved simply by resurrecting 'So Fine' or drawing amusing parallels between the taste of coke and cocaine. What was required were stunning new songs and a drastic reappraisal of their current approach to rock. Sadly, the extra-curricular activities of the individual members made it impossible for them to formulate another 'new' Byrds sound. The Byrds saw a fresh direction before them, but they were unable, and probably unwilling, to follow it.

One week after the release of *Farther Along* the front cover of *Disc And Music Echo* revealed an astonishing headline: 'Original Byrds To Reform?' Although it seemed totally speculative at the time, McGuinn had already received permission from Columbia to record an album on David Geffen's Asylum label. The album was to be recorded later in the year as a one-off project, and there was no question of the current Byrds disbanding – or so it seemed. McGuinn, however, later revealed that even during the recording of *Farther Along* his attention was being distracted by the plans for the reunion album. Roger's wavering commitment to the CBS Byrds at this point partly explained the aesthetic shortcomings and directionless nature of *Farther Along*:

'It was recorded at a time when we were having internal problems and were generally weak. So the attitude of all the songs was weak. Those guys were upset and threatened by the reunion album. Even then, we were talking about the project.'

The concern with solo albums, and Roger's unrevealed plans about the extent of the reformed Byrds venture, meant that some of the members were far from committed to the recording of *Farther Along* during that summer of 1971. McGuinn seemed to have allowed the sessions to proceed in order that the others could show their contempt for Terry Melcher by rushing out an unorchestrated album. White hinted that McGuinn's involvement in the project was far from committed and suggested that he was more interested in his latest love, Linda, than in the recording of the new album. McGuinn later accepted this criticism as fact:

'Yeah, I was in love and so I didn't care about the music. That's probably true. If my emotions were clouded I couldn't possibly function properly. I guess I was in love and just wasn't paying attention to my business. It's a pitfall.'

So, during the early months of 1972, the Byrds were in a very precarious position. There was no talk of a follow-up album to the disappointing *Farther Along*, but there was much discussion of the possibilities of a grand Byrds reunion later in the year. The latter-day Byrds felt threatened and uncertain about their future as a group, and McGuinn was unable to alleviate their fears.

21
The Creative Nadir

By early 1972, the Byrds appeared to be almost totally self-sufficient. Apart from achieving their ambition to produce their own albums, they were also free from managerial pressure. Following their involvement with Larry Spector, in 1968, they had initially re-enlisted Eddie Tickner but it was generally felt that his attitude was 'not progressive enough'. The return of Melcher had caused friction during the *Byrdmaniax* project and so the Byrds decided to manage themselves. They retained a business manager and a booking agent but the managerial decisions were taken almost entirely by the group. What seemed a good decision, however, had its disadvantages. Although the group had suffered due to bad management in the past, they had also benefitted from the experience of people such as Jim Dickson and Eddie Tickner. Dickson had played an important role in helping the group to determine its musical policy, and though it is easy to exaggerate his influence, it should be remembered that he was almost entirely responsible for projecting the Byrds to superstardom by insisting on the release of 'Mr Tambourine Man' in 1965. Although the Byrds were perfectly capable of managing themselves, the departure of Dickson and the loss of Melcher, as both producer and manager, placed greater pressures on them. There was now less opportunity to discuss their musical policy outside the sphere of the Byrds. Moreover, the departure of Melcher and Dickson meant that the group were without the two people whom they had recalled in the 1969-70 period to re-establish the original Byrds sound. Billy James had also moved on, to be replaced by an anonymous public relations agency. Even the extrovert Jimmi Seiter, who seemed to play such an important part in maintaining the Byrds' morale, had become another ex-Byrds road manager. McGuinn, weary of what he termed Seiter's 'outrageousness', lost his patience and fired the exuberant roadie.

Although the Byrds were tightening their control over the group, their efforts seemed to be counter-productive. The individual members of the group were, in fact, beginning to outgrow the band unit, and their particular desires to embark on solo projects were hardly conducive to the Byrds' unity. No Byrds album appeared in 1972 except a brief contribution to the *Earl Scruggs His Family And Friends* television special. McGuinn explained how the invitation from Earl Scruggs came about: 'His kids liked us. Gary Scruggs was a fan of the Byrds, and I was a friend of Earl's, so it came together'.

The Byrds contributed 'You Ain't Going Nowhere', which was recorded in collaboration with the Earl Scruggs Revue, and 'Nothin' To It', an old bluegrass number made famous by Doc Watson. The renowned veteran, Earl Scruggs, apparently had a high regard for the music of the Byrds, as Gene Parsons remembers:

'Oh, he enjoyed playing with the band. Earl is a good guy. We had dinner at his house a couple of times, unlike the commercial country stars who are afraid of our music. A lot of them are denouncing Earl Scruggs, I'm sure, for having anything to do with us. And Earl Scruggs, by the way, was the only country musician from Nashville that showed up for the Moratorium in Washington DC. Good fellow, Earl! His boys have influenced him and he has changed, expanded his musical interests.'

The Byrds continued to gig in the States during the first few months of 1972, but it seemed that they were encountering more problems. In a review of one of their concerts, at the Symphony Hall in the Atlanta Memorial Arts Center, their drummer received some heavy criticism:

'If there was a flaw in last week's performance, it was Gene Parsons' drumming. He seemed to be a bit too loose at times and often his runs and combinations would be too long or overly complicated to allow him to keep a solid rhythm. I had an image once during the show of three well-tuned athletes running effortlessly around a track, being followed by a slightly overweight kid with his shirt hanging out and his shoe untied. See what I mean? It's not always that way. Listen to the Byrds' *(Untitled)* album. There is a live segment on this two-record set that shows what fine drumming Parsons is capable of.'

Whether the Byrds, and more particularly, McGuinn, were affected by reviews such as these, it is difficult to determine. Whatever the real reasons, the fact was that, shortly after this, a whole series of gigs were cancelled, including projected performances in New York, Chicago and England. McGuinn was spending a lot of time on new projects, writing songs with Jacques Levy and planning to take part in a film script by his old friend, R.J. Hippard. Meanwhile, the other Byrds continued with their respective solo ventures, which were still in the planning stages.

A single, 'Born To Rock 'n' Roll', was scheduled for release in May, but failed to appear. According to Clarence White, the arrangement was substantially different from the version that later appeared on the Byrds' reunion album:

'We planned to record it as a single. But the way we did it was like an old rock 'n' roll song. It was nothing like McGuinn did it on the reunion album. With us he just sang it straight'.

By July, the rift between the members had become even greater and the first signs of a complete dissolution appeared when Gene Parsons was fired as Byrds' drummer. The official explanation for his departure was 'musical differences', but the reasons went a lot deeper than that. There had been a growing discontent within that line-up ever since *Byrdmaniax*, as Battin remembers:

'After *Byrdmaniax* things weren't so good. We got through *Farther Along* and then wandered off into our solo albums. Nobody seemed committed enough to cut another Byrds album'.

Apparently, the seeds of discontent had been sown by Terry Melcher, whose influence over Roger was stronger than anyone dared admit. Clarence White felt that McGuinn had fallen under the spell of his former producer:

'Melcher was turning everyone's heads round on the *Byrdmaniax* album. He was telling Roger, "You can get a better bass player and drummer for your records". Terry wanted Roger, Hal Blaine and Joe Osborne "to cut some good tracks". He'd go over to Skip and Gene and tell them they should cut their tracks by themselves during the week. And they felt that me and Roger had something going with a middleman, trying to screw up the whole thing. At that point I started to miss days and not go in, just to avoid any trouble. And I had to tell Roger, "Terry is taking you some place else. He's taking you away from the group". Then Terry would say, "Hey, Roger, – Gene, Clarence and Skip are ganging up on you". It was impossible. Melcher did what he pleased. Roger let him do everything.'

Melcher's respect for session musicians was well known, as was his own musical ability. If there were weaknesses in the Byrds he could certainly spot them and he was close enough to McGuinn to voice those views without reticence. There seems little doubt that Melcher's criticisms had a strong effect on Roger who, found it extremely difficult to measure the extent of his producer's influence: 'I don't know, maybe he did turn my head. Terry did hate Skip and Gene. He thought they were terrible musicians. He wanted to get more professional guys.'

The Byrds had tried, unsuccessfully, to revive themselves but the scar remained. While the others were willing to forget Melcher's words, McGuinn was beginning to lose faith in his musicians and, according to

Clarence, on one fateful day, he made the dramatic announcement: 'The time is right; we can get a better drummer'.

Although Gene Parsons was fired by McGuinn, there was disagreement on both sides. Roger remembers a dispute over wages, just prior to his dismissal:

'Gene's attitude was wrong and he wasn't trying his hardest. He was angry with me about the money, although he doesn't feel that anymore. We weren't ripping him off. We had a profit-sharing agreement, and there was a bit of misunderstanding about what constituted expense deductions. Gene didn't see the money he was making because he was spending it on the road. I was perfectly honest about the money.'

Roger's defence was supported by Skip Battin:

'McGuinn was definitely in the right on that occasion with Gene. If one person in the band is allowed more on the expense account, then everybody would want a share. But there was also some suspicion in the group that Roger was using the expense account for his own extravagances in a similar way to Gene.'

Gene Parsons' account confirms Battin's suspicions that the wages situation was breeding bad feelings in the group:

'I was fired, but I think Roger used the excuse that I wasn't playing well. He wanted to replace Skip and I with the original Byrds and keep Clarence. I was very vocal about the wages situation. I felt Roger was taking most of the money and we were supposed to have a profit-sharing agreement. We would get statements outlining draws for expenses and when it came time for profit-sharing there wasn't anything left. I feel Roger was more extravagant than the rest of us when you consider his portable telephone and the various gadgetry he would have on the road.'

It seems, then, that Gene's anger about the wages situation may have manifested itself in his bad playing at the Atlanta concert mentioned earlier. Although the decision to dismiss Parsons appeared a sudden move on McGuinn's part, there is much to suggest that the firing was preconceived:

'One night after a gig, John Phillips said to me, "Your drummer can't play 4/4 time. He can't play rock 'n' roll, he can only play country". After that I thought to myself, "Yes, he's right".

Like Melcher, John Phillips' opinion was not to be scoffed at, for he had already established his reputation as the musical mainman in the Mamas and the Papas. Once more, it seems that Roger fell under the influence of someone else's words, though he disputes this: 'I don't know. I wasn't that swayed by what John Phillips had said, it just got things moving'. With hindsight, the factors involved seemed threefold: firstly, Roger was growing tired of the Byrds; secondly, he was troubled by other people's comments on the ability of other members of the group; and, lastly, he was attracted by the implications of a full scale reunion of the original Byrds.

During the summer of 1972, Skip Battin recorded his solo album, which was finally released in Britain in January 1973. *Skip* was made up entirely of Fowley/Battin compositions, and among the guest credits were Roger McGuinn, Clarence White and John Guerin. According to Kim Fowley, the songs were written for inclusion on the next Byrds album, but Roger had wisely rejected them.

By September, the Byrds were still alive and had replaced Gene Parsons with John Guerin, although Michael Clarke had previously been tipped for the job. Guerin was already well known to the Byrds as a session musician, as Battin explained:

'Both Clarence and I had previously worked with John. He was pleased to join the Byrds in order to get some gigging experience. I think he wanted a break from session work for awhile.'

In the same week that Guerin joined, it was suddenly announced that the group had changed its name to Roger McGuinn and the Byrds. This was the strongest indication yet of the internal problems within the group. The McGuinn/White/Parsons/Battin Byrds had always seemed the most easy-going line-up, and each member had commended the democratic way in which Roger exercised his role as leader. Now, however, it seemed that in the ensuing paranoia surrounding Parsons' dismissal, McGuinn had felt the need to re-establish his leadership in the strongest possible fashion. The Byrds were no longer a four-piece unit but had been transformed into Roger McGuinn and his back-up band. Fortunately, the name was dropped at the last minute, thus saving McGuinn from further accusations of being a hirer/firer. That, in itself, would have been ironic for it was becoming increasingly clear that McGuinn's major mistake had been in allowing the subsidiary members too much say in the choice of songs.

The new-look Byrds began gigging at the end of September but failed to involve themselves in any extensive touring schedule. Guerin, it transpired, was not entirely devoted to the Byrds venture, and was still employed as a session musician during the week. McGuinn was tired of touring with the Byrds and seemed content to continue gigging on a weekend basis. At this point, of course, McGuinn was severely distracted by the recording of the Byrds' reunion album which began in October. Prior to the recording of the album, Roger revealed an overwhelming enthusiasm that few had seen in recent years. McGuinn was convinced that the project would be successful, even though he was aware that the expectations of the media and the public might be too high.

Fittingly, the first rehearsal of the reformed Byrds took place at Roger's house and the first song they performed was a new McGuinn composition. Roger vividly recalled the night of the musical reunion:

'It was really quite remarkable. The voices gelled together, and to me, it sounded like we'd never been apart. But then, that can often happen when you get back to a special place that you haven't been to in a very long time. Naturally, everyone was a little nervous. There was a feeling of apprehension among us all . . . some more than others. This was something both David and I were acutely aware of but, underneath the superficial nervousness that we all shared, both Gene and I felt positive that it would really work all over again.'

In spite of the nostalgic reunion, the Byrds played none of their old songs that evening, but concentrated their attention on selecting suitable material for the new venture. By the end of the first rehearsal, McGuinn and his former colleagues were convinced that the reunion was not only a viable proposition but had the potential to be an aesthetically pleasing venture. The Byrds had promised each other that if any member felt uncertain about his commitment to the project, then the reunion would be shelved. From the pleasing results of the rehearsal, however, the group unanimously agreed to proceed to the historic recording of their first joint album in seven years. Following the festivities of the grand reunion, Roger returned to White, Parsons and Guerin and continued to play at the weekends. Apart from his activities with the original Byrds, McGuinn had also completed a dozen tracks for his first solo album, which perpetuated rumours that a Byrds dissolution was at hand.

At this point, however, the Byrds were not quite ready for the death blow. Despite pressure from the original Byrds, and the enticement of a potential solo career, Roger kept the Byrds alive and even harboured ambitions of reaching even greater heights: 'We're getting away from country music towards the highest jazz'. This statement underlined the fact that Roger was unsure which direction would prove most beneficial. McGuinn was involved in so many projects that he seemed in danger of falling victim to his own imagination. He wanted to take the original Byrds back to *The Notorious Byrd Brothers* period, complete an historic solo album, and allow John Guerin to inspire him to play the highest forms of jazz. McGuinn was overreaching himself, and his ambition to take the Byrds into jazz remained a dream only:

'I just realized how much dedication it would take and I wasn't willing to put enough into it. I wasn't prepared to practise eight hours a day! I was into jazz when I was with Bobby Darin – from that time until "Eight Miles High", which was as close to jazz as I ever got. In fact, some people said the "Eight Miles High" break was good jazz. But I wasn't enough of a jazz singer or player to cut it, so I didn't take the 1972 Byrds into jazz. I think I had delusions of grandeur when I said that.'

In spite of McGuinn's confusion, the Byrds soldiered on and were lined up for gigs in Chicago and Texas in December. Since the dismissal of Parsons, in July, their future had been in the balance, but five months later they were still alive and gigging. However, most people agreed that **the Byrds had progressively declined since *(Untitled)* and, although their** albums were still selling, there was no sign of the exploratory spirit that had made them pioneers during the 1965-68 period. The Byrds had somehow struggled to the end of 1972 and were still in one piece, but it was plain that they were on their last legs.

22
The Final Dissolution

By the beginning of 1973, it seemed as though the Byrds were simply winding up their commitments before the final dissolution. Clarence White admitted: 'That ended up happening, but we didn't plan it. We were hoping for a new light, but things got worse. Roger's head got strange'.

The Byrds still had several bookings in the next three months, and McGuinn decided officially to disband the Byrds on 19 May at the Academy of Music, New York. The concert was a guaranteed sell-out but, regrettably, the Byrds disintegrated before their final performance. By the end of January, John Guerin decided that the Byrds' music did not suit his style of playing, so he moved on. In retrospect, McGuinn realizes that Guerin was not the ideal Byrds drummer:

'I liked working with John, but he was too jazz-orientated, and perhaps too good a drummer for what I wanted. He wanted more out of the deal. He was just doing it for a gig, he wasn't really part of the group. He had a funny attitude about the whole thing. He kind of looked down on us as something lesser than he was capable of doing. I guess that was true in a way. He's capable of another level of musicianship.

The sudden departure of Guerin meant that the Byrds had to find another drummer to fulfil their commitments. However, it was difficult to persuade musicians to join the unstable Byrds, who appeared likely to fall apart at any second. Denis Dragon, who had previously played with the Beach Boys, replaced Guerin but he was in and out of this unstable line-up at virtually every other gig, as White explained:

'He was only with us for four weeks, our last drummer. Another guy called Jim Moon filled in when John or Denis couldn't make it. But he didn't have enough experience at the time'.

The Byrds still looked as though they might struggle through to their final commitment until McGuinn suddenly decided to fire Skip Battin. Clarence White did not support McGuinn's decision:

'Roger said, "I think we could get a better bass player". Well, I said, "OK, maybe Joe Osbourne is technically a better bass player but even if he wanted to join the Byrds . . . can we relate to each other?" Skip knew our music and could change with us. After something like that has been together for nearly five years, you can't start replacing members. But Roger didn't believe me and had to find out for himself. I think he felt that Terry was right after all. I said, "If you feel like getting rid of those guys and don't like their musicianship, don't let me decide, you try it without them. You fire them!" So he did, and ended up with no band!'

McGuinn virtually admits that the dismissal of Skip Battin was nothing more than a whim: 'A lot of people had told me about Gene and Skip's inadequacies. I always felt funny about them. I thought Skip was kind of jive.' It seems incredible that, after playing with a fellow musician for over three years, McGuinn would suddenly discover that he was not up to standard. Yet, no other explanation has ever been given for the sackings of Parsons and Battin. McGuinn, while recognizing the contradiction in firing a musician for musical ineptitude after playing alongside him for over three years, cannot give any logical explanation for his own strange action except a flimsy excuse: 'Yeah, but I guess I didn't notice. I must have been getting complacent'. The complacency McGuinn refers to reflects his growing disenchantment with the final Byrds line-up. After Hillman had left, McGuinn had taken total control with the album *Dr Byrds And Mr Hyde* and had been censured for his tyranny. In the succeeding years, McGuinn gradually succumbed to the strong influence of Battin and White in an attempt to make the Byrds a democratic unit. By late 1972, however, McGuinn appears to have realized that his misplaced sense of democracy was, in reality, a form of complacency. His immediate reaction was to reassert his authority by promising to curb the number of Battin contributions, as well as indicating his intention to control the Byrds' musical direction. No doubt the reunion of the original Byrds played a crucial part in determining McGuinn's attitude and may even have made him realize that his current group, by comparison, simply wasn't good enough. Skip Battin believes that his dismissal was probably the result of McGuinn's desire to start afresh:

'McGuinn fired me. At the time I think he wanted to get Hillman and the original Byrds, but he also wanted to keep Clarence. He was probably right. The reunion seemed a good idea. We were falling apart. There was mild resentment and suspicion about the money. I wasn't surprised or

THE FINAL DISSOLUTION

annoyed. When Gene got it, I knew it was just a matter of time. I've had to fire people myself, sometimes it's necessary.'

McGuinn's last words on his role as hirer/firer within the group suggest that, by the end of the Byrds, he had once more achieved total control:

'The last band wasn't to my liking. Clarence and I fired each other as a joke, but nobody had the right to fire me as I was leader and I'd fired everybody by that time anyway'.

With several commitments left to fulfil, Roger took desperate measures and phoned Chris Hillman in an attempt to re-enlist him as a Byrd. Hillman recalled the day the 'Manassas Byrds' were formed:

'Well, Roger had a commitment in New Jersey, just before he ended the band. He had no bass player or drummer, so when he called me I suggested Joe Lala. Actually, Joe is more of a percussionist, and to be truthful, we didn't get a chance to rehearse. Now 50 per cent of the songs he was doing I'd played before but the rest were all new stuff from the (*Untitled*) album onwards. We played bad!'

Their weekend performances at the Capitol Theater in Passaic, New Jersey, on 24 February, were so untogether that the farewell performance in May was cancelled. Hillman and Lala were touring with Stephen Stills in April, so there would be no opportunity to improve their live performance through rehearsal. Prior to the Passaic gig, Roger was talking optimistically about forming a group with Clarence White and Chris Hillman, but the clash of personalities prevented the project from being realized. Although Chris and Clarence were old friends, all was not well that night at Passaic. A review of this final gig stressed the supposed animosity between Hillman and White, and Clarence's disappointment about the current state of the Byrds:

'Clarence enjoyed playing with Skip Battin because he said Skip was able to drive the band well. He was annoyed and angry when Skip was fired. It made him frustrated because it was clear that he didn't have any control over things that were going down in the group. Clarence said that at one time he felt that playing with the Byrds was consistent with what he wanted to be doing musically but that since Hillman and Lala joined, "It's become a drag." He has some hope, certainly a desire, for the Byrds to become a real group again and move forward, but if that doesn't happen then he isn't sure who he will get together with.'

The Free Aquarian reviewer seemed fairly certain who was responsible for the Byrds' substandard performance:

'It was Hillman who messed things up for the band. He is viewing the spring tour as a part-time job or a favour to Roger but he isn't thinking in terms of the music. He even admitted that he doesn't enjoy playing bass anymore but that fact didn't stop him from playing so loudly that he drowned out Clarence's guitar through most of the late show. Clarence asked him several times on stage to turn it down but Chris merely threw his head back, smiled and kept on playing. Hillman had also refused to rehearse with the band and it was evident that he didn't know most of the songs.'

Hillman received even greater censure when it was revealed that he had charged the Byrds $2,000 for his services that weekend. Yet, although McGuinn showed his displeasure at Hillman's actions during this period, Chris felt that the criticisms had been exaggerated:

'Roger asked me, "How much do you guys want to do this weekend?" Well, we had to cancel everything to do it, so I said, "How much are you grossing?" and the figure was $25,000 for the weekend. I said, "Give me and Joe $1,000 a night and we'll do the third night for free". We were making $500 to $1,000 a night with Stephen Stills, so I don't feel it was unfair. However, I must admit that we didn't play $2,000 worth of music. I wish I could have rehearsed with him but I just didn't know songs like "Chestnut Mare" and "Lover Of The Bayou".'

Hillman was especially annoyed at the press reports which had indicated his supposed refusal to rehearse:

'No! That was not true. I flew out there to rehearse but there was no time to. We only did a weekend. We flew out Friday morning from Colorado. We had a soundcheck for half an hour and that was the time we were supposed to learn those songs. We tried our damndest. If we'd only had six hours to rehearse, it would have been better.'

Following the gig, Roger spoke optimistically about the future and indicated that the present Byrds would complete their commitments:

'Unfortunately, we have to do things that are fairly familiar to our audience because we haven't had the time to get things together yet. It was a spur of the moment proposition that we all got together, and I think that what we can offer now is not technical perfection but spontaneity. Eventually, I hope to get technical perfection with the spontaneity, and get it filled out.'

These were brave words from Roger in the face of disaster but everybody had realized that the Byrds had died a death at Passaic. There was insufficient enthusiasm left in the band to consider the possibility of further gigs even though a McGuinn/Hillman reunion was something to be savoured. The real heroes that night at Passaic were the die-hard Byrd followers, who, despite being subjected to a poor performance, gave the group a rousing send-off. The critics were perplexed by the 'surprisingly appreciative response of the audience', who were obviously excited by the return of Hillman as well as paying tribute to the Byrds for the last time. After a year of indecision and dilemma, McGuinn at last dissolved the group that he had led for almost nine years.

23
The Phoenix Rises... And Falls

The disbanding of the CBS Byrds, in February, heralded the return of the original Byrds the following month. For, in March, the long-awaited Asylum album was at last released. While the dissolution of the group had passed almost unnoticed the previous month, the new-style original Byrds received their full share of publicity. The headlines proclaimed: 'The Byrds are dead . . . long live the Byrds', as speculation grew about the permanence of the reunion and possible touring plans for the summer. McGuinn was particularly excited about the venture, and it became clear that his strange and unpredictable moods throughout the previous year were the result of his desire to reinstate the original Byrds to their rightful position:

'It's a backwards step forwards and not a hype. Neither is it something that was scraped out of the bottom of a can. It's a brand new product and one which I'm certain will make a lot of people happy. From here on in, the only group of musicians who will be known as the Byrds, and who will record under that name, will be the original five. What I do on my own will be entirely different. You see, the major thing that the original band didn't accomplish was, simply, staying together. Or, at the very least, being open to each other and really attempting to work together. Personally, I always enjoyed the high moments of working with the original Byrds line-up, and this time around it feels like we're most definitely getting back to that.'

The strength of the reformed Byrds unit was seen to lie in the informality of its members' reunion. While the original Byrds had disintegrated because of the intensity of their interrelationships, it was hoped that the reformed group would avoid the problems of internal strife by reuniting on a yearly basis. In effect, the Byrds were to continue as a unit that would regroup at regular intervals in order to undertake tours and record albums. Thus, the members did not constitute a group in the traditional sense, but functioned as a gathering of individuals under the Byrds banner. The plan had its prototype in the Crosby, Stills, Nash & Young relationship, although that unit had not recorded together for over two years.

The press paid much attention to the Crosby/McGuinn relationship and spoke in grandiloquent terms about the ending of a feud which had raged between them for nearly seven years. In reality, of course, McGuinn and Crosby had long forgotten their differences. It was simply that their subsequent recording careers had taken two different roads which had seldom crossed until the reunion venture. Now, of course, their futures were inextricably bound together and, as part of the Columbia/Asylum exchange deal, Clive Davis had demanded that Crosby and McGuinn make a joint album for CBS, sometime the following year. Moreover, Crosby was already quite involved with Roger's solo album and had persuaded McGuinn to dispense with Terry Melcher, and take a more active role in the production of the work. Nothing, it seemed, could go wrong and negotiations were already underway for the proposed summer tour. Apparently, the Byrds had been offered $100,000 just to play one night in London, so a whole European tour could not be ruled out.

Many of these ambitious plans might have reached fruition were it not for one fateful twist: the critical reaction to the album. During and after the recording of the new album, Crosby and McGuinn had spoken with great enthusiasm about the high quality of the music, and the discovery of a new-found unity which the old Byrds had lacked. McGuinn had even suggested that the new album would take up where *The Notorious Byrd Brothers* had left off, implying that it would be another innovative album in the mid-Byrds tradition. Understandably, the critics were waiting for a classic Byrds album and may even have been expecting the group to surge forward in a new musical direction. In the light of these expectations, it was inevitable that the album would receive bad reviews. However, the criticism was so widespread that even McGuinn and Crosby began to doubt the merits of the new album and eventually dismissed it. As a result of the bad reception afforded the album, the individual members lost faith in the reunion idea, and this was enough to prevent the extensive touring plans from being realized. The Byrds returned to their various solo projects with half-hearted promises about the possibility of a second reunion album, to be recorded and produced in a different fashion.

In retrospect, the album hardly deserved the unanimous critical condemnation it received. Admittedly, it was no *Younger Than Yesterday* or *The Notorious Byrd Brothers*, but it was, undoubtedly, the most interesting album any Byrds line-up had recorded since *(Untitled)*, and that alone made it worthy of a reasonable review. However, due to the advance publicity, the over-expectant critics were not prepared for anything less than another *The Notorious Byrd Brothers*, and the whole project was dismissed prematurely. A re-evaluation of the album shows that it had several weaknesses but there was also evidence of a musical strength which the myopic critics of 1973 chose to ignore.

'Full Circle' was, originally, the projected title of the album before somebody decided on *Byrds*. No doubt Gene felt that the critics would mistakenly assume that he had written the song specifically for the reunion venture: 'I'd already recorded that song a couple of years earlier and it wasn't really written about anything specific. It was just an idea I had'. Nevertheless, the wheel of fortune idea was particularly applicable to Clark, who never really capitalized on the original Byrds status and subsequently fell from grace with the record-buying public for a period. Although undoubtedly one of the strongest cuts on the album, with some fine mandolin work from Chris Hillman, the song failed to receive the praise that it so obviously merited.

For his first contribution to the reformed Byrds, Roger stepped back into the style of his pre-flight folk days with 'Sweet Mary'. The whole approach to the song, with the nasal vocal and syllable stretching, conjures up visions of the old folk clubs in which Roger used to play before joining the Byrds. Hillman's mandolin work is, once more, effectively employed to enhance the folksy effect of the song.

The opening harmonica break to 'Changing Heart' immediately places the song in the tradition of 'Set You Free This Time'. This seems to be another autobiographical account centring on Gene's inability to convince the big business people that his work was valid, irrespective of its commercial potential. Whether the song was consciously autobiographical or not, the theme seems definitely applicable to Clark's musical career. He was lavishly praised by fans and media alike when he reached the top with the Byrds but, when he reverted to a solo career, in order to express his soul-searching more effectively, the bright lights deserted him. Although this is another strong number on the album, some excellent Rickenbacker work is unnecessarily mixed into inaudibility by Crosby.

The choice of a Joni Mitchell song, 'For Free', was hardly a great shock, since Crosby had stated on several occasions that she was his favourite songwriter. Their relationship, both personal and professional, was well known and he had previously produced her first album, *Songs To A Seagull*. His strong vocal performance on 'For Free' compensated for the fact that the harmonies are undeveloped. The stark, uncluttered instrumentation in this song works effectively and draws attention to the extent of Crosby's vocal range. Clarke's drumming is also exceptional and he even partly adopts the military style which he had previously pioneered on *Preflyte*. The song is certainly not irrelevant to this Byrds album, as some critics have suggested, since the theme fits in well with the subject matter of several other tracks. The point of the song is to stress the sad distinction between the famous superstar and the unsuccessful struggling performer. In this sense, the song is closely aligned to the Gene Clark songs mentioned earlier.

The closing cut on side one, 'Born To Rock 'n' Roll', is embarrassingly feeble, and McGuinn later admitted that he had a stronger song which he should have included. McGuinn appears to have attempted to write a semi-serious song about how he became a rock musician but suddenly changed his mind and concluded with a tribute to rock 'n' roll. Thus, the song is not to be regarded as too serious but should be enjoyed as a rousing rock number, with mildly amusing undertones. Unfortunately, the whole idea fails because the song is such a weak rock 'n' roll number. The enthusiasm it was designed to create, by preaching the merits of rock 'n' roll, is lost in a completely lacklustre performance. The high energy rock 'n' roll that McGuinn alludes to in the song is nowhere to be heard on this track. Having failed to cut an adequate version of this song with the CBS Byrds, and ruined the reunion album with a second unsuccessful attempt, McGuinn, for some inexplicable reason, even chose to inflict it on his followers again by including it on his third solo album. Once more, the song was a flop and, in retrospect, McGuinn recognizes its weaknesses:

'"Born To Rock 'n' Roll" was a dog. I tried to get it right again on my third solo album, but I've finally given up on it. I realize it's a total disaster. It's stilted and just doesn't work. The reason I tried it again was because it didn't work the first time. But I'll never try it again.'

The commercial 'Things Will Be Better' which opens side two is, in many respects, similar in content to the songs that Chris had contributed to *Younger Than Yesterday*. Although it lacked the strength of either 'Time Between' or 'Girl With No Name', it was, at least, substantially better than Chris' subsequent material with the Souther, Hillman, Furay Band. In common with several of the other tracks previously mentioned, this song reminds us that life is a wheel of fortune which can take you to the top in order to watch you fall.

The appearance of Neil Young's 'Cowgirl In The Sand' prompted many to assume that David Crosby had a strong hand in choosing the material. However, this was not the case. Gene Clark had long admired

Neil Young as a singer-songwriter and the inclusion of this song was a tribute from one artiste to another. Gene's vocal technique and harmonica playing brought the song an unusual country flavour. The harmonies from the other Byrds were the most effective thus far on the album, and the whole performance had a unified feel lacking elsewhere. This was the first track that could not instantly be characterized as a definite solo outing.

'Long Live The King' completed the Byrds' examination of the trials and tribulations of superstardom. The rock business is seen to produce super-heroes only to knock them down from their pedestals, when the appropriate time arrives. It seems unusual that an album which has generally been criticized as totally diffused should provide a thematic link over four separate songs by Crosby, Clark and Hillman. Ironically, the Byrds were unconsciously predicting the results of the whole reunion venture. They were encouraged to produce a star-studded album, only to watch it being publicly discredited along with the entire reformation concept. 'Long Live The King' at least demonstrated that the Byrds had the potential to produce an effective harmonic blend, complemented by some interesting guitar licks.

It is still debatable whether an essentially right-hand man, such as Chris Hillman, should have received an equal share in the distribution of songs on this album. Yet, his material on this album seems equal to that of the former leader, McGuinn. Although his bass work on the album was sadly ineffectual, this was at least compensated for by the impressive mandolin breaks on songs such as 'Borrowing Time'.

Crosby's decision to recut 'Laughing' for the album was made on the grounds that he had originally written it for the Byrds. The arrangement seems sufficiently different from his solo version to warrant inclusion. The 12 strings gel together to form a semblance of the old Byrds sound. This was a further indication that the group had the potential to create a unique sound of its own. Clarke's drumming on this track was the finest on the album and the stop/start technique at the end of each verse provided an interesting arrangement. The same technique can be heard on 'Cowgirl In The Sand', discussed earlier. The one criticism of this track is that, although it attempts to reintroduce traces of the Byrds 12-string sound, the overall effect is diminished because Crosby's voice is too instantly recognizable to be regarded as anything other than a solo effort. However, this seems an insoluble problem that will always apply when a former soloist chooses to sing lead on one of his own compositions.

The most fundamental criticism of the album was its disunity, and this objection about the failure to produce a distinguishable sound might have been entirely justifiable were it not for '(See The Sky) About To Rain'. Gene's lead vocal is strong, the harmonies are tight and the mandolin breaks provide an intriguing touch, adding a further layer of instrumentation to the enveloping sound. Significantly, Michael Clarke once more reverts to his unusual style of almost military drumming. In fact, all the components of the Byrds sound are mixed into this track. The high harmonies increase in prominence as the song progresses until the stop/start technique is re-employed at the end of the song. For just under one second there is complete silence, and this is followed by a sound which can only be described as pure Byrds. A legion of 12 strings fill the chasm of silence, while the voices attempt even greater heights. For even greater effect, Michael Clarke, the champion of 4/4, provides a final blast which is undoubtedly the finest drum roll heard on any Byrds song since those magic moments on 'Goin' Back'. The final line of the song is then drowned by a stream of reverberating 12 strings which create a magnificent wall of sound. At this precise moment, the Byrds succeed in creating a unique sound and, for this alone, the seven-year vigil for the reformation is proved worthwhile. Whatever criticism anyone has of the album, there can be no doubt whatsoever that, within the final minute of this song, five individual musicians combined to produce a stupendous sound that could have been successfully developed on subsequent albums.

The failure of the grand reunion, then, can be blamed equally on the comments of the over-zealous critics and the individual reactions of the over-sensitive Byrds. Of all the Byrds, only Gene Clark seemed even vaguely capable of placing the work in a critical perspective:

'I am disappointed in that album. Some of the harsh criticism is unjust, because, if you listen to it carefully, the album isn't that bad, but it just hasn't got the punch it could have had if we'd taken the time. Each member of the original Byrds has a lot of credibility and you can't discount them either as live performers or in the studio situation.'

It was clear that the reformed album was a rushed venture, and no critic should have expected a clearly distinguishable Byrds sound to emerge. A constructive review of the album should have attempted to discover whether an underlying Byrds sound was detectable beneath the individual contributions. Obviously, the Byrds could not be expected to dissolve their five personalities into a complete whole at the first attempt. It must be stressed that this was a first album and as such should have been regarded as transitional. The Byrds were aware of this and needed the necessary encouragement to record another. However, the critics proved destructive rather than constructive in their comments. The major points of contention were: Crosby's poor production; McGuinn's poor material; Hillman's inept bass work and the album's lack of cohesion. While the critics rightly stressed these faults, they chose to ignore all the elements which suggested that the Byrds were gradually formulating their own sound. Individual insights into the quality of the musicianship and the extent of the reformed Byrds' compatibility were sacrificed to preconceived notions about the worthlessness of the product.

Instead of attempting a constructive view of the work, the critics centred their discussion on such irrelevancies as the fact that the Byrds had failed to include any Dylan songs on the album. Of course, it hardly needed stressing that the last Byrds album to contain a Dylan song was (*Untitled*) back in 1970, and earlier works such as *The Notorious Byrd Brothers* and *Fifth Dimension* had shown that the group was certainly not dependent upon Dylan for its success. The critics, however, seemed to ignore the fact that the reunion album was a product of the 70's, rather than a nostalgic trip back into the mid-60's. The Byrds had chosen to perform the songs of Joni Mitchell and Neil Young because they were the important singer-songwriters of the 70's. In contrast, Dylan was a relatively non-creative force during the early 70's and it was not until *Blood On The Tracks*, in 1975, that his genius was fully rekindled. The Byrds had suffered at the hands of the critics for making the perfectly valid decision to not record a Dylan song. The total hypocrisy that underlines such criticism of the Byrds was made fully evident a couple of months later when Roger McGuinn's first album was greeted with critical acclaim. The same critics chose to ignore the fact that it also contained not a single Dylan song.

While the critics had helped to destroy the success of a long-term reformation by demolishing the album, the Byrds were equally guilty of accepting critical condemnation as a final judgement. From the date of the recording to the album reviews, the Byrds had revealed nothing less than total confidence in the final product. Crosby and McGuinn, in particular, had both stated that the album transcended their wildest expectations. Following the bad reviews, however, both Crosby and McGuinn were only too willing to admit that they had overestimated the album's worth. Looking back, Chris Hillman remembers that he was the only person who felt anything less than ecstatic about the album at the time it was recorded:

'At the time, I went to Elliot Roberts and told him it didn't sound right. I wanted to use Paul Harris on keyboards to fill out the sound but the others felt that we ought to keep it the Byrds. I talked to David three months after that and he said, "You were right". I said, "What the hell does that matter now?"'

Although the album was a relative chart success, the scathing reviews proved more than enough to destroy the enthusiasm and confidence of the over-sensitive Byrds. The plans to tour America and Europe that had seemed so definite weeks before the release of the album were now a bad dream, as Hillman recalled: 'We had plans to tour, but it never came about. It never even got down to discussing going out on tour after the release of that album'.

The Byrds returned to their individual projects and promised to rethink their approach before recording the next reunion album. In the meantime, the Byrds' public awaited the Crosby & McGuinn album with anticipation. It was generally accepted that the success or failure of another reunion venture depended upon the relationship between these two controversial figures. A joint album would, it was hoped, give them both the greatest opportunity to bridge the gap between their differing musical policies, and once such a fusion was created then the formulation of a new Byrds sound would be inevitable. Sadly, the much-vaunted Crosby & McGuinn album failed to materialize. Although it was originally a contractual necessity, the exchange deal was never completed, as McGuinn confessed: 'That was a Clive Davis idea and Clive got fired, so it was no longer valid. Crosby and I never bothered to record together. Nothing was cut'. By April 1973, it was clear that the Byrds would not be reuniting on a semi-permanent basis and all that remained was the hope of another reunion when the time was right.

Undoubtedly, 1973 was the tragic year in the history of the Byrds. Apart from the dissolution of the group and the retirement of the reformed unit, there were also two personal tragedies within the short space of three months. Clarence White, who had stayed by McGuinn's side until the final dissolution, was tragically killed by a drunken driver, on 14 July, while loading equipment into a van following a gig. The previous night he had been a guest at Roger's birthday party. Their relationship had survived the traumas of the Byrds' dissolution and they still hoped to record together sometime in the future. At the time of his death, Clarence had been involved in a host of projects, including a solo album, a Kentucky Colonels tour and a projected visit to Europe with a star-studded bill of ex-Byrds and Burrito Brothers. Having reached a new creative peak, White's life was tragically cut short. Gene Parsons' words expressed the feelings of musicians and friends all over the world: 'There isn't much to say except that we loved him very much, and we'll miss him for the rest of our lives. For myself, personally, I'll never be able to play music again without thinking of my friend Clarence'.

At the Catholic funeral service, an estimated 100 musicians were in attendance to say farewell to one of the most respected figures in country and rock music. Although no music was played during the service, Gram Parsons and Bernie Leadon remained at the graveside to sing 'Farther Along'. During the wake that followed, Gram Parsons was noticeably depressed about the funeral rites. On the same evening he and road manager Philip Kaufman went out to get drunk. According to a number of sources, Parsons and Kaufman made a ritual pact that night, agreeing that when either of them died the other would ensure that the body be taken to the desert and cremated.

On 19 September, tragedy struck once more when Gram Parsons died from reported heart failure. Ironically, Gram had been added to the ex-Byrds/Burritos tour of Holland, which was now set back once more, and finally cancelled. The bizarre circumstances of Gram's funeral were the subject of much publicity and were even reported in the English daily press. Following Parsons' tragic death, the corpse had been stolen and the FBI were called in to investigate what was suspected to be a ritual murder. The explanation, however, was not as sinister as the media had expected. Remembering the pact, Kaufman and group member Michael Martin had hijacked the coffin at Los Angeles Airport and taken it to the Joshua Tree National Monument, a place much loved by Parsons. There, they cremated the body, feeling that they had fulfilled Gram's dying wish.

The deaths of Clarence White and Gram Parsons had a profound effect on the progress of contemporary country music, to which they had each contributed so much.

24
We'll Meet Again

By 1974, Roger McGuinn was able to look back on the whole reunion venture and place it in a clearer perspective:

'I thought the album could have been a lot better. At the time we made it I was very excited. But that's how you always are when you write or record. It's not until later that you look back in perspective. In retrospect, the group should have been together more, rehearsed more.'

The idea behind the reunion was an interesting one, but McGuinn felt that it was a little too idealistic: 'A big square dance where everybody would play with everybody else over a period of 12 months; David and Graham, me and David, Chris and Stephen – but it won't work that way'.

McGuinn had diagnosed the situation correctly. Although the reformed Byrds unit seemed the perfect vehicle to allow friends to record together and extend their musical ideas without the usual problems of an established group set-up, the results were not pleasing. The Byrds had succeeded in negating their internal ego problems by allowing the individual members to record elsewhere and thus encouraging a non-claustrophobic situation. Unfortunately, with the loss of internal strife, the Byrds also ran the risk of losing the intense enthusiasm that had characterized their best work. Their finest albums, *Younger Than Yesterday* and *The Notorious Byrd Brothers*, were recorded at a time when either tempers were raging or the group was in the process of self-destruction. It almost seemed that their pleasure in reforming was somehow detrimental to the music. More importantly, however, the insistence that each member should continue a solo career and remain a Byrd seemed self-contradictory. The pursuit of individual projects by each member meant that the reformed Byrds would continue to grow away from each other rather than unify. They needed to place their musical ideas within the context of the Byrds, and this would be impossible if their minds were continually cluttered with solo projects. The concept of an annual reformation was not adequate. The Byrds needed more time to stay together as a permanent unit in order to rediscover each other as musicians and personalities. Only when this occurred could we expect to receive the innovative musical ideas that characterized their work in the mid-60's.

In spite of Roger's continued criticisms of the first reunion album, he remained confident that another would appear sooner or later:

'Maybe that'll be an anti-anti climax. It couldn't be worse than the last one. That one came out on the Asylum label because David was on Asylum and he was calling the shots and had the most power. Asylum were prepared to give us more money than Columbia too, so it didn't make any sense not to go with Asylum. Unfortunately, that was largely a business manoeuvre as opposed to a musical effort. It was very segmented.'

It seemed that McGuinn's criticisms of the album were not restricted to the performances, but also to the attitudes of some of the members: 'David is mostly concerned with how many dollars he can earn as a duo, a trio or whatever. He's out to make as many dollars as he can. But who isn't really?'

Certainly, McGuinn seemed willing enough to get involved in a business venture himself, and within months he was presented with one of the most lucrative propositions of his entire career. The reformed Byrds had never played a live gig, but Asylum Records was now on the point of persuading everyone to get together for one sell-out performance. Many felt that this was simply more speculation, until it was announced in the press that the gig had been set for 6 July at the Los Angeles Coliseum. McGuinn gave his full support to the idea of a reunion concert:

'It's a business move. Elliot Roberts and Bill Graham decided to promote that and get it together. They happened to have all the entertainers necessary to do that except me, and I'm willing to go along with it. If they can get the rest of the group on stage, I'll do it. It sounds like a lot of fun. It will be the Byrds, Buffalo Springfield and Crosby, Stills, Nash & Young in the chronological order they came in. I think it will all be recorded for an album.'

The ambitiousness of the project was gargantuan and somehow it seemed impossible. Three of the most legendary defunct outfits of all time staging a comeback on the same night was a thought that most people could not conceptualize. On the other hand, having reunited the original Byrds after a seven-year separation, it seemed that the Geffen/

Roberts starmakers were capable of anything. A reunion on this scale, however, would have meant nothing less than changing the face of rock history. The grand design remained unaccomplished, and all the speculation about a live album and a full length film of the gig were never realized. While the Bill Graham/Elliot Roberts amalgam had failed to reunite all three groups, their efforts were not wasted. In the summer, fans were overjoyed when the former superstars Crosby, Stills, Nash & Young reunited for a short season of gigs. The response was incredible, and the reformed group were in such great demand that they could only afford to play at football stadiums holding a minimum of 50,000 fans. On 14 September, they even managed to make a trip to England in order to appear at Wembley Stadium before 72,000 fans. The tour was a triumph and a new album was planned for the winter, but, like so many of these reformed projects, it failed to reach completion.

Rumours continued about another possible Byrds reformation, but as the years passed everyone gave up hope of ever seeing it realized. Apart from their commitments to solo ventures, the Byrds were still despondent about the failure of the first attempted reunion, as Chris Hillman explained:

'We only wanted to do it to get back together, to play and see what happened. We weren't really looking at it financially, even though it crossed our minds. We had plans to tour but the album turned out horribly. In all honesty, we didn't have enough time on the album. They gave us one-and-a- half months to do that album, expecting guys to regroup after a five to six year absence. We needed a producer, we needed at least three months to rehearse and we needed material, ours and someone else's. We had none of these, and everybody was so afraid of stepping on the other person's feet because of the tension that had gone down six years prior to that, that it became a bland album. Everybody was being too nice to each other. David recut "Laughing" for some reason, and I didn't put my good songs on the album as I was saving them for my solo album. I felt that everybody was doing the same. I think Gene had the best songs. "Full Circle" was great. If "(See The Sky) About To Rain" had been edited, it would have made a great single. But they didn't even do that.'

The failure of the 1973 reunion album was enough to keep the Byrds apart for a further four years. During that period each member went through a series of musical adventures, often interesting, but generally unspectacular. Crosby promised a second solo album to follow his brilliant, and surprisingly neglected, 1971 effort, *If I Could Only Remember My Name*, but circumstances continually persuaded him to postpone the idea. As the early 70's passed, Crosby appeared infrequently with Graham Nash and his other friends, but his creative output was relatively small. Following a three-year gap, the excellent

Wind On The Water indicated the possibility of a revival, but this was negated by the disappointingly average *Whistling Down The Wire*, released the following year. Although he appeared to be enjoying his musical escapades, Crosby had become complacent, and his work revealed little of the urgency or enthusiasm that had been shown at the dawn of the 70's.

For Roger McGuinn, the 70's were a far more productive period, but he also appeared to be falling into the same ennui as Crosby. His first two solo albums had been well-received, but for McGuinn this was not enough. Even his finest solo work was unfavourably compared to the old Byrds material, and his impatience was reflected in the increasing number of backing musicians whom he hired and fired in an attempt to compensate for the loss of the Byrds. By the end of 1974, it seemed that McGuinn's career had reached a new low. For some inexplicable reason, which he still cannot explain adequately, McGuinn released an appalling album titled *Roger McGuinn And Band*, which seriously dented his credibility. The album, consisting mainly of banal material from members of his backing band and ill-advised reworkings of 'Lover Of The Bayou' and 'Born To Rock 'n' Roll', suggested that McGuinn had lost all sense of musical direction. Fortunately for McGuinn, his reputation was salvaged the following year when he appeared as part of Bob Dylan's Rolling Thunder Revue. The successful tours that followed helped to re-establish McGuinn's reputation in the rock press, and inspired him sufficiently to record the much praised *Cardiff Rose*. McGuinn's plan to form a group with Mick Ronson, following the *Cardiff Rose* sessions, failed to reach fruition, however, and by the end of 1976 Roger had hired another bunch of backing musicians whom he dubbed Thunderbyrd. The Rolling Thunder venture had provided a much-needed shot in the arm for McGuinn, but the formation of Thunderbyrd hardly promised any innovative musical work in the future.

Like Crosby and McGuinn, Chris Hillman also appeared to be running short of fresh musical ideas. Having established a legendary reputation as a bassist and anchorman in the Byrds, Burritos and Manassas, Hillman allowed himself to be persuaded to form a group with Richie Furay and John David Souther. The Geffen/Roberts duo were convinced that this new superstar unit could produce platinum at will, and although their debut effort, *Souther, Hillman, Furay* did indeed go gold, it was far from aesthetically acceptable. The trio were less a group unit than three temperamental individuals, and by the time of the second album, *Trouble In Paradise*, the unit was in the process of collapse. That final album remains the least impressive record on which Chris has ever played as a permanent group member. The dissolution of the Souther, Hillman, Furay unit allowed Chris to concentrate on his long-awaited first solo album. The results were reasonable enough to encourage Chris to continue working as a soloist. Hillman's commitment to his career as a soloist, however, remained questionable. In the press, he freely admitted that his finest work had been accomplished in the role of a right hand man, rather than as a group leader. As the months passed, Chris spoke more and more about the possibility of becoming a full time producer and admitted that he was sick of playing the bass. Like his fellow ex-Byrds, Hillman was clearly becoming bored with his familiar role in the rock world.

Of all the original Byrds, it seemed that only Gene Clark was attempting to push forward towards any new musical horizons. Following a respectable showing on the Byrds reunion album, Gene stayed with Asylum and recorded the startlingly innovative *No Other*. Musically and lyrically, *No Other* was a masterpiece and a clear contender as one of the best albums of the decade. In spite of its brilliance, the work was not a commercial success, and after some disagreement with Asylum, Gene and producer Thomas Jefferson Kaye, moved to RSO, where they began recording a less complex work. In his determination to record a commercially successful yet aesthetically acceptable product, Clark was showing the first signs of an artistic compromise.

While the other four original Byrds were experiencing artistic problems, drummer Michael Clarke had finally found his perfect niche in Firefall. Apart from his working days in the Byrds and Burritos, Clarke had constantly ended up retiring to Hawaii, only once trying to retrace former glories in an obscure outfit known as the Dependables. With Firefall, however, he had found himself a secure future, and was now enjoying more commercial success than many of his fellow ex-Byrds.

Although it seemed unlikely that the Byrds would ever reassemble, a happy coincidence brought faith back to many disillusioned hearts. Three original ex-Byrds, McGuinn, Clark and Hillman, were lined up for a tour of Europe in May 1977, with each member fronting his own group. It was an ingenious idea on the part of the promoter to present the three ex-Byrds on one show but, unfortunately, all did not go according to plan. Throughout the first gig, in Dublin, they were plagued with sound problems, and their second concert, slated for Birmingham, was cancelled due to a series of delays caused by zealous customs officials. From the outset, it seemed that the whole tour was dogged with bad luck.

During the tour, there was much speculation about a reunion on stage, and, indeed, at the end of their first performance in London, the trio emerged to sing a medley of hits, much to the delight of a partisan audience. As the Thunderbyrd set reached its conclusion, Roger McGuinn casually announced, 'I'd like to bring on a couple of buddies', and out of the wings wandered Chris and Gene, their heads wrapped in tea towels in a hilarious parody of the Rolling Thunder Revue. They burst into an impromptu version of 'So You Want To Be A Rock 'n' Roll Star', and the previously unexpressive audience rushed to the stage in a desperate attempt to be part of this historical reunion. 'Feel A Whole Lot Better' followed, with Gene beckoning the audience to the front of the stage and encouraging them to clap and dance. Hillman had abandoned his rhythm guitar and switched to his more familiar role as bassist as they moved into 'Mr Tambourine Man'. The evening ended with a spectacular version of 'Eight Miles High', which left the audience gasping. The voices were a little flat, but there was a detectable magic in the strange combination of McGuinn and Clark's vocals. The trio had travelled back 12 years, and their performance that night had effectively transported a few of us into a different era.

What began as a mini-Byrds reunion, however, gradually became recognizable as a microcosm of the Byrds' history, complete with personality clashes and a premature dissolution. After that opening gig in London, the trio failed to reunite again, and the following evening I distinctly remember McGuinn beginning 'So You Want To Be A Rock 'n' Roll Star' with the words, 'Is Chris there?', only to be greeted by the reply from backstage, 'No, he's gone'. The following evening, McGuinn gave me his version of events:

'It was Gene's paranoia. He left and Chris left too. Gene got a little drunk and I guess he didn't want to stick around and stay sober and wait in the wings and watch Chris' set and my set in frustration'. The three groups performed separately at the next two gigs, Manchester and Leeds, and there was no more talk of a reunion.

Since the reformation venture seemed no longer plausible, each member proved more willing than before to discuss the controversial events surrounding the 1973 reunion. At the time of the reformation album, they had all stressed the fact that the personality problems within the group had been resolved. In the light of subsequent rumours, however, it seemed that David Crosby had taken too great a control in the production of that album. Many critics had blamed the supposed failure of the album on Crosby's production, but Chris Hillman now felt the need to deny this:

'No, it wasn't David's fault, it was all of us. David took the production credit and I'm sure he was sorry he did. I didn't realize he was the producer until the end of the album. I felt we were all the producers, but it came out that he took the credit, and he can have it.'

Although reticent about discussing Crosby's role in the reunion venture, McGuinn decided to break his silence, and spoke frankly about the strange relationship between himself and David Crosby during the recording of the album:

'My real feelings on the matter are that Crosby was trying to get back at me for firing him. Because he had David Geffen, Elliot Roberts and the financial power of Asylum, he had more say in the matter than he ever used to, and that's why Gene did more vocals than he normally would have. Crosby was calling the shots. It was Crosby's *coup d'etat*. He was being leader of the group.'

It soon became apparent that McGuinn had felt intimidated during the reunion album sessions:

'I think Crosby wanted Gene to do the vocals in place of me. It was one of those things. He wanted to minimize my importance in the group and maximize his, and other people's. In fact, he even stated as a joke, but I believe he meant it, that he wanted to put everyone on the cover except me, and wanted to put a horse in my place. The horse on the cover of *Notorious* was not done on purpose. It was an accident. That's just the way it came out.'

Crosby was more than a little incredulous about McGuinn's explanation: 'An accident? An accident! Do you believe that? It's bullshit. You know why he did it'. David was also sceptical about McGuinn's contention that he had intended to include a horse on the cover of the reunion album:

'That's his style not mine. That particular "joke" was not funny to me, and I wouldn't have said that to him . . . McGuinn I think was paranoid because he had done it, and I hope he was ashamed of himself'.

In concluding his comments on Crosby, McGuinn indicated that his words were not prompted by any feelings of bitterness:

'I'm still friendly with David. I'm just saying that David was trying to run the show on the Asylum album and it failed. I place the blame on him, though I was at fault too. I'm not saying it was entirely his fault. I was going on the road, Chris was going on the road, and the concentration was diffused. We were having too much of a good time at a party during it and weren't paying attention to our business. But David had a definite ego vendetta going on. I think Crosby was trying to prove that he should have been the leader of the band for the whole time, and with the Byrds reunion album it backfired on him. Especially when it came down to the mixing. That's when he panicked. I saw the beads of sweat on his forehead. That was the bottom line of the entire deal. Crosby does not subscribe to McGuinn's view:

'There was no panic and I didn't knife him hardly at all. Maybe I did a couple of times, but compared to what it could have been, it was enormously restrained.'

It seems then, that all the publicity about the vendetta between Crosby and McGuinn had some validity. Of course, the rivalry had not been sufficient to prevent their recording together. Prior to the reunion album sessions, McGuinn had been more than willing to follow Crosby's advice by firing Terry Melcher and taking full control of the production of his first solo album, *Roger McGuinn*. Crosby was allowed to make a guest appearance on three tracks and all five Byrds played on 'My New Woman', a song which many wish had appeared on the Byrds' reunion album. In spite of these friendly gestures, however, an underlying sense of rivalry remained and McGuinn believes that Crosby had to have the final say in avenging his dismissal from the Byrds. After stating his views about the ego problems surrounding the reunion venture, Roger seemed to realize the controversial nature of his remarks, yet he chose not to modify them: 'Crosby is going to hate me for what I said, but I believe in it'.

In replying to McGuinn's comments sometime later, Crosby was equally scathing about his former colleague:

'I think McGuinn's scared of me. I got too big, too fast and that's what he wanted to do . . . . I think that since CSN&Y he's resented me, being jealous of me, being afraid of me, and not wanted to be put beside me.'

Recovering his poise, Crosby argued that McGuinn probably misconstrued his actions on the reunion album:

'I got us a bad engineer, who didn't do that badly, but he was the wrong guy. One mistake I think I made was with the Neil Young song '(See The Sky) About To Rain'. I think it should have been sung by McGuinn, and not Gene. It should have been McGuinn lead. That was a definite mistake, not because of any ego trip, but because Roger could have sung it better. That was a mistake. I didn't have a vendetta with him then, and I don't now. It would be foolish to, because I did enormously better than he did, and both he and I know it. And he's got to live with the fact that he said he'd do better without me. That's his problem.'

The most important question of all, however, still remained to be asked. Would the Byrds be reuniting in the future? Gene Clark expressed a distinct joy at the prospect of another live reunion and felt sad that David and Michael were not part of the package tour:

'It could be done, but it has to be handled very gently, very carefully, and in such a way that everyone is still able to carry on their own careers. I know that Chris and Roger and I wouldn't want to split up our current bands and stop our individual careers just because we were doing a Byrds thing, but, if we handled it right, and took the right time, there's no reason why the Byrds shouldn't perform together, and even record something too.'

Chris Hillman seemed equally hopeful, and stressed the comparative ease with which such a move could be effected:

'I'd love to do it. I'd like to leave a better taste in everyone's mouth. People were expecting a good album and they didn't get it. People, to this day, will accuse us of doing it for the money, but we didn't make a dime! It was a bad album and it didn't sell.'

Hillman, of course, failed to mention the fact that the album reached the US Top 20 and, indeed, achieved gold status. Chris concluded that another reunion was probable:

'The contractual difficulties involved in getting us together are easy to fix. The problem is to coordinate it with each guy, which is something you have to set up six months in advance. The hardest part is getting everyone to agree to it and commit themselves. I've said it before and I'll repeat it now: I want to do it again! I know David and Roger do too.'

Behind the public mask of cameraderie, however, the mild dissatisfactions evident throughout the 1977 tour were shortly to result in a complete shambles. Firstly there was the minor problem of McGuinn and the press. As the tour progressed, Roger revealed signs of irritability when faced with microphones and familiar questions. Although sometimes curt with the press, his attitude during the 1977 tour bordered on the belligerent. Moreover, his increasing reliance on cocaine during this period led several of his colleagues to speculate upon his future as a creative musician. The unruly interviews merely led to further speculation that all was not well backstage.

Following these early problems, the promoters' worst fears were confirmed when it was officially announced that Chris Hillman had quit the tour. At first it seemed unbelievable. Chris Hillman, whose representatives claimed had never cancelled a concert in 15 years as a performer, was leaving his former colleagues in almost Gram Parsons fashion. The dramatic walkout concluded with some bitter statements about a misunderstanding over payments. For McGuinn, it must have provided a chilling reminder of the traumatic days of late 1968 when Hillman had left the Byrds due to a similar financial disagreement, smashing his guitar against the wall as a final comment on the situation.

Although McGuinn and Clark struggled on for one more show, the remainder of the tour was cancelled. Even the reviews of the final gig were far from complimentary, and there was discussion in the press of a drunken Gene Clark bounding onstage towards the end of the Thunderbyrd set to deliver an horrendous version of 'Mr Tambourine Man', much to McGuinn's annoyance. As the trio flew back to the States, the pundits were left shaking their heads and sighing, 'So much for the Byrds reunion'.

Before his departure, McGuinn expressed his true feelings about a Byrds reunion to me in a damning comment:

'It's not a great desire on my part at this stage. If the Byrds did reform again it would be so disastrous that I wouldn't want to think about it. I know I said before that I wanted to save the name, but I don't know if it's possible. It might be something that should be left alone. I guess I am putting it away. I feel it's something I don't need and I don't feel that the world needs it really. I think it's something that would gratify the egos of the other Byrds.'

25
McGuinn, Clark & Hillman

As if to underline the notorious unpredictability of the trio throughout their respective careers, yet another reunion took place in August 1977, only two months after the disastrous UK tour. Chris Hillman had dropped by Studio Instrumental Rentals and jammed with McGuinn. Both were sufficiently impressed with the results to take a long hard look at their respective futures. With McGuinn having recently left Columbia Records, he was free and willing to think in terms of a new project. Meanwhile, Gene Clark was showing similar signs of dissatisfaction with RSO so he flew down to join McGuinn and Hillman, in order to discuss the project. The dissolution of Thunderbyrd followed quickly and for the remainder of 1977 McGuinn and Clark went out on the road as an acoustic duo. Hillman appeared alongside them on a number of occasions and even David Crosby made a couple of guest appearances. Although David only sang a couple of songs, this was enough to add fuel to the notion that a Byrds reunion was in the offing. Crosby was particularly impressed by the brief onstage reunion:

'I tried to help them one time in San Francisco. Then they said they needed me at the Roxy because that's where most of the attention would be, so I flew down to Los Angeles to do it again. The best sound that I thought we ever got. It was me and Hillman both singing the same harmony in unison, and Gene and McGuinn singing the same melody in unison. So it was two vocal double lines. The best sound I heard us ever make. We used to do something very like that when Christopher wasn't singing. I would do the harmony, and Gene and Roger would sing the melody. Occasionally, Gene would work out a low harmony, but normally he would sing with Roger.'

As the months passed, however, the long hoped for reunion seemed less and less likely. With no official word from any source, and Chris Hillman apparently unable or unwilling to commit himself to the project, it seemed that the only possible outcome of the venture might be a joint Roger McGuinn/Gene Clark album. Towards the end of 1978, though, the trio embarked on an extensive tour of Australia and New Zealand, and were billed in many places as 'the Founders of the Byrds'. At first, it seemed that the group were unable to use the name Byrds because of a legal agreement, but McGuinn later told me otherwise: 'I made an agreement with David Crosby that I wouldn't use the name without him or Michael in the group. It was a gentlemen's agreement, but I decided to honour it'.

In February 1979, the 18 months of speculation ended with the release of an album under the banner of McGuinn, Clark & Hillman. McGuinn had kept his promise and it seemed that the group were accepting Crosby's contention that 'there were ever only five Byrds'. In subsequent interviews, it was stressed that the album *McGuinn, Clark & Hillman* was a new project, totally unconnected with the Byrds. Both press and public, however, continued to refer to the trio as the Byrds, and it was inevitable that the new work would be compared to their earlier efforts. How can we call the group who recorded the albums from *Dr Byrds And Mr Hyde* to *Farther Along* the Byrds, when they only contained one original member, while denying McGuinn, Clark and Hillman that same title? But were McGuinn, Clark and Hillman really the Byrds? Hillman clearly felt that they were not:

'We didn't approach this album as the Byrds. We didn't have David or Michael. There was more at stake. We didn't have our own personal little things happening at the time, as we did when we were doing the reunion album. I want everybody to realize that we're not the Byrds, and I'm sure they'll know that when they hear the record.'

Judging from the content of the album, many people might agree with Hillman's statement.

Perhaps the trio's determination to avoid the Byrds tag explains why they refused the services of David Crosby. According to Crosby, he was so pleased by the reformation idea that he immediately offered his services and made a special trip to ensure that he might be part of the historic reunion. Sadly, events did not turn out as he hoped:

'When they were cutting in Miami as McGuinn, Clark and Hillman, I flew there on purpose to see them, and to go in and ask them if I could sing. And I did. And they didn't want me to. I did it. I came in there real nice and I was humble. I didn't give anyone any shit. I just came in and asked if I could sing. I offered, and I even asked. They did a live gig and they didn't even call me. I went there to do it, to sing on the album. It was all three of them refused. They knew why I was there. I flew from Los

Angeles to Florida to sing some harmonies to help them. I wasn't trying to shine my own light. The emotion that was foremost in my mind was affection for them and a feeling that I could both focus attention on them and help them to make a better record. It hurt me that they didn't want me to sing because I wanted to do it. I think I could have helped them too.'

Without Crosby's assistance, the trio did manage to complete an album of tunes very unlike their previous Byrds recordings.

'Long Long Time', written by Hillman and Rick Roberts, would not have sounded out of place on a Firefall album. It had a slick 70's sound, unlike most of Hillman's previous Byrds contributions. Yet, in other respects, most discernible in the harmonies and tight instrumentation, it was clearly a development of his earlier work. Much the same may be said of 'Surrender To Me' (written by Rick Vito) which featured one of Hillman's finest vocal performances. The producers, the Albert Brothers, even borrowed an old Byrds trick from *Younger Than Yesterday* by using a backward tape introduction to the song. While it might seem that Hillman was in full flight on this album, his other contributions were less spectacular. 'Stopping Traffic' and 'Sad Boy' were average rock songs which lacked any real depth or originality. The presence of McGuinn and Clark failed to compensate for the weak material. Although Hillman was capable of fine writing during this period, particularly 'Rolling And Tumbling' (from the album *Clear Sailing*) the quality of his output on *McGuinn, Clark & Hillman* was decidedly erratic.

McGuinn's contributions to this 'reformation' album proved even less noteworthy. 'Don't You Write Her Off' (co-written with Bob Hippard) with its amusing references to desert islands and gurus, was commercial enough to provide the group with a long-overdue Top 40 hit, but even McGuinn agreed that the song was hardly of great portent: 'Oh, that was just me joking. It's a straight love song. The intent of the first verse is to establish credibility. It's just being silly too'.

McGuinn's only other contribution to the album, 'Bye Bye Baby', appeared to be a little more serious. Lyrically, it fell somewhere between 'Chestnut Mare' and 'Child Of The Universe', with its references to fillies running wild and a woman with the soul of a child. The inclusion of strings on the song was entirely due to Mike Lewis, string and horn arranger for Firefall and KC & The Sunshine Band, as Ron Albert co-producer explained:

'Lewis, without any prompting from us, came up with the string part for the track. Chris had his mandolin sitting in the studio all through the sessions, but we just never got round to using it. We thought about trying some mandolin on "Bye Bye Baby", but after we got the flute part on it, it was so special, so simple, that we just left it alone.'

In spite of Lewis' work, or perhaps because of it, one cannot escape the uneasy feeling the song is an extremely self-conscious attempt to capture the magic of 'Chestnut Mare'. It is almost as if McGuinn were searching for a quality song by distilling ideas from his previous classic compositions. The sentiments of the song, therefore, sound contrived and unconvincing, even if the track is perfectly recorded. As with the 1973 reunion album, McGuinn took a surprisingly low profile on this album and this time there was no David Crosby restraining him.

With Gene Clark dominating the album with the remaining four tracks, one might have expected some musical adventurousness, in the tradition of *No Other*. Sadly, this is not the case. 'Little Mama' is lyrically banal, and the melody seems too reminiscent of Smokey Robinson's 'You Really Got A Hold On Me'. In a vain attempt to improve the song, Ron Albert borrowed an idea from Paul McCartney:

'The first time Gene played this song for me, I heard something more drastic happening in the chorus – the "everybody's talking about it" part. It seemed a little too melodic, pretty, and I wanted to change the colour a bit. Finally, I figured we should try something really off the wall. I had this idea running around in my head for awhile to triple-track snare-drum parts, two cadences built around the straight 2/4 beat. We tried that on "Little Mama" and it worked great. The idea came from Paul McCartney's "Let 'Em In", so "Little Mama" is happening thanks to Paul. That's Blue Weaver on synthesizer. He works with the Bee Gees.'

'Backstage Pass' appeared to be a more serious composition, but, in an attempt to maintain a commercial sound, Gene included an embarrassing 'hey ho' chorus and standard orchestration. Even Ron Albert seemed confused by the conflicting elements in the song: 'It's sort of moody in the verses and more upbeat in the choruses and towards the end, maybe reflecting some of Gene's ambiguous feelings about being on the road.'

According to Hillman, 'Feeling Higher' was written after Clark had sighted a flying saucer. The UFO phenomenon obviously inspired Clark sufficiently to philosophize about spacemen who come into contact with us, but choose to hide from the 'dawning day'. The theme is subtle enough to be misinterpreted as a straight love song were it not for the speculations on extra-terrestrial life in the final verse. Musically, the song ends on an unusual note, with an extended piano and percussion fade-out, recalled by Ron Albert:

'Part of the magic of this track is the "Cuban Army" (Joe Lala and friends Ghia Farcia and Falco Falcore) on percussion. The whole track fell together because we had them set up live in the studio during the embryonic stages of the album. Lala's friends were just hanging around and he called them in for this song and it worked beautifully. Everyone just got to the end of the song and there was no ending, so Howard motioned Paul to keep playing and Lala and the Army just kept percussing. The whole outro was about 10 minutes long, and thanks to Howard's wonderful editing it works beautifully. We took the beginning and middle and end of that ending, edited out everything but the key piano lines and phrases and it was done. Howard's editing is seamless. We were listening to the final playback, watching the edits go by as the tape wound through the machine, and it all still sounds very spontaneous.'

Clark's final contribution, 'Release Me Girl', may well stand as the most controversial song he has ever recorded. Lyrically, it is one of his finest love songs, and a superb electric version was performed by Gene on the 1977 tour, and a fine acoustic adaptation was included in his 1978 concerts with McGuinn. The recorded version, however, is totally spoiled by insipid orchestration and excessive brass. Ron Albert recalls the changes that 'Release Me Girl' underwent during the stages of production:

'This is the one track that feels the most different from the takes the guys first got. It had a sort of Nashville kind of feel. As it turned out, we really altered it a lot, and now it has a much more up-to-date contemporary groove. We had Chris and Gene set up a different groove on bass and drums and then asked George to come up with a little guitar line that'd work better. The example I gave George was something sounding a little, but not a lot, like the guitar line in "Stayin' Alive", so he came up with a variation string part going, which ties it all back into the sound we were after. Then we added Lala's percussion and a Harris clarinet part with a weird sound and all the pieces just fell together. We did the backing vocals and gave it to Mike and turned him loose. The horn parts he came up with are almost like old-time big band, not slick disco style parts. We weren't too sure about them, though, but Gene loved the track when he heard the final mix so we stayed with it.'

Whether Clark's inexplicable acceptance of this new version was simply perverse experimentation or an unwholesome and blatant attempt at commercial appeal remains debatable.

What the album demonstrated most clearly was the determination of the trio to avoid what they believed to be a 'Byrds sound'. Thus, most of the original arrangements for *McGuinn, Clark & Hillman* were adapted to a slick 70's production, complete with obligatory brass and orchestration. In many respects, however, the desire to avoid the Byrds tag by experimenting with a new sound was self-contradictory. The most distinguishable feature of the Byrds' work had always been the desire to experiment with new ideas. From folk rock to space rock, from ragas to country music, the Byrds had always avoided any pigeonholing classification. Yet, from their comments, it seems that their greatest fear was of a public who were expecting a Byrds album with a distinctive 'Byrds sound'. But what precisely is this 'Byrds sound'? When we compare 'Mr Tambourine Man' with 'Eight Miles High' or *The Notorious Byrd Brothers* with *Sweetheart Of The Rodeo*, it becomes clear that the Byrds sound is hardly stylized. Ironically, it was the trio's very fear that the Byrds' music had become stylized which accounts for the aesthetic failure of *McGuinn, Clark & Hillman*. If the group had attempted to open new, unexplored areas in rock music, as they had done with virtually all their albums up to, and including, *Sweetheart Of The Rodeo*, then their efforts would deserve commendation. For example, an album such as *Sweetheart Of The Rodeo*, in spite of its flaws, remains a landmark in the history of rock music, signalling the death of psychedelia and indicating the move back to more traditional forms of music. *McGuinn, Clark & Hillman* may have been unlike any Byrds album, but it was hardly fresh or innovative. On the contrary, it was imitative of contemporaneous trends and production tricks which recalled the work of the Bee Gees, Firefall and other successful acts. Instead of looking forward, in the true Byrds tradition, McGuinn, Clark and Hillman were imitating their proteges. They wanted to be known as a late 70's group on record, but in concert they played their elaborately-arranged studio cuts with the old, familiar jingle-jangle sound, and also included a large sprinkling of old Byrds classics. It was an exercise in doublethink; McGuinn, Clark and Hillman were both a new group and they were also the Byrds revisited.

26
Circle Of Minds

As the 70's slowly wound to a close, the possibility of a second Byrds reunion looked likely. In April 1979, Michael Clarke followed David Crosby's lead by playing on stage with the Byrds for the first time since 1973. The reunions took place in Portland and Denver and by all accounts worked considerably well. The collaboration demonstrated that, in spite of his enormous success with Firefall, Clarke was still on friendly terms with his former colleagues. By the summer of 1979, a second incident occurred which seemed likely to influence strongly any reformation plans. The long-standing Crosby/Nash partnership temporarily dissolved in order that each artiste could concentrate on solo material. Capitol Records began negotiations to sign Graham Nash, and ended up signing both Crosby and Nash as solo artistes. With McGuinn, Clark, Hillman and Crosby on the same record label, some form of reunion suddenly appeared a distinct possibility. Even Hillman was optimistic about a reformation: 'Another reunion of the Byrds remains a very strong possibility. I know David and Michael want to do it, and when we have time maybe we'll do it right. And then, we'll just let the Byrds lie'. During the next few months, however, events took a strangely familiar turn as history began to repeat itself.

In August, McGuinn and Hillman began to appear without Gene Clark. The official explanation for Gene's absence was that he was 'extremely ill'. Students of ancient Byrds history, however, could not help remembering similar explanations prior to Clark's sensational departure in March 1966. In spite of such suspicions, there was strong evidence to suggest that Clark's absence might be merely temporary.

Hillman revealed that Clark's non-appearances were the result of an abscess of the mouth for which Gene was receiving treatment in a California hospital. Apparently, Clark had attempted some amateur surgery on his gum with an unsterilized needle and had, not surprisingly, poisoned his entire mouth. McGuinn and Hillman managed to perform with some competence without Clark, though they were besieged with screams of 'Where's Gene?' As the months passed, the public began to suspect that there were more profound reasons for Clark's lack of live appearances.

Adhering to their rigid schedule, McGuinn and Hillman entered the recording studio in November in order to cut their second Capitol album. Clark's appearances at the recording sessions were limited to a few hours, which left many people wondering whether his contributions would even appear on the final album. When, following the completion of the album, McGuinn and Hillman continued touring without Clark, there was no doubt in anyone's mind that a split had occurred. The reasons behind Clark's third departure from McGuinn and Hillman were all too familiar. Although he had tolerated the extensive touring schedules of the past year, it was evident that Gene simply could not adapt to life on the road. In many respects this had always been his primary problem as a performer, dating back to the days of the New Christy Minstrels. While Clark has frequently attempted to come to terms with his distaste for the road, the results have invariably been a series of failures. On each occasion, Clark has allowed contributory factors to irritate his neurosis to such an extent that he has been brought to the edge of a complete breakdown.

Throughout 1979, Gene's domestic problems had hardly been conducive to the unity of McGuinn, Clark and Hillman. One might have thought that with their history of divorces the group would have been more than capable of dealing with such a problem, but apparently this was not the case. Clark's familiar excesses further led to a lack of reliability and efficiency which could not easily be tolerated in a group that was still trying to recapture past glories. The inevitable decision was reached that Clark would no longer appear on the road with McGuinn and Hillman. Although the decision seemed a sudden one, it was hardly unexpected. Hillman, in particular, was well aware that Clark might not be able to hold things together for very long. Apparently, Chris' reluctance to commit himself to the McGuinn, Clark and Hillman project during the latter half of 1977 was not entirely due to contractual problems. He had been extremely wary of joining Clark in a permanent unit for fear that past problems would be resurrected. It was only after long thought that Hillman realized the potential of the group, with or without Clark's commitment. When the split finally occurred, McGuinn and Hillman initially looked capable of surviving as a duo.

The problem of surmounting Clark's departure had last occurred around the time of the recording of *The Notorious Byrd Brothers*. With the sacking of Crosby, the future of the Byrds had appeared to rest on Clark's contribution to the group. On that occasion, Clark had survived only three weeks and contributed nothing. Without him, the Byrds had managed to create one of their greatest albums. Twelve years later, McGuinn and Hillman found themselves under similar pressure and although they could not produce another *Notorious*, they at least proved themselves capable of re-establishing their rock 'n' roll credibility.

The album, *City*, was rush released in January 1980 under the banner of 'Roger McGuinn and Chris Hillman featuring Gene Clark'. The work had been completed less than two months earlier during a 20-day spell at Criteria Studios in Miami. While the recording had been cut quickly, everything had run far from smoothly. Apart from the problems with Clark, McGuinn and Hillman found themselves in direct conflict with their producers, the Albert Brothers. Since recording their last album both McGuinn and Hillman had come to realize their mistake in allowing the Albert Brothers so much creative control. In spite of the hit single, 'Don't You Write Her Off', and the relative commercial success of *McGuinn, Clark & Hillman*, both Roger and Chris felt that the elaborate production was an artistic error. Fresh from the concert platform, they recorded some very strong rock songs which they presented to their producers. The demos failed to impress the Alberts who continually argued in favour of a more professional production. McGuinn and Hillman held their ground, however, and the album was completed in the way that they had originally envisaged. Hillman explained their approach to the project:

'We went in with a bunch of new songs to record a rock 'n' roll album using the same kind of fast, basic, hold-the-overdubs, strings and horns approach we used 15 years ago. Add to that the recording technology available today and we cut an album that's really fresh, uptempo and full of energy.'

In analysing the album, it is difficult to disagree with Hillman's claims. The duo made a concerted attempt to recreate the freshness of their 1965 debut by returning to basics. With McGuinn finding fresh inspiration as a songwriter, and Hillman producing some inspired hard-rock items, the album showed reasonable potential for the future. Unlike their recent offerings, *City* revealed McGuinn, Clark and Hillman working together as a group, rather than as three individuals.

The title of the album was, to some extent, an indication of the theme of the work. However, *City* was certainly not a concept album in the usual sense of the term since only four of the 10 tracks reflected the urban theme. Most of the songs of city life came from Hillman's collaboration with Peter Knobler, and were written in a similar vein to 'Stoppin'

Traffic' on the previous album. Fortunately, some thought had gone into the musicianship on *City* and what might otherwise have sounded fairly average songs were given extra bite. 'Who Taught The Night' proved a very strong number, displaying the group's aggressive musicianship in a way that had not been heard for many years. Much the same could be said of the other Hillman/Knobler collaboration on side one, 'Street Talk', with its Shadows' 'Man Of Mystery'-style opening, dramatically followed by a rock number of fine quality. At the time, McGuinn explained why he and Hillman were thinking more in terms of urban life than the pastoral settings of yore:

'It's time to get back to the city. Chicago is my home town and I almost moved to New York. I need the urban environment, that's why I live in a Century City high-rise. I find that energy really stimulating. Sure, the city can be overwhelming and frightening, but there are ways of dealing with it. It's like the ocean: you can drown or sail across the surface. You can enjoy it as long as you respect its power.'

McGuinn's tendency to relate drawn-out analogies was continued in his discussion of the album's first US single, 'One More Chance':

'It reminds me of the old parable about the knight in armour who thought he was invincible, but he was killed when an arrow found its mark in a crevice between his armour plates. The idea is no matter how hardened you think you are, you're still vulnerable somehow.'

In many respects the song is a celebration of McGuinn's new life as a born-again Christian. However, it is also possible to interpret the composition as a love song, without any specific spiritual implications. McGuinn himself wisely chose to leave the interpretation open to the listener. Musically, 'One More Chance' is an example of McGuinn and Hillman's attempt to channel the 60's Byrds sound into an 80's format. Thus, there is the familiar Rickenbacker break of old coupled with a white reggae riff, similar in feel to the Police's 'Walking On The Moon'. This clearly showed McGuinn attempting to incorporate something new into his dated repertoire.

Clark's 'Won't Let You Down' emerged as another of the album's highlights, showing the ease with which the trio could capture the sound of the original Byrds when they chose to. Although McGuinn has often attempted, with a modicum of success, to recapture the sound of the first Byrds album on songs such as 'The Lady', he has never come as close as this to succeeding. 'Won't Let You Down' was not only 'Feel A Whole Lot Better' revisited but even included snatches from other Byrds classics such as 'Chimes Of Freedom'. Although 'Won't Let You Down' appeared to be a standard love song directed at an individual, manager Al Hersh maintained that it was written about the group during their period of crisis. What might have seemed a fairly ordinary lyric becomes a little more intriguing when examined from this point of view. In spite of its optimistic tone and singalong chorus, the events surrounding Clark's departure from his former colleagues transform the song into a statement of some depth. The composition opens with Clark presenting to the group a new and as yet untitled song for consideration. What follows is nothing less than an admission of Clark's fall into near alcoholism over the years ('a life of whiskey and wine') and the way in which the group 'made a new moon' by giving him the opportunity to begin a new phase in his life. Clark's promise as stated in the title of the song is severely qualified as early as the second line of the chorus, in which he acknowledges that all he has left to give them is his music, 'his world'. As Al Hersh explained, "Clark promised that he would not let them down, but in the end he blew it!"

The highlight of *City* turned out to be its striking title track. With its strong Rickenbacker work, including shades of 'Eight Miles High', and a lyric that is a cut above any of his recent compositions, 'City' revealed McGuinn reviving from a creative atrophy. Roger's wife, Camilla, who co-wrote the song, explained how the work was composed:

'"City" was a thing that came about rapidly. We talked about the words that we wanted to use. Roger had this tune and we both sat down and worked together on some suitable lyrics'. According to Roger, the idea came to him while gazing at a photo of tall buildings, a scene which is depicted on the album sleeve:

'The photo was taken at night when light was streaming out of the office windows. A Lear jet was parked downstairs on ground level. Starting with just the word "City", Camilla and I started kicking around ideas and came up with someone being lost in the city, something we can all identify with.'

Perhaps the only criticism one might have of the song is that it could have been even better if McGuinn had not been so sparing with the Rickenbacker break. The snatch of 'Eight Miles High'-style guitar work is immediately striking but remains undeveloped, almost as if McGuinn were teasing the listener with tasty morsels from his past.

A less fortunate remnant from Roger's past opens side two in the form of 'Skate Date'. Camilla explained why Roger decided to write a song about roller skating:

'Roger wanted to do a roller-skating song. Ever since he was a kid he's always loved roller skating. He and Chris worked on the song and I completed it. It was written in two separate stages. It's not particularly heavy of course, but I enjoy it.'

Camilla's last sentence more or less sums up the song, which is little more than a throwaway. It is rather ironic that three writers are credited for such a banal composition. Novelty recordings are always a critical problem and usually succeed as either one-off items by one-off artistes or as light relief from a major artiste's more important work. However,

McGuinn and Hillman were neither novelty exponents nor major recording stars and could ill afford the luxury of a humorous excursion on what was meant to be an important album.

McGuinn's recording of Tom Kimmel and Lynn Tobola's 'Givin' Herself Away' proved another high point of *City*. The aggressive vocal style brilliantly highlights the irony of the song, in which a guy callously sets out in search of a perfectly submissive woman only to discover a domineering mistress who reduces him to sycophancy. It is the old tale of the hunter becoming the hunted, and the theme allows McGuinn to spit out the words with pure venom.

'Deeper In' showed Hillman employing another co-writer, his La Jolla, California, next-door neighbour, Douglas Foxworthy. The song is little more than average, however, and generally as unspectacular as Hillman's work on the first McGuinn, Clark and Hillman album.

Inevitably, it was Gene Clark who provided the album with its strangest cut, 'Painted Fire'. The rock 'n' roll-style piano and drums give the song a 50's feel which admittedly sounds totally out of place on the album. In some ways, the song's lack of instrumentation is reminiscent of the work that Clark was pursuing on the second Dillard and Clark album. Structurally, the song appears to be incomplete, almost as though Clark originally had an interesting idea but decided to abandon it during the writing process. The contrast between the country girl who loves to sit out drinking beer at the weekend and the fashion queen who becomes 'everybody's dream' is never fully realized. Having employed the metaphor 'Painted Fire' (referring to an enticingly made-up and dangerously passionate nymphet) Clark failed to create a dramatic situation as a vehicle for the theme. As a result, the song appears to be extremely fragmentary.

The closing cut on the album, 'Let Me Down Easy', is another reminder of past days, harking back to the style of mid-period Flying Burrito Brothers. The employment of the steel guitar completes the mixture of musical styles on this album. More importantly, the song demonstrated, both musically and lyrically, that Hillman and Knobler were not restricted to composing thematically repetitive rock songs, as might have been supposed from their contributions.

Overall, *City* denied the group's statement of intent voiced during the recording of the first McGuinn, Clark and Hillman album. At that point, the members of the group were anxious to avoid their 'old' sound, but on *City* it seemed that they were pleased to record a Byrds album 80's style. For once, the trio were looking back at their history in order to make sense of their present. Rather than imitating their former colleagues and allowing themselves to become a product of late 70's producers, they had decided to use their familiar sound as a springboard to greater achievements. Such a decision might have brought favourable rewards, but it was also a dangerous ploy. The old Byrds Rickenbacker sound meant ripe pickings in the 70's for imitators such as Tom Petty, who effortlessly capitalized on McGuinn's pioneering work. Unfortunately, it did not follow that McGuinn, Clark and Hillman would necessarily cut into Petty's market. In the early 70's, an album such as *City* by three ex-Byrds might have broken through, but by 1980 the market had been milked by a plethora of pretenders.

Sadly, *City* did not even receive any compensatory critical commendation. Having produced their finest work in years, the group lacked one crucial quality: innovation. It was obvious that the trio knew they were in trouble artistically, and set out to rectify that situation on *City*. McGuinn's typical reaction was to attempt a sampler of past achievements, a trick he had previously used to good effect on *(Untitled)* and his first solo album. Since then he had treaded dangerous waters and occasionally overused old formulas as can be heard on the ironically titled 'Same Old Sound' and the blatantly self-imitative 'Bye Bye Baby'. For McGuinn, retrospection had become an almost Pavlovian reaction to bad record sales. In this respect, it was not too surprising that, worried by their faltering artistic credibility, McGuinn and company should attempt to override unsympathetic producers and take creative control. It was a wise move and *City* showed that the familiar jingle jangle sound could still be put to good use. McGuinn, Clark and Hillman answered their critics by recording the best of the Byrds as the best of McGuinn, Clark and Hillman. But it was neither enough for critical nor commercial success.

Without Gene Clark, McGuinn and Hillman continued the never-ending struggle of proving themselves on the road. After completing a European tour, more changes took place when they parted with manager Al Hersh, who had worked with McGuinn for more than a decade. By early 1980, it seemed that McGuinn and Hillman were determined to carry on and another album, produced by Jerry Wexler, was scheduled for release later that year. Any hopes of a full scale reunion, however, seemed fanciful. Even Camilla McGuinn was dubious about her husband's involvement in such a project:

'It's remote. Perhaps it's still possible for a short period. But each of the original Byrds has grown in different ways. Roger and Chris are probably the most stable, so much would depend on them'.

Crosby, alone and already heavily into drugs, seemed an unlikely candidate for any recordings with the newly born again McGuinn, but provided some hope of another reconciliation with his old partner:

'I frankly like the guy. I feel more distant from him now because of this Jesus thing, but I like him. The Christianity wouldn't necessarily keep us apart. I could still work with him, easily'.

The prospects of a reunion were slim but proved enough to convince a very small core of followers that the Byrds were not dead. And so, against incredible odds, we stubbornly chose to place our faith in another miracle – The Third Coming.

27
The Dark Decade

Any hopes that McGuinn and Hillman might continue recording together in the 80's were virtually shattered following the release of their lacklustre swansong, *McGuinn/Hillman*. At a time when the duo most needed a strong album to convince Capitol of their worth, they produced what sounded like a tired and uninspired contract filler. The hackneyed artwork, complete with the overdone image of a bird spreading its wings, was reflected in the music which largely consisted of mediocre cover versions of songs by Graham Parker, Rodney Crowell, Will MacFarlane and Robbie Steadman. McGuinn and Hillman managed to co-write three numbers, of which only the closing 'Turn Your Radio On' impressed. McGuinn later explained that the duo had a number of suitable compositions ready for inclusion on the album, but these were vetoed by producer, Jerry Wexler, in favour of extraneous material. The vain hope that one of the covers might produce a fluke hit was a long shot, which missed by a mile. Instead, the album gave the impression that the duo had run embarrassingly short of ideas and brought the validity of their partnership into question. Although they continued to play low-key gigs together, there was a jaundiced air about those performances as though they had accepted that this latest collaboration had run its course. At one gig, Hillman was spotted wearing a badge imploring: 'How do I get out of this thing?' It was an apposite comment. What had seemed such a promising reunion back in 1977 was now limping towards an anti-climactic disbandment. During the final days of the group, the fiery Hillman crossed swords with a Capitol promotions man, while McGuinn was obviously disillusioned with the entire set-up. Following a plane trip, Roger expressed his annoyance by informing Hillman that he did not wish to work with him in the future.

The decade had barely begun and suddenly the original Byrds were as far away from each other as they had ever been. Talk of further reunions were summarily dismissed as either artistically irrelevant ventures or time-wasting cash-ins. David Crosby, upset by the others' reluctance to allow him to contribute vocals during the Miami sessions, had evidently hardened in his attitude. 'It's history', was his weary riposte to any reunion queries. Chris Hillman seemed equally dismissive and was betraying a discernible antipathy towards big label schemes by uncompromisingly pursuing his interest in bluegrass music. Gene Clark was still willing to tour as the Byrds, but knew that Hillman and McGuinn were none too keen on working with him again. Mike Clarke, for all his recent successes with Firefall, still had problems convincing his fellow-Byrds that he was God's gift to the drum-kit. Finally, McGuinn was absolutely adamant: the Byrds was dead. He could not envisage a time when the five would reconvene. In the few interviews that he sat through, there seemed a marked reluctance even to talk about the Byrds. It was now the great irrelevance.

The 80's was to prove the darkest period in Byrds history as the individual members either ceased recording or restricted their output to small, independent record labels. The greatest American group of all time were now nothing more than five former legends without a major record contract between them. Godhead had retreated into culthood.

Surprisingly, it was the less prestigious members of the group who fared best during the next few belt-tightening years. The ever-practical Chris Hillman was not content to live on the memories of stardom with the Byrds, Burritos and Manassas, but elected to seek new avenues. Prior to the McGuinn, Clark and Hillman project, he had told me of his desire to forego the rock 'n' roll circus and retire gracefully to become a producer. Confusingly, he also spoke of the possibility of recording a traditional bluegrass album and re-investigating his pre-Byrds roots. Following the split with McGuinn, he ceased playing altogether for about a year before signing to the specialist label, Sugar Hill. After arranging the re-release of his archive album with the Hillmen, Chris re-established contact with former mentor Jim Dickson and set about recording a new work in a traditional vein. Backed by a trio of country cousins (Bernie Leadon, Al Perkins and Herb Pedersen) Hillman performed some reasonable covers of songs by Bob Dylan, Gram Parsons and others. The predominantly bluegrass *Morning Sky* was obviously a refreshing experience for Hillman who sounded as confident as ever. Without the hype and over-expectation of the Byrds' associated projects, he was rewarded with a clutch of positive record reviews. That, at least compensated for his reduced stature as a 'minor label' recording artiste.

During the same period, he teamed up with former Burrito/Firefall lead singer Rick Roberts for a short tour which ably showed off their talents as acoustic musicians. The gigs were pleasantly informal with the duo relishing the opportunity to display their rapport in a spontaneous series of humorous one-liners. At one show a cheeky member of the audience shouted 'Where's Gram?', only to be told 'How would you like to personally meet him?' Offstage, Hillman repeatedly stressed his pleasure at rediscovering the mandolin after too many years as a rock bassist and guitarist and seemed intent on continuing the retreat into pre-Byrd territory. His turntable choice in 1982 consisted largely of old bluegrass material and songs that he had first learned 20 years before. Although no longer a major label recording star, Hillman was pleased with his music and outwardly seemed reasonably content.

That same year, Hillman completed another traditional country album, *Desert Rose*, which again received fair reviews. Hillman was cleverly using the independent circuit to record his favourite music without having to conform to the dictates of a commercial major label. Although he had only recorded a couple of his own compositions during this period, the critics seemed pleased enough with the covers. Modest ambitions bring their own critical rewards, as Hillman's early 80's career gratefully reflected.

In common with McGuinn, Hillman put aside the excesses of the 70's and began to take greater care of himself physically. He was now known to rise at 5 am to jog along beaches and also took up cycling, sometimes travelling up to 40 miles across the coast. The healthiness is next to godliness philosophy was emphasized in his involvement with an evangelical Christian group. In 1985, he collaborated with Bernie Leadon and Al Perkins on a project entitled *Ever Call Ready*, which resulted in an album of Christian bluegrass. Given his past association with McGuinn, some people presumptuously assumed that Hillman was 'born again', but he expressed concern about the right-wing political aspects of Fundamentalist Christianity and refused to be labelled.

By the mid-80's, Hillman was still playing regular concerts and formed a new group, the Desert Rose Band, with a cavalcade of country talent, including Herb Pederson, Jay Dee Manass, John Jorgenson, Bill Bryson and Steve Duncan. Given Hillman's recent history, it seemed likely that this new group would struggle in the twilight musical arena of small bars and clubs, with only limited distribution on their records. Fortunately, their live performances attracted the interest of the majors and their new label, Curb Records, received the corporate clout of MCA Records. Two albums, *The Desert Rose Band* and *Running* were surprisingly strong with a freshness and bite reminiscent of the best of the early Flying Burrito Brothers. One of the highlights of the first album was a reworking of 'Time Between', which compared reasonably well with the version on *Younger Than Yesterday*. The revitalization of Hillman as a mature performer was reflected in a self-revealing aside to *Music Connection*:

'Songwriting and royalties have kept me real comfortable. I don't have a mansion in Palm Springs and a mansion in Malibu but I'm very comfortable and I'm not excessive in my lifestyle. I'm still here, 25 years later, and I'm still working. There are a lot of people my age who aren't. There were a lot of people that were bigger than me and I never had to fall. I was never a big star. I'm real fortunate . . . we didn't get a great record deal, millions of dollars of advance money or a limousine. We got a chance, and that's all I ever wanted.'

Optimistic as he sounded, even Hillman could not have envisaged the commercial success which awaited the Desert Rose Band. As the decade wound to a close, they were being tipped for Grammy awards and zooming to the top of the country charts. From small label obscurity, the irrepressible Hillman had worked his way up the ladder to emerge unexpectedly as a big draw on the ever-profitable country circuit. Chris' true feelings about his success were aptly summed up in a comment to an old friend: 'I'm finally getting what I *deserve*'.

In common with Hillman, Gene Clark found the 80's a tough decade, with major labels no longer wishing to take a chance on 70's singer songwriters. Clark had been through CBS, A&M, Asylum and RSO as a soloist and produced a formidable body of work, including the awesome *No Other*, yet the sales invariably failed to reflect the artistry. Without the other Byrds, Clark's currency with corporate record companies was weak and so he too was forced to opt for the obscurity of the independent circuit. He briefly teamed up with Hillman, Perkins and the rest to record some stylish demos with Jim Dickson, including the excellent 'No Memories' and a revamped 'Feel A Whole Lot Better'. Unfortunately, the experiment was discontinued. In 1984, Takoma Records released *Firebyrd*, a pleasant enough album which saw Clark browsing through the Byrds back pages with reworkings of 'Feel A Whole Lot Better' and 'Mr Tambourine Man'. The latter was particularly interesting for Clark chose to include the verses that the Byrds had omitted from their hit version. The reliance on Byrds' material, though no reflection on Clark's output, indicated the way he was thinking, and it came as no great surprise when he announced his involvement in a '20th Anniversary' tour. Neither McGuinn, Crosby nor Hillman were remotely interested in resurrecting the Byrds name so Clark was forced to form his own curiously-selected 'supergroup'. The participants were Gene, Michael Clarke, Rick Roberts, Rick Danko and Blondie Chaplain, and the billing carefully announced '20th Anniversary Tribute To The Byrds'. An unintentionally macabre poster amusingly noted: 'Also appearing with their *original* line-up: The Flying Burrito Brothers'. Although the tour was opportunist in intent, few who had witnessed Clark's lack of sales over the years could deny him the chance to make some quick money. Regrettably, the qualifying remarks prior to the Byrds name were not strictly adhered to by every promoter and news reached England that Clark was intending to tour simply as 'the Byrds'. Fortunately, this sacreligious 1985 British Byrds invasion never materialized. Instead, Clark appeared in London on a solo mission and played one of the best sets I ever saw in my life. A packed audience at Dingwalls was treated to an acoustic 'best of Gene Clark' which included a stunning rearrangement of 'Eight Miles High', which was quite remarkable. Affable, and more communicative than usual, Clark agreed to play a private gig for the author and sample some California wines on his next visit. He promised to return soon with his amorphous band of anniversarians, but, ever unpredictable, he changed his plans and remained in the States.

Although generally accepted as the most underrated of the original Byrds, Clark retains a substantial cult following, particularly in Europe. At home, he enjoys the respect of younger musicians and was pleased to guest on albums by the Long Ryders and the Three O'Clock. He even gained some retrospective Don Juan notoriety when Michelle Phillips belatedly made public her affair with the tambourine man back in the mid-60's. In 1987, Clark recorded the well-received *So Rebellious A Lover* with Carla Olson, but all in all it was a very quiet decade for the most prolific member of the Byrds.

Michael Clarke had ended the 70's on an absurdly high note. While the careers of his former colleagues were beginning to founder, Clarke's latest group Firefall was enjoying spectacular commercial success. It couldn't last, however, and by the early 80's Clarke had left the group, which rapidly plunged downhill. For several years, he worked for Jerry Jeff Walker, then joined Clark's 'Byrds' tour and finally set about establishing himself as an impressionistic painter. After years of artistic frustration playing behind America's finest group, Clarke was revealing creativity in an area beyond the scope of his more illustrious former compatriots. Like Hillman, Clarke had come full circle and delved back into his pre-Byrd career for new inspiration. When Crosby had first 'discovered' the fledgling drummer playing congas at Big Sur, Clarke's other main pastime was painting on the beach. Now he was pursuing his second career with vigour. Like everyone else in this story, however, Clarke was still haunted by the legacy of the Byrds and so decided to revive the name. It was a presumptuous move which was to have startling repercussions. Michael Clarke, for perhaps the first time in his life, was about to prove the unlikely catalyst for a serious Byrds' reunion.

Roger McGuinn remained something of an enigma during the 80's when his once prolific recorded output evaporated altogether. Like the other Byrds, he avoided the trap of attempting to form another major label superstar aggregation and reverted to his coffee house troubadour persona of the early 60's. His motives were not entirely nostalgic. Burned out from a diet of booze and cocaine during the 70's, McGuinn changed drastically following his re-conversion to Christianity. Gone was the Dylanesque cynicism, replaced by a beautific impenetrability. Some of the old coolness remained, however, and many felt that behind the man's polite exterior there lurked a sense of resignation. McGuinn's account of his conversion was particularly revealing and characteristically idiosyncratic. He claims that he felt severe stabbing pains in his chest and was convinced that he was being pulled down to the lower regions of hell. Gradually, he became extremely wary of aligning himself with non-believers and was in need of spiritual advice. The elders in his Church agreed that he was 'unequally yoked' and counselled him against the 'darkness' of agnostic attachments. As a result, McGuinn studiously avoided reuniting with his former associates and continued as a solo act. At some gigs his wife, Camilla, replaced the standard sound engineer at the mixing desk. Drugs and alcohol were conspicuous by their absence as spirituality reigned. Several of McGuinn's new songs, including 'Light Up The Darkness' testified obliquely to his faith but the evangelical tone seldom permeated his onstage raps or altered a familiar repertoire.

Armed with a Rickenbacker and a smiling, confident stage persona, McGuinn transformed himself into a one-man travelling show. He toured the States and Europe, usually appearing at small clubs and halls and treating his followers to a formidable selection of past hits, peppered with the occasional new song. At times, the performances seemed rather clinical and stagey, as though McGuinn were settling into a new role as an anaesthetized, middle-aged trouper on the supper club circuit. However, such reservations would usually be shattered by moments of genius, most notably in the ambitious and dramatic arrangement of 'Eight Miles High'. Not content to play the easy, singalong tunes, McGuinn would climax his set with a virtuoso performance on the Rickenbacker, complete with the complex interweaving guitar breaks that were always the highlights of this remarkable composition. It says much for McGuinn's faithful and searing solo rendition of 'Eight Miles High' that he could pull off those effects so impressively.

One of the more entertaining and amusing aspects of McGuinn's 80's performances was the re-introduction of the *Gene Tryp* saga. The play had never been adapted for radio, let alone reached Broadway, but, two decades on, the stubborn McGuinn finally incorporated the tale into his stage act. Audiences expecting the usual, polite, hackneyed song introductions would smile benignly as McGuinn warmly invited them to imagine a scene set in nineteenth-century America. A wedding is taking place, Gene Tryp appears on the horizon, abruptly whisks away the bride and they live happily together until one day an enormous force field envelops their house, causing Tryp to travel the world. McGuinn would next picture his protagonist on the campaign trail, atop a wagon painted red, white and blue. The catchy 'I Wanna Grow Up To Be A Politician' naturally followed. The scene would then shift to document Tryp's cowboy adventures in which he captures, and finally loses, a beautiful 'Chestnut Mare'. Next he travels down to New Orleans and confronts a sinister character who calls himself the 'Lover Of The Bayou'. Finally, Tryp grows weary of his travels and muses on his eventful life in the elegiac 'Just A Season'. At this point, McGuinn would take some amusing liberties with the original script in order to throw in a couple of older Byrds hits. Tryp is pictured on a farm and one night a flying saucer lands in his corn field. Several extra-terrestrial beings emerge and cordially invite our astonished hero to accompany them on a ride into space. The words of 'Mr Spaceman' provide an apt reply. After whizzing around in a flying saucer, Tryp returns to Earth only to discover that a century has elapsed. It is now July 1965 and Tryp turns on a radio to be greeted by the familiar strains of . . . 'Mr Tambourine Man'. The scene ends.

Audiences responded loudly and appreciatively to McGuinn's witty narrative while he, no doubt, felt relieved to have partly exorcized the troubled ghost of Gene Tryp – the most fanciful and frustrating of all his schemes. An exorcism of a different kind was evident in McGuinn's decision to update one of his old Byrds songs as 'Tiffany Queen II'. Sounding better than ever on acoustic, the song boasted new lyrics which were especially noteworthy. McGuinn remembers a summer back in the early 70's when he threw parties for 'half a million friends', but soon drugs and alcohol took their toll, fistfights ensued, and his mate left to 'marry a guy named Carradine'. This was a clear reference to his ex-wife Linda Gilbert, who subsequently wed *Kung Fu* star David Carradine. In the final verse of 'Tiffany Queen II', McGuinn pays tribute to his new bride (Camilla) and presents an idyllic portrayal of life in sun-drenched Florida, swimming daily in the Gulf of Mexico and learning from all his past mistakes. What had seemed a rather ordinary song on *Farther Along* is given a completely new life by the sharp arrangement and explicit autobiographical lyrics.

By the late 80's McGuinn had amassed a backlog of unreleased titles, stretching back a decade. Never a prolific writer, he reckoned that at least 15 new songs were completed, most of which were included in various solo concerts. The quality of the material was decidedly patchy and some compositions, such as 'Woman' and 'The Tears', sounded somewhat mawkish. 'Sunshine Love', a poppy cousin to 'Don't You Write Her Off', was insubstantial but catchy, while 'The Price You Pay' sounded like a country rock singalong. 'Living Legend', the story of a washed-up rock star reduced to working in a factory, was a return to strength while the plaintive 'Sweet Memories' recalled the haunting melody of 'Kathleen's Song'. There were also some passable covers, including a pleasing reading of the Dream Academy's 'Life In A Northern Town'. Perhaps the most intriguing of the lot, however, was the impressive arrangement of 'America For Me', a patriotic verse borrowed from nineteenth-century poet Henry Van Dyke. Although this new repertoire lacked any songs as startling as 'Chestnut Mare' or 'Just A Season', there was some evidence to suggest that McGuinn's songwriting flair had returned.

The commitment to solo performances did not prevent McGuinn from making several prestigious guest appearances during the 80's. He toured the world with Bob Dylan and Tom Petty and the Heartbreakers and there was much speculation about a possible collaboration. McGuinn even co-wrote a song with Petty, 'King Of The Hill', which they performed on several dates. Another group whom McGuinn joined onstage was REM, a highly respected outfit whose work had already been compared to that of mid-period Byrds. With further guest appearances on records by the Beach Boys and Elvis Costello, McGuinn ensured that his name was not forgotten by music scribes and, as the decade wound to a close, it seemed only a matter of time before a major label signed the Rickenbacker wunderkind for a well-publicized and overdue comeback album.

David Crosby's career during the 80's was less a question of darkness than the prospect of a complete eclipse. The most commercially successful Byrd of the previous decade soon discovered that he was no more capable of securing a major contract than any of his former partners. Always an excessive, he fell victim to cocaine addiction on a grand scale. I witnessed the extent of his dependency over a couple of days when the freebase pipe was seldom away from his lips. 'Please don't mention the drugs', he confided, 'it's bad enough as it is'. Despite this, Crosby remained lucid, sharp and thoroughly in command of proceedings, as though the drug was no more potent than a packet of cigarettes. One of the more remarkable aspects of Crosby's addiction was his ability to carry it off. His colleagues later recalled ghoulish tales of ether-filled rooms and unprecedented degeneracy, but at the beginning of the decade Crosby still looked in good shape, dressed casually but cleanly, ate well and was conducting his business affairs with assiduous skill and clarity. His acoustic performances were a joy to behold and his articulacy onstage and off was undiminished by his habit. He could still talk for entire afternoons and evenings, answering often difficult questions with a precision and perspicuity beyond the power of his fellow Byrds. His creativity had not yet been stymied by drugs and three of his new songs, 'Delta', 'Distances' and 'Drive My Car' all sounded impressive. After the shows, he dug into his bag to produce some new handwritten compositions: 'Melody', 'Paper Glider' and 'Stand Up And Be Counted'. In reserve, he still had 'King Of The Mountain', 'Samurai' and 'Jigsaw', and Neil Young had recently offered him 'Little Wing' and the old CSN&Y favourite 'Pushed It Over The End'. There were also some wordless melodies and plans for a choral work. It was difficult to escape the conclusion that Crosby's compositional skills remained intact. Sadly, the creative drought was closer than either of us imagined.

Always a barometer of emotion, Crosby could be arrogant, immodest, humble, aggressive and loving. Temperamentally, he was the perfect foil to McGuinn. It was difficult to imagine two more strikingly different personalities: passionate forcefulness versus cool deliberation. Crosby's love/hate passion for the Byrds, as for all his music, was positively tangible. He felt frustrated, held back, at times unforgiving and contemptuous of his fellow Byrds and yet simultaneously affectionate and respectful towards them. Their status was shifting sand, depending on the time period in question; conquering heroes in 1965, brilliant experimentalists during the 'Eight Miles High' period, villains of the piece throughout 1967, and bitter enemies in the wake of *The Notorious Byrd Brothers*.

In spite of his criticisms, Crosby genuinely believed that he could work with the Byrds again and the state of his career in 1980 suggested that this was far from unlikely. Temporarily estranged from Stills and Nash, his only artistic outlet was a long-awaited second solo album. The fact that Capitol Records (McGuinn, Clark and Hillman's label) had signed Crosby indicated that somebody in the company was thinking 'Byrds'. Unfortunately, the flock would soon disperse, in parodic imitation of previous disputes.

By 1981, Capitol had effectively humiliated Crosby by rejecting his new album on the grounds that it was musically anachronistic. It was a bitter blow to Crosby and a sad indication of his declining commercial appeal. He was about to go the way of McGuinn, Clark and Hillman. Starved of a major record label, there was nothing else to do but survive on the revenue offered by small club dates, while patiently awaiting an upswing of fortune.

The vestiges of control that Crosby exercised over his art and life in 1980 were systematically eroded during the succeeding years, as his free basing intake reached new and dangerously high levels. Professional commitments sapped his energy, while the all-consuming addiction robbed him of vital sleep. During bouts of exhaustion, Crosby would occasionally lose control of his propane torch and accidentally burn holes in his clothing or set alight hotel mattresses. Although his drugs were top quality, increased dependency meant an ever-present danger of scoring impure base. Following one gig, Crosby's body finally cried out for help and he suffered a seizure which might have taken his life. When this horror bulletin reached his remaining friends in California, they decided to act.

One of the more remarkable aspects of Crosby's character is his ability to win the love and loyalty of those who feel they should know better. Jim Dickson describes him as 'one of the greatest salesmen of the 20th century'. Crosby's personal absorption has an enticing quality which is difficult to rationalize. It is easy for people to believe in him, partly because he emanates such a powerful sense of self-worth. So it was that a posse of long-suffering friends invaded his house in 1981 and attempted to press gang the erring egotist into seeking medical assistance. An emotionally cathartic evening ended with Crosby reluctantly agreeing to enrol in a drug programme at Scripps Hospital in La Jolla. His commitment is best exemplified by his insistence on freebasing copiously en route. The fiasco was completed 24 hours later when Crosby discharged himself.

When his once loyal friends finally abandoned him as a lost cause, Crosby found a new supporter in the unlikely figure of Jack Casanova. The mysterious Casanova had virtually no experience of the rock world but he convinced David that he could continue to make a living as a 'functioning' base head. To a large extent Casanova was correct. He kept Crosby on the road, found investors and became the key figure in the singer's drug-centred existence. Crosby paid a high price for his voracious cocaine appetite. As his dependency increased, he found that he could no longer sleep or even eat without an accompanying blast from his ever-present pipe. On commercial air flights he would surreptitiously light up his propane torch and somehow dodge the normally vigilant eyes of suspicious stewards. Even his driving technique was carefully adapted to facilitate his freebase usage; astonished passengers would watch in open-mouthed astonishment as Crosby skilfully steered the car with his knees while gluttonously toking from the pipe that refused to leave his hands. The private doper had now crystallized into a public menace.

Crosby's flagrant self-abuse became national news on 23 March 1982 when he suffered a potentially deadly seizure at the wheel of his car. He was extremely fortunate to escape with his life. Upon regaining consciousness, he discovered to his horror that his car had careered into a freeway divider. A police search of the vehicle unearthed a veritable Pandora's box of narcotics: cocaine, quaaludes and an assortment of drug paraphernalia. To make matters worse, Crosby was carrying a loaded colt .45. When asked why he carried a gun, the still bemused singer offered the wry reply: 'John Lennon'. That comment was a revelation in itself. Here was a guy without a record contract whose self-esteem was still high enough to believe that he might attract a superstar assassin.

Hadn't the Byrds once been called 'America's Answer To The Beatles'?

Crosby was immediately released on $2,500 bail but the shock of arrest had no salutary impact on his drug consumption. Fifteen days later, he was again arrested, this time in the dressing room of a Dallas nightclub. The charges were virtually identical: possession of cocaine and illegally carrying a loaded firearm. While legal preparations and appeal procedures tortuously dragged on, Crosby continued to feed his ravenous addiction. His self belief was reinforced by an unexpected approach from Stills and Nash. Under pressure from Atlantic Records, they requested his assistance in converting their joint album into a three-way affair. The *volte face* made good commercial sense. Soon, Crosby, Stills & Nash were back on the charts and plans were hatched for a major tour. For Crosby, it was a financial lifeline and a means for further self abuse.

Court rooms, concert tours and continuous cocaine consumption characterized Crosby's chaotic career hereafter. In September 1982, he was arrested once more on an outstanding warrant for an alleged assault and battery suit dating back to 1980. The case was quickly dismissed and soon afterwards the driving and drug offence was plea bargained by his formidable attorneys. Crosby was fined $750.00 and placed on three years' probation, a period in which he agreed to enter a drug counselling programme. The Dallas charge, however, would not go away.

The following summer, Crosby found himself back in court in Texas and newspapers reported that he consistently fell asleep and snored during the proceedings. What seemed a contemptuous gesture was probably nothing more than drug-related exhaustion. Indeed, Crosby was far from nonchalant about his fate and at one point rose to his own defence with an impassioned plea:

'Jail is no joke. Handcuffs are no joke. It's real serious. It's been very lonely. Those bars are real. I spent a lot of nights thinking about it. It frightened me. I don't want to do anything ever again that puts me in jeopardy. I want to feel proud of myself and stand for something again.'

Judge Patrick McDowell may have been impressed by Crosby's eloquence, but the dispassionate legal arguments of Dallas District Attorney Knox Fitzpatrick proved decisive. On 5 August 1983, Crosby was sentenced to five years' imprisonment. An appeal was immediately lodged and the singer was freed on bond. The case was far from over.

Throughout this nightmarish period, Crosby somehow managed to fulfil his professional obligations. Like the chronic alcoholic who miraculously gets to work every morning, Crosby pulled his weary body through a gruelling series of solo tours arranged by the ever present Jack Casanova. In order to supplement his income, Crosby was reduced to selling drugs as a sideline. His backing musicians rapidly resigned themselves to the extent of his addiction and even armed themselves with personal fire extinguishers. Meanwhile, their pyrogenous boss continued to leave a trail of burn stains in his wake.

Although Crosby had been ordered to undergo drug counselling his efforts in this direction were either lacklustre or unsuccessful. For a brief period he was hospitalized in Marin County but the treatment was not to his liking. Incensed, he ripped an intravenous tube from his arm and marched out of the hospital leaving a trail of blood behind him. Thereafter, the news worsened. His girlfriend, Jan Dance, was arrested for attempting to board a plane with a handgun. A subsequent search of her luggage revealed small traces of cocaine, marijuana and heroin residue. Jan was released on probation and reunited with David in Marin County. Now they both lived in fear of imminent incarceration.

Crosby's carelessness seemed certain to prove his undoing. In October 1984, he was arrested yet again for recklessly driving on a motorcycle. A dip into his bag brought forth a rubber tube, Bunsen burner, pipe, and, inevitably, more cocaine. For good measure there was another offensive weapon, this time a dagger. Attorneys disputed the legality of this latest search and Crosby escaped with a fine for reckless driving. Back in Texas, Knox Fitzpatrick had intensified his attempt to enmesh the beleaguered singer, but Judge McDowell, realizing the extent of Crosby's addiction, took a firm but compassionate stance and ordered the defendant to enter a closed institution to undergo drug rehabilitation.

Faced with a choice between imprisonment or hospitalization, Crosby decided to enrol at the Fair Oaks Hospital in New Jersey. This institution was widely regarded as one of the finest of its kind in America and had achieved considerable prestige among the rock community following the rehabilitation of John Phillips, whose drug problems were arguably even more horrific than those of Crosby.

Hostility and denial characterized Crosby's mood during the early days of treatment at Fair Oaks. He was also in considerable physical pain. His ankles resembled balloons, his mouth was full of abscesses and he could not breathe properly while asleep. In spite of these handicaps he made slow but steady progress and might have pulled through but for the psychological dependence on drugs. During the sixth week of his treatment, while walking in the hospital grounds, Crosby abruptly made a break for the hospital walls, climbed over and sped off with a friend in an awaiting car. Within 48 hours he was arrested in Greenwich Village on another charge of cocaine possession.

Realizing the seriousness of his predicament, Crosby volunteered to return to hospital but his conciliatory gesture had come too late. He was held at the chillingly-named Riker's Island before returning to Texas for another trial. His defence attorney made a fresh appeal for hospitalization but Judge McDowell finally denied bond and despatched Crosby to Lew Sterrett County prison. For four months, the erring singer suffered gruesome withdrawal symptoms, spending most of his time in solitary confinement. He frequently phoned his business manager, Jack Casanova, and begged him to arrange his release at any cost. Eventually, Graham Nash and CS&N manager Bill Siddons produced the $15,000 to secure his release. David assured them of his intentions to stay straight but, less than two days later, he was freebasing again.

Crosby's inexorable slide back into the narcotic netherworld was tempered by an ever-present fear of returning to prison. He became more cautious than before and for a time attempted to convince sceptical journalists that he could conquer his addiction. He accompanied Stills and Nash on tour, even appearing at Live Aid alongside the perpetually reluctant Neil Young. The televised performance betrayed how much Crosby had already surrendered to drugs. Visually and vocally, he seemed but a shadow of his once ebullient self. Yet, his celebrity outlaw status continued to attract ghoulish multitudes eager to witness what might prove the *last* performance by Crosby, Stills & Nash. By this time, Crosby had erected his own prison in the form of a backstage van surrounded by his own prison officers – burly minders whose job was to keep him relatively straight. The freebasing still went on, however. Even his best friends had run short of excuses and explanations for David's behaviour. Graham Nash, once loyal almost to a fault, now seemed convinced that his partner was doomed and informed the press: 'David will eventually die, it's only a question of when'.

The Grim Reaper showed a strange reluctance to ensnare Crosby but the police authorities had no such reservations. In late 1985, David suffered a flash of *déjà vu* when he drove into a fence on the road to Mount Talmalpais. On this occasion, he remained conscious and unwisely decided to flee from the scene. A car chase ensued and Crosby was arrested for hit and run driving. Police again found a gun in his possession, plus the usual assortment of drug paraphernalia. In spite of his countless string of arrests, Crosby again received bail at $5,000.

Judge Patrick McDowell wearily scheduled another hearing in Dallas but this time Crosby failed to appear. Fearing almost certain imprisonment, he decided to become a fugitive. Accompanied by Jan Dance, he fled in search of an impossible redemption. Rather fancifully, he convinced himself that he could escape justice by sailing into the sunset on his boat, the *Mayan*. The plot bore a striking resemblance to his classic fantasy tale 'Wooden Ships'. Now reality was imitating art. The elaborate get away was ultimately thwarted by the state of the *Mayan*, which had fallen into disrepair following years of neglect and was no longer seaworthy.

The wreck of the *Mayan* appeared to symbolize Crosby's own final defeat. In despair, he abandoned the futile struggle for freedom and turned himself in. He had once equated prison with death in his own mind but now it offered blessed release. Rather than destroying Crosby, his tenure in jail provided salvation. Initially, he suffered severe withdrawal pangs which seemed insurmountable but gradually, almost imperceptibly, his health improved. He was assigned a job in the prison mattress factory as if to atone for all the beds he had torched during a decade of addiction. As the months passed, Crosby slowly adapted to life behind bars and even began writing new songs, as well as appearing in the prison band. His progress was duly noted and, one year on, his old friends began campaigning for his release. The Texas board of parole were similarly impressed and, in August 1986, Crosby was freed. The following year, the Texas Supreme Court concluded that the invasion of his dressing room at Cardi's nightclub in Dallas had been illegal and his conviction was retrospectively overturned.

Crosby emerged from custody overweight, drug free and reformed. Inevitably, there were great changes in his life to face. The recondite Jack Casanova disappeared from his circle without pursuing any claim for a live album and Bill Siddons assumed full managerial responsibilities. He sagaciously encouraged Crosby to sever his old ties in San Francisco and move to Los Angeles. Siddons next tackled his client's tangled business affairs which included a hefty $1,000,000 debt to the IRS. Crosby responded to the crisis by declaring himself bankrupt and seeking a fresh start. The ever-loyal Graham Nash purchased his songs, thereby ensuring that his copyrights remained in safe and responsible hands. Since 1986, Crosby has been successfully rebuilding his shattered psyche, attending AA meetings and lecturing on the dangers of addiction. He married Jan Dance and reunited with Stills, Nash & Young to record the impressive *American Dream*, the quartet's first studio album since *Déjà Vu* in 1970. The flurry of activity continued with a best-selling autobiography, *Long Time Gone*, and the completion of that seemingly lost second solo album, retitled *Oh Yes I Can*. After all that, there was only one avenue that still remained unexplored: the Byrds.

28
Tomorrow Is Never Before

Although the individual Byrds remained on hold for most of the 80's, their influence on the music scene was as pervasive as ever. A wealth of fresh, young groups including REM, the Smiths, the Long Ryders and the Bangles acknowledged the pre-eminence of the Byrds, while Tom Petty, Husker Du and even Roxy Music found themselves borrowing material from the quintet's back catalogue. Music critics accepted that the Byrds were now of classic stature; like the Beatles, early Elvis and mid-period Stones, their best work was deemed above criticism. Pat phrases such as 'Byrds-like Rickenbacker breaks' and 'jingle-jangle guitar work' became common journalistic similes that were in danger of becoming cliches. Although never superstars in their time, the Byrds found themselves belatedly eulogized as indisputable greats. Independent record companies recognized their lasting appeal and specialist labels such as Edsel, Rhino, Sierra and Murray Hill kept the group's musical legacy alive by both re-opening old catalogues and re-issuing the best of their subsequent solo work.

The most ambitious and intriguing archivist adventure was undertaken by Murray Hill, which determined to scour the tape shelves of Columbia in search of unreleased material from the 1965-67 period. The man behind the project was Bob Hyde, who had the foresight to employ Jim Dickson to remix various cuts, thereby ensuring that the Byrds not only gave their blessing to the project but became actively involved in improving the unearthed material. The most difficult task in the entire archivist expedition was actually finding the tapes and persuading Columbia to sanction their release. Several crucially important unreleased tracks were lost, seemingly forever, while other songs were unavailable in their original multi-track format. Approximately 50 per cent of the unreleased gems were finally discovered, with RCA Records apparently digging out the vintage cuts of 'Eight Miles High' and 'Why' in the space of an afternoon. Meanwhile, back at Columbia, trouble was brewing. The archive album, so near to completion, looked likely to be neutered. The RCA versions were vetoed on the grounds that they weren't recorded at Columbia, while 'It Happens Each Day', 'Old John Robertson' and others met corporate resistance because 'foreign' instruments had been added to the original tracks. Eventually, the political obstacles were largely overcome and, in December 1987, Murray Hill released the appropriately titled *Never Before*.

Superbly packaged in a pastiche mid-60's sleeve, the contents included a tantalising sessionography, previously unseen photographs from 1965, a track-by-track breakdown by Bob Hyde and some personal reminiscences from Jim Dickson. Fittingly, the album commenced with that most famous of all Byrds songs, 'Mr Tambourine Man', finally presented in a crisp, previously unreleased, stereo mix. Jim Dickson was very impressed with Terry Melcher's work on this track and felt that his decision to create a great mono cut was perfectly sound. It was hoped that the piano work of Leon Russell and the distinctive counter vocal from Gene Clark could be retrieved from the mix but, unfortunately, they had been buried into inaudibility. Dickson concluded that 'Mr Tambourine Man' was the least changed track on the album:

'Outside of "Mr Tambourine Man" I never put up any of the original mixes. I did with "Tambourine Man" because it had been sped up and I wanted to get the same pitch. I respected Terry Melcher's mix so much that I didn't want to lose anything he'd gotten in mono. We couldn't really make much of a stereo recording out of it so the only thing we really split was the voices. I took that military drum and put it slightly off-centre to open up the drums a little bit because they were all on one track, except for that overdub of the military drum. I spread it out a little bit so that maybe people might hear it.'

The new stereo mix of 'I Knew I'd Want You' was considerably better, highlighting the excellent musicianship of Hal Blaine, Larry Knechtel, Jerry Cole and Leon Russell. Another Gene Clark song followed, 'She Has A Way', last heard in more primitive form on *Preflyte*. The Columbia version was a vast improvement with McGuinn's Rickenbacker work particularly evident and Michael Clarke in top form. Like so many Gene Clark songs from the period, 'She Has A Way' was eventually rejected in favour of extraneous material. Ironically, Bob Dylan, whose work largely replaced that of Clark on the first two albums, proved a great admirer of the underrated Kansas songwriter.

The irreverent 'It's All Over Now, Baby Blue' revealed McGuinn at his most acerbic, the exaggerated Dylanesque vocal creating an almost comic effect. As he would later do with 'You Ain't Going Nowhere', McGuinn took poetic licence with Dylan's lyrics, this time as early as the first line: 'You better go now, take what you want you think will last'. The track ultimately emerges as vintage, Byrds folk rock – fast and raucous with some ferocious drumming from Clarke, a distinctive Rickenbacker break that still tingles, and a delightfully offhand arrangement which captures the group at their most playfully arrogant.

The title track of the album was apparently the last song that Clark recorded with the Byrds. The densely-packed verses, full of portentous Dylan-inspired lyrics, were typical of the period and indicated the direction Clark would take in his later solo career. Unfortunately, Clark's involvement in the *Never Before* project was not as extensive as it might have been, as Dickson revealed:

'Gene disappeared. He refused to be interested in any way until right at the end when he found that his song was going to be the title track, and it wasn't as bad as he remembered it. He has more embarrassing cuts to worry about than that, but it was rough on the tape. The ones that got bootlegged would lead you to believe that it was worse than it was. It turned out kind of funky. I liked it because I enjoy hearing Michael play that way. It's the way he likes to play – chunky and hard.'

One of the highlights of *Never Before* was the belated unveiling of the RCA version of 'Eight Miles High'. McGuinn, Hillman and Crosby voiced their own views on this version earlier in the book and, looking back, I tend to support McGuinn. The guitar work does sound more spontaneous on the RCA cut and it will prove difficult, if not impossible, to dislodge the power of the classic released version from the collective memory. 'Why', with its sitar-like guitar breaks, recalls the original single track, rather than the less spectacular cut issued on *Younger Than Yesterday*. The song is aptly placed on *Never Before*, prefacing three other David Crosby songs which testify to his creative ascendency in 1967.

'Triad', the controversial *menage a trois* ode, emerges with a striking arrangement and a cool yet sexually beguiling vocal. Crosby actually re-recorded a vocal line but, according to Dickson, the substitution was so precise that it is virtually undetectable. Even more impressive is 'It Happens Each Day', one of the first Crosby songs to include his new characteristic use of sea imagery. An irresistible candidate for *Younger Than Yesterday*, it was inexplicably omitted and effectively abandoned by its writer. On the recording included on *Never Before* considerable work was done on the old tapes, including some excellent additional acoustic guitar, courtesy of Chris Hillman. Remarkably, Crosby admitted to me that he had completely forgotten the song existed. There was no such memory lapse over 'Lady Friend' which Crosby has always felt passionately about, deeply resenting its omission from *The Notorious Byrd Brothers*. The long-awaited stereo version is a soaring *tour de force*, with some previously unheard scat singing to accompany the epical brass fade-out. Unfortunately, the original drum work was not deemed strong enough to translate into stereo, so a session drummer was employed by Murray Hill to embellish the sound. For the sake of authenticity, it was regrettable that Michael Clarke did not take up sticks. Nevertheless, 'Lady Friend' remains a staggering work and a perfect conclusion to a commendable album.

Such was the impact of *Never Before* that the demand for further material prompted Murray Hill to empty their cupboards and add seven additional tracks to the CD version of the work. The luckless Chris Hillman lost some glory, not to mention songwriting royalties, when two of his tracks were abruptly deleted from the CD. CBS refused to sanction 'Old John Robertson' on the grounds that a 'foreign instrument' (a tastefully applied mandolin) had been belatedly added. Meanwhile, 'Have You Seen Her Face' lost out because the new stereo mix added so little to the original track. McGuinn then intervened and took time out to remix the remaining cuts with Ken Robertson. New stereo mixes of the b-sides 'Why' and 'She Don't Care About Time' may have added some clarity to the originals but generally underlined weaknesses rather than highlighting strengths. The 45 version of 'Why', for example, lost most of its punch in the diffused stereo mix, exposed Clarke's previously unobtrusive drumming to embarrassing effect and totally buried Hillman's wonderfully subtle gulping bass line. In these instances, at least, the mono mixes were better left in their original state. 'Don't Make Waves', a suspect choice anyway, was not only passable but largely vindicated by the cheeky inclusion of Crosby's sarcastic studio comments at the end of the song: 'Great, let's double it! Masterpiece!'

The real meat of the *Never Before* CD was to be found in those long-awaited five unreleased tracks. Chief amongst these was the legendary 'I Know My Rider', a wonderful example of Byrds folk rock with an astonishing Rickenbacker break from McGuinn. Recorded several times during the making of *Fifth Dimension* and *Younger Than Yesterday*, the song was successively rejected by the Byrds, but its charm and vibrancy is undeniable.

The once predominantly instrumental 'Psychodrama City' appears in edited form on the CD but the recording quality is excellent. The song, a revealing example of the jazz-influenced Crosby attempting some talking blues, is an apt comment on the 'psycho dramas' that the Byrds underwent during the 1965-67 period. In the first verse, a blonde fan threatens suicide if she can't have the delectable Crosby, an apparently not uncommon occurrence. Later in the song, there is an an oblique reference to Gene Clark's departure from the Byrds, including the incident outlined in Chapter Eight in which he freaked out on a plane. Crosby casually concludes: 'To this day, I don't know why, why he got on at all if he didn't want to fly'. Prior to the release of the CD, while promoting his autobiography *Long Time Gone*, Crosby vehemently denied that he had ever written or sung a composition entitled 'Psychodrama City'. The vocal and the writing credits tell a different story, however, which underlines the amnesiacal disregard that the Byrds often betrayed towards their past work.

From Crosby eccentricity to McGuinn whimsy is a clever way of completing a Byrds compilation and the instrumentals 'Flight 713' and 'Moog Raga' are both intriguing. The former was discovered at the end of the studio tape of 'Get To You' under the rather unimaginative title 'Song Number 2', until McGuinn belatedly rechristened the composition 'Flight 713'. An effective instrumental that might have been developed into a strong song, 'Flight 713' provides us with a welcome insight into what McGuinn and Hillman were attempting in the studio in the immediate wake of Crosby's departure. Infinitely more bizarre is the closing 'Moog Raga' which, along with the later and still unreleased 'Moog Experiment (Jenny Comes Along)', may be the only examples credited to the Byrds of McGuinn's extravagant essays into synthesizer rock. In combining a raga break with an otherworldly synthesizer drone, McGuinn creates a delightful work which simultaneously prompts respect for its innovation, while provoking mild laughter at its obvious novelty. More than anything it stands alongside '2-4-2 Fox Trot (The Lear Jet Song)', 'Oh Susannah' and 'We'll Meet Again' as a wonderfully whimsical way to complete an important work.

While Murray Hill were turning back the pages of history, Rhino Records re-assembled the *Preflyte* tapes for another intriguing retrospection: *In The Beginning*. Jim Dickson benignly handed over approximately 45 tracks of various cuts recorded in primitive conditions at World Pacific Studios in 1964. The tapes included many different versions of familiar Byrds songs, including three renditions of 'Boston' and, incredibly, six takes of 'You Movin''. The latter two tracks were the Byrds' early attempts at composing derivative r'n'b influenced material, specifically for live performance. Dickson stresses that these were never seriously considered for recording purposes though they were rehearsed *ad infinitum* so that the Byrds' dancing followers would not be disappointed.

What is most fascinating about *In The Beginning* is the brave decision to include as many alternate takes as possible, irrespective of their quality. Indeed, far more than previous releases, this CD captures the very genesis of the Byrds. On 'Mr Tambourine Man' the primitiveness is taken to its retrospective extreme. The sound is so raw and the vocal so wayward that it makes even the previously issued take sound sophisticated by comparison. On 'I Knew I'd Want You', McGuinn picks out a delicate arrangement which was subsequently altered on all the later takes. There's a wonderfully bizarre attempt at Liverpudlian diction on 'Please Let Me Love You' and a ramshackle 'You Showed Me', which even the Byrds would be shocked to hear. 'It's No Use', never previously issued in its pre-Columbia state, is another interesting artefact, proving that the group were experimenting with a dense guitar sound even as early as the summer of 1964. The highlights of the CD, however, are the acoustic and electric treatments of a song never previously released in any form: 'Tomorrow Is A Long Ways Away'. Written by Gene Clark, who rather generously surrenders co-writing royalties to David Crosby and Jim McGuinn on the minimally altered electric version, the song is a veritable revelation. The melody is fascinating with a lilt reminiscent of an Elizabethan madrigal. Clark transforms his composition into a folk rock torch song with a heart-rending solo vocal in the Scott Walker/P.J. Proby school. Unfortunately, it was this aberrant quality which doomed the song to obscurity. Never mind. The song was worth the 25-year wait and like the rest of *In The Beginning* allows us a unique opportunity to re-investigate and appreciate the very essence of the Byrds sound.

The timely retrospectives, *Never Before* and *In The Beginning* emphasize the point that the magical entity that was the Byrds cannot be 'recreated' but only rediscovered in a lost past. This will probably prove the hardest lesson of all for the group to appreciate. For, whatever they achieve in the future, it seems virtually certain that no Byrds reunion album could hope to capture the emotional intensity or critical acclaim that those rejected outtakes from the mid-60's captured so effortlessly.

29
The Third Coming

Over the years, the Byrds have become victims as well as celebrants of their own history. They have tried, not without some success, to confine their illustrious name to the past, but the monstrous myth continually returns to haunt and injure their present day projects. Roger McGuinn nobly attempted to close the book on the Byrds in 1973 and, along with Crosby, appeared to concur with the proposition that 'there were ever only five Byrds'. McGuinn claimed that he owned the Byrds monicker and intended to trademark the name to prevent its misuse. Unfortunately, his application was turned down and although the group name remained unused it was, theoretically at least, up for grabs. McGuinn's disbanding of the Byrds did not mean that he was disowning or ignoring his past. On the contrary, he continued to play Byrds standards in concert and even christened one of his 70's groups 'Thunderbyrd'. Gene Clark fleetingly betrayed a similar dependence and re-recorded two old Byrds classics, 'Mr Tambourine Man' and 'Feel A Whole Lot Better' for the ominously titled *Firebyrd*. In 1985, Clark became bolder and decided to set out on a '20th Anniversary Byrds Tour'. He received short shrift from the remaining originals, with the exception of drummer Michael Clarke, who was obviously feeling the pinch since the glory days of Firefall. Without McGuinn, Crosby or Hillman, Clark's anniversary tour was decidedly low-key, though mildly interesting for its peculiar tendency to chronologically mismatch latter day Byrds with the two original members. McGuinn was displeased by the tour but charitable enough not to begrudge Clark the chance of picking up some money. In the end, Clark became the victim of wily promoters who felt it made economic sense to jettison the 'Anniversary' mouthful and simply bill the ensemble as 'The Byrds'. Eventually, Gene Clark returned to solo work, but Michael Clarke sporadically soldiered on under the banner 'A Tribute To The Byrds'. Again, the inevitable abbreviation followed. At one point, a parodic Byrds line-up turned out comprising Michael Clarke, Skip Battin, John York and Carlos Bernal. Die-hard fans were mortified, Hillman was dismissive, McGuinn seemed saddened. Crosby, incapacitated by cocaine addiction, and later prison, had more important things to worry about.

When David Crosby walked out of Huntsville Prison, Texas, corpulent and clean, he looked like a man ready to reclaim his past. After reforming CSN&Y, he observed the current state of the Byrds and was less than pleased. A passionate, fiercely opinionated man, David Crosby has the unique ability to stir up the emotions of others to such a degree that they become part of his own drama. McGuinn and Hillman had good cause to listen to his pitch and suddenly decided that the good name of the Byrds should be salvaged for the sake of history – not to mention integrity, reputation and money.

The new Byrds triumvirate had briefly tested the prospect of a reunion in June 1988 when they appeared as soloists at a celebratory concert for the reopening of the legendary Ash Grove folk club. A wealth of Ash Grove alumni turned up at the Wiltern Theatre and anticipation was high for an onstage Byrds get together. The audience was not disappointed. As the house lights blinkered, impresario Ed Pearl welcomed 'McGuinn, Crosby, Hillman'. Backed by John Jorgenson and Steve Duncan of the Desert Rose Band, the trio provided a wonderful greatest hits repertoire consisting of 'Mr Tambourine Man', 'Turn! Turn! Turn!', 'Eight Miles High' and 'So You Want To Be A Rock 'n' Roll Star'. Cheering them on from the audience was Gene Clark, whom Crosby explained was unable to appear due to a recent stomach operation. It was not anticipated that the reunion would be taken any further but, several months later, David Crosby learned about a very different Byrds tour:

'Michael Clarke had fallen on hard times and was in the hands of some people who put him on the road as the Byrds. Then I had this horrible paranoid flash. I called up McGuinn and Hillman and said: "What if these guys who have a band on the road copyright the name and then we can't use it?" They said: "What an awful idea! Do you take special pills to come up with these bad thoughts?" I said: "I really think they might do that". And, sure enough, that's what they were up to, so we beat them to it!'

The man behind Michael Clarke was Artists International manager, Steve Green, a specialist in repromoting classic 'oldies' acts. He accepts Crosby's contention that a trademark was sought, but denies that there was anything remotely surreptitious about such a move:

'Sure, we tried to trademark the name. If they weren't going to use it, which they hadn't, why shouldn't we? We didn't go about it to hurt them. We were in contact with their attorneys from day one. We didn't try to trademark the name to blow them out of it. We just wanted to get legitimate ownership. We're not trying to steal the name. Even if we'd got the trademark, they'd have had time to oppose it. When you get a trademark, it's not written in concrete. There's a five-year period of opposition. You can oppose it at any time in those five years. We're not trying to pull over anything on anybody. We went about our business to protect our rights.'

Green maintains that on the very same day Michael Clarke applied for a federal trademark, a similar application was despatched by Gene Clark. It was an uncanny coincidence and another subplot to a story which was becoming more bizarre by the minute.

One of the more amusing ironies in this whole book is that the undemonstrative Michael Clarke should dramatically emerge as the key figure in effecting another Byrds reunion. For, in order to strengthen their rights to the name, McGuinn, Crosby and Hillman elected to revive the Byrds and play three shows during January 1989 in San Juan Cappistrano, Bacchanal in San Diego and Ventura Theatre in Ventura. Backed by John Jorgenson and Steve Duncan, the streamlined Byrds performed a plethora of old hits. The set began with a shaky, but stirring, 'Chimes Of Freedom', with Hillman featuring strongly on backing vocals. At the time the song was recorded Chris was known as the stage shy Byrd but, 24 years later, he was ready and willing to sing along with the others. A ragged 'It Won't Be Wrong' followed, with Crosby overworking his vocal part to distracting effect. This was probably the one noticeably disappointing rendition in the set. Despite the absence of Gene Clark, the trio still managed a surprisingly impressive version of 'Feel A Whole Lot Better', which had previously featured frequently during McGuinn's latter days with the Byrds. The surprise inclusion of Crosby's 'Everybody's Been Burned' was especially moving and possibly the highlight of the show. Although the Byrds could not hope to reproduce the superb quality of the recorded version without endless rehearsal, their late 80's rendition was nevertheless worthy. Another *Younger Than Yesterday* track followed with the evergreen 'My Back Pages'. Even though McGuinn had sung the song for 22 years, he somehow managed to mistakenly transpose the second verse into the final stanza. A worryingly hoarse Crosby next appeared at the microphone to defend the 1966 hit, 'Mr Spaceman', from accusations of being a novelty number. 'We were serious!', he exclaimed, before the Byrds broke into an excellent version of the song. This was succeeded by a solo 'The Bells Of Rhymney', which only lacked those wonderfully bell-ringing cymbals of Michael Clarke. The mischievous Hillman then decided to inject some humour into the proceedings by introducing a Byrds song on which Crosby had failed to appear. In a wonderfully sarcastic rewriting of Byrds history, Chris informed the audience:

'About 1968, David left and we begged and begged him not to leave. He went off with Stephen and Graham and he made a million dollars, and Roger and I went to Nashville and we decided we'd crack the country 'n' western market. We missed you on that record!'

With Crosby making shovelling movements in the background, the group launched into the singalong 'You Ain't Going Nowhere'. It proved an interesting version, not only because Crosby was heard for the first time, but also due to Hillman being allowed to sing lead vocal on alternate verses. McGuinn completed this new revisionism by altering the lyrics to 'pick up your money and pack up your tent' in retrospective deference to the once aggrieved Bob Dylan.

The most famous Byrds song of all time was saved for late in the set. While introducing 'Mr Tambourine Man', McGuinn credited Dylan's former road manager Victor Maimudes for introducing the song to the group, thereby adding a further erroneous twist to an already complicated story. The song itself provided a high moment of nostalgia and was swiftly followed by another US number 1 hit 'Turn! Turn! Turn!', during which Crosby's voice sounded hoarser than ever. The rush of hits continued with 'Eight Miles High'. 'They thought it was a drug song, but it isn't', confirmed McGuinn for the umpteenth time. Crosby's chunky upfront rhythm guitar sounded excellent, though the impact of Hillman's bass work was less pronounced. Steve Duncan's drumming was unquestionably solid and strong, but lacked the aural authenticity of the exiled Michael Clarke. McGuinn, having played 'Eight Miles High' consistently in solo concerts, naturally gave a strong performance which inspired the crowd to cheer loudly. The encore began with McGuinn asking, 'Do you all know how to scream?' as the Byrds' greatest hits repertoire ended with a rousing refrain of 'So You Want To Be A Rock 'n' Roll Star'. In striking contrast to 1967, the Byrds came off stage hugging and back-slapping each other and although there were no plans for additional shows, they were clearly pleased by the performances. Two months later, Crosby was still enthusing about those gigs and told me:

'We got up there, man, and tore it up! We hit "Chimes Of Freedom" and I got chills going up my back. And the audience went: "Whoop! Up for grabs! Totally nuts!" I'm being very immodest but I'm telling you the truth. We got reviews from people that normally wouldn't give you the sweat off their brow, and they were raves. It was really exciting and, more importantly, it was a hell of a lot of fun.'

In spite of his past disagreements with McGuinn and Hillman, Crosby was obviously in a magnanimous mood and spoke of his partners with the exuberance of a fan who had just rediscovered old heroes:

'When I started playing with Roger and Christopher, I'd forgotten how strong they were. Especially how strong McGuinn is. I confess it. I'm guilty. I didn't remember he was that good. He was fantastic. He's better now than he ever was. We all know that he's got this guitar style which can't be duplicated, but I'd forgotten what a great tale teller he is. Also, the last time I played with Chris Hillman he was just a kid. Now he's Manassas, Burritos and the Desert Rose Band with three number 1 (country) singles in a row. He's a very strong, polished, mature, confident guy.'

As the superlatives flowed, Crosby revealed that the new Byrds were intending to record a live album, thereby suggesting that touring plans were afoot. When pressed on the non-involvement of Gene Clark, he replied somewhat obliquely:

'I don't think Gene's ready to do that. Roger and Christopher had an awkward time with Gene when they tried to work with him last. I'm not the one to make a decision about Gene. The other guys made their decision. I'm real happy with it and would like to work with Roger and Christopher.'

Contrary to Crosby's suggestion, Gene Clark certainly seemed more than ready to join his colleagues, if the opportunity arose. He had already tried to make his peace by promising that he would not tour under the name Byrds again. In speaking of his previously troubled adventures with McGuinn and Hillman, he stressed with unnecessary humility: 'I feel a lot of remorse about that'. As paragons of physical health and ageing advocates of non-excessive lifestyles, Crosby, McGuinn and Hillman are obviously choosy about their partners, but it must be stressed that in the wake of this new puritanism, Clark has also reformed his ways. He has not had a drink in the past two years, enjoys a stable lifestyle and has even attended the same AA meetings as Crosby. If there is some form of underlying moral criterion to this reunion, then the new Gene Clark cannot justifiably be faulted. While diplomatically sitting on the fence, he clearly felt that a full reunion would be the most sensible solution: 'The best thing would be for the five people to sit down and come to some sort of agreement'.

Since the streamlined reunion concerts, the stakes have been upped and as Crosby promised: 'We beat them to it'. Events reached a head when Clarke's Byrds arrived in Tucson, Arizona, hometown of McGuinn's family. Posters appeared advertising the Byrds 'featuring Roger McGuinn'. Although the flyers were removed when the mistake was pointed out, the Tucson Garden was flooded with calls and according to the club owner many people said they would attend despite McGuinn's absence. When a reporter called the club on the day of the concert enquiring if the billed Byrds were the original group, the wry answer was 'as original as we're going to get!' For McGuinn and company, this mix-up was clearly the final straw. During the spring a lawsuit was filed in federal court by the three Byrds suing Michael Clarke, Artists International Management, Steve Green and John Does 1-10 for allegedly false advertising, unfair competition and deceptive trade practices. Crosby and manager Bill Siddons seemed confident about the outcome of the legal proceedings but gave the impression that they were underestimating Green, who had previously fought and won cases involving rival groups of Platters and Drifters. Not surprisingly, Green counter-sued, employing the argument that McGuinn had abandoned the name Byrds and that the last person to use it for a number of years was his client, Michael Clarke. McGuinn, Crosby and Hillman consistently stressed that Clarke never wrote or sang with the Byrds and therefore his contribution was minimal. Green, rather than making a big deal out of his client's collaborative work on 'Captain Soul' or 'Artificial Energy', bypassed the musical arguments to suggest that Clarke's primary importance to the Byrds was as a sex symbol. Did Michael's good looks ultimately sell as many records as McGuinn's Rickenbacker or Crosby's harmony and green-suede cape? Much appeared to depend on the perspective of a 69-year-old judge. In any case, the entire question of musical authenticity was underplayed by Green, who argued:

'We think we're going to win. We're not idiots. We don't say that we can recreate what they did in 1965. We're hoping to bring the group into the 90's and do what Little Feat and others have done by replacing members and going on and having a hit record. We're not sure that we can, but we're getting a tremendous amount of interest.'

For Hillman, the above scenario must have seemed a nightmare guaranteed to provoke the same antipathy he has voiced against the various refried Burritos, who have aesthetically cheapened a once great name.

Michael Clarke's reply to the criticisms of his ex-colleagues was the weary: 'I won't be denied a living and I don't like to be harassed'. Green claimed that he had attempted to come up with endless permutations of the name that might be acceptable to McGuinn and the others:

'We tried "Michael Clarke salutes the Byrds", "The Byrds with Michael Clarke", "An evening with the Byrds featuring Michael Clarke". It sounded all right to us! We tried everything to make them understand that we're not trying to misrepresent them, but their egos are so big that they think we're making money out of them. They don't want parity. I'll go with them being the Byrds if Michael can be the Byrds. I'll go with them "saluting the Byrds" if Michael can "salute the Byrds". Anything they want to do is all right with me.'

In defence of McGuinn, Crosby and Hillman, Bill Siddons countered:

'We tried to set up meetings with the five musicians and Steve Green refused to let Michael go to the meeting'. Detached observers seemed strongly divided on the issue and, not surprisingly, their opinions were governed by whomever they had spoken to during the dispute. On aesthetic grounds, Michael Clarke clearly seemed out of order, but the trio were also censured in some quarters for using the name Byrds and not inviting their former colleagues to participate in the reunion. Crosby brushed aside such criticisms along with Green's rhetoric by stating that the one member with an indisputable claim to the name was his former rival, McGuinn:

'My contribution aside, if it doesn't have Roger McGuinn in it, it's not the Byrds. I don't care what anybody says. That's the truth. He's the heart and soul of the Byrds. He always has been and he always will be. If he's not there, it isn't the Byrds.'

Hillman and Siddons concurred with Crosby's viewpoint in separate statements and it seemed likely that this would be the crux of their case.

The most frustrating realization for McGuinn was that he lost his right to the name Byrds otherwise, as Green admitted, Michael Clarke would have no possible claim. Clarke signed away his rights to the Byrds name in January 1968, but so had Crosby several months before and, in any case, all five reconvened officially as 'Byrds' in 1973. Green, wisely, did not underestimate the strong association in the public's mind between McGuinn and the Byrds, but pinpointed a number of possible flaws in their argument:

'We're not denying that McGuinn was the Byrds or a major force in the group. His problem is that he lost his trademark as the Byrds and made so many public statements that he doesn't want to be the Byrds anymore. His abandonment seems clear. Roger was only as good as his players. He can't prove that on his own he was successful. They say Michael was marginal but the Byrds didn't have any real success after he left. Plus, their royalties have actually gone up in the last five years since he went out as the Byrds. They don't seem to want to do anything except stop Michael. That's why their position is weak. Eventually, the courts are going to ask them what they want to do with the name. You can't just take away somebody's living and stop it because you want to bury the group. That will never wash. If McGuinn thought the name was sacrosanct he should have stopped in 1968, but he went on with whomever he could find. That was OK for Roger McGuinn to do, but it's not OK for Michael.'

Green has a point here, though he ignores the important fact that the Byrds were still an 'ongoing' group when McGuinn used the name. With hindsight, Roger might concede that ideally he should have ended the Byrds at a somewhat earlier date, though they were still a lucrative proposition when he diplomatically dissolved the final CBS line-up in

1973. Since then, he has resolutely, many feel nobly, withstood any financial temptations to turn back the clock by trading off the Byrds name. Even during the 80's, when he had no record contract, he chose not to use the Byrds as commercial leverage. Clearly, what he now sought was not simply to stop Michael Clarke, but to regulate the use of the name, and decide if and when the Byrds should reconvene. It was probably the impending legal battle which persuaded him to modify his previous stance in 1973 when he and Crosby agreed that the only Byrds were the original five.

McGuinn, Crosby and Hillman may have seen themselves as the true guardians of the Byrds, but as the talk of a possible live album and tour continued, where did that leave the presently neutral Gene Clark? Cynics felt that money would eventually topple morality in this scenario, especially as the three Byrds could command a massive advance without Clark and Clarke and, thereby, split the cake three ways rather than five. However, such expediency would not only have been an affront to history but myopic economics. Big-time promoters would always offer far more money for the complete set of original Byrds, rather than a 'best of compilation'. The original quintet had not performed live since early 1966 and their complete reformation would have been a mouthwatering prospect for any astute impresario. Unlike their great contemporaries, the Beatles, the Beach Boys, the Rolling Stones and the Who, the Byrds have a complete line-up still alive 25 years on. Both Michael Clarke and Gene Clark appreciated the enormous commercial potential of the original Byrds and remained eager to tap that source. While fighting for Michael's rights, Steve Green knew that the real jackpot would be won by masterminding a full scale reunion:

'There should be five or none, but Michael has to make a living. I'd like to see them all own the trademark: one fifth each. My position has always been consistent. If they want it for five of them, we don't have to go to court. Put it in one name: The Byrds Inc. They tour whenever they want to tour. Nobody's left out. If they trademarked it five ways, we'd drop our application. All we want is a resolution. Even if these guys hate each other, let them do their show, go home, make $10,000,000 for each tour they go on, and split it five ways. It may take only 30 days a year. Michael will then have to find some other way to pay his bills.'

Green's fanciful idea about an annual Byrds get together was surely out of the question, but even a single live album and one-off reunion tour would probably earn Clarke more than years of playing small time gigs throughout the States with his bastardized version of the Byrds. I would wager that Clarke and Green would agree to the Byrds remaining in indefinite suspended animation if McGuinn, Hillman and Crosby agreed to a one off album/tour and five-way split under the right conditions. With such an incentive Clarke and Green were obviously intent on fighting on. As Green concluded: 'If we win the injunction, McGuinn and Hillman are done for'.

The injunction hearing, for all its importance, looked like being little more than the first round of an extremely bloody battle ending in a full trial. Such a course of action would have meant a judge ultimately unravelling the complex history of the Byrds in order to reach a solution. Clarke's role in the various comings and goings would no doubt have made particularly interesting reading. We know that Crosby received $10,000 compensation from the Byrds following his dismissal in October 1967. A couple of months later, Clarke was also out, but in signing away his rights all he received was his drumkit and his royalties. Whether he should have asked for compensation for surrendering the value of the name Byrds at that point was a factor that Green's lawyers intended to focus upon in the event of a trial. Within two months of Michael's leaving, on 29 February 1968, McGuinn and Hillman signed a new agreement with CBS Records for which they received an advance of $150,000. Clarke thereby missed a welcome windfall by a matter of weeks. How relevant these factors could become was a matter of debate but with Green collecting affidavits like cigarette cards, and even securing the assistance of former Byrds manager Larry Spector, everything seemed set for one of the most exciting and revealing court cases in rock history. Days before the injunction hearing, Green ominously warned:

'When everybody's background is brought into this and all the quotes come out, nobody wins. We all lose! Let's figure out what these guys want to do with the Byrds or how Michael can make a living. End of lawsuit.'

The injunction hearing finally proved not so much a body blow as a complete knockout awarded to Michael Clarke. The District Judge William J. Castagna, after hearing both sides of the argument, emerged with an unequivocal judgement:

'The Court has considered the parties' legal memoranda and affidavits, and has heard oral argument. Preliminary injunctive relief is appropriate if the plaintiffs demonstrate: (1) a substantial likelihood of their success on the merits; (2) their own irreparable injury absent injunctive relief; (3) that the plaintiffs' threatened injury outweighs whatever damage the injunction may cause the opposing party; and (4) that the public interest will not be harmed if the injunction issues. Because the plaintiffs have failed to establish their own irreparable injury absent injunctive relief, their motion is declined. Plaintiffs may establish irreparable injury by showing that the defendants' acts will cause a likelihood of public confusion. Here, the plaintiffs' affidavits attempt to demonstrate instances of actual confusion, but these instances are at best minor and inconsequential, and, in addition, are recited by individuals with a bias toward the plaintiffs. The plaintiffs' most significant and unbiased example of actual confusion involves an advertising flyer misidentifying defendant Clarke's band as 'The Byrds featuring Roger McGuinn'. But, rather than suggesting a likelihood of confusion, this isolated incident is the best evidence of a lack of confusion. Since 1984, the defendant Clarke has performed over 300 times throughout the United States using the Byrds name. And yet the plaintiffs can only credibly identify one incident of confusion. When the sparsity of incidents of confusion is compared to the wide exposure the defendants have received in over 300 concerts over four years, it is apparent that the likelihood of confusion caused by defendant Clarke's actions is indeed remote. But perhaps most important, the plaintiffs have, by their delay, rendered incredible their claim to irreparable injury. As indicated, the plaintiffs have known for at least four years that defendant Clarke has used the name the Byrds in over 300 concert performances. And until now the plaintiffs have taken no meaningful steps to prevent Clarke's continued performances. Under these circumstances, where the plaintiffs have delayed applying for injunctive relief for approximately four years, their claim of irreparable injury is simply not credible. For the reasons stated, the plaintiffs have failed to establish their own irreparable injury absent injunctive relief, and it is therefore ordered that plaintiffs' motion for a preliminary injunction is declined.'

Not surprisingly, Michael Clarke's reaction to the news was a combination of excitement and relief: 'I've been on pins and needles since the court date but we won a monumental decision. I'm back in business and my life is wonderful'.

The news from the other Byrds camp was not so wonderful for they were still under threat from Green's counter-lawsuit. Within 26 days of Castagna's ruling, McGuinn, Hillman and Crosby voluntarily dismissed their action without prejudice. The great Byrds trial would not now be taking place after all. A stoical Siddons concluded: 'It just cost too much money to force Michael to stop abusing the Byrds name'. Many fans would reiterate his lament. A delighted Steve Green disagreed and felt that his side were magnanimous in their victory:

'I was confident we'd win but what they did to Michael really damaged us and it's going to take a lot of time to recover. I wanted them to pay my lawyers' fees but I'm going to let it go, and I'll tell you why. We're all talking now and maybe we'll reunite the band for 30 days this year. That might be the best thing. That's all we really wanted anyway. We always wanted that first but, if they didn't want to play we still wanted to have the ability to go out and play. So if they want to reunite, they'll reunite and if they don't then Michael will be out there for as long as he wants to be. That's how it finally wound up.'

Green's explanation left several questions unanswered. Although

Clarke was in a position to counter-sue and free to perform as the Byrds, McGuinn, Crosby, Hillman and the neutral Clark retained the talent and drawing power to make the real money. This would seem to be their crucial ace card. Surely, Michael would forgo any rights to the name Byrds in return for a slice of that full scale reunion cake, which could take the form of large record company advances plus royalties and substantial concert receipts. Green accepted the logic, but was extremely wary of surrendering his client's hard fought victory so easily:

'We don't think that will ever happen. It may be their last card but it wouldn't work for Michael because if the album's a bust nothing happens and the tour might not be as big as expected. Michael's still got to work for the rest of his life. It's too much of a gamble. Unless some promoter guarantees them $30,000,000 over the next four to five years for a certain number of dates per year, then of course he'd be fine. But, until that happens, it'd be real touchy whether he would want to be in a situation where it was all or none of them. We're not looking to hurt them. Hopefully, they'll all start talking and get back together and go about their business.'

Bill Siddons seemed confident that three or four of the original Byrds (minus Clarke) would possibly get together for a brief reunion and added: 'Our intent all along has only been that if a fan bought a ticket to see the Byrds, at least Roger McGuinn would be in the band.' Siddons' perspective underestimated the full implications of Clarke's victory. For now that Clarke had won the injunction proceedings, he was in a strong position to dictate the future of the Byrds name and the terms of any reunion. Without legal redress, the trio's only chance of convincing Clarke to forgo the Byrds name would be to invite him back into their camp, agree to a reunion and hope that he accepted. In spite of Green's reservations about surrendering the name, even he realizes that the value of the title Byrds is merely relative. One big reunion killing would be worth years of struggling around the oldies circuit, especially when you consider that Clarke does not yet have a contract with a major company. Despite his earlier comments, Green probably knows that it would be foolhardy to decline a reunion offer on any terms simply to retain a prestigious name that cannot of itself make big money:

'Michael won't make a fortune unless he can come up with a hit record. That way he would make more money than any kind of reunion. You just don't know. You've got to weigh it up. We're sitting on it now because the lawsuit has been dismissed. We could file a counter-lawsuit against each and every one of them for what they did. But instead of doing that, in the hope that maybe we can recreate some of that magic, let's try and get back together, play some dates, and if they don't want to, Michael can go out and do it. Now that everybody's under a certain amount of their own control I think you might see more out of it than you ever saw in the past. They're all going in their own directions, and that's good. Maybe now the channels can be opened and we can talk to each other and go out and make some money.'

In spite of all the conflict, Hillman and McGuinn were talking to Clarke within days of the court hearing. Like five separate companies, the Byrds and their representatives continued to exchange views in the hope of finalizing a world tour and live album. Clarke's representatives are still optimistically talking about reforming the quintet and playing a 30 day tour for ten consecutive years! At the time of writing at least one full scale reunion seems tantalizingly close. but whether it will reach fruition remains to be seen. The good news is that the old acrimony is past . . . at least for the present.

Discography

The following Byrds discography is essentially UK based. All references are to original CBS UK serial numbers unless otherwise stated. Please note that reissues and various artiste sampler albums are not included. For related US releases from the CBS years see the sessionography.

SINGLES

1964 (As the Beefeaters)
'Please Let Me Love You'/'Don't Be Long' (Pye International 7N-25277)

1965
'Mr Tambourine Man'/'I Knew I'd Want You' CBS 201765
'All I Really Want To Do'/'Feel A Whole Lot Better' CBS 201796
'Turn! Turn! Turn!'/'She Don't Care About Time' CBS 202008

1966
'Set You Free This Time'/'It Won't Be Wrong' CBS 202037
'It Won't Be Wrong'/'Set You Free This Time' CBS 202037*
'Eight Miles High'/'Why' CBS 202067
'5-D (Fifth Dimension)'/'Captain Soul' CBS 202259
'Mr Spaceman'/'What's Happening?!?!' CBS 202295
*(CBS switched sides are the first week of release)

1967
'So You Want To Be A Rock 'n' Roll Star'/'Everybody's Been Burned' CBS 202559
'My Back Pages'/'Renaissance Fair' CBS 2468
'Lady Friend'/'Don't Make Waves' CBS 2924
'Goin' Back'/'Change Is Now' CBS 3093

1968
'You Ain't Going Nowhere'/'Artificial Energy' CBS 3411
'I Am A Pilgrim'/'Pretty Boy Floyd' CBS 3752

1969
'Bad Night At The Whiskey'/'Drug Store Truck Driving Man' CBS 4055
'Lay Lady Lay'/'Old Blue' CBS 4284
'(I) Wasn't Born To Follow'/'Child Of The Universe' CBS 4572
'Jesus Is Just Alright'/'It's All Over Now Baby Blue' CBS 4753

1970
'Chestnut Mare'/'Just A Season' CBS 5322

1971
'I Trust (Everything Is Gonna Work Out Alright)'/'(Is This) MyDestiny' CBS 7253
'Glory Glory'/'Citizen Kane' CBS 7501

1972
'America's Great National Pastime'/'Farther Along' CBS 7712

1973
'Things Will Be Better'/'For Free' Asylum AYM 516
'Full Circle'/'Long Live The King' Asylum AYM 517

1974
'Full Circle'/'Things Will Be Better' Asylum AYM 545

EPs

1966
Times They Are A-Changin' CBS EP 6069
'Times They Are A-Changin''; 'The Bells Of Rhymney'; 'It's No Use'; 'We'll Meet Again'

Eight Miles High CBS EP 6077
'Mr Tambourine Man'; 'All I Really Want To Do'; 'Turn! Turn! Turn!'; 'Eight Miles High'

1983
The Byrds Pickwick SCOOP 33 7SR 5016
'Lay Lady Lay'; 'Turn! Turn! Turn!'; 'So You Want To Be A Rock 'n' Roll Star'; 'Chestnut Mare'; 'All I Really Want To Do'; 'Goin' Back'

ALBUMS

The following is a list of the Byrds official albums, excluding greatest hits compilations which can be found under the entries for individual artistes. Record companies have been slow in adapting the Byrds back catalogue to compact disc. Although Edsel Records have, at the time of writing, issued three of the group's albums in CD form and numerous others have appeared in the US on Columbia, a definitive series of scheduled releases has yet to emerge, but should be forthcoming in the early 90's. CD tracks currently released but unavailable on disc are highlighted in the albums section of this discography.

Mr Tambourine Man CBS SBPG 62571
'Mr Tambourine Man'; 'Feel A Whole Lot Better'; 'Spanish Harlem Incident'; 'You Won't Have To Cry'; 'Here Without You'; 'The Bells Of Rhymney'; 'All I Really Want To Do'; 'I Knew I'd Want You'; 'It's No Use'; 'Don't Doubt Yourself Babe'; 'Chimes Of Freedom'; 'We'll Meet Again'

Turn! Turn! Turn! CBS SBPG 62652
'Turn! Turn! Turn!'; 'It Won't Be Wrong'; 'Set You Free This Time'; 'Lay Down Your Weary Tune'; 'He Was A Friend Of Mine'; 'The World Turns All Around Her'; 'Satisfied Mind'; 'If You're Gone'; 'The Times They Are A-Changin''; 'Wait And See'; 'Oh! Susannah'

Fifth Dimension CBS SBPG 62783
'5-D (Fifth Dimension)'; 'Wild Mountain Thyme'; 'Mr Spaceman'; 'I See You'; 'What's Happening?!?!'; 'I Come And Stand At Every Door'; 'Eight Miles High'; 'Hey Joe (Where You Gonna Go)'; 'Captain Soul'; 'John Riley'; '2-4-2 Fox Trot (The Lear Jet Song)'

Younger Than Yesterday CBS SBPG 62988
'So You Want To Be A Rock 'n' Roll Star'; 'Have You Seen Her Face'; 'CTA-102'; 'Renaissance Fair'; 'Time Between'; 'Everybody's Been Burned'; 'Thoughts And Words'; 'Mind Gardens'; 'My Back Pages'; 'The Girl With No Name'; 'Why'

The Notorious Byrd Brothers CBS S 63169
'Artificial Energy'; 'Goin' Back'; 'Natural Harmony'; 'Draft Morning'; 'Wasn't Born To Follow'; 'Get To You'; 'Change Is Now'; 'Old John Robertson'; 'Tribal Gathering'; 'Dolphin's Smile'; 'Space Odyssey'

Sweetheart Of The Rodeo CBS S 63353
'You Ain't Going Nowhere'; 'I Am A Pilgrim'; 'The Christian Life'; 'You Don't Miss Your Water'; 'You're Still On My Mind'; 'Pretty Boy Floyd'; 'Hickory Wind'; 'One Hundred Years From Now'; 'Blue Canadian Rockies'; 'Life In Prison'; 'Nothing Was Delivered'

Dr Byrds And Mr Hyde CBS S 63545
'This Wheel's On Fire'; 'Old Blue'; 'Your Gentle Ways Of Loving Me'; 'Child Of The Universe'; 'Nashville West'; 'Drug Store Truck Drivin' Man'; 'King Apathy III'; 'Candy'; 'Bad Night At The Whiskey'; 'Medley: My Back Pages; B.J. Blues; Baby, What Do You Want Me To Do'

Ballad Of Easy Rider CBS S 63795
'Ballad Of Easy Rider'; 'Fido'; 'Oil In My Lamp'; 'Tulsa County Blue'; 'Jack Tarr The Sailor'; 'Jesus Is Just Alright'; 'It's All Over Now, Baby Blue'; 'There Must Be Someone'; 'Gunga Din'; 'Deportee (Plane Wreck At Los Gatos)'; 'Armstrong, Aldrin And Collins'

(Untitled) CBS S 64095
'Lover Of The Bayou'; 'Positively 4th Street'; 'Nashville West'; 'So You Want To Be A Rock 'n' Roll Star'; 'Mr Tambourine Man'; 'Mr Spaceman'; 'Eight Miles High'; 'Chestnut Mare'; 'Truck Stop Girl'; 'All The Things'; 'Yesterday's Train'; 'Hungry Planet'; 'Just A Season'; 'Take A Whiff'; 'You All Look Alike'; 'Well Come Back Home'

Byrdmaniax CBS S 64389
'Glory Glory'; 'Pale Blue'; 'I Trust'; 'Tunnel Of Love'; 'Citizen Kane'; 'I Wanna Grow Up To Be A Politician'; 'Absolute Happiness'; 'Green Apple Quick Step'; '(Is This) My Destiny'; 'Kathleen's Song'; 'Jamaica Say You Will'

Farther Along CBS S 64676
'Tiffany Queen'; 'Get Down Your Line'; 'Farther Along'; 'B.B. Class Road'; 'Buglar'; 'America's Great National Pastime'; 'Antique Sandy'; 'So Fine'; 'Lazy Waters'; 'Bristol Steam Convention Blues'

Byrds Asylum SYLA 8754
'Full Circle'; 'Sweet Mary'; 'Changing Heart'; 'For Free'; 'Born To Rock 'n' Roll'; 'Things Will Be Better'; 'Cowgirl In The Sand'; 'Long Live The King'; 'Borrowing Time'; 'Laughing'; '(See The Sky) About To Rain'

In addition to the above there have been several archive albums released retrospectively as follows:

Preflyte Together ST-T-1001 (US) Bumble GEXP 8001
'You Showed Me'; 'Here Without You'; 'She Has A Way'; 'The Reason Why'; 'For Me Again'; 'Boston'; 'You Movin''; 'The Airport Song'; 'You Won't Have To Cry'; 'I Knew I'd Want You'; 'Mr Tambourine Man'

The Original Singles Volume I CBS 31851
'Mr Tambourine Man'; 'I Knew I'd Want You'; 'All I Really Want To Do'; 'Feel A Whole Lot Better'; 'Turn! Turn! Turn!'; 'She Don't Care About Time'; 'Set You Free This Time'; 'It Won't Be Wrong'; 'Eight Miles High' ; 'Why'; '5-D (Fifth Dimension)'; 'Captain Soul'; 'Mr Spaceman'; 'What's Happening?!?!'; 'So You Want To Be A Rock 'n' Roll Star'; 'Everybody's Been Burned'

The Original Singles Volume II CBS 32103
'My Back Pages'; 'Renaissance Fair'; 'Have You Seen Her Face'; 'Don't Make Waves'; 'Lady Friend'; 'Old John Robertson'; 'Goin' Back'; 'Change Is Now'; 'You Ain't Going Nowhere'; 'Artificial Energy'; 'I Am A Pilgrim'; 'Pretty Boy Floyd'; 'Bad Night At The Whiskey'; 'Drug Store Truck Drivin' Man'; 'Lay Lady Lay'; 'Old Blue'

Never Before Re-Flyte MH 70318 (US)
'Mr Tambourine Man'; 'I Knew I'd Want You'; 'She Has A Way'; 'It's All Over Now, Baby Blue'; 'Never Before'; 'Eight Miles High'; 'Why'; 'Triad'; 'It Happens Each Day'; 'Lady Friend'; plus bonus tracks available on CD only: 'I Know My Rider (I Know You, Rider)'; 'Why'; 'She Don't Care About Time'; 'Flight 713 (Song Number 2)'; 'Psychodrama City'; 'Don't Make Waves'; 'Moog Raga'

In The Beginning Rhino R1 70244 (US)
'Tomorrow Is A Long Ways Away'; 'Boston'; 'The Only Girl I Adore'; 'You Won't Have To Cry'; 'I Knew I'd Want You'; 'The Airport Song'; 'Please Let Me Love You'; 'You Movin''; 'It Won't Be Wrong'; 'It's No Use'; 'You Showed Me'; 'She Has A Way'; 'For Me Again'; 'Here Without You'; plus bonus tracks available on CD only: 'The Reason Why'; 'Mr Tambourine Man'; 'Tomorrow Is A Long Ways Away (acoustic)'

ALBUM CONTRIBUTIONS
The following is a complete list of albums on which each of the Byrds has played as a permanent group member.

James Roger McGuinn

Albums with the Limeliters:
Tonight In Person RCA RD 7237/SF5114

Albums with the Chad Mitchell Trio:
Mighty Day On Campus Kapp KS 3262 (US)
The Chad Mitchell Trio At The Bitter End Kapp KS 3281 (US)

Albums with the Byrds:
Mr Tambourine Man CBS SBPG 62571
Turn! Turn! Turn! CBS SPBG 62652
Fifth Dimension CBS SBPG 62783
Younger Than Yesterday CBS SBPG 62988
The Byrds' Greatest Hits CBS SBPG 63107
The Notorious Byrd Brothers CBS S 63169
Sweetheart Of The Rodeo CBS S 63353
Dr Byrds And Mr Hyde CBS S 63545
Preflyte Together ST-T-1001 (US)
Ballad Of Easy Rider CBS S 63795
(Untitled) CBS S 66253
Byrdmaniax CBS S 64389
The Byrds' Greatest Hits Volume II CBS S 64650
Farther Along CBS S 64676
Byrds Asylum SYLA 8754
History Of The Byrds CBS 68242
The Byrds Play Dylan CBS 31795
The Original Singles Volume I CBS 31851
The Original Singles Volume II CBS 32103

Never Before Re-Flyte MH 70318 (US)
In The Beginning Rhino R2 70244 (US)
The Byrds Collection Castle Communications CCSLP 151

Isolated appearances with the Byrds:
Early LA Together ST-T-1014 (US)
Don't Make Waves MGM 4483 ST (US)
Candy Stateside SSL 10276 (US)
Easy Rider Stateside SSL 5018
Homer Atlantic 2400137
Earl Scruggs, His Family And Friends CBS 64777
Banjoman Sire SRK 6026
Elektrock (as the Beefeaters) Elektra 60403

With the exception of *Homer*, *Easy Rider* and *Elektrock* the above albums contained Byrds tracks generally not available elsewhere, including different mixes of 'Don't Make Waves' and 'Candy' for movie scores, and the latter day CBS Byrds performing two songs ('You Ain't Going Nowhere' and 'Nothin' To It') on the Earl Scruggs television special. *Banjoman* also contains one new track, 'Roll Over Beethoven', and an acoustic version of 'Mr Tambourine Man'.

Solo and post-Byrds recordings:
Easy Rider Stateside SSL 5018
Roger McGuinn CBS 62574
Peace On You CBS 80171
Roger McGuinn And Band CBS 80877
Cardiff Rose CBS 81369
Thunderbyrd CBS 81883

The contributions on *Easy Rider*, 'Ballad Of Easy Rider' and 'It's Alright Ma (I'm Only Bleeding)', were the only solo recordings released by McGuinn during his stay with the Columbia Byrds.

As McGuinn, Clark & Hillman:
McGuinn, Clark & Hillman Capitol EST 11910
City Capitol EST 12043

As McGuinn/Hillman:
McGuinn/Hillman Capitol EA ST 12108

In addition to the above, McGuinn has also played on several guitar and banjo albums: *The 5-String Story* (Delyse Envoy VOY 9158), *The 12-String Story* (Delyse Envoy VOY 9159), *The 12-String Story* (London SH-F 8285), *Feuding Banjos* (Olympic 7105), *Anthology Of The Banjo* (Bellaphon BJS 4036), *Anthology Of The 12-String Guitar* (Bellaphon BJS 4044) and *Anthology Of The Blues Guitar* (Everest TR 2071). He has also appeared as a contributor on albums by the following artistes: Hoyt Axton, Judy Collins, the Irish Ramblers, Bob Gibson, David Hemmings, Skip Battin, Earl Scruggs, Charles Lloyd, Bob Dylan, Susan Lynch, Vern Gosdin, Peter Case, the Beach Boys, Kinky Friedman, Crowded House, Elvis Costello and the Nitty Gritty Dirt Band.

Gene Clark

Albums with the New Christy Minstrels:
Merry Christmas CBS SBPG 62287
Land Of Giants CBS CS 8987 (US)

Although he is pictured on the album sleeve of the New Christy Minstrels' *Ramblin'* (SBPG 6269) the album was recorded before Gene's arrival in the group.

Albums with the Byrds:
Mr Tambourine Man CBS SBPG 62571
Turn! Turn! Turn! SBPG 62652
Fifth Dimension CBS SBPG 62783
The Byrds' Greatest Hits CBS SBPG 63107
Byrds Asylum SYLA 8754
Preflyte Together ST-T-1001 (US)
History Of The Byrds CBS 68242
The Byrds Play Dylan CBS 31795
The Original Singles Volume I CBS 31851
The Original Singles Volume II CBS 32103
The Byrds Collection Castle Communications CCSLP 151
Never Before Re-Flyte MH 70318 (US)
In The Beginning Rhino R1 70244 (US)

Isolated appearances with the Byrds:
Early LA Together ST-T-1014 (US)
Homer Atlantic 2400 137
Roadmaster Edsel ED 198*
Elektrock Elektra 60403

* The original Byrds line-up performed two songs on *Roadmaster*: 'She's The Kind Of Girl' and 'One In A Hundred'. This album was for many years only available as a Dutch import (A&M 87584).

Solo and post-Byrd recordings:
Echoes (With the Gosdin Brothers) CBS 62934
White Light A&M AMLS 64292
Early LA Sessions Columbia KC 31123 (US)*
Roadmaster Edsel ED 198
American Dreamer Soundtrack Mediarts 41-12 (US)**
No Other Asylum SYL 9020
Two Sides To Every Story RSO 2394 176
Firebyrd Making Waves SPIN 122

* This was a remixed, re-recorded version of the 1967 *Echoes (With the Gosdin Brothers)*. The track sequence has been altered and one cut, 'Elevator Operator', deleted.
** Gene contributed two tracks to the soundtrack: 'Outlaw Song' and 'American Dreamer'.

As Dillard and Clark:
The Fantastic Expedition Of Dillard And Clark A&M AMLS 939
Through The Morning Through The Night A&M AMLS 966
Kansas City Southern A&M 86436 ZT (Holland)*

* This Dutch release is included here because it contains three rare tracks previously only available on single: 'Why Not Your Baby', 'Lyin' Down The Middle' and 'Don't Be Cruel'.

As McGuinn, Clark & Hillman:
McGuinn, Clark & Hillman Capitol EST 11910
City Capitol EST 12043

As Gene Clark and Carla Olson:
So Rebellious A Lover Demon FIEND 89★

★The CD version of *So Rebellious A Lover* contains one extra track: 'Lovers Turnaround'.

In addition to the above Gene sang lead vocal on the Flying Burrito Brothers' single 'Tried So Hard', which was re-recorded without his voice for the group's third album. Clark also wrote several songs never recorded by himself but picked up by other artistes. These included 'Back Street Mirror' (originally titled 'How Hard It Would Be') which appeared on David Hemmings' *Happens* (MGM E-4490) in 1967 and 'Till Today' and 'Long Time', which ended up on the eponymous album by Rose Garden (Atco FD 33-225) in 1968. Clark also guested on recordings by Merry Go Round, Steve Young, Long Ryders, Primitive Future and Three O'Clock.

David Crosby

Albums with Les Baxter Balladeers:
Jack Linkletter Presents A Folk Festival Crescendo 196 (US)

Albums with the Byrds:
Mr Tambourine Man CBS SBPG 62571
Turn! Turn! Turn! CBS SBPG 62652
Fifth Dimension CBS SBPG 62783
Younger Than Yesterday CBS SBPG 62988
The Byrds' Greatest Hits CBS SBPG 630107
The Notorious Byrd Brothers CBS S 63169
Preflyte Together ST-T-1001 (US)
Byrds Asylum SYLA 8754
History Of The Byrds CBS S 68242
The Byrds Play Dylan CBS 31795
The Original Singles Volume I CBS 31851
The Byrds Collection Castle Communications CCSLP 151
Never Before Re-Flyte MH 70318 (US)
In The Beginning Rhino R1 70244 (US)

Isolated appearances with the Byrds:
Early LA Together ST-T-1014 (US)★
Don't Make Waves MGM SE 4483 ST (US)
Homer Atlantic 2400 137

★ As well as containing two tracks by the Jet Set ('The Only Girl' and 'You Movin'') *Early LA* also featured a couple of solo cuts recorded by Crosby prior to joining the Byrds: 'Willie Gene' and 'Come Back Baby'.

As Crosby, Stills & Nash:
Crosby, Stills & Nash Atlantic 588 189
So Far Atlantic K 50023
CSN Atlantic K50369
Replay Atlantic K 50766
Daylight Again Atlantic K 50896
Allies Atlantic 78-0075-1
Bread And Roses Fantasy 79011

As Crosby, Stills, Nash & Young:
Déjà Vu Atlantic 2401 001
Woodstock Atlantic 2657 001
Four Way Street Atlantic 2657 007
Woodstock II Atlantic 2657 003
SWALK Polydor 2383 043
So Far Atlantic K 50023
American Dream Atlantic WX 233 781888-1

As David Crosby:
If I Could Only Remember My Name Atlantic 2401 005
Oh Yes I Can A&M AMA 5232

As Crosby & Nash:
Crosby & Nash Atlantic K 50011
Wind On The Water Polydor 2310 428
Whistling Down The Wire Polydor 2310 468
Crosby & Nash Live Polydor 2310 165
Crosby & Nash's Greatest Hits Polydor 2310 626

In addition to the above, David Crosby has also guested on a number of albums by such artists as Jefferson Airplane, Joni Mitchell, Bob Gibson, John Sebastian, Stephen Stills, Jefferson Starship, Paul Kantner/Grace Slick, Rick Roberts, Graham Nash, Jackson Browne, Dave Mason, Paul Kantner/Grace Slick/David Freiberg, Neil Young, Phil Lesh and Ned Lagin, James Taylor, Carole King, and Bonnie Raitt.

Michael Clarke

Albums with the Byrds:
Mr Tambourine Man CBS SBPG 62571
Turn! Turn! Turn! CBS SBPG 62652
Fifth Dimension CBS SBPG 62783
Younger Than Yesterday CBS SBPG 62988
The Byrds' Greatest Hits CBS SBPG 63107
The Notorious Byrd Brothers CBS S 63169
The Byrds' Greatest Hits Volume II CBS S 64650
Preflyte Together ST-T-1001 (US)
Byrds Asylum SYLA 8754
History Of The Byrds CBS 68242
The Byrds Play Dylan CBS 31795
The Original Singles Volume I CBS 31851
The Byrds Collection Castle Communications CCSLP 151
Never Before Re-Flyte MH 70318 (US)
In The Beginning Rhino R1 70244 (US)

Isolated appearances with the Byrds:
Early LA Together ST-T-1014 (US)
Don't Make Waves MGM SE 4483 ST (US)
Homer Atlantic 2400 137

With the Flying Burrito Brothers:
Burrito Deluxe A&M AMLS 983
The Flying Burrito Brothers A&M AMLS 64295

DISCOGRAPHY

Last Of The Red Hot Burritos A&M AMLS 64343
Close Up The Honky Tonks A&M AMLH 63631
Honky Tonk Heaven A&M 87585 XDT (Holland)*
Sleepless Nights A&M AMLH 64578

* This Dutch release included various tracks unreleased elsewhere.

With Firefall:
Firefall Atlantic K 50260
Luna Sea Atlantic K 50355
Elan Atlantic 50494
Undertow Atlantic SD 16006 (US)

The last Firefall album on which Clarke appeared *Undertow* did not receive a UK release. In addition to the above, Michael also guested on albums by Gene Clark and Dillard and Clark. Between leaving Firefall and reviving the Byrds name, Clarke worked for several years on the live circuit with Jerry Jeff Walker.

Chris Hillman

Albums with the Scottsville Squirrel Barkers:
Bluegrass Favorites Crown CLP 5346 (US)

Albums with the Hillmen:
The Hillmen Together ST-T-1001 (US)

Although never released at the time of its recording in 1964, tapes of the Hillmen were compiled for this retrospectively released album on Together in 1969. The album was later reissued on the Dutch label Negram and included the previously unheard 'Copper Kettle'. In 1981, the work was remixed and reissued on Sugar Hill Records (SH-3719) complete with another unissued track, 'Back Road Fever'.

Albums with the Byrds:
Mr Tambourine Man CBS SBPG 62571
Turn! Turn! Turn! CBS SBPG 62652
Fifth Dimension CBS SBPG 62783
Younger Than Yesterday CBS SBPG 62988
The Byrds' Greatest Hits CBS SBPG 63107
The Notorious Byrd Brothers CBS S 63169
Sweetheart Of The Rodeo CBS S 63353
Preflyte Together ST-T-1001 (US)
The Byrds' Greatest Hits, Volume II CBS S 64650
Byrds Asylum SYLA 8754
History Of The Byrds CBS S 68252
The Byrds Play Dylan CBS 31795
The Original Singles, Volume I CBS 31851
The Original Singles, Volume II CBS 32103
The Byrds Collection Castle Communications CCSLP 151
Never Before Re-Flyte MH 70318 (US)
In The Beginning Rhino R1 70244 (US)

Isolated appearances with the Byrds:
Early LA Together ST-T-1014 (US)
Don't Make Waves MGM SE 4483 ST (US)
Homer Atlantic 2400 137

With the Flying Burrito Brothers:
Gilded Palace Of Sin A&M AMLS 931
Burrito Deluxe A&M AMLS 983
The Flying Burrito Brothers A&M AMLS 64295
Last Of The Red Hot Burritos A&M AMLS 64343
Close Up The Honky Tonks A&M AMLH 63631
Honky Tonk Heaven A&M 87585 XDT (Holland)
Sleepless Nights A&M AMLH 64578

With Manassas:
Stephen Stills/Manassas Atlantic K 60021
Down The Road Atlantic K40440

As Souther, Hillman, Furay:
Souther, Hillman, Furay Asylum SYLA 8758
Trouble In Paradise Asylum SYLA 8760

As Chris Hillman:
Slippin' Away Asylum K 53041
Clear Sailin' Asylum K 53060
Morning Sky Sundown SDLP 053
Desert Rose Spindrift SPIN 113

As McGuinn, Clark & Hillman:
McGuinn, Clark & Hillman Capitol EST 11910
City Capitol EST 12403

As McGuinn/Hillman:
McGuinn/Hillman Capitol EAST 12108

With Ever Call Ready:
Ever Call Ready A&M WR 8310 (US)

With the Desert Rose Band:
The Desert Rose Band Curb 90202
Running Curb/MCA 42169 (US)

Hillman has also guested on numerous albums including those of Don Parmley, David Hemmings, Gene Clark, Dillard and Clark, Bob Gibson, Marc Ellington, Cherokee, Barry McGuire, Roger McGuinn, Rusty Weir, Poco, Dan Fogelberg, Stephen Stills and the Nitty Gritty Dirt Band. In 1981, he contributed to the compilations *God Loves Country Music* and *Down Home Praise*. Chris has also done production work on records by the Gosdin Brothers, Rick Roberts, Dan McCorison and Street Talk.

Kevin Kelley

With Fever Tree:
For Sale Ampex 10113 (US)

With the Byrds:
Sweetheart Of The Rodeo CBS S 63353
The Byrds' Greatest Hits, Volume II CBS S 64650
History Of The Byrds CBS 68242
The Byrds Play Dylan CBS 31795
The Original Singles, Volume II CBS 32103
The Byrds Collection Castle Communications CSLP 151

With Jesse Wolff & Whings:
Jesse Wolff & Whings Shelter SW 8907 (US)

Kelley was previously a member of the Rising Sons, but it is conjectural whether the recordings released by them contain his drumming. Since leaving the Byrds, Kelley's musical endeavours have been slight, though he was still playing around LA in the late 70's. Today, he claims to enjoy tinkering in the studio and says that music is still very much a part of his life.

Gram Parsons

With the Shilos:
The Early Years 1963-1965 Sundown SDLP 008

With the International Submarine Band:
Safe At Home LHI 12001 (US)

This album was remixed and reissued on Shiloh (SLP4088) as *Gram Parsons* and finally received a UK release in 1985 under its original title on Statik Records (STATLP 26).

With the Byrds:
Sweetheart Of The Rodeo CBS S 63353
The Byrds Greatest Hits, Volume II CBS S 64650
History Of The Byrds CBS S 68242
The Byrds Play Dylan CBS 31795
The Original Singles, Volume II CBS 32103
The Byrds Collection Castle Communications CCSLP 151

With the Flying Burrito Brothers:
Gilded Palace Of Sin A&M AMLS 931
Burrito Deluxe A&M AMLS 983
Close Up The Honky Tonks A&M AMLH 62631
Honky Tonk Heaven A&M 87585 (Holland)
Sleepless Nights A&M AMLH 64598

As Gram Parsons:
G.P. Warners/Reprise K44228
Grievous Angel Warners/Reprise K 54018
Gram Parsons WEA K 57008

Gram Parsons has also made guest appearances on records by the Byrds, Rolling Stones, Rick Gretch, Delaney and Bonnie, Steve Young, Fred Neil and Jesse Ed Davis.

Clarence White

With the Kentucky Colonels:
New Sounds Of American Bluegrass Briar 109 (US)
Appalachian Swing World Pacific (US)
The Kentucky Colonels United Artists UAS 29514*
Livin' In The Past Briar SBR 4202 (US)
The Kentucky Colonels With Scotty Stoneman, Live In LA, 1965 Briar SBR 4206 (US)
Kentucky Colonels 1965-66 Rounder 0070 (US)

* This was a re-release of *Appalachian Swing*, with the addition of two songs previously available on single only: 'That's What You Get For Loving Me' and 'The Ballad Of Farmer Brown'.

With Nashville West:
Nashville West Sierra SRS 8701 (US)

With the Byrds:
Sweetheart Of The Rodeo CBS S 63353
Dr Byrds And Mr Hyde CBS S 63545
Ballad Of Easy Rider CBS S 63795
(Untitled) CBS S 66253
Byrdmaniax CBS S 64389
The Byrds' Greatest Hits, Volume II CBS S 64650
Farther Along CBS S 64676
History Of The Byrds CBS S 68242
The Byrds Play Dylan CBS 31795
The Original Singles Volume II CBS 32103
The Byrds Collection Castle Communications CCSLP 151

Clarence White also made guest appearances on *Younger Than Yesterday* and *The Notorious Byrd Brothers*, as well as appearing on countless other albums as an uncredited session musician.

Isolated appearances with the Byrds:
Banjoman Sire SRK 6026

N.B. White's work along with the other Byrds instruments is not evident on the cut 'Child Of The Universe' from the *Candy* soundtrack, which featured McGuinn backed by an orchestra.

With the White Brothers:
The White Brothers, The New Kentucky Colonels, Live In Sweden (1973) Rounder 0073 (US)

Other albums:
Muleskinner Warner Brothers BS 2787 (US)
Silver Meteor Sierra SRS 8706 (US)*

* This compilation contains four tracks that Clarence had recorded for the solo album he was working on immediately prior to his death: 'Never Ending Love', 'Last Thing On My Mind', 'Alabama Jubilee' and 'Why You Been Gone So Long'. Two further tracks from those sessions, 'Waterbed' and 'Lucky Me' have yet to obtain an official release.

Gene Parsons

As Cajun Gib and Gene:
Cajun Country Ariola 87 143 HT (Holland)*

* This was released as a solo Gib Guilbeau album in 1973 but was, in fact, the previously unreleased album which Cajun Gib and Gene had recorded for Bakersfield International.

With Nashville West:
Nashville West Sierra SRS 8701 (US)

With the Byrds:
Dr Byrds And Mr Hyde CBS S 63545
Ballad Of Easy Rider CBS S 63795
(Untitled) CBS S 66253
Byrdmaniax CBS 64389
The Byrds' Greatest Hits Volume II CBS S 64650

Farther Along CBS S 64676
History Of The Byrds CBS S 68242
The Byrds Play Dylan CBS 31795
The Original Singles Volume II CBS 32103
The Byrds Collection Castle Communications CCSLP 151

As Gene Parsons:
Kindling Warner Brothers K 46257
Melodies Sundown SDLP 008

With the Flying Burrito Brothers:
Flying Again CBS 69184
Airborne CBS 81433

As Parsons Green:
Birds Of A Feather Sierra SE 4223 (US)

John York

With the Byrds:
Dr Byrds And Mr Hyde CBS S 63545
Ballad Of Easy Rider CBS S 63795
The Byrds' Greatest Hits, Volume II CBS S 64650
History Of The Byrds CBS S 68242
The Byrds Play Dylan CBS 31795
The Original Singles Volume II CBS 32103

Following his departure from the Byrds, York retired from active recording to study piano. He occasionally recorded demos, including 'Don't Jump Baby', 'Waves Of Jealousy' and 'Driving Into The Sun'. He returned to the Byrds story after joining up with Gene Clark and Michael Clarke on the various 'reunion' tours.

Skip Battin

With the Evergreen Blueshoes:
The Ballad Of Evergreen Blueshoes London SHU 8399

With the Byrds:
(Untitled) CBS S 66253
Byrdmaniax CBS S 64389
The Byrds' Greatest Hits, Volume II CBS S 64650
Farther Along CBS S 64676
History Of The Byrds CBS S 68242
The Byrds Play Dylan CBS 31795
The Byrds Collection Castle Communications CCSLP 151

Isolated appearances with the Byrds:
Banjoman Sire SRK 6026

As Skip Battin:
Skip Signpost SB 4255
Navigator Appaloosa 014 (Italy)
Don't Go Crazy Appaloosa 034 (Italy)

With the Flying Burrito Brothers:
Airborne CBS 81433
Live From Tokyo Regency REG 79001*

* This album was originally released in Japan under the title *Close Encounters To The West Coast*.

With New Riders Of The Purple Sage:
Brujo CBS 80405
Oh What A Mighty Time CBS 69182
New Riders MCA 2196

CD RELEASES

At the time of writing, the Byrds are poorly represented in the CD market and only a small proportion of their back catalogue is available worldwide. As the compact disc market continues to grow CBS will no doubt eventually reissue most or all of the Byrds recordings. So far, only one CBS Byrds CD has been issued in Britain *The Byrds' Greatest Hits* (CBS 63107/32068). Fortunately, Edsel Records have successfully licensed *Younger Than Yesterday* (Edsel ED 227), *The Notorious Byrd Brothers* (Edsel ED 262) and *Sweetheart Of The Rodeo* (Edsel ED 234). The only other UK release, as at September 1989, is Castle Communications' *The Byrds Collection* (CCS CD 151). American releases are more extensive and a full scale reissue programme cannot be far away. Columbia have so far released the following: *Mr Tambourine Man* (CK 9172), *Turn! Turn! Turn!* (CK 9254), *The Notorious Byrd Brothers* (CK 9575), *Sweetheart Of The Rodeo* (CK 9670), *The Byrds' Greatest Hits* (CK 9516), *(Untitled)* (CGK 30127), *The Original Singles, Volume I* (CK 37335), *Best Of The Byrds* (CK 31795), *Fifth Dimension* (CK 9349) and *Ballad Of Easy Rider* (CK 9942). More should follow soon.

Previously unissued Byrds material is available on *Never Before* (Murray Hill D 22808) and *In The Beginning* (Rhino R2 70244), and the tracks are documented in the albums section. Three other CDs have appeared on the Continent, where the copyright laws are considerably less stringent, featuring material previously available only on bootleg tapes:

The Monterey Pop Festival 1967 Volume I Living Legend LLR CD 017/018
Released by Living Legend Records, this 17-track excellent quality CD features three tracks by the Byrds taken from their appearance at the Monterey Pop Festival: 'He Was A Friend Of Mine', 'Hey Joe' and 'So You Want To Be A Rock 'n' Roll Star'. Crosby provides his own inimitable introductions to the songs, including the famous reference to the Kennedy assassination. The compilers have erroneously credited Bob Dylan with the authorship of 'He Was A Friend Of Mine'. Although Dylan did record a song of that name as a demo for Leeds Music in early 1962, the lyrics to the Byrds version were written entirely by McGuinn.

The Live Byrds Bulldog BGCD 022
'You Ain't Going Nowhere'; 'Old John Robertson'; 'You Don't Miss Your Water'; 'Hickory Wind'; 'Feel A Whole Lot Better'; 'Chimes Of Freedom'; 'The Christian Life'; 'Turn! Turn! Turn!'; 'Medley: My Back Pages/B.J. Blues/Baby, What Do You Want Me To Do'; 'Mr Spaceman'.
Subtitled 'It was more than 20 Years Ago . . . recorded live at Piper Club Roma May 2, 1968' this CD is a below average quality reproduction of the famous Piper Club tape which has been in circulation on the bootleg tape market for years.

Live In Stockholm 1967 Swinging Pig TSP CD 006
Introduction; 'Hey Joe'; Introduction; 'My Back Pages'; Introduction; 'Mr Tambourine Man'; Introduction; 'He Was A Friend Of Mine'; Introduction; 'So You Want To Be A Rock 'n' Roll Star'; Introduction; 'Roll Over Beethoven'.
This excellent quality recording was taken from a live broadcast on Radiohuset (Studio 4), Stockholm. A brief note mentions that the recording took place in April 1967, though I suspect it may have been between 29 February and 3 March when the group visited Stockholm on a promotional tour. Once again, McGuinn loses the writing credit of 'He Was A Friend Of Mine' to Bob Dylan.

VIDEOS

The Byrds have yet to appear on any video compilation but a number of their television appearances are still in existence and will surely one day be released by an enterprising company. The Byrds were filmed extensively in 1965 and footage still exists from these early experiments. The group also performed their hits on a number of television shows, both in America and Europe. The following is a selective listing of taped performances:

1965
11 May 1965	*Hullabaloo*: 'Mr Tambourine Man', 'Chimes Of Freedom'.
19 June 1965	*Hollywood A-Go-Go*: 'Mr Tambourine Man','All I Really Want To Do', 'Feel A Whole Lot Better'.
23 June 1965	*Shindig*: 'Mr Tambourine Man', 'Not Fade Away'.★
20 July 1965	*Top Of The Pops*: 'Mr Tambourine Man'.
10 August 1965	*Top Of The Pops*: 'All I Really Want To Do'.
11 August 1965	*Ready Steady Go!*: Special edition devoted to the Byrds during their summer tour of Britain.
– August 1965	*Where The Action Is*: 'All I Really Want To Do', 'The Bells Of Rhymney'.
– August 1965	*French television*: 'Mr Tambourine Man', 'Chimes Of Freedom', 'Feel A Whole Lot Better'.
16 September 1965	*Shindig*: 'Chimes Of Freedom', 'Feel A Whole Lot Better'.
21 October 1965	*Shindig*: 'Turn! Turn! Turn!'.
– October 1965	*Hollywood A-Go-Go*: 'Turn! Turn! Turn!'.
19 October 1965	*The Big TNT Show*: 'Mr Tambourine Man', 'The Bells Of Rhymney','Turn! Turn! Turn!'.
29 November 1965	*Hullabaloo*: 'The Times They Are A-Changin'', 'Do You Believe In Magic?'.★
12 December 1965	*Ed Sullivan Show*: 'Turn! Turn! Turn!', 'Mr Tambourine Man'.
25 December 1965	*Top Of The Pops*: 'Mr Tambourine Man'.
26 December 1965	*Top Of The Pops*: 'Mr Tambourine Man'.

★The covers of the Rolling Stones' 'Not Fade Away' and the Lovin' Spoonful's 'Do You Believe In Magic?' were never attempted in the studio by the Byrds.

1966
– January 1966	*Where The Action Is*: 'It Won't Be Wrong', 'Set You Free This Time'.
Date Uncertain	*Smothers Brothers Show*: 'Mr Spaceman'.
– December 1966	ABC documentary: 'Milestones' (excerpt filmed during a studio rehearsal).

1967
Date uncertain: *Beat Club*: 'Eight Miles High', 'Chestnut Mare', 'Bristol Steam Convention Blues', 'So You Want To Be A Rock 'n' Roll Star'.
Date uncertain: *Midnight Special*: 'Mr Tambourine Man', 'So You Want To Be A Rock 'n' Roll Star'.

★The Byrds did not record 'Rolling In My Sweet Baby's Arms'.

1973
28 March 1973   *Midnight Special*: 'Turn! Turn! Turn!', 'Ballad Of Easy Rider', 'It Won't Be Wrong', 'The Water Is Wide'★, 'Mr Tambourine Man', 'Nashville West', 'Lover Of The Bayou', 'Jesus Is Just Alright', 'Mr Spaceman', 'So You Want To Be A Rock 'n' Roll Star'.

★The Byrds did not record 'The Water Is Wide' though it was subsequently cut by Roger McGuinn and included on his first solo album.

BOOTLEG ALBUMS

Byrds Live At Buddy's In England Fly Records 502
'You Ain't Going Nowhere'; 'Lover Of The Bayou'; 'Old Blue'; 'Well Come Back Home'; 'Medley: My Back Pages/B.J. Blues/Baby, What Do You Want Me To Do'; 'He Was A Friend Of Mine'; 'Willin''; 'Soldiers Joy'/'Black Mountain Rag'; 'Take A Whiff'.
Originally released in the UK in 1971, this was the first known Byrds bootleg. The actual date and recording venue remains in doubt for the concert was taped from a radio broadcast. The quality is reasonable/good and would probably receive a grade 7 on the old 'Trademark of Quality' scale.

Hey, Mr Tambourine Man
'Old Blue'; 'Soldier's Joy/Black Mountain Rag'; 'Take A Whiff'; 'Chestnut Mare'; 'You Ain't Going Nowhere'; 'Truck Stop Girl'; 'Medley: My Back Pages/B.J. Blues/Baby, What Do You Want Me To Do'; 'Jamaica Say You Will'; 'So You Want To Be A Rock 'n' Roll Star'; 'Roll Over Beethoven'.
Released in Holland in 1971. The compilers have erroneously credited John York as bassist instead of Skip Battin. In terms of quality, this album is equal to the more famous *Buddy's*. The recording date is again uncertain but judging from the material I would suspect that it was taped during the group's May 1971 tour.

Byrds Live At Lincoln Straight Records
'Willin''; 'Antique Sandy'; 'Soldier's Joy'/'Black Mountain Rag'; 'I Wanna Grow Up To Be A Politician'; 'Mr Spaceman'; 'Buglar'; 'You Ain't Going Nowhere'; 'Medley: My Back Pages/ B.J. Blues/Baby, What Do You Want Me To Do'; 'Jesus Is Just Alright'; 'Glory Glory'.
Recorded live at the Lincoln Folk Festival on 24 July 1971. The quality varies from barely acceptable to absolutely atrocious. This is partly explained by the fact that a portion of the album was not recorded at Lincoln at all but pirated from *Live At Buddy's*. This easily ranks as the worst ever Byrds bootleg.

BOOTLEG ALBUMS

1972	
– January 1972	*Country Suite*: 'Rolling In My Sweet Baby's Arms', 'Soldier's Joy/Black Mountain Rag', 'Mr Tambourine Man', 'Farther Along'.
2 March 1967	*Top Of The Pops*: 'So You Want To Be A Rock 'n' Roll Star'.
3 March 1967	*Popside*: 'Mr Tambourine Man', 'So You Want To Be A Rock 'n' Roll Star', 'Eight Miles High'.
30 March 1967	*Drop In*: 'So You Want To Be A Rock 'n' Roll Star', 'Mr Tambourine Man', 'Eight Miles High'.
13 July 1967	*Johnny Carson Show*: 'Renaissance Fair', 'Lady Friend', 'Have You Seen Her Face'.
29 July 1967	*American Bandstand*: 'Lady Friend', 'Have You Seen Her Face'.
29 October 1967	*Smothers Brothers Show*: 'Goin' Back', 'Mr Spaceman'.
1968	
– April 1968	*Sam Riddle's Ninth Street West Show*: 'Eight Miles High', 'So You Want To Be A Rock 'n' Roll Star'.
11 May 1968	*American Bandstand*: 'You Ain't Going Nowhere'.
– May 1968	*Where The Girls Are*: 'Renaissance Fair', 'Lady Friend', 'Have You Seen Her Face'.
1969	
Date uncertain:	*Playboy After Dark*: 'You Ain't Going Nowhere', 'This Wheel's On Fire'.
1970	
– January 1970	*Memphis Talent Party*: 'Jesus Is Just Alright', 'Mr Tambourine Man'.
Date Uncertain	*Johnny Carson Show*: 'Mr Tambourine Man'.
– December 1970	*Flatt And Scruggs Show*: 'You Ain't Going Nowhere', 'Nothin' To It'.
1971	
9 May 1971	*Top Of The Pops*: 'I Trust (Everything Is Gonna Work Out Alright)'.
23 June 1971	*Midweek*: 'Old Blue', 'Soldier's Joy/Black Mountain Rag'★, 'Mr Tambourine Man', 'Pretty Boy Floyd', 'Take A Whiff', 'Chestnut Mare', 'You Ain't Going Nowhere', 'Truck Stop Girl', 'Medley: My Back Pages/B.J. Blues/Baby, What Do You Want Me To Do', 'Jamaica Say You Will', 'So You Want To Be A Rock 'n' Roll Star', 'Roll Over Beethoven'.
– July 1971	*David Frost Show*: 'So You Want To Be A Rock 'n' Roll Star', 'Mr Spaceman', 'Soldier's Joy/Black Mountain Rag', 'Mr Tambourine Man', 'I Wanna Grow Up To Be A Politician', 'Citizen Kane'.
Date uncertain:	*Beat Club*: 'Soldier's Joy/Black Mountain Rag', 'Chestnut Mare', 'Mr Tambourine Man', 'So You Want To Be A Rock 'n' Roll Star'.

★The Byrds did not record 'Soldier's Joy/Black Mountain Rag'.

Kralingen Triple album set
'You Ain't Going Nowhere'; 'Medley: My Back Pages/B.J. Blues/Baby, What Do You Want Me To Do'; 'Jesus Is Just Alright'; 'All The Things'; 'So You Want To Be A Rock 'n' Roll Star'.
Recorded at the Netherlands open-air festival on 26 June 1970, this bootleg was released during 1971. The triple album set also included material by the Jefferson Airplane and It's A Beautiful Day. In terms of quality the album is below the standard of *Live At Buddy's* but infinitely superior to *Live At Lincoln*. The festival was later transformed into a movie *Stamping Ground* (also known as *Love And Music*) which included the Byrds' performance of 'Old Blue'. Additional footage from the movie features the group playing 'Soldier's Joy'/ 'Black Mountain Rag'; 'All The Things'; 'Nashville West'; 'Turn! Turn! Turn!'; 'Mr Tambourine Man'; 'Buckaroo'; 'Eight Miles High'; 'So You Want To Be A Rock 'n' Roll Star'; 'Mr Spaceman'; and 'Amazing Grace'.

Byrds: Older Than Yesterday Cocaine Records
Side A. London Hammersmith Odeon, September 1977.
Gene Clark Band:
'Release Me Girl'; 'Hula Bula Man'.
Chris Hillman Band:
'Quits'; 'The Witching Hour'; 'It Doesn't Matter'.
Side B. London Hammersmith Odeon, September 1977.
Roger McGuinn Band:
'Lover Of The Bayou'; 'American Girl'; 'Mr Spaceman'; 'Golden Loom'; 'It's Gone'.
Side C. London Hammersmith Odeon, September 1977.
'Dixie Highway'; 'Shoot 'Em'.
McGuinn, Clark & Hillman:
'So You Want To Be A Rock 'n' Roll Star'; 'Mr Tambourine Man'; 'Eight Miles High'.
Side D. Studio (1964-70).
'Willin'' (from an English concert 1970); Beefeaters: 'Please Let Me Love You'; 'Don't Be Long'. Byrds: 'Don't Make Waves'; 'Don't Make Waves' (alternate take); 'She Don't Care About Time'; 'Lady Friend'; 'Lay Lady Lay'; 'Willin''.
Released in Holland in 1979. According to the information on the sleeve, this was a special product by Cocaine Records in celebration of the Byrds' 15th anniversary. As explained above, the material is taken primarily from the 1977 Hammersmith Odeon concert, plus some rare, but previously released, items. The 'Roger McGuinn Band' is, of course, the short-lived Thunderbyrd. The quality is excellent, largely due to the fact that the concert portions were taped from a BBC radio broadcast.

Doin' Alright For Old People Excitable Recordworks 4506-1
'Jolly Roger'; 'Chestnut Mare'; 'Mr Tambourine Man'; 'You Ain't Going Nowhere'; 'Turn! Turn! Turn!'; 'Knockin' On Heaven's Door'; 'Bye Bye Baby'; 'So You Want To Be A Rock 'n' Roll Star'; 'Eight Miles High'; 'Feel A Whole Lot Better'.
The sleeve notes claim that this was recorded at the Boarding House, San Francisco on 10 February 1978, though I suspect that the true date was 2 February 1978. This is an important album as it contains the work of four Byrds (McGuinn, Clark, Hillman and Crosby). Crosby appears on 'Mr Tambourine Man', 'Eight Miles High' and 'Feel A Whole Lot Better'. The excellent quality is again explained by the fact that the show was taped from a KSAN radio broadcast. See the 'Bootleg Tapes' section for a longer version of the concert.

BOOTLEG ALBUMS

Easy Riders Penguin EGG 5
'He Was A Friend Of Mine'; 'Willin''; 'It's Alright Ma (I'm Only Bleeding)'; 'Ballad Of Easy Rider'; 'Chestnut Mare'; 'Chimes Of Freedom'; 'Get Out Of My Life Woman'; 'Mexico' (sic); 'Come Back Baby (From Way Behind The Sun)'(sic); 'Drug Store Truck Drivin' Man'.
Released in 1981, this reasonable quality recording is particularly interesting for its second side, taken from the Boston Tea Party concert at Massachusetts in February 1969. A rare glimpse of the *Dr Byrds And Mr Hyde* period Byrds sees John York taking lead vocal on 'Tulsa County Blue' (mistitled as 'Mexico' on the album) and the unreleased '(Going Back Baby) Way Behind The Sun'.

Live In Washington 9/12/71 Black Cat Records (picture disc)
'Lover Of The Bayou'; 'So You Want To Be A Rock 'n' Roll Star'; 'Mr Spaceman'; 'I Wanna Grow Up To Be A Politician'; 'Soldier's Joy'/'Black Mountain Rag'; 'Mr Tambourine Man'; 'Pretty Boy Floyd'; 'Nashville West'; 'Tiffany Queen'; 'Chestnut Mare'; 'Jesus Is Just Alright'; 'Eight Miles High'; 'B.J. Blues'; 'Roll Over Beethoven'; 'Citizen Kane'.
Another 80's retrospective release, this bootleg was taken from a live broadcast on Radio WANU. The quality is at best mediocre and the material, with the exception of 'Citizen Kane', is over familiar and duplicated on many other bootlegs and tapes.

Mr Tambourine Man
'Jamaica Say You Will'; 'Old Blue'; 'Soldier's Joy/'Black Mountain Rag'; 'Mr Tambourine Man'; 'Pretty Boy Floyd'; 'Take A Whiff'; 'Chestnut Mare'; 'Jesus Is Just Alright'; 'You Ain't Going Nowhere'; 'Truck Stop Girl'; 'Medley: My Back Pages/B.J. Blues/Baby, What Do You Want Me To Do'; 'Jamaica Say You Will'; 'So You Want To Be A Rock 'n' Roll Star'; 'Roll Over Beethoven'.
An average and unspectacular collection featuring the McGuinn, White, Parsons, Battin Byrds. The inclusion of a second live 'Jamaica Say You Will' is an interesting anomaly.

Boston Tea Party Handmade Records FC 002
'You Ain't Going Nowhere'; 'Old Blue'; 'Long Black Veil'; 'Goin Back'; 'Get Out Of My Life Woman'; 'Ballad Of Easy Rider'; 'Jesus Is Just Alright'; 'Tulsa Country Blue'; 'Sing Me Back Home'; 'Lay Lady Lay'; 'Time Between'; 'Medley: My Back Pages/B.J. Blues/Baby, What Do You Want Me To Do'; 'Take A City Bride'; 'It's All Over Now, Baby Blue'; 'Turn! Turn! Turn!'; 'Mr Tambourine Man'; 'Eight Miles High'; 'I Shall Be Released'; 'Drug Store Truck Drivin' Man'.
An excellent quality double album taken from the belatedly available Boston Tea Party tape (22 February 1969). This collection omits the following tracks: 'He Was A Friend Of Mine', 'Mr Spaceman', 'This Wheels On Fire', 'Jesus Is Just Alright', 'Nashville West', 'Fido' and, most strangely in view of its rarity, John York's 'Way Behind The Sun'.

Goin' Back D541
'You Don't Miss Your Water'; 'Hickory Wind'; 'Feel A Whole Lot Better'; 'The Christian Life'; 'Turn! Turn! Turn!'; 'Medley: My Back Pages/B.J. Blues/ Baby, What Do You Want Me To Do'; 'Mr Spaceman'; 'Lay Lady Lay'; 'Medley: My Back Pages/B.J. Blues/ Baby, What Do You Want Me To Do'; '(Goin Back Baby) Way Behind The Sun'; 'Jesus Is Just Alright'; 'Turn! Turn! Turn!'; 'Mr Tambourine Man'; 'Eight Miles High'; 'Goin' Back'.
Another fine quality album combining the Piper Club concert and the Boston Tea Party. In other words nothing particularly new. The first two tracks from the Piper Club gig, 'You

Ain't Going Nowhere' and 'Old John Robertson', are omitted and in selecting the cuts from the Boston Tea Party the compilers fall into the trap of repetition by electing to use the 'Medley' twice in the space of one album.

The Byrds Back Pages Colombia Guinn 202
'She Has A Way'; 'It's All Over Now, Baby Blue'; 'Tabernacle Hillside' (sic); 'It Happens Each Day'; 'John Riley' (sic); 'I Know You Rider'; 'Psychodrama City'; 'Triad'; 'Hey Joe'; 'My Back Pages'; 'Mr Tambourine Man'; 'He Was A Friend Of Mine'; 'So You Want To Be A Rock 'n' Roll Star'; 'Roll Over Beethoven'; 'The Bells Of Rhymney'.
A bootleg of British origin released in 1987, this was compiled from the rough tapes of *Never Before* that had been circulating among collectors prior to the album's release. Thus, the vocals on a couple of the cuts are barely audible and 'Triad' is an instrumental backing track only. Not knowing the actual title of Gene Clark's 'Never Before' at the time of the bootleg's release, the compilers jokingly called it 'Tabernacle Hillside' (borrowed from the lyrics of 'So You Say You Lost Your Baby' on Clark's first solo album). The otherwise unavailable and untitled instrumental from the rough tapes is erroneously called 'John Riley' on the album. 'Psychodrama City' includes the lengthy instrumental introduction deleted from *Never Before*. Side two consists of the Radio Hus 1967 Stockholm performance, now available on CD, and the final track, 'The Bells Of Rhymney', is taken from an unidentified US television show *circa* early 1966. Finally, the cover artwork boasts some bogus liner notes from Derek Taylor, cleverly designed in the style of the rear cover of *Turn! Turn! Turn!*.

The Byrds Back Pages: A Collector's Guide B 6470
'Please Let Me Love You'; 'Don't Be Long'; 'Hey Joe'; 'My Back Pages'; 'Mr Tambourine Man'; 'He Was A Friend Of Mine'; 'So You Want To Be A Rock 'n' Roll Star'; 'Roll Over Beethoven'; 'Don't Make Waves'; 'Child Of The Universe'; 'You Ain't Going Nowhere'; 'Turn! Turn! Turn!'; 'Ballad Of Easy Rider'; 'It Won't Be Wrong'; 'The Water Is Wide'; 'Mr Tambourine Man'; 'Nashville West'; 'Lover Of The Bayou'; 'Jesus Is Just Alright'; 'Old John Robertson'; 'So You Want To Be A Rock 'n' Roll Star'; 'He Was A Friend Of Mine'.
A mish-mesh of an album containing the Beefeaters single, the Radio Hus tracks, and a couple of cuts from the Piper Club. Haphazardly put together, 'Jesus Is Just Alright' is not actually listed on the sleeve whereas a second 'So You Want To Be A Rock 'n' Roll Star' and 'He Was A Friend Of Mine' are, but do not appear on the album! The inclusion of 'The Water Is Wide' is of potential interest but sadly the track has been taken from a slow-running tape. Finally, the title and liner notes are pirated from my own work, with a cursory thanks to John R! The source of the article was a piece I did in issue 13 of *Dark Star* titled 'The Byrds Back Pages: A Collector's Guide To The Byrds'. Needless to say, I had no involvement in the bootleg and was not aware of its existence until it was pointed out to me by the ever vigilant Barry Ballard.

Byrds On The Wyng Wally Jig 001
'You Won't Have To Cry'; 'She Has A Way'; 'Turn! Turn! Turn!'; 'I Don't Believe Me' (sic); 'Eight Miles High'; 'Why'; 'Ways To Show It' (sic) ; 'Triad' (instrumental)'; 'I Knew I'd Want You' (sic); 'Eight Miles High'; 'Hey Joe'; 'I Know You Rider'; 'Disembodied Spirit' (sic); 'Scrambled Egg Jam' (sic); 'Mr Tambourine Man'; 'Thoughts And Words'; 'It's All Over Now, Baby Blue'.
Undoubtedly the best and most interesting Byrds bootleg to date this includes material from the CBS archives not generally available elsewhere. 'You Won't Have To Cry' and 'She Has A Way' are taken from the first CBS album sessions and feature a brief snatch of Terry Melcher on instruction vocals. 'Turn! Turn! Turn!' and 'Triad' are instrumental

BOOTLEG TAPES

backing tracks. The RCA versions of 'Eight Miles High' and 'Why' are the same as those on *Never Before* and there are some brief segments from the *Younger Than Yesterday* sessions. 'I Knew I'd Want You', although listed on the sleeve, does not appear on the album. 'It Happens Each Day' (mistakenly titled 'Disembodied Spirit') is the original version, unimproved by Crosby and Hillman, while 'Scrambled Egg Jam' is another fictitious coinage for the instrumental with no name that appeared on one of the CBS tapes. The remaining material is so far exclusive to this album. 'I Know You Rider' is a rougher take than the one included on *Never Before* but McGuinn's lead guitar breaks still sound effective and there is the delightful bonus of some scat singing from Crosby. An alternate take of 'Eight Miles High' from the Columbia sessions is a minor revelation, mainly because it sounds so rough, spontaneous and unfocussed. Michael Clarke's drumming is extremely heavy handed and very different from his work on the completed single version. Most chaotic of all, however, is a truly shambolic rendition of 'Hey Joe' with Crosby all over the place and Clarke sounding as though he is banging a dustbin lid. Unbelievable. The album also contains a real mystery. A girl singer complete with a Byrds-sounding back-up group provides a couple of Dylan covers: 'I Don't Believe You' (which the producer insists on calling 'I Don't Believe Me') and 'It's All Over Now, Baby Blue'. It turns out that these were guide vocals and demos specifically imported by Terry Melcher to encourage the group to increase its Dylan repertoire. The group were an unknown local combo and the producer Jack Nitzsche. The overall result is a fascinating insight into what was happening to the Byrds in the studio during one of the most interesting phases of their career.

BOOTLEG TAPES

The continued interest in the Byrds will probably ensure that more obscure bootlegged taped material will continue to be released in the future. The following is a list of live/studio tapes generally known to be available. This section does not include lists of songs that are previously listed in the videos category.

1964 *The World Pacific Recordings*

'Tomorrow Is A Long Ways Away (acoustic)'(I); 'Tomorrow Is A Long Ways Away'(I); 'I Knew I'd Want You'(I); 'I Knew I'd Want You'(U); 'I Knew I'd Want You'(P); 'I Knew I'd Want You'(U); 'Boston'(U); 'Boston'(U); 'Boston'(P/I); 'The Airport Song'(P/I); 'It Won't Be Wrong'(B); 'It Won't Be Wrong'(I); 'Please Let Me Love You'(B); 'Please Let Me Love You'(I); 'The Only Girl'(E); 'Mr Tambourine Man'(I); 'Mr Tambourine Man'(P); 'The Reason Why'(U); 'The Reason Why'(P/I); 'You Won't Have To Cry'(P); 'You Won't Have To Cry'(I); 'She Has A Way'(U); 'She Has A Way'(U); 'She Has A Way'(U); 'You Movin''(E); 'You Movin''(U); 'You Movin''(U); 'You Movin''(U); 'You Movin''(P/I); 'You Movin''(U); 'For Me Again'(U); 'For Me Again'(P/I); 'For Me Again'(U); 'You Showed Me'(I); 'You Showed Me'(P); 'You Showed Me'(U); 'It's No Use'(U); 'It's No Use'(I); 'It's No Use'(U); 'It's No Use'(U); 'It's No Use'(U); 'Here Without You'(U); 'Here Without You'(P); 'Here Without You'(I).

This extraordinary tape represents what was left from the World Pacific recordings. For the sake of convenience, I have provided a key to the tracks as follows: (I)= tracks released on *In The Beginning*; (P)= *Preflyte*; (B)= Beefeaters; (E)= *Early LA* and (U)= previously unreleased. The only problem that the tape presented to me was the identification of the *Preflyte* and *In The Beginning* version of 'She Has A Way'. The ending of version two of the song on the tape sounds the same as the cuts on *Preflyte* and *In The Beginning* but the opening appears noticeably different. It may be that there was a fourth version which has not been included here. Also missing is 'Maybe You Think', which appeared on the original tapes that were licensed in 1969, but has since disappeared. For anyone intrigued by the Byrds early experiments at World Pacific these recordings are mandatory listening.

1965-67 *The Columbia Recording Sessions*

'You Won't Have To Cry'; 'She Has A Way'; 'Turn! Turn! Turn!' (instrumental backing track); 'It's All Over Now, Baby Blue'; 'Never Before'; 'Eight Miles High'; 'Why'; 'It Happens Each Day'; Untitled Instrumental; 'Mr Tambourine Man'; 'I Knew I'd Want You'; 'I Know My Rider'; 'Psychodrama City'; 'Triad' (instrumental backing track); 'Moog Raga'; 'Everybody's Been Burned' (version one); 'Everybody's Been Burned' (version two); 'Everybody's Been Burned' (version three); 'Everybody's Been Burned' (version four); 'Everybody's Been Burned' (version five); 'Everybody's Been Burned' (version six); 'Everybody's Been Burned' (version seven); 'Thoughts And Words'(version one); 'Thoughts And Words' (version two); 'Thoughts And Words' (version three); 'Thoughts And Words' (version four); 'Thoughts And Words' (version five); 'Thoughts And Words' (version six); 'Thoughts And Words' (version seven); 'Thoughts And Words' (version eight); 'Thoughts And Words' (version nine); 'Thoughts And Words' (version ten); 'Thoughts And Words' (version eleven); 'Thoughts And Words' (version twelve); 'Thoughts And Words' (version thirteen); 'Renaissance Fair' (version one); 'Renaissance Fair' (version two); 'Renaissance Fair' (version three).

The most complete of the bootlegged rough tapes from which the majority of *Never Before* was compiled, this is a treasure trove of Byrds ephemera. The tracks are roughly in chronological order and the recording dates span early 1965 to early 1967. The familiar voice of Terry Melcher introduces the first take of 'You Won't Have To Cry' from the *Mr Tambourine Man* album sessions. This version is a little more restrained than the final LP cut, but immediately reveals how far the group have progressed since those tentative World Pacific demos only months before. The musicianship is noticeably tighter and the vocal harmonies far more effective as a result of endless hours of rehearsal. But the recording is far from perfect or complete. The pounding tambourine featured on the album is conspicuous by its absence here, and was probably overdubbed separately by Melcher after the session had finished. As the track fades, the still dissatisfied producer suggests: 'Let's take one more'.

The tape next cuts to a Columbia take of Gene Clark's 'She Has A Way', one of several World Pacific songs that failed to win a place on their first album. The listener is allowed to eavesdrop on a fascinating studio conversation in which the participants attempt to pull the song into shape. Melcher seems unsure how many parts there are in the harmony, while Crosby disputes the merits of an earlier take.

Crosby: 'They put a fade-out on the ending!'

Melcher: 'Hold it! You don't have to keep singing over the fade. Right. You just stop somewhere.'

Melcher then proceeds to sing several lines of the song himself, and his rendition is pretty good. Thumping his hands on the studio mixing desk to provide a percussive accompaniment, he instructs Crosby to 'just let go after "wanna settle down, whoa, whoa".' A much improved version of the song follows, with McGuinn's guitar particularly evident. The drumming is even more astonishing. Months before, Michael Clarke had played the number like a schoolboy in a military cadet band. Suddenly, he has transformed into a competent studio musician. Clarke's rapid improvement and unquestionable involvement in all these songs is one of the many surprises on the tape, especially to those cynics who had suspected that session drummers were recruited at crucial moments.

The instrumental 'Turn! Turn! Turn!' follows and although it sounds strange without McGuinn's distinctive vocal, it is nonetheless pleasant and instructive. 'It's All Over Now, Baby Blue' is the same take used for *Never Before* as is the succeeding 'Never Before'. Here, however, the vocal is buried so low in the mix that it is barely audible. Thankfully, it was later rescued and tidied up for inclusion on *Never Before*. The RCA versions of 'Eight Miles

High' and 'Why' are good quality recordings and I can still recall the shock of pleasure upon hearing them for the first time over two decades on. 'It Happens Each Day' underwent significant alteration before being included on *Never Before*. Both Hillman and Crosby worked on the track adding guitar and bass. The drumming also sounds different on the *Never Before* version.

Arguably the only carping omission from the *Never Before* CD round-up of unreleased tracks was the amazing instrumental that now exists on tape only. Erroneously titled 'Circle Of Minds', 'Milestones' and even 'John Riley' it is none of these, but an untitled work that sounds like a studio warm-up. There is some strong banjo work on the track, possibly from Doug Dillard, although it could equally be McGuinn. The instrumental steams along at a tremendous pace before falling apart after several minutes. A splendid tour de force.

The version of 'Mr Tambourine Man' on this tape is the same as the number one single apart from an elongated fade-out and the sound of Hal Blaine clicking his drumsticks and counting to six in the lead-in to the song. 'I Knew I'd Want You' offers no such extras and sounds the same as the original flip-side. 'I Know My Rider' is the version chosen for the *Never Before* CD rather than the other outtake on *Byrds On The Wyng*. Even this rough version is nothing less than astonishing. Crosby's vocal is prominent, the harmonies are well executed and McGuinn lets rip with two Rickenbacker solos which combine judicious economy with maximum power. At the end of the take, an evidently excited Crosby enthuses: 'Let's do it again!' Suddenly, you find yourself wishing they had done just that on the tape.

'Psychodrama City' suffers from a low audibility vocal which was vastly improved on the *Never Before* CD. The redeeming feature of this rough version is that we get to hear the lengthy introduction which was later edited out of the recorded track. Following 'Psychodrama City' we get to hear an amusing interlude during which Michael Clarke treats us to a drum solo, just to prove that he can play with the best of them. An impatient Gary Usher interrupts: 'Hold it! Hold it, Mike!', and the tape cuts to the next recording. The instrumental backing track for 'Triad' demonstrates the quality of the Byrds' playing to moving effect. Towards the end of the track, Usher reveals that this is a ninth take. Unfortunately, we do not get to hear the vocal part which was slightly amended on *Never Before*. The eerie 'Moog Raga', with its ethereal droning is a slightly longer version of the track that McGuinn remixed for the *Never Before* CD. It brings the first side of this lengthy tape to an appropriate close.

The remainder of the unreleased tape consists of approximately 40 minutes of studio backing tracks from the sessions for *Younger Than Yesterday*. Although tedious listening at times, these tortuous retakes provide an interesting insight into the way in which the Byrds fashioned and improved their albums. 'Everybody's Been Burned', one of the greatest Byrds songs, requires several attempts before McGuinn masters the tricky arrangement. Clarke, meanwhile, is having great problems keeping time, and Usher is finally moved to complain: 'Michael, it's falling down before you even get started'. After restarting for the umpteenth time, they finally produce a much improved backing track with Hillman's solid bass lines high in the mix. But Gary Usher is still not satisfied with the results and turns his polite wrath on the tousled-haired bassist: 'Chris, would you turn your volume down a little please! Not on your guitar, but on your amplifier!' Ten minutes into the tape we leave the Byrds still struggling with the intricacies of 'Everybody's Been Burned' and move to another song.

'The mike sounds good', chirps Hillman, as the Byrds launch into the instrumental backing track of 'Thoughts And Words'. The first take sounds good, but there is some hesitation about halfway through. Two more completed takes follow, but Usher is still not entirely satisfied. 'Keep this sound, it sounds good that way', he advises Crosby before spurring on the flagging Hillman.

Usher continually frames his questions and criticisms in disarmingly polite rhetorical asides: 'Chris, are you driving as hard as you can, please?' The fourth take begins spectacularly enough with the cleanest sound yet, but unfortunately it breaks down. Two more takes follow in quick succession until a frustrated Mike Clarke terminates the proceedings with a heavy-handed drum roll. The ferociously polite Usher responds with a schoolmasterly enquiry: 'Michael, may I hear for a minute what you're going to play?' The errant drummer obliges and a seventh take ensues. This too ends in an explosion of drums, and Clarke receives further advice from his producer.

Take eight features some great bass playing by Hillman, while Clarke also suddenly hits form. But it is still not quite right. Take nine is perfunctory, take ten reveals Hillman experimenting with the bass line. Take eleven falls apart before it has even begun. Take twelve sounds like the big breakthrough. Usher goes for the killer take, but cannot resist ticking off Clarke one last time: 'Mike, make sure you hit the very last note with the band. Can you hear me? You didn't do it this time'.

'I don't want to do it', retorts the exasperated drummer, who clearly has his own ideas about how he should sound.

'Oh, you don't want to do it! All right. Thirteen!' Usher sounds surprised but content. The thirteenth take includes vocals, and it is a stunner. Although identical to the version on *Younger Than Yesterday*, its appearance after a dozen frustrating and tortuous takes allows us to appreciate the song in an entirely new way. Although the familiar backwards guitar break is incorporated into the track, it no longer sounds a studio trick, but appears to be happening live, and Crosby's interweaving harmony with Hillman is wondrous to behold. Even Usher is sufficiently moved to offer a congratulatory understatement: 'It's not bad'.

The final few minutes of the tape present 'Renaissance Fair', complete with delicately precise guitar work and a surprisingly driving rhythm from Hillman and Clarke. Three fragmented takes follow before the tape abruptly ends.

1967 *Radio Hus, Stockholm*
As documented in the CD section, this tape contains six tracks recorded for radio in 1967. Some tapes include an additional cut, 'The Bells Of Rhymney' but this was taken from a US television show in early 1966.

1967 *Monterey Extract*
Now superseded by the Continental release of a CD featuring most of the Byrds' set at Monterey, this short tape consisted of a radio broadcast from KMET (1973) which included a brief segment of 'So You Want To Be A Rock 'n' Roll Star' and 'He Was A Friend Of Mine'.

1967 *Monterey: The Audience Tape*
'Hey Joe'; 'He Was A Friend Of Mine'; 'Lady Friend'; 'Chimes Of Freedom'; 'I Know My Rider'; 'So You Want To Be A Rock 'n' Roll Star'.

While the Continental CD on Living Legend Records contains 'He Was A Friend Of Mine', 'Hey Joe' and 'So You Want To Be A Rock 'n' Roll Star', here we get the original set in all its glory. The quality of the tape is surprisingly good given the time of its recording. There is a rough, almost aggressive quality about the Byrds' performance which reflects the tensions in the group at the time. Highlights of the tape are the rarely heard live versions of 'Lady Friend' and 'I Know My Rider' which betray a hard metallic edge. McGuinn's sitar-like guitar break still entrances, almost creating a wall of sound effect. The startling addition of live brass on 'So You Want To Be A Rock 'n' Roll Star' ends the performance on a high note.

1965-68 *Rhythm Track Mixes*
'So You Want To Be A Rock 'n' Roll Star'; 'Have You Seen Her Face'; 'CTA-102'; 'Renaissance Fair'; 'Time Between'; 'Everybody's Been Burned'; 'Thoughts And Words'; 'Mind Gardens'; 'My Back Pages'; 'Girl With No Name'; 'Why'; 'Eight Miles High'; '(I) Wasn't Born To Follow'; 'All I Really Want To Do'; 'You Ain't Going Nowhere'; 'Draft Morning'.

These recordings are rough studio mixes with the vocals turned down to the level of barely audible. As a result the Byrds' rhythm work is highlighted to remarkable effect. There are some real revelations on this tape. Crosby's chunky rhythm guitar work on 'Eight Miles High', herein transformed into a lead instrument, is nothing less than astonishing. 'Time Between' features Crosby's harmony vocal in the chorus separated and presented in an entirely new way. 'Draft Morning' is another surprise for buried underneath the sound of gunfire is an extremely attractive Hillman mandolin break which you can now hear independently for the first time. Even 'Mind Gardens' has a few surprises, the raga-like guitars creating a swirling ethereal feel which is emphasized by the absence of Crosby's vocal. It would be fascinating to hear the remainder of the Byrds canon in this format.

1968 *Middle Earth*
'Tribal Gathering'; 'Eight Miles High'; 'You Don't Miss Your Water'; 'The Christian Life'; '5-D (Fifth Dimension)'; 'Turn! Turn! Turn!'; 'Medley: My Back Pages/B.J. Blues/Baby, What Do You Want Me To Do'; 'Foggy Mountain Breakdown'; 'Pretty Boy Floyd'; 'Hickory Wind'; 'Under Your Spell Again'; '(Excuse Me) I Think I've Got A Heartache'; 'So You Want To Be A Rock 'n' Roll Star'; 'Mr Tambourine Man'; 'Chimes Of Freedom'; 'Goin' Back'; 'Feel A Whole Lot Better'; 'The Bells Of Rhymney'; 'We'll Meet Again'; 'Sing Me Back Home'.

A poor quality recording, although it does contain four unreleased songs. In fact, only one of these, 'Sing Me Back Home', is known to have been attempted in the recording studio. Gram Parsons plays electric piano on some cuts, which helps to improve the quality of the rock songs.

1968 *Roundhouse*
This is of similar quality to the Middle Earth tape, and most of the songs are duplicated with the exception of 'You Ain't Going Nowhere' and 'Space Odyssey'.

1968 Venue unknown
'So You Want To Be A Rock 'n' Roll Star'; 'Chimes Of Freedom'; 'You Ain't Going Nowhere'; 'Medley: My Back Pages/B.J. Blues/Baby, What Do You Want Me To Do'; 'Hickory Wind'; 'Sing Me Back Home'; 'The Christian Life'; 'You've Got Me Under Your Spell Again'.

A fair quality recording with some hard drumming from the little heard Kevin Kelley. The set is similar to that performed at the Royal Albert Hall gig in 1968 although this appears to have been recorded at a small club.

1968 *The Piper Club, Rome*
Now available on CD on Bulldog Records, the original rough taped version offers a better quality reproduction. See CD section for the full track listing.

1968/69 *Avalon Ballroom*
'So You Want To Be A Rock 'n' Roll Star'; 'Goin' Back'; 'This Wheel's On Fire'; 'Jesus Is Just Alright'.

A good quality stereo recording from a radio broadcast of the Byrds' performance at the Avalon Ballroom (2 November 1968). Bob Cohen, owner of the Avalon, allowed KSAN to broadcast three of the songs in their *What Was That – Suddenly Lost Summer* documentary.

'Jesus Is Just Alright', taken from a Fillmore West gig (15 June 1969) was donated by Bill Graham. The Byrds line-up at both concerts was McGuinn, White, Parsons and York.

1969 *Boston Tea Party*
'You Ain't Going Nowhere'; 'He Was A Friend Of Mine'; 'Old Blue'; 'Long Black Veil'; 'Goin' Back'; 'Get Out Of My Life Woman'; 'Ballad Of Easy Rider'; 'Jesus Is Just Alright'; 'Tulsa County Blue'; 'Mr Spaceman'; 'Sing Me Back Home'; 'This Wheel's On Fire'; 'Lay Lady Lay'; 'Time Between'; 'Medley: My Back Pages/B.J. Blues/ Baby, What Do You Want Me To Do'; 'Take A City Bride'; 'It's All Over Now, Baby Blue'; '(Going Back Baby) Way Behind The Sun'; 'Jesus Is Just Alright'; 'Turn! Turn! Turn!'; 'Eight Miles High'; 'I Shall Be Released'; 'Drug Store Truck Drivin' Man'; 'Nashville West'; 'Fido'.

Not to be confused with the famous Boston Tea Party at which the Byrds and Burritos united, this was recorded in Massachusetts on 22 February 1969. John York takes lead vocal on 'Long Black Veil', 'Tulsa County Blue' and '(Going Back Baby) Way Behind The Sun'. The recording quality is excellent and the material is of particular interest as it includes non-recorded items such as Bob Dylan's 'I Shall Be Released' and Lee Dorsey's 'Get Out Of My Life Woman'.

1970 *Bath Festival*
'Turn! Turn! Turn!'; 'Mr Tambourine Man'; 'Eight Miles High'; 'Just A Season'; 'So You Want To Be A Rock 'n' Roll Star'; 'You Ain't Going Nowhere'; 'Willin''; 'Soldier's Joy'/ 'Black Mountain Rag'; 'Goin' Back'; 'Drug Store Truck Drivin' Man'; 'You Don't Miss Your Water'; 'Amazing Grace'.

Recorded on 28 June 1970, this tape documents one of the Byrds' most acclaimed gigs of the period. Although the recording fails to capture the power of the group, it serves as a reminder of the festival for those who attended.

1970 *Live In Amsterdam*
'You Ain't Going Nowhere'; 'Lover Of The Bayou'; 'Old Blue'; 'Well Come Back Home'; 'Medley: My Back Pages/B.J. Blues/Baby, What Do You Want Me To Do'; 'He Was A Friend Of Mine'; 'Willin''; 'Soldier's Joy'/'Black Mountain Rag'; 'Take A Whiff'; 'This Wheel's On Fire'; 'It's Alright Ma (I'm Only Bleeding)'; 'Ballad Of Easy Rider'; 'Jesus Is Just Alright'; 'All The Things'; 'Buckaroo'/'Nashville West'; 'Turn! Turn! Turn!'; 'Mr Tambourine Man'; 'Eight Miles High'; 'Positively 4th Street'; 'Mr Spaceman'; 'You Don't Miss Your Water'; 'Chestnut Mare'; 'Chimes Of Freedom'; 'Amazing Grace'.

This was the full tape from which *Live At Buddy's* was taken. The quality is excellent and far superior to the bootleg album it spawned.

1971 *Manchester: 11 May 1971*
'Lover Of The Bayou'; 'You Ain't Going Nowhere'; 'Truck Stop Girl'; 'Medley: My Back Pages/B.J. Blues/Baby, What Do You Want Me To Do'; 'Jamaica Say You Will'; 'Mr Tambourine Man'; 'Pretty Boy Floyd'; 'Take A Whiff'; 'Chestnut Mare'; 'Jesus Is Just Alright'; 'Hold It!'; 'So You Want To Be A Rock 'n' Roll Star'; 'Mr Spaceman'; 'It's Alright Ma (I'm Only Bleeding)'; 'Ballad Of Easy Rider'; '(I) Wasn't Born To Follow'; 'Hold It!' (reprise).

A typical Byrds set of its era, complete with their stagey theme tune 'Hold It!' This is a rather poor recording but others on the UK tour at Liverpool, Sheffield and Croydon were slightly better. The stable Byrds line-up of McGuinn, White, Parsons and Battin performed so frequently during this period that it would be pointless and repetitious to list all the illegal tapes in circulation. There were also several concerts recorded direct from the mixing board which will no doubt appear at some future point.

1972 *Live At The Olympia, Paris*
'Lover Of The Bayou'; 'So You Want To Be A Rock 'n' Roll Star'; 'Mr Spaceman'; 'Rolling In My Sweet Baby's Arms'; 'Medley: My Back Pages/B.J. Blues/Baby, What Do You Want Me To Do'; 'Eight Miles High'; 'Amazing Grace'.

The standard Byrds' set of the period, complete with the elongated 'Eight Miles High'. This tape is notable for its fine quality and the inclusion of 'Rolling In My Sweet Baby's Arms'.

1972 *Fairleigh Dickinson Hall, New Jersey*
'Lover Of The Bayou'; 'So You Want To Be A Rock 'n' Roll Star'; 'Mr Spaceman'; 'Buglar'; 'I Wanna Grow Up To Be A Politician'; 'Medley: My Back Pages/B.J. Blues/Baby, What Do You Want Me To Do'; 'Soldier's Joy'/'Black Mountain Rag'; 'Mr Tambourine Man'; 'Pretty Boy Floyd'; 'Rolling In My Sweet Baby's Arms'; 'Tiffany Queen'; 'Chestnut Mare'.

Subtle changes in the set are notable here, as the Byrds head inexorably towards their final dissolution.

1972 *Curtis Hixon Hall, Tampa, Florida*
'Lover Of The Bayou'; 'Buglar'; 'America's Great National Pastime'; 'Chimes Of Freedom'; 'I Wanna Grow Up To Be A Politician'; 'Medley: My Back Pages/B.J. Blues/Baby, What Do You Want Me To Do'; 'Soldier's Joy/'Black Mountain Rag'; 'Mr Tambourine Man'; 'Take A Whiff'; 'So You Want To Be A Rock 'n' Roll Star'; 'Mr Spaceman'; 'Chestnut Mare'; 'Eight Miles High'; 'Nashville West'; 'Feel A Whole Lot Better'; 'Roll Over Beethoven'.

Recorded on 1 November 1972, this tape is of particular interest as it includes the work of John Guerin, who had recently been recruited to the group following the dismissal of Gene Parsons. The quality is very good and the Guerin version of 'Eight Miles High' is particularly interesting.

1978 *Boarding House, San Francisco*
'Release Me Girl'; 'Silver Raven'; 'Bound To Fall'; 'Ballad Of Easy Rider'; 'Jolly Roger'; 'Chestnut Mare'; 'Crazy Ladies'; 'Train Leaves Here This Morning'; 'Mr Tambourine Man'; 'You Ain't Going Nowhere'; 'Turn! Turn! Turn!'; 'Knocking On Heaven's Door'; 'Bye Bye Baby'; 'So You Want To Be A Rock 'n' Roll Star'; 'Eight Miles High'; 'Feel A Whole Lot Better'.

Of the many concerts by McGuinn and Clark during this period, this recording is of importance because it features both Hillman and Crosby, and was the nearest thing from the period to a full Byrds reunion. Crosby wanders on and off stage but can be heard clearly on 'Mr Tambourine Man' and 'Eight Miles High'.

1989 *Ventura Theatre*
'Chimes Of Freedom'; 'It Won't Be Wrong'; 'Feel A Whole Lot Better'; 'Everybody's Been Burned'; 'My Back Pages'; 'Mr Spaceman'; 'The Bells Of Rhymney'; 'You Ain't Going Nowhere'; 'Mr Tambourine Man'; 'Turn! Turn! Turn!'; 'Eight Miles High'; 'So You Want To Be A Rock 'n' Roll Star'.

As documented in the main text, this concert in Ventura (6 January 1989) was part of a brief series of Byrds reunion gigs, featuring three-fifths of the original group: McGuinn, Hillman and Crosby. The quality of the tape is excellent but has yet to be transformed into a vinyl bootleg.

SESSIONOGRAPHY

The Columbia Recordings, 1965-72
Usual Personnel: Jim McGuinn (lead 12 string and six string guitar, vocals); David Crosby (six string, occasional 12-string guitar, vocals); Gene Clark (vocals, tambourine); Chris Hillman (bass, mandolin) and Michael Clarke (drums, percussion, harmonica).

Mr Tambourine Man Columbia CS 9172
Released 21 June 1965
Recorded at Columbia Studios, Hollywood
Producer: Terry Melcher
Engineer: Ray Gerhardt

Singles from the LP sessions:
'Mr Tambourine Man'/'I Knew I'd Want You' Columbia 43271
(released 12 April 1965)
'All I Really Want To Do'/'Feel A Whole Lot Better' Columbia 43332
(released 14 June 1965)

Sessions:
20 January 1965. Jim McGuinn (12 string guitar); Jerry Cole (rhythm guitar); Larry Knechtel (bass); Leon Russell (electric piano); Hal Blaine (drums).
72245 'Mr Tambourine Man' single 43271, LP
72246 'I Knew I'd Want You' single 43271, LP

8 March 1965. Usual personnel.
72425 'All I Really Want To Do' LP
72426 'It's No Use' (version I) rejected
72427 'You And Me' unreleased
72428 'You Won't Have To Cry' (version I) rejected
— 'She Has A Way' unreleased

14 April 1965. Usual personnel.
72493 'It's No Use' (version II) LP
72494 'The Bells Of Rhymney' LP
72495 'Feel A Whole Lot Better' single 43332, LP
72496 'Words And Pictures' unreleased
72497 'You Won't Have To Cry' (version II) LP
72498 'Spanish Harlem Incident' LP
72499 'I Love The Life I Live' unreleased
72500 'We'll Meet Again' LP
— 'All I Really Want To Do' alternate take single

22 April 1965. Usual personnel.
72501 'Chimes Of Freedom' LP
72502 'Don't Doubt Yourself Babe' LP
72503 'Here Without You' LP

Turn! Turn! Turn! Columbia CS 9254
Released 6 December 1965
Recorded at Columbia Studios, Hollywood
Producer: Terry Melcher
Engineer: Ray Gerhardt

SESSIONOGRAPHY

Singles from the LP sessions:
'Turn! Turn! Turn!'/'She Don't Care About Time' Columbia 43424
(released 1 October 1965)
'It Won't Be Wrong'/'Set You Free This Time' Columbia 43501
(released 10 January 1966)

Sessions:
28 June 1965. Usual personnel.
72646 'The Flower Bomb Song' unreleased
72647 'The Times They Are A-Changin'' (version I) rejected
72648 'She Don't Care About Time' (version I) rejected
72649 'It's All Over Now, Baby Blue' (version I) rejected

23 August 1965. Usual personnel.
72728 'The Times They Are A-Changin'' (version II) rejected
72729 'She Don't Care About Time' (version II) single 43424
72730 'The World Turns All Around Her' (version I) LP

– August 1965. Usual personnel; produced by Jim Dickson and the Byrds; engineered by Tom May.
— 'It's All Over Now, Baby Blue' (version II) unreleased

Note: announced on the radio as a new single release but withdrawn before release.

1 September 1965. Usual personnel.
72732 'The Times They Are A-Changin'' (version III) unfinished
(72734) 'Turn! Turn! Turn!' unfinished

10 September, 14-16 September 1965. Usual personnel. Add harmonica -1 (Michael Clarke)
72733 'The World Turns All Around Her' (version II) rejected
72734 'Turn! Turn! Turn!' single 43424, LP
72736 'It Won't Be Wrong' single 43501, LP
72737 'Satisfied Mind' unfinished
72738 'Set You Free This Time' -1, single 43501, LP
72739 'I Don't Ever Want To Spoil Your Party' unreleased
72740 'Stranger In A Strange Land' unreleased

1 October, 4 October 1965. Usual personnel. Add banjo -1 (McGuinn)
87510 'Wait And See' LP
87511 'Oh! Susannah' -1, unfinished

18 October, 20 October, 22 October 1965. Usual personnel.
(87511) 'Oh! Susannah' LP
87518 'If You're Gone' LP
87519 'Lay Down Your Weary Tune' LP

27 October, 28 October 1965. Usual personnel.
— 'Circle Of Minds' unreleased
(72732) 'The Times They Are A-Changin'' (version III) LP
(72737) 'Satisfied Mind' LP

1 November 1965. Usual personnel.
87528 'He Was A Friend Of Mine' LP

Fifth Dimension Columbia CS 9349
Released 18 July 1966
Recorded at Columbia Studios, Hollywood, except where noted
Producer: Allen Stanton
Engineer: Ray Gerhardt

Singles from the LP sessions:
'Eight Miles High'/'Why' (alternate take) Columbia 43578
(released 14 March 1966)
'5-D (Fifth Dimension)'/'Captain Soul' Columbia 43702
(released 13 June 1966)
'Mr Spaceman'/'What's Happening?!?!' Columbia 43766
(released 6 September 1966)

Sessions:
22 December 1965. Usual personnel. Recorded at RCA Studios, Hollywood. Producer: Jim Dickson. Engineer: Dave Hassinger. Final mix 4 January 1966.
— 'Eight Miles High' (version I) unreleased
— 'Why' (version I) unreleased
— 'The Times They Are A-Changin'' (version IV) unfinished

24 January, 25 January 1966. Usual personnel
87687 'Why' (version II) single 43578
87690 'Eight Miles High' (version II) single 43578, LP
— 'Never Before' unreleased

Gene Clark leaves the group at this point.

21 February 1966. Usual personnel. Add banjo -1.
87722 'John Riley' (version I) -1, rejected
(87796) 'I Know My Rider' (version 1) unfinished

28 April, 29 April, 3-6 May 1966. Usual personnel. Add strings -1, clavia -2, harmonica -3 (Clarke), sound effects -4, cowbell -5.
87796 'I Know My Rider' (version 1) unfinished
87800 'Mr Spaceman' single 43766, LP
87801 'What's Happening?!?!' single 43766, LP
87802 '2-4-2 Fox Trot (The Lear Jet Song)' -4, LP
87803 'John Riley' (version II) -1, unfinished
87804 'Wild Mountain Thyme' -1, unfinished
87805 'Hey Joe' -5, unfinished
87806 'I Come And Stand At Every Door' unfinished
(87876) 'I See You' unfinished
(87877) 'Captain Soul' -3, unfinished

12 May, 16-19 May 1966. Usual personnel.
(87796) 'I Know My Rider' (version 1) unreleased
(87804) 'Wild Mountain Thyme' unfinished
(87805) 'Hey Joe' LP
(87806) 'I Come And Stand At Every Door' LP
87876 'I See You' LP
87877 'Captain Soul' single 43702, LP

SESSIONOGRAPHY

24 May, 25 May 1966. Usual personnel, plus Van Dyke Parks (organ, electric piano -1)
(87804) 'Wild Mountain Thyme' LP
(87803) 'John Riley' (version II) LP
87883 '5-D (Fifth Dimension)' -1, single 43702, LP

Younger Than Yesterday Columbia CS 9442
Released 20 February 1967
Recorded at Columbia Studios, Hollywood
Producer: Gary Usher
Engineer: Tom May

Singles from the LP sessions:
'So You Want To Be A Rock 'n' Roll Star'/'Everybody's Been Burned' Columbia 43987
(released 9 January 1967)
'My Back Pages'/'Renaissance Fair' Columbia 44054
(released 13 March 1967)

Sessions:
28 July 1966. Usual personnel. Producer: Allen Stanton. Engineer: Ray Gerhardt.
87993 'I Know My Rider' (version II) unreleased
87994 'Psychodrama City' unreleased

28-30 November, 1 December 1966. Usual personnel plus Clarence White (pull string guitar -1), Vern Gosdin (guitar -1), Hugh Masekela (trumpet -2). Add oscillator -3.
88324 'So You Want To Be A Rock 'n' Roll Star' -2, single 43987, LP
88329 'Have You Seen Her Face' single 44157, LP
88331 'Milestones' unreleased
88388 'Time Between' -1, LP
88389 'Mind Gardens' LP
88390 'CTA -102' -3, LP

5-8 December 1966. Usual personnel plus 'Jay' (sax -1), Clarence White (pull string guitar -2)
88395 'My Back Pages' single 44054, LP
88396 'Thoughts And Words' LP
88397 'Renaissance Fair' -1, single 44054, LP
88398 'Everybody's Been Burned' single 43987, LP
88399 'It Happens Each Day' unreleased
88400 'The Girl With No Name' -2, LP
— 'Why'(version III) LP

3 February 1967. Usual personnel. Add overdubbed organ.
(88395) 'My Back Pages' rejected

The Notorious Byrd Brothers Columbia CS 9575
Released 3 January 1968
Recorded at Columbia Studios, Hollywood
Producer: Gary Usher
Engineers: Tom May and Don Thompson except where noted.

Singles from the LP sessions:
'Have You Seen Her Face'/'Don't Make Waves' Columbia 44157
(released 22 May 1967)
'Lady Friend'/'Old John Robertson' Columbia 44230

(released 13 July 1967)
'Goin' Back'/'Change Is Now' Columbia 44362
(released 20 October 1967)

Sessions:
26 April 1967. Usual personnel.
94793 'Don't Make Waves' single 44157
— alternate take MGM LP 4483 (released September 1967)
94794 'Lady Friend' unfinished

Note: various overdubs were attempted on 'Lady Friend' on 4 May, 10 May, 23 May and 5 June, all incomplete.

14 June, 21 June 1967. Usual personnel, except Crosby plays bass and Hillman six-string guitar (-1). Add string quartet. Add trumpets (-2).
(94794) 'Lady Friend' -2, single 44230
94897 'Old John Robertson' -1, single 44230
— alternate mix with phasing added on LP

31 July, 1-3 August 1967. Usual personnel, plus Clarence White (pull string guitar -1). Add mandolin, brass (-2). Gunshots (-2) courtesy of Firesign Theater.
94922 'Change Is Now' -1, unfinished
94923 'Draft Morning' -2, LP

Note: further work on 'Change Is Now' was done on 14 August 1967.

14-18 August 1967. Usual personnel, except Jim Gordon replaces Michael Clarke (drums). Add piano (-1).
94926 'Dolphin's Smile' LP
94927 'Tribal Gathering' -1, unfinished
94928 'Triad' unreleased

Note: further overdubs of 'Tribal Gathering' were attempted on 29-30 August and 29-30 November 1967, all unfinished.

29-30 August 1967. Usual personnel.
(94922) 'Change Is Now' single 44362, LP

5-6 September 1967. Usual personnel, except Jim Gordon replaces Michael Clarke (drums), and David Crosby, although present, did not participate. Add Red Rhodes (pedal steel guitar), Paul Beaver (Moog synthesizer), unknown celeste, harp and cello.
95118 'Goin' Back' (version I) rejected

9, 11, 16 October 1967. Personnel as above.
95175 'Goin' Back' (version II) single 44362, LP

David Crosby leaves the group at this point and Gene Clark returns for live performances but leaves again within three weeks.

23, 30 October, 1 November 1967. Usual personnel. Add Moog synthesizer. Add conga, resinators, electric bongo, electric tabla (-1). Roy Halee, engineer.
95281 'Space Odyssey' LP
95287 'Moog Raga' -1, unreleased

13 November 1967. Usual personnel, except Jim Gordon replaces Michael Clarke (drums). Add Clarence White (pull string guitar), strings. Vocal processing 'through Lesly speakers'.
95296 'Get To You' LP

29, 30 November 1967. Usual personnel, except Jim Gordon replaces Michael Clarke (drums). Add Clarence White (pull string guitar -1). Add Moog synthesizer, strings (-2).
93504 'Natural Harmony' -2 LP
93588 'Wasn't Born To Follow' -1, LP

5 December, 6 December 1967. Usual personnel. Add piano, brass (-1). Roy Halee, engineer.
(94927) 'Tribal Gathering' LP
93508 'Artificial Energy' -1, LP

Michael Clarke leaves the group at this point.

Due to the various comings and goings throughout this turbulent period complete line-ups were not present during the final stages of the recording of *The Notorious Byrd Brothers*. Gene Clark did not appear on the succeeding 'Space Odyssey' or 'Moog Raga', while some of Crosby's contributions consisted of a mixture of vocals and backing tracks. As explained in the main text, the Byrds completed 'Draft Morning' with their own lyrics and vocals but Crosby now confirms that he played on the cut, thus verifying the above information: 'We cut the track before I left. As I remember we did, then they redid the vocals. They changed the lyrics, but we cut the instrumental track first. That would explain it. That's what happened'. An interview with McGuinn at the time of the album's release (when he could accurately remember the participants' individual contributions) also tallies with the information contained herein: 'Crosby's on nothing on the first side of the album. He's on "Change Is Now" singing harmony, "Old John Robertson" on high harmony, singing lead with Chris on "Tribal Gathering" and singing harmony on "Dolphin's Smile".'

Sweetheart Of The Rodeo Columbia CS 9670
Released 22 July 1968
Producer: Gary Usher
Engineers: Roy Halee and Charlie Bragg

Singles from the LP sessions:
'You Ain't Going Nowhere'/'Artificial Energy' Columbia 44499
(released 2 April 1968)
'I Am A Pilgrim'/'Pretty Boy Floyd' Columbia 44643
(released 2 September 1968)

New Personnel: Roger McGuinn (guitar); Chris Hillman (bass and mandolin); Gram Parsons (guitar); Kevin Kelley (drums). Augmented by Earl P. Ball (piano); Jon Corneal (drums); Lloyd Green (steel guitar); John Hartford (banjo, guitar, fiddle); Roy M. Huskey (bass); Jaydee Maness (steel guitar); Clarence J. White (guitar).

Sessions:
9 March 1968. Usual personnel.
98261 'You Ain't Going Nowhere' single 44499, LP
98262 'Hickory Wind' LP

11 March 1968. Usual personnel.
98263 'Lazy Days' unreleased

12 March 1968. Usual personnel.
98264 'Pretty Boy Floyd' single 44643, LP

13 March 1968. Usual personnel.
98265 'I Am A Pilgrim' single 44643, LP
98266 'Pretty Polly' unreleased

14 March 1968. Usual personnel.
98267 'Reputation' unreleased
98268 'Nothing Was Delivered' LP

4 April 1968. Usual personnel.
97169 'Life In Prison' LP

15, 17, 24 April 1968. Usual personnel.
97220 'You Don't Miss Your Water' LP
97260 'The Christian Life' LP
97319 'You're Still On My Mind' LP
97323 'Blue Canadian Rockies' LP

27 May 1968. Usual personnel.
97335 'One Hundred Years From Now' LP
— plus overdubbing on 97220

Gram Parsons, Kevin Kelley and Chris Hillman leave during the time between this and the next recording.

Dr Byrds And Mr Hyde Columbia CS 9755
Released: 3 February 1969
Producer: Bob Johnston
Engineer: Roy Halee

Single from the LP sessions:
'Bad Night At The Whiskey'/'Drug Store Truck Drivin' Man' Columbia 44746
(released 7 January 1969)

New personnel: Roger McGuinn (guitar, vocals); Clarence White (lead guitar); Gene Parsons (drums, guitar, five-string banjo); John York (vocals, bass).

Sessions:
7 October 1968. Usual personnel.
97734 'Old Blue' single 44868, LP
97735 'King Apathy III' LP

8 October 1968. Usual personnel.
97736 'Drug Store Truck Drivin' Man' single 44746, LP
97737 'This Wheel's On Fire' unfinished

14 October 1968. Usual personnel.
97749 'Your Gentle Ways Of Loving Me' LP

15 October 1968. Usual personnel.
97750 'Nashville West' LP
97751 'Bad Night At The Whiskey' single 44746, LP

16 October 1968. Usual personnel.
97752 'Stanley's Song' unreleased

4 December 1968. Usual personnel.
97857 'This Wheel's On Fire' LP
97858 'Medley: My Back Pages/B.J. Blues/Baby, What Do You Want Me To Do' LP
97951 'Child Of The Universe' LP
100506 'Candy' LP

Ballad Of Easy Rider Columbia 9942
Released: 27 October 1969
Producer: Terry Melcher
Engineer: Jerry Hochman

Singles from the LP sessions:
'Lay Lady Lay'/'Old Blue' Columbia 44868
(released 2 May 1969)
'Ballad Of Easy Rider'/'Oil In My Lamp'* Columbia 44990
(released 1 October 1969)
'It's All Over Now, Baby Blue'/'Jesus Is Just Alright'
Columbia 45071
(released 15 December 1969)

* Note: some copies of Columbia 44990 were released with '(I) Wasn't Born To Follow' in place of 'Oil In My Lamp'.

Usual personnel: Roger McGuinn (vocals, guitar, synthesizer); Clarence White (lead guitar, vocals); Gene Parsons (drums, guitar, vocals, five-string banjo); John York (vocals, bass).

Sessions:
27 March, 18 April 1969. Usual personnel. Add female chorus.
105809 'Lay Lady Lay' single 44868

17 June 1969. Usual personnel.
106034 'Jesus Is Just Alright' single 45071, LP

18 June 1969. Usual personnel. Add strings.
106035 'Ballad Of Easy Rider' single 44990, LP
106036 'Jack Tarr The Sailor' unfinished

19 June 1969. Usual personnel.
106039 'Oil In My Lamp' unfinished
106040 'Deportee (Plane Wreck At Los Gatos)' unfinished

23 June 1969. Usual personnel.
(106040) 'Deportee (Plane Wreck At Los Gatos)' LP
106041 'Build It Up' unreleased
106042 'Way Behind The Sun' unreleased

24 June 1969. Usual personnel.
106043 'Moog Experiment (Jenny Comes Along)' unreleased
106044 'There Must Be Someone' unfinished

1 July 1969. Usual personnel.
(106039) 'Oil In My Lamp' single 44990, LP
(106036) 'Jack Tarr The Sailor' LP

2 July 1969. Usual personnel.
(106044) 'There Must Be Someone' LP

22 July 1969. Usual personnel.
106139 'It's All Over Now, Baby Blue' single 45071

23 July 1969. Usual personnel. Add Byron Berline fiddle.
104002 'Tulsa County Blue' LP

24 July 1969. Usual personnel.
104003 'Gunga Din' LP

28 July 1969. Usual personnel.
104027 'Mae Jean Goes To Hollywood' unreleased

15 August 1969. Usual personnel.
104030 'Fido' LP

26 August 1969. Usual personnel.
104040 'Armstrong, Aldrin And Collins' LP

John York leaves at this point.

(*Untitled*) Columbia G 30127
Released: 16 September 1970
Producers: Terry Melcher and Jim Dickson
Engineer: Chris Hinshaw

Single from the LP sessions:
'Chestnut Mare'/'Just A Season' Columbia 45259
(released 23 October 1970)

New personnel: Roger McGuinn (vocals, guitar, synthesizer); Clarence White (vocals, guitar); Gene Parsons (drums, guitar, vocals, five-string banjo); Skip Battin (bass, vocals).

Sessions:
26-28, May, 31 May 1970. Add Gram Parsons, backing vocals (-1); Byron Berline, fiddle (-2), Sneaky Pete Kleinow, steel guitar (-3).
106946 'All The Things' -1, unfinished
107027 'Lover Of The Bayou' unfinished
107032 'You All Look Alike' -2, unfinished
107036 'Yesterday's Train' -3, LP
107037 'Hungry Planet' LP
107038 'Willin'' unfinished
107039 'Well Come Back Home' LP

1-5 June, 9 June, 11 June 1970. Usual personnel. Add Gram Parsons, backing vocal (-1), Byron Berline, fiddle (-2).
106946 'All The Things' -1, LP
106996 '15 Minute Jam' unreleased
107011 'Willin'' unreleased
107012 'Take A Whiff (On Me)' LP
107630 'Just A Season' single 45359, LP
107631 'Chestnut Mare' single 45259, LP
107633 'Kathleen's Song' unfinished
107642 'Truck Stop Girl' LP
107645 'Amazing Grace' unreleased
107646 'Eight Miles High' rejected
107667 'Eight Miles High' LP
107668 'Mr Tambourine Man' LP
107669 'Mr Spaceman' LP
107670 'It's Alright Ma (I'm Only Bleeding)' unreleased
107671 'Nashville West' LP
107672 'So You Want To Be A Rock 'n' Roll Star' LP

107673 'Positively 4th Street' LP
107674 'Lover Of The Bayou' rejected

Byrdmaniax Columbia KC 30640
Released: 23 June 1971
Producer: Terry Melcher
Engineer: Chris Hinshaw

Single from the LP sessions:
'Glory Glory'/'Citizen Kane' Columbia 45440
(released 20 August 1971)

Sessions:
6 October 1970. Usual personnel. Add Terry Melcher (piano) and female chorus.
107894 'I Trust (Everything's Gonna Work Out Alright)' LP

9 January 1971. Usual personnel.
110643 '(Is This) My Destiny' LP

11 January 1971. Usual personnel. Add Paul Polena, horns (-1); Paul Polena, string arrangement (-2), Larry Knechtel, organ (-3)..
110650 'Citizen Kane' -1, single 45440, LP
110652 'Absolute Happiness' -2, LP
110655 'Tunnel Of Love' -3, LP

17 January 1971. Usual personnel. Add Paul Polena, string arrangement (-1), female chorus (-2).
110640 'Jamaica Say You Will' -1, LP
110641 'Glory Glory' -2, single 45440, LP

19 January 1971. Usual personnel.
110638 'I Wanna Grow Up To Be A Politician' LP

24 January 1971. Usual personnel. Add Byron Berline, fiddle and Eric White, harmonica.
110649 'Green Apple Quick Step' LP

26 January 1971. Usual personnel. Add Paul Polena, string arrangement (-1).
110658 'Pale Blue' -1, LP
(107633) 'Kathleen's Song' -1, LP

Farther Along Columbia KC 31050
Released: 17 November 1971
Recorded: London
Producer: The Byrds
Engineer: Mike Ross
Single from the LP sessions:
'America's Great National Pastime'/'Farther Along' Columbia 45514
(released 29 November 1971)

Sessions:
August 1971. Usual personnel.
115543 'Farther Along' single 45514, LP
115585 'So Fine' LP
115586 'Get Down Your Line' LP
115587 'Precious Kate' LP
115588 'Lazy Waters' LP

115589 'Buglar' LP
115590 'Antique Sandy' LP
115591 'America's Great National Pastime' single 45514, LP
115592 'Bristol Steam Convention Blues' LP
115594 'Tiffany Queen' LP
115595 'B.B. Class Road' LP

Earl Scruggs, His Family And Friends Columbia 30584
Released: 20 October 1971
Recorded: Doug Underwood Ranch, Nashville
Producer: Neil Wilburn
Engineers: Ed Hudson and Freeman Ramsey

Sessions:
26 April 1971. Usual personnel, augmented by Earl and Randy Scruggs and the Earl Scruggs Revue.
108783 'You Ain't Going Nowhere' LP

28 April 1971. Usual personnel, augmented by Randy Scruggs.
108784 'Nothin' To It' LP

The Final Sessions
12 January 1972. Usual personnel.
115709 'Drivin' Wheel' unreleased

18 April 1972. Usual personnel.
115930 'Born To Rock 'n' Roll' unreleased

Gene Parsons leaves the group at this point.

July 1972. Recorded at Wally Heider's Studio. Usual personnel, except that John Guerin replaced Gene Parsons on drums.
— 'Bag Full Of Money, unreleased
— 'Draggin'' unreleased
— 'I'm So Restless' unreleased

Note: 'Born To Rock 'n' Roll' was intended as a single and would probably have been backed by 'Drivin' Wheel'. The tracks recorded during July 1972 were later salvaged and re-recorded for McGuinn's first solo album.

UNRELEASED MATERIAL

Following the release of the archive albums *In The Beginning* and *Never Before* there are still several songs that remain unissued. The list below is a breakdown of the still unreleased tracks that the Byrds completed in the studio between 1964-72. Although many of the tapes of the early songs appear to have been lost or destroyed, there is clearly enough material from the latter day Byrds to warrant another archive collection.

'Maybe You Think'. Recorded in 1964 at World Pacific, this track survived the period and was a contender for *Preflyte* along with 'Tomorrow Is A Long Ways Away'. Since then it appears to have been mislaid and was not on the tapes presented to Rhino for *In The Beginning*. Apart from this track, no other previously unreleased songs are known to be still in existence from the pre-Columbia days even though the group cut numbers by the Beatles and the Searchers, amongst others, during rehearsals.

'You And Me'. The Byrds performed this song onstage frequently during early 1965 and it was recorded for their debut album on 8 March 1965. It was later deleted in favour of newer material. The tape of the song could not be found in the CBS archives.

'Words And Pictures'. Recorded on 14 April 1965 for *Mr Tambourine Man* this was also missing from the tape shelves at CBS and is unlikely ever to be found.

'I Love The Life I Live'. Recorded the same day as 'Words And Pictures', this Crosby favourite was written by Mose Allison and appeared on a Georgie Fame EP during the same period. Once again, the original tape could not be found.

'Flower Bomb Song'. One of the earlier examples of Crosby's songwriting, this was regarded as totally inappropriate by both Dickson and the group, yet it was recorded for *Turn! Turn! Turn!*. When I reminded Crosby of the song he burst into defensive laughter and admitted that it was not only 'very bad' but one of his worst compositions. Written in free verse, it contained such memorable lines as 'I'm going to make the love gun that will blow your mind'. It would certainly be intriguing to hear Crosby's hippie philosophizing at such an early period, but the tape has been lost, feared destroyed.

'Stranger In A Strange Land'. Another Crosby song, this time scheduled for a movie that never appeared. Inspired by the Robert Heinlein book of the same title, Crosby admitted that it was a fairly naive piece of work. Tickson Music even sold the copyright of the song, such was their lack of confidence in the piece. In many ways, these unreleased Crosby songs are a key missing chapter in the early history of the Byrds. Apart from 'The Airport Song' on *Preflyte* there are no examples of his lead vocal work during 1964-65 nor any indication of his songwriting, good or otherwise. Even Crosby at his most excessive was never less than interesting and the loss of these tracks is therefore all the more regrettable. Since this song was ultimately intended for release on a soundtrack album it is possible that copies were taken from the tape and sent to the proposed filmmakers. No tape exists at CBS but perhaps a copy lies dormant in the attic of some would-be film producer from the mid-60's. We can only hope.

'I Don't Ever Want To Spoil Your Party'. Yet another Crosby favourite which bore the kiss of death. This was written by his good friend Dino Valenti and recorded at the same session as 'Stranger In A Strange Land'. The tape was again lost, but listeners anxious to hear what the original might have sounded like should check out the first Quicksilver Messenger Service album where it was re-recorded under the title, 'Dino's Song'.

'Circle Of Minds'. Although listed in the CBS files as having been recorded by the Byrds, no session number was assigned to this track. If the song was anywhere near as interesting as its title, then it was another serious loss to the Byrds canon.

'Milestones'. Recorded for *Younger Than Yesterday* at a time when Hillman was hitting form having just returned from a Hugh Masekela session, this was a tantalizing example of the Byrds' determined excursion into jazz territories. According to Hillman and his colleagues, this instrumental was taken from the album of the same name by Miles Davis. However, nobody has previously pointed out that 'Milestones' was not a track but an album title. It is rather like a new group announcing that they had recorded a Byrds song called 'Younger Than Yesterday'. The instrumental that Chris is referring to was probably 'Miles', which the Byrds presumably mistitled 'Milestones' after the album. Certainly, 'Miles' could have been adapted by the Byrds very effectively. Sadly, this tape was also missing from the CBS archives.

'Untitled Instrumental'. The mystery instrumental that appeared on the rough tapes of the *Never Before* sessions has never been identified by the participants and even Dickson could not recall its origin. Essentially a warm-up number, it did sound pleasant enough in its own right to deserve a place on the CD of *Never Before*.

'Lazy Days'. Recorded on 11 March 1968 for *Sweetheart Of The Rodeo* and reputedly still in existence as a completed tape, this song was later recorded by the Flying Burrito Brothers and included on their second album, *Burrito Deluxe*.

music for a possible album. His colleagues were less than entranced with his synthesizer forays, but this particular one, aptly named 'Moog Experiment', took place during an actual Byrds recording session. The weight of objection no doubt accounted for its non-appearance on *Ballad Of Easy Rider*.

'Mae Jean Goes To Hollywood'. Recorded on 28 July 1969, this was a serious contender for both *Ballad Of Easy Rider* and *(Untitled)*. Indeed, some of the early sleeves of *(Untitled)* actually list the song as appearing on the album. The track was written by Jackson Browne and subsequently appeared on Johnny Darrell's *California Stopover*. Larry Murray, composer of 'Buglar' and a former colleague of Hillman, produced the album on which Clarence White also played guitar.

this stage, it is debatable whether McGuinn actually intended these last couple of cuts to appear under their aegis.

Inevitably, there are some songs, assumed to have been recorded by the Byrds, which do not appear in CBS files. Of the latter tracks the most surprising omission is 'Just Like A Woman', which more than one of the group recalled cutting with Jackson Browne on piano. Whether this was some form of warm-up session that was never captured on tape is conjectural. The same applies to 'Sing Me Back Home' which was strongly rumoured as a recorded song prior to *Sweetheart Of The Rodeo*. Although it featured heavily in the Byrds' sets of the period, it may not, in retrospect, have been attempted in the studio. The session listing also fails to elucidate the complete story of the recording of *Sweetheart Of The Rodeo*. None of the details of the scrapped vocals and warm-up sessions are provided and it would require a detailed listening of all the rough tapes to learn more. Finally, it is interesting to note that several of the songs that the Byrds performed live or on radio or television were not apparently attempted in the studio. These predominantly cover songs, spiced with material recorded by various personnel after the group split, included 'Things We Said Today', 'When You Walk In The Room', 'Do You Believe In Magic?', 'Not Fade Away', 'Roll Over Beethoven', 'Get Out Of My Life Woman', '(Excuse Me) I Think I've Got A Heartache', 'Foggy Mountain Breakdown', 'Sing Me Back Home', 'Under Your Spell Again', 'Long Black Veil', 'Take A City Bride', 'I Shall Be Released', 'Six Days On The Road', 'Close Up The Honky Tonks', 'California Blues', 'Rolling In My Sweet Baby's Arms', 'Buckaroo', 'Soldier's Joy'/'Black Mountain Rag', 'The Water Is Wide' and 'Salt River'.